BOUND & CONTROLLED

THE COMPLETE SERIES

SHAW MONTGOMERY

THE OWNERS

A BOUND & CONTROLLED PREQUEL

"They all look so unhappy, Master." Conner snuggled deeper into Ben's lap, resting his head on Ben's shoulder.

"I know. They're smiling and talking, but it's only on the surface." Ben rubbed his hand absentmindedly up and down Conner's naked back. "Something's changed over the past couple of months. I'm just not sure what."

Ben felt Conner tracing circles on his chest as they watched the four brothers sitting across the room. Well, four brothers and Calen, who was with them so often he might as well have been another sibling. They came to the club every couple of weeks, sometimes in groups and sometimes individually.

It had been odd at first, knowing all of them were involved in the BDSM scene. But watching them laugh and tease each other, it was soon easy to see why it wasn't strange for them. They loved each other and honestly wanted what was best for their siblings.

Dom, sub, or switch, it didn't matter. They were a family.

And a lot of their family time was spent together at Bound & Controlled.

Bound & Controlled was a private gay BDSM club in Washington, D.C., and was Ben's baby. He'd never pictured it growing as big as it had in just a few short years, much less getting to celebrate the start of the second club in Baltimore.

"They're all single, that's the problem."

Ben snorted; his boy always thought being in love was the answer to everything. Ben happened to agree, but that wasn't the point. "They've dated and had fun. Hell, you've seen several of them have *lots* of fun in different demos."

"It's not the same." Conner lifted his head up, giving Ben a sweet, mischievous smile. "You know we could help—"

"No matchmaking. Remember, we agreed."

Conner sighed. "But Garrett would be perfect with—"

"Nope. We're going to stay out of it." He tried to sound stern, but his resolve was failing and Conner knew it.

"And Bryce—there are a few couples looking for a third. I'm sure we could—"

"Conner." Ben drew out his sub's name, giving him a look.

Conner blinked at him innocently. "But, Sir…"

Ben laughed. "I'm not falling for that. And if you want your spanking tonight, you have to stop. We said we weren't going to meddle."

"We wouldn't have to if they could see what was right in front of them." Conner huffed and curled back into Ben. "Garrett especially, but Brent isn't any better. They make me crazy."

Ben had to agree. "Garrett did say he was tired of casual scenes and dating."

Conner sat up and grinned. "He was practically asking us to help."

They really shouldn't. It was almost taking advantage of their positions at the club. Being the owners, they had insider knowledge that most people wouldn't want to get out. They were very good at keeping secrets, but if that information could be used to help members of the club, then it couldn't hurt.

"It's not really meddling if we push things in the correct direction." Ben's resolve went right out the window.

Conner nodded enthusiastically, then reached over to take a long sip of his drink. "Just a nudge." He glanced over across the room to the bar. "A little one. Tiny."

Ben agreed. "When the time is right. It can't be too obvious or the little thing will get nervous."

Conner giggled, already feeling the effects of the alcohol. "He's already nervous or they would have met ages ago."

"Only if Garrett wasn't so blind." Ben shook his head, still not sure how the Dom couldn't see what was right in front of him. "That other sub nearly killed himself tripping over the chair trying to get Garrett's attention last time they came in, but he didn't even notice."

"Poor Tony, he was so embarrassed." Conner tried to be serious, but he couldn't do it. Laughing, he took another sip of his drink. "But falling right into Allen's lap was perfect. They've gone out several times since then."

Conner's smiles were getting bigger and his giggles louder. His boy was only halfway through one of the bright red, fruity concoctions, but he was well on his way to being lit. Conner didn't drink much and had almost no tolerance for alcohol at all. Normally, Ben didn't let him have any, but they were celebrating, and Conner's schedule had been so hectic lately that he'd relaxed the rules.

Conner helped at the club when he could, but he owned a custom construction company, so most of the time he was incredibly busy. He'd recently finished up several big projects, so they'd decided to relax and have fun before the work on the new club started.

"Allen kept saying he wasn't looking for anything serious, but I think Tony is changing Allen's mind."

Nodding, Conner giggled, taking another sip before glancing over at the bar. "They'd be *perfect* together."

"Wyatt and Garrett?"

Sighing, Conner nodded seriously, which was cute considering how tipsy he was. "We have to help."

Unable to deny his boy anything, or mind his own business, Ben smiled. "We'll talk to Wyatt soon. He's doing the furniture for the new club, and there is some paperwork he needs. Since Garrett does his insurance, it might be the push they need."

Garrett and his brothers owned an insurance company in Richmond, and when Wyatt had moved down there, they'd casually mentioned Garrett's business to the sweet sub. If Wyatt purchased new coverage from the Dom he quietly stalked with his eyes every time they were in the building together, it wasn't anything they'd done.

They watched as the brothers got up and started wandering toward other parts of the club. The lounge area near the bar was fairly tame, with most people casually sitting around talking. Although with some subs kneeling by their Masters and everyone in various stages of dress, no one would ever call it vanilla.

Brent and Calen stayed and continued to talk, but the rest of the family headed off in different directions. They both grimaced as Grant went up to a cute sub at the bar. Grant was never the most subtle Dom. He charged right in and didn't shy away from saying whatever he was thinking. For subs looking for a suave, sophisticated Dom, he looked more like a thug.

"That's never going to—Oh dear." Conner frowned.

The new sub had taken one look at Grant and made a hasty retreat. A little more flamboyant and almost feminine in appearance, the sub was exactly the kind of guy Grant liked. But as usual, it rarely worked out in his favor.

If Ben remembered correctly, the new boy was some kind of

aide to a congressman and thought very highly of himself and his position. Ben hadn't been impressed with the guy, but nothing in his application or interview had made him think that he'd be a bad fit for the club.

He was just a bad fit for Grant.

"We might have to...do something with him." Ben wasn't sure what to say. Grant was a wonderful guy, but there weren't that many subs that caught the Dom's eye. "Maybe we can find someone to introduce him to."

Conner scrunched his face up and earnestly nodded, the alcohol clearly going to his head. "He wants a pretty guy. Do you remember the Halloween party last year?"

That had been impossible to forget. There had been quite a few subs who'd dressed up in cute little costumes Grant loved, but he'd been disappointed when he'd realized it had just been fun for the guys and none of them were actually interested in the more feminine look they'd chosen for the night.

"We'll see what we can do. The new club will bring in more people. Maybe we'll find his Mr. Right up there." Ben hoped they'd find someone for Grant. Even if he looked like a biker or some kind of Hells Angel, he was interesting and a well-established businessman.

"They need to like pretty things." Conner waved his hands around enthusiastically.

"But they can't be too submissive. Grant needs someone who'll keep him in line and not let themselves get flattened by his personality."

"Or his size. The guy is huge." Conner was eyeing Grant like he was undressing him in his head.

"You looking to trade me in? I think you'd look sexy in frilly lingerie." Ben was teasing, but he laughed when Conner threw his arms around him enthusiastically.

"I love you." Conner then ruined the sweet declaration by grinning and saying, "He's built like a truck, though."

Then Conner frowned, like his brain was just catching up to what he was saying. "I don't like frilly things, so you have to keep me."

"I'll keep you, my drunk little sub."

"I'm not drunk yet." Conner looked down at his drink and seemed confused. "It's empty?"

"Yes."

"That's terrible. I need another." Shaking his head, Conner blinked up at Ben and pouted prettily. "Can I have another one, Master? I've been so good."

"Good enough for two drinks? Do you remember what happened last time?" Ben knew his stern words were ruined by the grin he couldn't quite suppress.

"No dancing on the table. Honest." Conner blinked at Ben, looking very sincere while he traced his finger over his chest in a cross-my-heart gesture. "I'll keep my clothes on and everything."

Ben laughed, not believing it for a second. Conner was an exhibitionist and it came flooding out when he drank. The club was a safe space for him to indulge in it, though, and most of their friends and members had gotten an eyeful at some point or another in the past.

The two drink maximum was supposed to keep things in check, but with Conner's level of tolerance, it didn't help. They had no plans to play tonight beyond a spanking, so he just leaned back and enjoyed his giggly sub.

"As long as your clothes stay on. If you're naughty, I'll have to punish you tomorrow, and you don't want that, do you?"

Ben smiled as Conner tried to cover his wicked grin. "No, Master. I'm going to be good. You won't need to spank me or tie me up and flog me or even get out the *crop*." Conner shivered and licked his lips, his hard-on pressing against the tight leather shorts he wore. "I'll be *very* good."

"All right, I want you to remember that. You don't want to have to bend over tomorrow and get spanked or paddled because you were naked and naughty tonight." Ben watched as Conner squirmed, squeezing his legs together.

They'd been a couple for years, but he never got tired of seeing his boy needy and aroused, right on the edge of being wonderfully wicked. Conner leaned in, giving him a kiss. "I'll be s-o-o-o good."

He'd be so bad, but they'd both love it.

"Come on. Let's get you that drink and we'll see what everyone is up to. We need to see how the demo is going, anyway." They had staff that monitored the scenes and play areas, but he liked to check on special demonstrations and scenes personally.

"Oh, the sounds! I forgot." After they stood up, Conner threw his arms around Ben. "I love watching that!"

His enthusiastic sub grinned wildly and looked around excitedly. "We can go watch?"

"Yes, just watch, though. It's their scene and you have to be good." Ben gave him a firm look, meaning it that time.

Conner nodded sincerely. "I'll be good. Oliver *loves* sounds."

"All right, let's get your drink before I change my mind." He was going to have the bartender ease up on the alcohol for the next one. Conner didn't need that much more, or he'd never be able to behave.

"One more, you promised." Taking Ben's hand, Conner started leading them over to the bar.

Giving Conner a quick swat on the ass, Ben pulled him close. "Are you being bossy?"

Conner stopped moving and looked back at Ben, thinking harder than he should have had to. "No, I'm...I'm being cute?"

Laughing, Ben gave his boy's tempting ass another pop. "Let's be less cute and better behaved."

Realizing Ben wasn't angry and his drink wouldn't be taken away, Conner smiled. "Yes, Master."

Heading over to the bar, they walked up and stood beside a frustrated Grant. Conner gave him a big smile, probably trying to cheer him up. "Hi, Master Grant."

Grant grinned, but it came out looking forced. "Hey, guys."

"Are you going to see the sounding demo? Sir is getting me my second drink and then we're going to head over. Do you want to come with us?" Conner was trying to remember his manners, but his excitement was starting to bubble over.

As Grant tried to figure out how to respond, Ben gestured to the bartender for another drink for Conner, making sure the guy knew to ease up on whatever was in the drink. Grant, seeing the exchange, couldn't quite keep a straight face. Ben was just happy to see him smile.

"So you're going to come?" Conner perked up like an excited little bird.

"Um, not this time, but I think Bryce wandered over that way." Grant tried to smooth over the rejection, but Conner didn't seem to mind. He immediately jumped to the idea of finding Bryce.

"Oh, he'll love it. Troy is so...so...he's so Troy, and Oliver is so..." Smiling at the new drink that appeared in front of him, Conner must have lost track of what he was saying because even to Ben it didn't make sense.

Grant just grinned and nodded. "Yes, he is." Turning his focus to Ben, Grant gave him a nod. "I heard about the new club. Congrats. I can't wait to see it."

"Thanks. We've been able to finalize it quicker than I thought. Conner is starting on the building renovations next week." They'd had a few delays and frustrations, but overall, Ben was pleased with how it was coming along.

"That's great." Grant looked around the room. "Will it have the same feel?"

Conner looked up, setting his drink down carefully. "Yes, we're going for the same feel, but it's going to be more open... opener...more opener...not as closed off. It's going to look amazing."

Trying not to snort out laughter, Ben nodded, pressing his lips together. Grant didn't have the same restraint. He burst out laughing, then looked down at Conner's drink. "What's in that?"

Conner shrugged in an awkward, disjointed manner. "It's new." He gestured over to the bartender with sweeping hand gestures. "Jack is trying out special drinks for the other club. It's good stuff."

"I can see that." Grant nodded his head toward Conner and grinned at Ben. "I'm betting he's on the table in the next half hour."

Conner peeked at Ben guiltily, then shook his head at Grant. "I'm supposed to be good. Shh."

"Come on, before you get yourself in trouble." Reaching out, he gave Grant's shoulder a squeeze. "We'll see you later. And you have to visit and see the new club as soon as it's done."

"Absolutely."

"I'm going to hold you to that." Taking Conner's free hand, Ben led him away from the bar. Making their way toward the hallway that led to the public scene areas, they weaved between couples and groups. The club was always busy, but lately, it had been almost too full.

He was hoping that opening the second location would help bring the numbers in the D.C. location down to a more manageable size. It was going to mean more traveling for them, but they'd talked about it and it seemed like the best investment.

They had members who traveled from a variety of locations, and if they could steer some of their northern members to the new Baltimore club, it would give them some breathing room. Maybe then they could even do some remodeling—

No, he wasn't going to let himself think it. One ridiculously massive project at a time.

As they crossed the room, he noticed Brent and Calen. Something about their body language and the way they were looking at each other pulled at his attention. He'd always thought of Calen as another one of the brothers, but it wasn't brotherly affection he was seeing as they talked.

There was a barely restrained passion radiating from both of them. He'd seen enough scenes and couples engaged in all kinds of activities to know when two people were hot for each other. No matter what they were talking about, that kind of genuine desire only happened when the emotion was there as well.

Not wanting to intrude, he steered Conner around them without interrupting their conversation. Next time he saw either one of them, he wasn't going to be so restrained. At the very least, he wanted to know if they realized how apparent their yearning for each other was. There had to be a way to ask about it without seeming obvious. He would have to think about it.

The hallway to the back of the building always made Ben feel like he was heading to another universe. The areas were distinct, but they never felt out of place. Most of the time, he could almost see the change that came over people as they headed toward the more risqué side of the club.

He loved the sounds that echoed from the demonstration areas. The sound of a flogger, the moans of pain and pleasure...it took every desire someone was feeling and amped it up. Conner could feel it, too. The way he walked subtly changed, and his whole body seemed to vibrate with excitement.

Making their way over to the main demo area, Ben was

pleased to see several staff members monitoring the scene. Troy and Oliver were a well-established couple that had done public scenes before, so he wasn't worried, but he liked to be careful. His club had never had any kind of safety issues, and he wanted to keep it that way.

The space around the stage was so packed they had to stand at the back of the area. They could still see the stage, but it gave them a good view of the crowd as well. Sometimes he felt that was the best view. Watching the emotions play across the faces of the people observing could be incredible if the scene was done right.

Troy and Oliver always got the best reactions.

Their desire for each other was obvious, but so was their love and connection. They pulled to each other, and somewhere in that whirl of emotion they pulled the audience in with them. Ben loved when they agreed to do a scene, and the times that they'd asked to do one had been even better.

The sounds had been their idea, and Ben knew it would be incredible.

Oliver was normally cheerful and bouncy; there was so much barely restrained excitement in him it seemed like he might explode at any minute. Troy was the exact opposite. The strong, silent type, he was broad and always looked a little stern until you got to know him. They complemented each other, even though physically and personality-wise they were complete opposites. Sometimes Ben couldn't understand why they were looking for a third.

Oliver was naked, strapped down to a table. His only coverings were a collar and cuffs that wrapped around his ankles and wrists. As sexy as he looked, what caught Ben's attention was his face. The anticipation and arousal he showed was even more striking than his long, lightly muscled frame.

Troy stood beside him, gentle touches helping to soothe

Oliver. Conner had described him as a sexy Norse god, which Ben had to agree with. As tough as the Dom looked with his broad frame and serious expression, he always looked at Oliver with an intense passion that made it clear how much he loved his sub.

Pulling his mind away from the scene, Ben tugged Conner in close and glanced around at the other people watching. Some were focused on Oliver's straining erection that was held upright by a cock ring. Some were focused on Troy's leather pants that even Ben had to agree looked painted-on. Some, like Bryce, were focused on the two men as they quietly talked, completely ignoring everything around them.

Ben wasn't surprised to find Bryce watching the demo. As a switch, it would probably appeal to him on many levels. What did surprise Ben was the look on his face. His need was so strong and clear it almost hurt to see. It was in the line of his body as he propped himself against the wall, trying to seem relaxed. It was in the intensely beautiful way he watched the two men, focusing on their expression and their love, not their bodies.

"Oh, Master. They're so..." Conner lost his train of thought again, but he gripped Ben's arms tight and leaned into his chest, watching the stage.

Ben tightened his hold on Conner, letting his fingers casually caress the smooth skin of his boy's chest. Bending down, he whispered, "I agree. We're going to have to do a scene soon. Would you like that? Being tied up and helpless while everyone watched?"

Conner shivered in his hold. Nipples puckering tight, he pressed his ass into Ben's groin. "Yes, Master...Please."

Ben didn't mind being watched, but it wasn't something he especially needed. Conner craved it. Strapped down so he was helpless, or dancing on the table, it didn't matter, he loved it. Maybe Ben would have had an issue with it if Conner needed to include other people in their play or wanted to be touched by someone else, but it had never gone that far. He just soaked up the desire as people watched and it lit him up. It gave him a spark that made him shine, and Ben loved watching him.

Sliding his fingers up Conner's chest, Ben circled his nipples, getting closer and closer. "You have to be good now if you want me to let everyone watch you later."

Conner's whispered pleas went right to Ben's dick. "Yes, Master. I'll be good."

"Good boy." Then he closed the final gap and flicked Conner's nipples with his fingers, loving the soft inhale that was the only hint of Conner's arousal.

Teasing and pulling on Conner's sensitive tips, Ben watched as Troy moved slowly down Oliver's body. Low, whispered words were drowned out by the quiet hum of the crowd, but whatever Troy was saying to Oliver, it was making him crazy.

Whimpered pleas broke out as Troy fisted Oliver's straining erection in one long stroke. The straps that held him down for safety wouldn't let him move much, but Ben could see the tension in the leather as he writhed and begged. Troy gave him a wicked smile, and his response made Oliver even more erratic.

"God, Master, what's he saying?" Conner arched into Ben's touch, letting out a low whimper as Ben pulled on the dark, now puffy tips.

"Do you think he's telling him how sexy he looks, or is it something naughtier?"

"It has to...Master...has to be something *wicked*..." Conner sounded envious, and Ben knew that Conner would have loved to have been the one up on the stage.

Ben watched as Conner's glass wobbled in his hand. "Don't spill your drink, or no spanking for you."

"But, Master..."

"If you're good, I might even spank you in the club. Would

you like that? Do you want your master to pull down your shorts and bare your bottom, then redden it while you beg for more?" Ben flexed his hips, rubbing his cock against Conner's ass. "Everybody would be able to see you...see your red bottom while you squirmed."

"Oh...please...yes..."

Not wanting to get Conner any more excited, Ben eased off on the teasing and let his boy come down from the pleasure he knew had been building. Moving off Conner's nipples, he felt his boy sag into him. Conner took a deep breath and went back to looking at the scene as he took another long drink of the red concoction that smelled like juice.

Bringing his focus back to the couple, Ben watched as Troy took the long, prepared rod and teased at the head of Oliver's cock. Beautiful noises and impatient begging echoed from the stage as Oliver tried to push his dick closer to the toy.

More of the Dom's muffled words had Oliver shaking, frantic words sending shivers through the audience. "Please, Master! Yes!"

The absolute need in his voice had everyone on edge. Ben could almost see the audience leaning in to get closer to the desperate emotion. The two men were even more incredible than usual. Ben couldn't help but wonder what was pushing their emotions so high.

Troy's smile was pure sin as he held Oliver's cock steady and eased the sound just inside the tip of Oliver's slit. The lubed rod went in easily, but Oliver's wailing pleasure ratcheted up the pulsing arousal in the room.

Looking over, Ben saw that Bryce was just as affected. Ben couldn't tell if Bryce wanted to be the one on the table or the one teasing Oliver mercilessly, but he was clearly mesmerized by the sight. Tension gripped his body, and Ben knew the sheer will it took to stand there and just watch had to be tearing Bryce apart.

A start running through Bryce had Ben looking back toward the stage. The sound was fully seated in Oliver's cock and Troy was leaning down, whispering to his boy again. The crowd watched as Oliver shook and mewled under Troy's gentle, careful caress of his dick.

Even the lightest touch would be magnified by the intense sensation surging through the sub. When Troy reached up and started carefully using the rod to fuck Oliver's slit, Ben thought the boy would come right off the table.

Chest heaving, tremors racked Oliver's body as he watched his Master slowly slide the sound in and out of his cock. Red and thick, his erection was impressive as it pulsed and enveloped the rod. They all watched, barely breathing as Oliver was pushed closer to the edge.

Hovering on the verge of insanity and orgasm, he called out frantic pleas to his Master. Troy's intense focus never wavered from his boy, but his pleasure was obvious. He loved making his boy crazy. Troy had once told Ben that when they played, it felt like he held the most basic part of who Oliver was in his hands.

When Oliver finally broke, rambling words tumbling out and beautiful frenzied sounds wrapping their way through the crowd, Troy took pity on his boy. Leaning down, Troy's face was angled just right for Ben to be able to see his lips as he spoke low to Oliver.

The last part was a loud, firm command. "Come!" Then he pulled the sound out in one long stroke.

The audience was focused on the exquisite screams that drowned the rooms as Oliver shouted out his orgasm, but Ben was still trying to piece together what had sent Oliver flying. He'd been hovering right at his orgasm, just close enough to almost reach it but not quite find it, when something Troy said sent him careening into pleasure.

To Ben, it looked like he'd told Oliver to let "him" see him come. But Troy hadn't been looking at Oliver when he spoke. He hadn't been telling Oliver to come for his master. Saying that one word was the only time his focus had broken from his boy. Ben could have sworn he'd looked up at Bryce as he'd ordered Oliver to orgasm.

Conner was shaking in his arms as they watched Oliver come down from his pleasure, sinking into subspace as the blissful sensations rolled through him. He didn't even move as Troy unstrapped him and gathered him into his arms.

The crowd broke away as Troy carried him over to a couch set deep in the shadows off the stage. As Ben turned his tipsy, horny sub in his arms, he watched out of the corner of his eye as Bryce inched closer to the darkened corner.

Telling himself it wasn't his business, he focused on how frustrated Conner would be when he realized he'd been too distracted to see how the three men interacted. His boy was going to hate it. Ben fought his growing grin as he leaned down and kissed Conner.

Conner was swaying back and forth, rubbing his cock against Ben's to music only he could hear. "Master, I need you."

People around them started to grin as Conner began to move. Ben's smile faded to something more erotic. "Does my boy want to put on a show for his master?"

Conner's head dropped back, exposing the long, beautiful line of his neck. Ben leaned down and nibbled up the tender column, loving the little gasps that escaped his boy. "Please, Master."

He'd behaved a lot longer than he usually managed to, and Ben knew the need had to be ready to explode out of him. Looking around, Ben saw one of the smaller stages off to the other side of the room was free. Taking Conner's hand, Ben led him through the crowd of knowing grins. He gave a nod to Gerald, a staff member who'd been with them for several years.

Gerald spoke into his earpiece, and within seconds, a low bass was thumping from hidden speakers near the elevated platform. A dirty rhythm that made Ben think of grinding bodies in a dark dance club came on as Conner stepped on the stage. The sway of his hips and the way he moved reminded Ben of the first time he'd seen Conner.

He'd been scoping out gay clubs, trying to see if there were enough people interested in kink to make a predominantly gay BDSM club worthwhile in the D.C. area. Conner had been a go-go dancer in a cage mounted over the dance floor in one of the edgier clubs on the outskirts of town.

He'd been incredible.

His lean, sexy body writhed to the music, lost in his own world as the dancers down below stared and begged for his attention. Most people would have assumed Conner would have been easy, but it had taken weeks of Ben showing up at the club to watch before he'd let Ben even approach him. Ben had been surprised to learn that the sexy dancer actually owned a construction company and used the dancing as a way to let off stress when things became too much.

Eventually, Ben had an incredible time showing his sexy boy new ways to relax.

Conner's body moved to the music. Not quite dancing, it was almost like he was making love with the sounds. His boy knew every eye was on him, but his gaze never strayed from Ben's. His sultry smile focused on his master, his eyes sending wicked promises for the evening to come.

Dancing for Ben was the only time Conner was allowed to touch himself freely and his boy took full advantage of it. Flicking his nipples and rolling his hips, his head bowed back. It looked like he was being fucked in time to the music, riding the beat like it was taking him right there on the stage.

Hands slid down his torso and Ben heard the inhale from

the crowd that watched as Conner's fingers found the button on his tiny leather shorts. They were so small he could have never worn them in public. Even if they could have been called a bathing suit, people would have been scandalized.

Ben loved the way they cupped every curve and bulge, and Conner loved the way eyes would follow him as he walked past. Dom or sub, it didn't matter, something about his sexy boy captivated them. And never more so than when he was tipsy and turned on.

As the little shorts fell to the floor, Ben had to grin at the frustrated moans around him. Sometimes he had Conner go naked under them, but that night he'd dressed Conner in a sexy G-string with a silken pouch that barely hid his boy's hard length.

It was stretched to the max, wet spots showing just how turned on Conner was. Ben felt his own erection straining at the confines of his pants, and he knew his control would only hold so much longer. As much as he loved to see Conner shine, he was ready for his boy.

Teasing at the strings, pulling them away from his body just enough to hint at the perfection that was hiding under the silk, Conner turned and writhed, sexier than any dancer or stripper Ben had ever seen. Something about the way his boy's passion came through held everyone captivated every time his wicked side ventured out to play.

Finally he couldn't wait any longer. A growl escaped as Ben strode up on the stage, pulling Conner's nearly naked body against his. Eyes wide and pupils blown with need, Conner threw himself into Ben's arms.

"Master." His needy whimper sent shivers down Ben's spine.

"I'm going to wear you out, boy." Ben slid his hands down to cup Conner's ass. "You won't be able to walk tomorrow, much less work. You'd better hope you can take the day off."

He'd make sure his boy was too worn out to overwork himself, even if he had to make love to Conner all night long. Conner was beyond caring what would happen in the future. Ben could see that everything in him was focused on his arousal and the need pulsing through his body.

Conner's erection was so hard it was pushing out of the pouch, showing off the thick base of his cock. He pushed it up against Ben, desperately trying to get enough friction through the soft fabric to orgasm. Ben lifted a hand and brought it back down against one round cheek. The pop made a delicious noise.

"Naughty boy."

Conner gasped, then groaned as the heat from the spank spread through him. "Thank you, Master."

Ben grinned; he knew it was wicked and full of heat. "I've got one of the private rooms reserved. Oh, the things I have planned for you, boy."

A little moan escaped as Conner bit his lip and fought to be still in Ben's arms. "Master, I want to be good, but..." His hips thrust and he gasped as his cock rubbed against Ben's. "Master, it just won't listen."

Laughing, because Conner was completely serious, lost between the pleasure and the drink, Ben squeezed the cheek he'd smacked. "I'm going to have to help it listen, then."

The dark threat growled out should have made Conner nervous, but if anything it made him even more turned on. Conner loved all kinds of toys, even ones that made it almost impossible for him to come. "The next time we come to the club and you get to have fun, I'm going to make you all turned on, then put your cock ring on under your clothes. I'm going to let everyone see how hard you get and what a sexy package you have."

Conner flushed with arousal and he blinked up at Ben, words no longer working. Ben smiled again. "Let's go, boy."

Leading Conner off the stage, still cupping his nearly naked ass with one hand, Ben glanced over to the corner where he could just make out Troy through the crowd. Shadows moved beside him in the dark, and if it weren't for Troy's size and blond hair, they would have blended into the walls. He wasn't sure what the men were doing, but he hoped that they'd found what they were looking for.

Knowing Bryce, it wouldn't be easy.

Ben turned back to focus on his boy, squeezing Conner's ass and loving the way he moaned and squirmed. "I think I still owe my boy a spanking."

Conner looked up at Ben and shivered, pleasure and need wrapped up in a sexy, delicious package. Breathy and low, his words dripped with sex and desire. "Thank you, Master."

They'd see if Conner was still thanking him in the morning when he was exhausted. Until then, he was going to enjoy sending his boy right into orbit. They had a room full of toys at their disposal and he knew just how to please Conner.

He brought his hand down hard on Conner's naked ass, loving the way his handprint bloomed on the pale skin. Conner went up on his toes, cock jerking, and beautiful whimpers flowing out of him. "Oh, Master. Oh, I love you."

"I love you too, boy. And you're going to feel how much I love you tomorrow." Ben growled out the words, loving the blissful expression on Conner's face.

Giving the luscious bottom one more squeeze, Ben started moving them back toward the private rooms. He knew how lucky he was to have found Conner. Ben just hoped that Garrett, Brent, Grant, and Bryce were as fortunate as he was.

GARRETT

FIRST EDITION JUNE, 2017

1

GARRETT

"Furniture? He wants a small business policy for custom furniture?"

"Yup."

He couldn't picture the bouncy guy being focused enough to have a business, much less one that made custom furniture. Maybe that was just his perception of him, but it wasn't completely baseless. From what Garrett had seen, Wyatt was polite and perpetually cheerful but forgetful and constantly in motion. The two opposing pictures didn't mesh.

"You're sure?" He should have known better than to ask.

"How often am I wrong?" Calen gave him a look that spoke volumes. Bossy Dom. He should have known better than to have hired another Dom as an office manager. But when his closest friends were all in the scene he didn't have much of a choice.

"You're right. I'm sorry. Send him in, thanks." Garrett tried to remember anything else he knew about him as Wyatt came in. Usually before he met with an insured, he reviewed their policies and had everything organized. This was very last-minute which was not his preferred method.

Wyatt Matthews had been with them since he moved to

Richmond about a year ago. Garrett thought he'd moved from somewhere up north but he wasn't positive. Most of the time, Wyatt dealt with Calen or Melissa, the front office assistant. He came in more than just about any other insured.

Some of those visits made sense.

He came in about once a month to pay his auto insurance, sometimes more if another policy was due. Then a week or two later, he'd come in with a question on one of his policies. Garrett had only gotten the questions a couple of times. It was like Wyatt did nothing but read the fine print in his policies.

If he hadn't been so damned earnest...and sweet, Garrett would have thought the guy was up to something. Nobody wanted to talk to their insurance company that often. Hell, he was an agent, and he didn't even look at his own policies that often. The guy was too nice to be up to something.

Garrett looked up from where he'd been making notes when someone cleared their throat at his door. Damn the kid was cute. No, not kid or boy or anything else like it. Wyatt was a customer and Garrett didn't want him to think he didn't respect him.

It wouldn't matter that Garrett didn't mean any offense. The sexy bo—insured, was young but not too young. He looked so innocent and he was almost ten years younger than Garrett. Something about the combination brought out the Dom in him.

He looked so adorable. The way he'd peek at Garrett, when he thought no one was watching, called to Garrett. However, not enough to take the risk of alienating or offending an insured. It was getting close, though. Heaven help them both if he came in many more times this month.

Garrett always needed time to talk himself out of saying anything inappropriate and Wyatt had already been in there on Monday. It was only Friday, of the same week, it was too soon to test his control. No Dom was perfect, especially when a body like that was wrapped around such a delightful personality.

"Hello, Mr. Matthews, come on in. Calen said you need a business policy."

"Hi. Call me Wyatt, please."

Garrett stood and gestured to the chair in front of his desk before walking around to shake Wyatt's hand. He usually preferred it when he kept the desk between them, but it would probably seem rude if he didn't greet him appropriately. Especially since he was coming to talk to Garrett specifically. Hopefully, the sexy man wouldn't notice the constant interest Garrett's body tried to take when they were in the same room.

"Wyatt. So tell me about your business." With most people, Garrett would have spent more time on pleasantries and catching up on all that had happened since the customer was last in. But in this case, with how often he actually came in, it would be ridiculous. Garrett also couldn't take the risk of dragging out their conversation. It was too much temptation.

"Well, it's just gotten out of the hobby stage really. I mean, before I was working another job and now I'm doing this full-time." Wyatt was trying to sit still but his leg kept bouncing up and down. It looked like he was dying to pace around the office.

"That's great. It sounds like things are taking off. I couldn't remember you ever saying anything about the furniture before." Garrett was sure he wouldn't have forgotten something like that. His memory when it came to the cute little—customer, when it came to the customer was pretty good.

"I probably didn't mention it. I'm only working at my day job a few hours a week now because the business has started to take off into a real...well, real business." Wyatt blushed as he stumbled through the explanation. "I was going to come in and talk to you guys eventually because, well, I know there's probably other insurance I need but this just came up and well..."

His leg was bouncing all over the place. The longer he stammered his way through his little speech, the worse it got. Garrett wanted to reach over and grab him up—just to help him calm down of course. That wasn't an option. No matter how incredible the fantasy.

Nice, well-mannered insurance agents did not cuddle their clients or do anything else he could see doing to the cute little— to the gentleman. He had to keep reminding himself that, or he was going to end up calling the customer something that would seem insane.

He wasn't going to survive this.

Wyatt was starting to look like he wanted to sink into the floor. The sheepish expression and blush that still tinted his cheeks looked so damned...Garrett had to get himself back on topic or he would look like a moron. He had to act like the Dom he was. His control was better than this.

He cleared his throat. "So you need something specific today? Then you want to come back and go over more options for the business?" That sounded like what he'd been trying to say. Then it clicked.

Dear God, he was going to have to meet with him again next week.

Wyatt nodded, looking grateful that Garrett had deciphered his rambling. "Yes. I need...they said...Well..." He took a deep breath and tried again, this time with more success getting the words out in complete sentences. Just confusing ones. "I'm working on some furniture for a...restaurant up in Washington, D.C. and even though I know the owner, I'm still being listed as a subcontractor. At first, they thought I wouldn't be required to have it. I need to have a bond so that all the insurance stuff is in order. He said just to talk to whoever does my other insurance and they should be able to help. So here I am."

"I'd be happy to help. This won't take very long to get together." Garrett could write this policy in his sleep but what captured his attention was the little hesitation right before Wyatt had said "restaurant." Had he been going to say something different or was it just his overactive imagination when it came to this... client. This client.

Maybe if he said it enough times, he'd remember what to call Wyatt.

They talked for a few minutes about how much coverage the client had requested. As he filled out the information on the policy, Garrett was making small talk about other business insurance Wyatt might find useful. Things were going well until Garrett turned to him to get the business name and address.

That's when things went strangely pear shaped, as his mother liked to say.

"Um, oh...Um, I guess I forgot the address. Let me just...Yes, let me just email that to you later." Wyatt grabbed a business card off the desk and waved it around. "I'll call...or email...or something in just a little while about the address. Um, thank you. I'll call...Um, yes..." Then he was gone.

Garrett sat there for a long time looking at the door. "What the hell?"

"Everything okay?" Calen asked, poking his head around the door, clearly not working. Hell, it was Friday afternoon. He was lucky anyone was still in the office. "He left in a hurry."

"I don't know." Garrett wasn't sure what happened.

"Did you finish the policy?" Calen came in and sat down, propping his feet up on the desk. "You scare him off?" It was a running joke around the office that one day Garrett was going to frighten the poor...customer...that Garrett would frighten Wyatt away.

"Almost and I don't think so."

Now Calen perked up. To Garrett, he looked like a shark smelling blood. "You don't think you scared him off or you don't think you got the policy done?"

Nosey gossip. "The policy is almost done. We got to the part about the business name and he went all rabbit and panicked. He dashed out making all kinds of excuses about calling back with the address later this afternoon. I didn't even get the chance to tell him that I needed his business address or take a payment, damn it."

"Man, I know you said he wasn't—"

"He's not shady. He's just...skittish. I must have done something to make him nervous." Garrett just couldn't think what.

"This is the third time he's been in this week. Come on, no one visits their insurance company this much unless they're shady or they like the view." Now Calen smirked, giving him a nod. "You know what Brent said."

"Brent's crazy. There's no way...he's just wrong. Besides, all we need is a sexual harassment lawsuit because I came on to someone." There was a good chance Wyatt was gay. However, gay and a sub, or at least, open-minded enough to consider it, probably not. "Three times?"

"Yup. He paid the auto policy on Monday then came back on Wednesday to pay the life insurance. And don't distract me, nobody blinks at you guys anymore. You're paranoid."

Cautious.

He preferred the term cautious. When he and his three brothers had all come out in college, things had been fine at home. However, when they'd taken over his dad's insurance company after he passed, they'd ruffled a few feathers in the local business community. If word got out he was not only gay but a Dom as well, things might get interesting again.

"Your brothers—"

"All agreed that we would be discreet in town. That's why when we want to play we go elsewhere. If I start making waves, then it would affect not only myself but the business as well." That was the deal when they'd taken over. They wouldn't go back in the closet, or anything absurd, but with all of them interested in kink in one way or another, they'd agreed that discretion was a must.

That meant being very careful when dating in town.

"Your dad would have told them all to go take a flying fuck and then told you to do whatever the hell you wanted." Calen shook his head.

He was right about Dad. "It was a different time when my dad started building the business. People minded their own business back then." His dad had been unique in more ways than one. Not only in his acceptance of his boys but in his own personal life. Martin Ryder would have understood the need for privacy but not hiding.

"I'm not willing to risk everything we've built up on a *maybe he's gay* and *maybe me being a Dom won't make him freak*." Garrett needed to get up to the club and find someone to play with. He'd been thinking about going up this weekend, but suddenly, the idea didn't sound as good as it usually did. He probably just needed some time off.

Calen shook his head. "You're making a mistake."

"Bossy Dom."

"Takes one to know one," he said in a sing-song voice as he waltzed out of the office.

"Go get some work done!"

"It's four o'clock on Friday, you should be grateful I'm here at all," he hollered as he went down the hall. Garrett hoped Calen was heading back to his office to get work done, but it sounded more like he was heading for the kitchen to get a beer.

"Too many damn Doms in one place."

Shaking his head, Garrett tried to clear his mind. He still had a few more things to wrap up before he could quit for the day. Hopefully, Wyatt would call him back shortly with the information and maybe even finish the policy so he could get it sent off today.

"*Back to work*! No more mooning over the client. You have a lot to do before the meeting at six. Get your ass in gear." Garrett didn't think the reminder would help.

"Talking to yourself is a sign of senility!" Calen yelled from the back of the building. Yup, he was in the kitchen.

"Go back to work!"

It was going to be a long afternoon.

"You're sure this is the information he gave you?" Garrett looked at it then had to read it again.

"Are you *kidding*? I just forwarded you the email!" It sounded like Calen was well into his "It's five o'clock somewhere" Friday afternoon ritual. Well, it was after five here so Garrett thought he probably shouldn't complain. At least Calen was getting a little work done. Maybe.

"This doesn't make sense." Garrett thought he was talking to himself so he jumped when Calen huffed.

"What doesn't? I should have read the damned email. So much for respecting your privacy." Calen had this look like he wasn't going to be the last to know next time. Nosy Dom.

"You're right, you should have looked. You wouldn't have believed it either." Even on his third time reading through the email, he still couldn't believe it.

"What did it say!" Calen demanded impatiently.

"He's asking for the paperwork to be sent to B & C Corporate Holdings in Washington, D.C." Garrett watched Calen to see if he could make the connection.

"B & C, why does that sound familiar?" Calen flopped down in one of the chairs then propped his feet up in the other. Garrett mentally shrugged, at least it wasn't his desk this time.

"Because you've seen it on a sign several times a month for

the past couple of years. Maybe longer." Garrett watched as the lightbulb started to go off over Calen's head. He could see the slightly tipsy office manager almost had it.

"Man, no!"

"Yup."

"He's doing custome furniture for Bound & Controlled?"

"That's what it looks like."

"What kind of custom...Ohhh." Then Garrett could tell that Calen had finally caught up with the rest of the class. "Ha, and you were worried he'd be shocked."

"Hell, now I'm the one who's shocked." That sexy little thing...and Bound?

Bound & Controlled, or B & C, was a BDSM club in D.C. that primarily catered to the LGBTQ crowd. If Wyatt was designing anything for that club, it was going to be interesting. Garrett had been going there since it opened about five years ago. The only thing he could picture in the club that might fit Wyatt's vague description was the BDSM furniture the club was famous for.

"Oh, man, he makes the spanking benches and stuff! Those are damn steady. Last time I was up there, I had this sub—"

"Calen! Not the time."

"Oh, right." Calen tried to get serious but he couldn't do it. "You were so worried he'd like sue or something if you flirted with him. That's why he was so nuts this afternoon."

That brought to mind other questions.

"I shouldn't know what this means. No vanilla guy, even a gay one, would know B & C Corporate Holdings was the business name for a gay BDSM club. I probably wouldn't even know except we've got some of the owners' personal insurance here. Why would he even assume I'd know what this meant?"

Calen looked at him questioningly, clearly not following the logic. It had Garrett a little concerned. "How many beers have you had?"

He snorted. "Not enough. I'm keeping up. It seems crazy. Like one of Melissa's romance novels or maybe a spy thriller if we're lucky." Calen looked like he found that idea entirely too appealing.

"He's not a spy."

"You don't know *what* he is."

Evidently. "Well, I know he's not a spy. How could he know this would ring any bells for me at all?"

"Have you thought about calling?" Calen said in this deadpan voice like it was obvious. The delivery was ruined by his shit-eating grin.

"Call who?" He couldn't call Wyatt until he knew what to say.

"Ben and Conner. Duh!"

"What are you, twelve?" It should have been obvious. At this point, calling the owners of the club might be the only way to get more answers. Hadn't Wyatt said something about the company telling him to call his insurance agent? Maybe there had been more to that conversation than Wyatt had confessed because the boy...client seemed to have a hard time telling Garrett everything.

2

WYATT

"I'm an idiot! Like completely–out–of–my–mind–moron kind of idiot!" Wyatt dashed into the shop nearly crashing into a customer who was leaving. "Sorry, Mrs. Jenkins."

The sweet older lady gave him an understanding smile. "That's all right. Whatever you did this time will work out. It always does." Then she gave his arm a pat. "Remember the case of doorknobs? That worked out, didn't it? All right, dearies, I'm late for tea."

Watching the classy lady with her little Jackie O. hat and gloves, nobody would have ever thought tea meant liquor and cards with her group of naughty little old ladies. "Yes, ma'am. Thank you."

Mrs. Jenkins was the classic Southern lady. Wyatt was starting to realize that didn't mean what he thought it did. She was polite, proper, and always looked so put together, but looks were deceiving. It wasn't until she'd been coming into the shop for months that her daughter had stopped in to pick something up and spilled the beans.

Once she was out of the store, he took a quick look around to see if they were alone. When he was sure there were no customers, he threw himself down in a small upholstered chair that was some kind of antique reproduction, sighing dramatically.

When all he got from Carter was a snort, he looked over and frowned. "That's not enough sympathy for this situation."

"Honey, I grew up down south. That was not nearly dramatic enough if you want my sympathy." Carter cocked his hip and pretended to flutter his lashes. "Now, would you care to explain, or do I have to show you what a real drama queen does for attention?"

"You're not a queen. You're sweet and loving and under-standing and perfect and you're going to regret not giving me a better response." Wyatt closed his eyes and tried to calm down.

"You were just supposed to...Oh...What did you do this time? You actually had to talk to Sexy Agent Man, didn't you?"

"Yes!" It came out more of a wail than a real word. "And stop calling him that."

"You didn't actually kneel, did you?" Carter asked in a hushed tone filled with worry and probably suppressed laughter.

"No, but it was close. He's just so sexy and hot and powerful and did I mention sexy? He's the perfect Dom and I'm an idiot who can't function around him!"

Carter giggled. "Well, at least you stayed in your seat."

"Yes, but I still ended up looking like an idiot."

"What did you do?"

"When he asked about the address and company informa-tion I panicked and said I didn't have it with me. I could hardly get a sentence out. I was so nervous. Now it looks like I don't know what I'm doing. I was so afraid he was going to know once I said it out loud...and he was wearing that red tie again! I've got to stop going in there on Fridays!"

"I think the better vow would be to stop going in there so

often." Carter moved around from behind the antique desk to sit beside Wyatt in another of the weird little chairs. Wyatt thought he really should learn the name of them if he was going to sell them.

"That would be a lie and we both know it. I'm hopeless." He couldn't help it. Garrett, Wyatt didn't even let himself think of the sexy Dom as anything other than that just in case he actually said it out loud, was perfect. Going into the office to get his fix of the hot Dom was the highlight of his month. Okay, sometimes his week, but still, a guy had to have some eye candy in his life.

"I thought you said the guys who own the club weren't going to mention they knew you? Something about respecting your privacy. Ring any bells?" Carter had dated on the edge of the BDSM community but had never been up to the club in D.C. He admitted to being a sub but always said he was more than most Doms could handle.

Wyatt thought it was more likely that he didn't want to have to explain his quirks to a Dom.

"Yes, they won't tell, but I looked like such a spaz he's got to think something's wrong with me." The guys had said that more than likely Garrett wouldn't even connect the corporate name to the club but Wyatt wasn't so sure. They'd known Garrett well enough to recommend him as a new insurance agent to Wyatt when he'd told them he was moving down to Richmond. Something about the whole thing seemed fishy.

"I still don't understand why you didn't get everything out in the open when you first got your insurance there. A simple '*Hi, I'm Wyatt. I picked you guys because I've seen you at the club,*' and you wouldn't be in this situation."

"Because when I practiced it, I sounded like some kind of stalker! Then when I went in, I could barely talk to him and it all went to pieces." He couldn't function when Garrett was around.

He was able to do a reasonable job when the Dom was out of the office but since the goal of going in was to see him, that didn't work out so well.

Carter couldn't control how funny he thought the situation was. Giggling and shaking his head, he just looked at Wyatt. "What did you do when he asked you about the address?"

"I ran out in nearly a panic, promising to give it to him later this afternoon. I can't call him back!" That wasn't going to be an option.

"Then email him. Send the address and thank him for his help. That's it. Nothing else and...Hell, give it to me and I'll email him. You'll just do something dumb and it will go all kinds of wrong." Carter held out his hands for Wyatt's papers and phone.

Handing them over, Wyatt sighed again. "Just email the office manager. He's nice and will pass on the information."

Carter took a minute to email the information from Wyatt's phone. "All right. Done."

"You should come in next time I have to go pay my bill. You'll see. He's the *perfect* Dom." Carter didn't believe him, but Wyatt knew it would only take one look to change his friend's mind.

"I'm not going to go with you to stalk your insurance agent. I need to be able to bail you out when you're arrested." Carter made it sound like he was planning *when* not *if* it happened.

"I'm not stalking him. I'm paying my bills and asking questions." Mostly. Maybe asking a lot of questions but he didn't go in there for nothing. *That* would be stalking.

"Sure. Keep telling yourself that." Carter made it clear he wasn't buying that line of BS.

"What are the chances that he won't connect the dots?" Wyatt looked hopefully to Carter, but his friend, and almost boss, just shook his head.

"Slim to none. But then, I thought he would have realized he'd met you before by now. So you might get lucky."

"We only met once, and that was a couple of years ago when I was still dating my old Dom. He was polite, and it was quick before he moved off to talk to other people. He wouldn't have had any reason to remember it." Wyatt had still been enamored with his previous Dom at that point and while he'd noticed Garrett, it hadn't turned into an obsession yet.

Wyatt didn't develop his crush until later when his relationship had fallen apart. His Dom had taken a job overseas. It wasn't until Wyatt realized he had no desire to go with him that he had taken a good look at his relationship. Ending things had been hard, but it had been for the best.

He'd hung around Baltimore for another six months or so until Carter had told him it was time to stop moping and do something new. Which is why he ended up moving to Richmond and trying to turn his furniture hobby into a business. Carter had been wonderful enough to let him work in the antique store he owned until Wyatt could get settled.

He'd known Carter since their freshman year in college when they'd bonded over being a bit outside the box. Wyatt had already figured out he was a complete bottom and was starting to research the BDSM community. Carter had been trying to uncover his more flamboyant side and was experimenting with all kinds of different things.

He toned things down more now that he was a *successful business owner* but it had taken some of their more conservative customers a while to get used to the occasional skirt and guyliner. Today he was *really* toned down in black pants that looked almost masculine and a neutral sweater. The only noticeable thing was a little bit of makeup.

"You look strangely normal today. Why?"

Carter sighed. "I have a date. I thought I'd tone it down a little."

"With the online guy?" Wyatt didn't have high hopes for that one. The guy sounded entirely too vanilla for Carter. "Well, from what you've told me, he seems...nice."

That was about the only good thing Wyatt could say. The two met on an online dating site but he'd turned out to be the most tragically normal gay man Wyatt had ever heard of. Carter snorted. "That's what I'm afraid of, but it seemed mean not to at least give it a go. There's nothing wrong with him."

To Wyatt, the fact that the guy wasn't a Dom was reason enough not to date him but it was up to Carter. "I'm sure it will go fine. Where are you guys going?"

Carter perked up a little. "He said he was feeling like steak. Hopefully, dinner should be good."

"See, that's a good start." At least his friend would get a nice meal out of it.

"Fingers crossed. What are you up to tonight?"

Now it was Wyatt's turn to get excited. "I'm finishing up some of the final pieces for the new club."

When Ben and Conner decided to open up a second club in Baltimore, they'd called Wyatt to see if he could make the furniture for the new site since he'd already done the benches and a few more intricate pieces in the other one. Between that and some private commissions he'd started picking up lately, it looked like he was going to be able to do it full-time in the next couple of months.

"That's great. They're going to love them." Carter couldn't have been more supportive of Wyatt and he'd be forever grateful. If it hadn't been for his enthusiasm, Wyatt might have never tried to make a go of it.

"They're over the moon about the pieces that have already been delivered. I'm heading over to the garage as soon as I'm done moping." Wyatt gave Carter his best puppy dog eyes. "When do you have to go to your date?"

"Not for another hour," Carter laughed. "You can stay here and beg for attention."

"Good!" That's what friends were for—sympathy when you were a moron.

3

GARRETT

"Whatdo you mean you plead the fifth? I just asked if he was making the furniture for the new club. He came in today and it was...odd." It had taken three phone calls before Ben had picked up the phone. Garrett was going to be late for his meeting. With the damned thing being in his conference room that wasn't going to make him look good.

"*Well*, I can't tell you why I can't tell you." Ben's slow Southern drawl made Garrett want to reach through the phone and strangle him. Hearing the noise and music from the club in the background didn't help either. It had been ages since he'd had time to go up.

"What the fuck!"

"No need for that kind of language." Garrett could hear Conner losing his mind laughing in the background. "We made some promises to some of our *subcontractors* about privacy, that's all."

Privacy? "They're subcontractors *not submissives* why would they need privacy! Especially from their insurance agent!"

There was a long pause on the other end of the phone and if

it weren't for the laughter and occasional "Hush, Conner" he would have thought he'd lost the call. What had he said that—

"He's a sub! From the club?"

More laughter and noise came from the other end of the phone. "Conner, hush, he doesn't care if that rhymes. Sorry, Garrett, he was good this week and got permission to have a couple of drinks. They've gone right to his head. Now what were we saying? Oh, right. You're going to be a good agent and send any paperwork a customer requests, without asking me things I can't answer."

He was a sub. Things were starting to make more sense.

"If you've promised someone privacy, I can't ask you to break that. Club guidelines officially list respecting members' privacy as a primary rule of the group." Garrett tried to word that as carefully as he could.

Evidently it was enough, because Ben chuckled. "Very true. Listen, I have to go. He's trying to talk me into another drink and if I don't keep an eye on him he's going to be dancing on the tables again. Naughty boy. Keep that up and you're not going to get spanked tonight!" The smile in his voice, and the odd nature of the threat, didn't make it sound very terrifying.

"Have fun. I have a meeting I need to get to."

"Oh, I'm going to have fun. You should too. Maybe go buy furniture or something." Then the infuriating man hung up.

"Go buy furniture..." Garrett was still mumbling and trying to work through everything he'd learned and everything that he hadn't learned when he walked back to the conference room. What Ben hadn't said was just as interesting now that Garrett wasn't tempted to kill him.

He was still trying to figure out what to do next when he walked into the conference room. Normally, he didn't mind meeting with everyone. It was only one Friday a month and he liked getting together with his family. Today, though, he wasn't in the mood to deal with anything.

It would have been too much to ask for Calen to have kept his mouth shut.

As soon as Garrett stepped into the room, Calen called out. "So what did you find out from Ben and Conner? The little one is more than meets the eye, isn't he?"

How many beers had he consumed?

Of course, that was too much for his nosey family. Just enough of a tease to make the hounds smell blood. Or in this case, good gossip. Between his three brothers and an assortment of office managers, the room was packed. They all started talking but Brent was the closest to the door and the least likely to say something obnoxious, so Garrett focused on him.

"Everything okay at the club?" Brent was always calm and had this feeling about him that you could depend on him. Garrett always found him the easiest of his brothers to talk to.

"Yeah, I had a question about some insurance for the new one they're opening and talking to them was frustrating." That was an understatement but Garrett knew if he went into more detail it would just lead to endless questions.

"Were they already at the club?" Brent looked nearly as jealous as Garrett felt. They'd all been working too hard lately and hadn't taken nearly enough time off. Maybe in the next couple weeks he could make everyone take a weekend off and they could all go up.

"Yeah, Conner was already three sheets to the wind as a reward." That part had honestly been funny so Garrett's smile was genuine.

Brent laughed and leaned back in his chair, ignoring everyone else. "Was he on the table already?"

"Just about. Ben had to hang up and go chase him down. That's why I'm running late."

"Conner probably needed the stress relief. I know with the second club going up he's been under a lot of pressure to keep things on schedule." Brent frowned and shook his head. "With that, plus his normal projects he's probably bouncing off the walls."

Ben and Conner owned the club together but Conner also owned a small construction company that primarily did custom homes. He was always crazy busy and incredibly stressed. When Ben said Conner had been good, he'd meant that his boy hadn't overworked himself and had actually slept.

"If he's earned this big of a reward then things can't be going that bad."

Brent nodded and then came back to what he'd probably wanted to know to begin with. "Little one? Am I safe in assuming that he's talking about Wyatt?"

What?

"Why would you assume that?"

That had everyone laughing hard enough that Garrett couldn't ignore them anymore. "Hey!"

He loved his family, he really did, but some days he just wanted to—taking a deep breath he tried to focus on anything else besides where he'd hide the bodies. Sometimes he wasn't sure what made him think going into business with his brothers was a good idea.

His parents had built up an incredibly successful insurance business but things were so much more difficult now. Instead of one branch, there were now three, and Brent, who was the claims manager for the area. The fact that they all had such strong personalities didn't help either.

Things would have been easier if they were all more traditional but with everyone being bossy, nosy, opinionated, and into the lifestyle in one way or another, meetings were always interesting. He was at the point of saying to hell with the meeting when Brent cleared his throat and gave everyone the look that said he was done with the clowning around.

For someone who identified as a sub, he always got everyone else in line.

They settled down pretty fast, but Grant, the oldest, just started shaking his head and wouldn't let it drop. "He's not kidding? He has no idea how you knew it was Wyatt?"

Oldest always knows best. Garrett didn't have the patience for that today. He loved Grant, he really did, his older brother would do anything for any one of them, but Garrett wasn't in the mood to butt heads with him today.

There was a chorus of laughter and the general consensus was that he was stupid. "*What?*"

With everyone shouting over each other, it was a few minutes before they were all quiet enough for him to talk. "Would someone like to explain now?" He was getting frustrated.

Grant looked over at Bryce, the baby of the family. "You explain it. You saw it first."

"Saw what?"

Bryce grinned and cleared his throat before turning to Garrett. "Do you remember when I came in a few weeks ago and we were talking about the Murphys' retirement plans?"

"Yes." He wasn't a moron.

"Wyatt came in that day to pay a bill, right?" Bryce's voice was careful and measured.

Garrett felt like he was being led along one step at a time. "Just get on with it."

Bryce cocked an eyebrow at him, waiting for Garrett to answer the question.

Stubborn bastard was all Garrett could think. "Yes, damn it. I remember."

Grinning, Bryce kept going. "Do you remember how he was acting?"

"No odder than usual." Wyatt was always a little bit different. Garrett wasn't one to throw stones but something about the bo— customer was unique. Garrett's answer had everyone in stitches.

Even Bryce just looked at him, confused. "He's like that all the time?"

"He's been like that since the first time he came into the office." The conversation was going nowhere fast.

Now they were looking at him like he was an idiot again. "*What*?"

"He's head over heels for you...or in this case ready to kneel for you." Then Bryce paused like he was waiting for something.

It took Garrett a minute to really hear what he'd said. Huh? Ready to...With his earlier conversation with Ben fresh in his mind, things were looking a little different.

Brent evidently wasn't sure that Bryce had gotten through to their thick-skulled brother because he cheerfully chimed in. "If you had met him at the club the first time instead of here in the office what would you have thought?"

That was easy. "That he needed a master to settle him down. The boy's a mess."

"There you have it!" Bryce had a fake cheerful tone like Garrett was a child who'd done something impressive, like add two plus two.

"Bingo." He was going to throw something at Grant if he didn't stop the sarcastic bullshit.

"Yup." Brent was nodding and trying not to smile.

"You following now, moron?" The last comment came from Calen. Drunken ass.

"Yes, I'm following now." He just wasn't sure what he was going to do now. "He's still a customer."

"Who was ready to jump you. I'm not sure there's going to be a problem." Bryce responded in a deadpan expression. Then he looked over at Brent. "Maybe it was easier for us to notice because we see things differently."

Bryce was the switch in the family so he thought he was smarter than Garrett and Grant who had a tendency to see things with "Dom-vision" as they called it. Basically, it was like tunnel vision but with the Dom tendency to always believe they're right. Garrett thought it was insane. He was just always right, it didn't matter if he was a Dom or not.

There was no way he was going to let them believe they were right.

"He can't possibly have been attracted to me for that long." It wasn't possible. Was it? If he was honest, he'd been fighting the attraction to the...hell, to the boy for that long.

The general consensus was that he was an imbecile. A blind one who'd missed a sexy sub in desperate need of a Dom. "Do you think I could have met him at the club before? He seemed anxious that I would know the business name of the club when he came in today."

Grant piped up, obviously very curious. "What did he need?"

"He's working as a subcontractor, building the furniture in the new club. Evidently, he makes *custom* pieces."

Calen evidently thought Garrett was being too subtle because he called out. "He makes the spanking benches and stuff. Hey, I wonder if he did the cross too. The one with the carvings and the cut out for—"

"Enough. We have real things we need to get to. Garrett's love life will have to wait." For once he was grateful for Grant's need to take charge and run the show. At least it would get him out of the spotlight.

And give him a chance to think.

Wyatt was a submissive who evidently was as interested in

Garrett as Garrett was in him. He had to fight to keep the smile off his face. That still didn't answer the question about how he knew Garrett was a Dom. It wasn't something he went around advertising.

Ben and Conner wouldn't have randomly told someone his personal information. Had he met Wyatt before? Nothing came to mind right off the bat, but he knew it was possible. It had been months since he'd been up, but he couldn't remember anyone like Wyatt.

If he'd met the boy before, why wouldn't he have said something? Hell, why wouldn't Ben and Conner have said something? Privacy was normal, but this felt like more than that. Wyatt had said the "owners" had told him to go to his insurance agent…and those asses hadn't been surprised at all that Garrett was the agent.

He was trying to keep things in perspective but he was starting to feel like Calen acted, suspicious and a little crazy. Everyone else thought Wyatt had been attracted to him for a long time because of the behavior. If that was true, he would have been interested since he'd first moved down.

Suddenly, Garrett had a feeling that he needed to be a conscientious agent and take the papers down to Wyatt. It would only be the right thing to do. Without a signature and a payment, the policy wouldn't go into effect anyway and he'd wanted it to start as soon as possible. Yup, taking it down personally was the only right thing to do.

"Are you listening?" Bryce's voice broke through Garrett's thoughts.

"No." No point in lying. He hadn't the foggiest idea what they were talking about.

Grant sighed and leaned back in his chair. "This is going to take forever. Can you please stop mooning over the guy and pay attention?"

"Fine. What were you guys discussing?"

"Damn it! He wasn't listening at all!" Grant's voice got louder when he realized Garrett hadn't just missed part of the conversation, he had no idea what was going on.

"You are entirely too wound up." Garrett wasn't going to take shit from Grant. The guy needed a weekend off and to get laid. It would probably help if he didn't look like a biker or bouncer at a club. He'd never attract the guys he wanted looking like that.

Brent broke in giving them both an exceptionally well-done version of their mother's stink eye. "Enough." Then he turned to Garrett. "We were trying to discuss the advertising campaign we were going to be doing on the local radio station."

Damn. He actually had to pay attention. This was supposed to be his part of the meeting. He looked over at the clock on the wall. This was going to take forever.

4

WYATT

Wyatt jumped and nearly dropped the sander he'd just turned off when the voice came from the door of his workshop.

"You know, you should lock the door."

He would know that voice anywhere, it even gave him butterflies in his dreams. Garrett. What was he doing here? Wyatt took several deep breaths and put down the tool before he let himself turn around. Every good intention to try and look like a normal person went right out the window the second he caught sight of the sexy Dom.

If Wyatt had thought Garrett looked good in a suit, the man was incredible in jeans and a t-shirt. The pants molded to his body like a second skin and the shirt was even worse. How was he supposed to be able to make his brain work when the man looked like *that*?

"I...um...you...and...um..." He sounded like an idiot. Taking another deep breath, he focused over Garrett's shoulder at the street light outside the door. Hoping it would help if he wasn't looking directly at the sexy Dom, Wyatt tried again. "Um...Well, hello...Um...Can I help you?"

It came out too formal and still stuttered but it was at least a sentence. Most of one at least. Wyatt fought the urge to kneel and just look up at him. He probably looked even more ridiculous now than he had earlier.

Just thinking about the meeting had Wyatt's stomach in knots. The butterflies had turned into giant sci-fi-sized moths. Had he figured it out? Even if he had, Wyatt knew he shouldn't be panicking. So he designed furniture for interesting activities. The guy was a Dom for goodness sake, it wasn't like he was going to judge.

But the idea of Garrett knowing made his knees weak.

Garrett grinned and leaned against the doorframe. He crossed one leg over the other highlighting his—Giving his head a little shake, Wyatt went back to focusing on the soft glow of the light. When had it gotten so dark?

"I wanted to come bring you the papers. I needed a signature." There was a little pause then his voice got a little deeper, rougher. "I also wanted to see your...furniture."

That little pause told Wyatt more than anything else the Dom had said. He knew. Now what? Pretend he didn't know that he knew? That didn't make enough sense. Most of the blood in Wyatt's body was *not* in his brain.

The Dom must have known he'd fried Wyatt's brain. His grin got bigger and he straightened up. Wyatt watched as the Dom quietly moved closer. This wasn't the same insurance agent he'd been dealing with for the past year. This was the Dom he'd been fangirling over. What changed?

He decided, he probably didn't want to know.

Maybe he did. It was too confusing. Garrett tossed some papers down on a table but didn't stop. He kept getting closer until he was almost touching Wyatt. Wyatt had a weird bubble. Sometimes he liked having people close and sometimes it made him crazy. With Garrett, Wyatt wanted to climb all over him or kneel at his feet. Neither one was an option so his body couldn't decide what to do.

That made his normally twitchy body even worse.

Hands clenched then opened. They went in his pockets and then came out. When he started biting his fingernail, he knew he looked nuts. The wiggling and shifting didn't help either. He couldn't decide what to do. Everything was always easier when he didn't have to fight his instincts.

Garrett took the decision away from him.

"Hands behind your back." His voice sent shivers through Wyatt, and he instinctively obeyed. "Very good."

Hearing the pleasure in Garrett's voice made Wyatt's cock even harder than it already was. This had been his fantasy for months, probably longer. He wanted to pinch himself to see if it was real but he kept his hands clasped tightly. Disobeying the Dom was out of the question. Even a fantasy version.

Wyatt didn't even realize he'd been staring at the man's sexy chest until Garrett spoke again. "Look at me."

Obeying that order was harder. Wyatt knew he wouldn't be able to hide his desire from the Dom. His eyes moved up the sculpted body until he was looking into his eyes. "That's a good boy."

Shivers raced through him and he couldn't help the little moan that escaped. Garrett didn't seem to mind. His devilish grin got wider, heat flared in his eyes. The Dom liked making him nuts. Wyatt wasn't sure what to make of it but that expression didn't lie.

"Here's what we're going to do. We're going to take a few minutes and finish up the paperwork so I can send this up to Ben and Conner. Oh yes, boy, I know what that business is. That's what you were so nervous about, wasn't it?" Garrett waited and it took Wyatt a minute to figure out he had to respond.

"Um, yes..." That was one of the things he'd been nervous about. So technically he'd been honest. And what was he supposed to call the man now? Garrett was too informal now and Sir seemed presumptuous. Master would be even worse so maybe Sir wasn't that bad. "Sir?"

"That will do...for now. Once we've gotten that out of the way you're going to show me your *custom furniture*." Oh yeah, he knew. The Dom looked like he was *very* interested in a tour of the workshop. Wyatt couldn't decide how he felt about that.

He wasn't sure if a response was required so he simply nodded, waiting. Garrett wrapped one hand around Wyatt's waist and rested it on his back. It was like electricity shooting right through Wyatt and another little sound escaped.

Garrett's smile got almost wolfish. Pressing his hand tighter, he steered Wyatt over to the table where the papers were lying. Once he had Wyatt positioned where he wanted, he removed his hand and took a step back.

Wyatt had to take a deep breath to clear his head as Garrett started explaining what everything meant and what was spelled out in the bond. He was glad Garrett was taking it seriously, but even on a good day he only understood about half the insurance paperwork. Today wasn't even a good day, but he tried to follow along as best he could.

Garrett must have realized Wyatt wasn't following because his voice softened and he smiled almost tenderly. "We'll get this ready to be sent off today so you've got everything in order for the contract, but I want you to email me this weekend with any questions you have. You're going to read it through several times. Are we clear? I want you to understand what everything means."

Nodding, he looked up at the Dom and tried to smile. "I'll read it."

"And email me with any questions. I think doing it that way might be easier for you to stay focused. Calling might be...difficult." His smirk made Wyatt want to blush. He was right though. Calling the sexy man with real questions would be nearly impossible.

"Yes, Sir. I'll email questions." Wyatt signed the papers and agreed to call the office Monday to make the payment.

"That's all set then. Now for my tour." That wolfish look was back. "I'm very curious to see your work. I've seen it *first-hand*, but this is very different."

He'd never seen the Dom using anything he'd made but just the idea made his knees weak. "Um, yes...sure...I'd...I'd be happy to show you."

Garrett put his hand back on Wyatt's back, this time making slow caresses up his back. "Why don't you show me what you were working on when I came in?"

It had to be that.

Wyatt's face lit up like a bright red Christmas bulb but he couldn't think of any reason to say no. It wasn't that he was ashamed of the piece. He wasn't sure he'd be able to find the words to describe it. The warm hand, rubbing his back only made his focus worse.

Leading them back over to the bench where Wyatt had been working, Garrett looked down at the pieces. It probably looked like a big 3-D puzzle, but when it was all put together it was going to be a beautiful—

"That's going to be an incredible spanking bench. Almost like the ones in the D.C. club but not exactly." Garrett's eyes lit up. He reached out to run his fingers down the unfinished wood. "It's very smooth."

"It has to be." He got some of it out before his nervousness clicked back in. "Um...Well, you know...because of the use and all...I'm really careful..." He sounded like an idiot again.

Garrett's fingers dipped low on his back for a second teasing at his senses. Then the Dom grinned a sexy wicked smile. "Oh, with something like this you'd have to be *very* careful. So much tender bare skin that you wouldn't want injured—at least, not by the wood."

His face was so red it hurt, but he did his best to respond, "Yes, Sir." It was almost a sentence.

He didn't even realize his hands were fidgeting again until the order came again. "Hands behind your back. Good boy."

His cock jumped at the firm control in the Dom's voice. He thought it would be possible to come from just hearing the man. Smooth and sexy, he sounded incredible. One of Wyatt's favorite guilty pleasures was to go in and ask questions to hear him talk.

When the Dom reached down to wrap his hand over Wyatt's clasped ones, he almost did come. A needy little whimper escaped, it was all he could do not to beg for more. It was a ridiculous reaction to such a small touch. But it was so much more than he'd ever expected. Each little thing sent his body into overdrive.

"Aren't you so cute." His hand tightened on Wyatt's, not enough to make him feel bad trapped or anything...just enough to make him feel crazy sexy good trapped. "So responsive, aren't you?"

It *might* have been a question, so Wyatt nodded. He was desperate for more but Garrett just left his hand holding Wyatt's as he looked around. "How about you show me more? I've never met anyone who does such beautiful work."

He had to walk? And talk?

His brain and body both protested loudly, but he cleared his throat a couple of times then managed to croak out a short response. "Sure."

Wyatt didn't seem to mind his fried brain though because he just smiled. "Lead the way...this time."

That didn't help his coordination any.

Just the images that popped into his brain were enough to

make his dick start leaking precum. He had to get a hold of himself. His mind wanted to fantasize about everything the Dom might do to him. It didn't help that every time Wyatt started talking about a piece or answered a question, Garrett's fingers would start caressing the top of his ass.

Still holding on to Wyatt's hands, Garrett would let a few fingers trail over the bottom of his back, right at his crack. Just enough to make his breath catch and he had to fight the urge to beg. He was a better sub than that though. He needed to show Garrett how good of a sub he was.

There were only so many things he could explain as they walked around the warehouse. Sooner than he wanted, he'd run out of projects to talk about. Finally, he gave a little shrug and looked around. "That's about it."

"You have some incredible designs. You said you do custom work for individuals as well?" He honestly seemed to be interested and Wyatt couldn't help but get a little shy talking about his work. He still wasn't used to sharing it with people.

"Yes and sometimes I'll make something just because I get an idea. Then I'll put that on my website to show people." Setting up the site hadn't been as hard as he'd been afraid it would. Carter had been a huge help. He'd set up the shop's website, and he hadn't minded showing Wyatt how to do it too.

"When you get done with the pieces for the club, I'll have to see about getting you to make something for me. Do you have any finished pieces I could look at that aren't going to the club?" There was something in his voice that sent shivers down Wyatt's spine.

"Um, nothing here but...I um...Um, I have...Well, I have a few pieces at home I ended up liking too much to sell." He couldn't decide if it was a good idea to confess that or not.

"Hmm, interesting." The Dom looked like he wanted to say

more but he stopped. Looking around, he seemed to switch gears completely. "Do you have anywhere to sit?"

Sit?

"Um, there's just...it's..." He pointed over to an overstuffed chair in the corner that was covered by a sheet. He only used it when he got too tired to go home and needed to sleep there.

"Ah." Then he started leading Wyatt over to it. Pulling back the sheet, he grinned at Wyatt. Then Garrett gave him a little wink that made Wyatt try to hide a giggle. "There's only one seat, so I guess you'll have to sit on my lap."

Then he gave Wyatt a gentle, questioning smile. It was clear Garrett wouldn't force the issue if it made him uncomfortable, but there was no place else Wyatt wanted to be. This was dream-come-true time. "Yes, Sir. Um, I want to...Um."

That wolf grin was back as Garrett sat down and pulled Wyatt onto his lap. Still holding tight to his clasped hands, Garrett set his other hand on Wyatt's legs after he got him settled. Wyatt wanted Garrett to hold him tighter...and to move his hand higher. Just a few more inches up his leg and Wyatt would be in heaven.

Garrett seemed to be content not to rush things. He leaned back and relaxed, watching Wyatt closely. "I have some questions for you."

It wasn't a question but Wyatt nodded anyway. He'd been expecting some questions, probably even some embarrassing ones. Garrett had to have tons, unless Ben and Conner had told on him. That wasn't likely. Although, the two must have said something.

He had a question before Garrett started. "How did you... How did you find out about the business?"

Garrett chuckled. "I have several of the club's policies as well as some of their personal ones. I'm probably the only insurance agent who would have known right off the bat what B & C Corporate Holdings was."

He could feel the heat rising on his face. "They didn't tell me that." Those two had set him up.

"They told you to go see your agent, huh? Did they know you did everything through me?" It was clear Garrett could see the set-up too.

"Yes, they recommended you when I told them I was moving down." That was mostly the truth. They'd just been the ones to clue him into the fact that his crazy major crush was also an insurance agent.

"Those two. They wouldn't tell me anything about you. I think I've filled in some of the gaps, however." His fingers started drawing little circles on Wyatt's legs making him want to squirm. "I'm assuming you're single?"

"Yes." That was an easy one.

"How long has it been since you've had a Dom?"

"About a year and a half."

"That's a long time. Have you played with anyone since then?" He didn't look like he was judging, only curious.

This one was harder to answer. "No...I...I like...I'm more on the full-time end of the spectrum and a lot of Doms don't want to deal with that." Did Garrett? Would Wyatt end up being too much for him?

"That's fine. How full-time do you prefer?" Again, no judgment, just open curiosity.

It took him a few deep breaths before he could start. He wanted to show Garrett he could do this. "I need to be able to work. I like what I'm doing but I like for my Dom to take control over things. I...I...I'm a complete sub in the bedroom. Like my Dom would control everything in there."

This was the part that started making some Dominants wary. He couldn't meet Garrett's eyes any longer, so he looked down to watch Garrett's fingers trace patterns on his legs. "I also like to have my Dom be in charge of things outside of sex." He felt a ridiculous amount of pride when he'd managed to say it without stumbling. "Asking permission to go out with friends...Um... Having him approve my schedule...Serving him when we're together...That kind of stuff."

"Look up at me." His voice was firm but still warm and sexy.

Wyatt peeked up and tried not to squirm. "Yes, Sir."

"That's good. Now, I've never had a full-time submissive but I'm not opposed to the idea. There would have to be negotiations and extensive discussions first before I would take over as your full-time Dom, but it's not a deal breaker for me, Sweet." It was such a different response than what Wyatt had been expecting. At first, he didn't get it.

"You're not? I mean, it's not?"

"No. Now, would you like to have dinner with me tomorrow?"

Huh?

"*Dinner*?"

"Yes, the meal where you generally take a date so you can get to know them better." Garrett was laughing at him, but it made shivers dance down his spine so the Dom could laugh all he wanted.

"You want to get to know me? I mean..." He wasn't sure what he meant. It had been so long since a Dom hadn't made polite excuses when Wyatt explained what he was looking for, he wasn't sure what to do now. A date hadn't been what he was expecting.

"Yes. I want to get to know you before we take things too fast. I want to take you out and ask you stupid questions about what kind of movies you like and what your favorite dessert is. Then I'm going to drop you off at home and give you a good night kiss to remember." The last part came out almost as a growl and Garrett's hand had tightened on his leg making it hard to think.

The crazy level of sexual arousal was the only thing Wyatt had to blame his impulsive offer on. "Would you like to have dinner at my house instead? I could show you the things I made."

Garrett licked his lips, making Wyatt's cock even harder. He couldn't believe he said it, but he wasn't going to take it back. He loved to cook, and they'd be able to talk more openly, if they had privacy. Garrett must have thought it was a good idea as well because his fingers started wandering higher up Wyatt's leg, almost to his cock but not quite.

Garrett was going to be a Dom that loved to tease. Wyatt couldn't wait.

"I would love to, cutie. Is tomorrow too soon? I don't want to wait."

"No, that's fine." He looked down at his lap again, shyness getting the better of him. "I don't want to either."

"Very good. Is six o'clock good for you?"

"Yes, I have to work at the store for a few hours tomorrow. Then I have some things to do here but that should be good." He was in shock. The sexiest Dom he'd ever seen wanted to have dinner with him.

"Wonderful. And, Wyatt?"

"Yes." Wyatt glanced up at him. He shouldn't have. There had to be all kinds of naughty things going through Garrett's head. The look on his face was pure sex.

"I said I didn't want to go too fast...That doesn't mean I want to go slow."

5

GARRETT

"Couldn't stay away, huh?"

"Yeah. You're just that awesome. Let me in or I'll call Mom and tell her you've found Mr. Right." Brent grinned, he knew how terrible that threat was. He might have been trying to look happy but something seemed off. The normally laid-back brother seemed...sad, maybe.

"What did I do to you?" Garrett was sure it was too early to have to deal with family. Especially, someone who was being vague about why they were there.

"You made me get up at a ridiculous hour to check on your sorry ass since you wouldn't answer the phone last night." Then Brent shouldered by, inviting himself in. "Where's the coffee?"

Oh yeah, something was very wrong.

"Where it always is. What has you in a mood this morning?" Garrett was starting to think the morning visit had less to do with his love life and more to do with Brent. He ignored his family on a regular basis. It was the only way to get peace and quiet some days.

"Nothing. You should have answered the phone. You dashed out of the meeting last night saying you had to get the papers signed, then nothing. I got calls all night asking if I knew what the hell you were up too." Wandering into the kitchen, Brent made himself at home. Pouring coffee, he started rummaging around for the goodies he knew Garrett would have hidden somewhere.

Garrett watched as his disgruntled brother poked around the well-appointed kitchen until he found the chocolate chip muffins Garrett had hidden with the pots and pans. It might be his house but enough people dropped by that if he didn't put them some place weird they'd be gone before he got one. He was going to have to find a new hiding spot. They had been entirely too easy to find.

When his brother was settled with caffeine and sugar, Garrett walked over to the table. Sitting down with his own cup, he folded up the paper he'd been reading. For international and national news he used the computer or his tablet but for local stuff the paper seemed more fitting.

He'd also been having a pretty good fantasy about what he would have loved for Wyatt to have been doing. If things kept moving like he thought they would, one day he was going to have that sweet sexy sub on the floor warming his master's cock while Garrett read the paper. But his fantasy would have to wait. Thank God he'd already gotten dressed this morning or Brent would have gotten an eyeful when Garrett opened the door. Pajamas didn't hide an erection.

Grabbing another muffin, Garrett thought it might be safe to approach his normally calm brother. "So, what's really up?"

Brent picked some of the chocolate off and shrugged.

Well, that hadn't been helpful. "I stopped by and saw Wyatt last night. I'm not saying anyone was right, but he and I *might* have a date this evening."

That at least got Brent to smile. "So he's really a sub?"

"*Oh yes.*" Garrett thought *that* was an understatement. "He's looking for more of a lifestyle relationship so it's been difficult for him. It was easy to tell he was expecting me to take off when he said he wasn't just looking for a play-on-the-weekend kind of guy." Brent winced as Garrett finished. He hoped they might finally be getting somewhere with whatever was making Brent nuts.

"Yeah, that's hard. Guys are willing to fool around and play a little but that's about it. When it comes to someone who wants a serious relationship in the lifestyle, and not just inside the bedroom, that's harder to find." Brent started taking his muffin apart again. Still not eating anything but the chocolate.

"Your evening not go well?" That would explain things but Garrett wasn't sure if he should ask.

"Oh, it was a spectacular failure." Brent slumped down in the chair and took a sip of his coffee.

"You've been talking to that guy, the one you met on the kink site?" He thought that was right. Brent was a little shy sometimes, so he didn't always volunteer information on who he was dating. Leftover shit from growing up with mostly Dominants in the house.

"Yeah."

Garrett was still getting one-word answers, but the tone was starting to change. A little softer and Brent's frustration was starting to ease because he actually took a bite of the mangled muffin. "I thought things were going pretty good. He said he wasn't into something completely lifestyle but he didn't want to just keep stuff in the bedroom."

"Well, that's what you've been looking for. Y'all have been talking for a while, right? Like about real life stuff first?" At least, that's what he thought Brent said. Something about wanting to take things slow. It had helped that the guy lived a few hours away. No way to rush a three-hour car trip.

"Yeah, good thing too. We were on FaceTime last night and

his *wife* came home early from her business trip." Brent said it so matter-of-factly that it took Garrett a minute to get what he'd said.

"*What!*"

"Yup, turned out he was married. His wife and *Domme* called me back about an hour after he hung up unexpectedly. He's a sub who evidently does this every couple of months if she has to travel too much for work. She apologized and said she thought she'd found all the fake accounts.

"Are you sure? That sounds weird." It sounded less real life BDSM and more like something on TV.

"Yeah, he even got on the phone too. He's bi, and she was gone for a couple of weeks with some kind of international business deal. It didn't seem like anything was off. He was trying to get her attention, but she'd been too busy to notice. She said that usually she catches on in a few days. Recently her work hours have been crazy, it just got out of hand." Now Brent was back to picking apart the rest of the muffin.

"Man, you have the worst luck. I'm sorry." He reached over and gave Brent's shoulder a squeeze. His brother closed his eyes and took a deep breath.

"It's not like I loved the guy. We hadn't even met in real life. I'm frustrated more than anything. It sucks." Brent really did have terrible luck with men. If there was a loser in a hundred-mile radius, he'd tried to date Brent.

It wasn't even like Brent was ugly or something. Average height, trim and muscular without being too big, he looked like the rest of the guys in the family. Even Garrett could see he was cute. Other Doms had to find him attractive. But Brent didn't come across like most guys thought a sub should. He wasn't a twink, and he was so calm and in charge at work and with regular day-to-day stuff most people in the lifestyle thought he had to be a Dom.

"We need to get you back to the club. D.C.'s dripping with Doms." They'd all been too busy to relax lately. He wondered how long it'd been since Brent went up to even hang out.

"That doesn't help. Going up there alone is boring. Most of my friends are either vanilla or paired off with the *perfect* partner. And when I go with you guys, people either assume I'm taken by the sheer number of Doms I'm with or that we're all *really* kinky." Brent was starting to come out of his funk because he started laughing. "Remember that old guy with the bad hairpiece. He was so sure we were in some kind of incest relationship when he realized we were brothers."

Garrett shuddered. "That guy was weird. Just the look on his face. It went way beyond being open-minded to creepy giddy."

Brent nodded. "Ben and Conner said they had to banish him not long after that. He was making some of the other couples uncomfortable."

There was only one couple Garrett could think of that the guy would have upset. "You mean Aubrey and Lincoln?"

"Yeah, as soon as someone outed them as brothers to the douche he wouldn't leave them alone. It was creepy."

"I hadn't heard."

"You've been busy. And possibly avoiding the club?" Brent looked like he was fishing for more information.

Maybe.

Not that he would admit it. Something about going up there without his own sub hadn't been appealing lately. Sure there were other guys looking for serious relationships, but he always attracted subs who were just looking for a good time before they went back to their high-powered jobs. He didn't have a problem with subs who had full-time, important jobs. It just meant they couldn't relocate. His life was in Richmond. Between family and the business, leaving wasn't an option.

"I hope whoever outed them got in trouble too. It was so easy to see the guy was disturbed, whoever mentioned it had to be doing it on purpose." That shit was wrong. A few members had a problem with them, but anybody who remembered what happened didn't begrudge them happiness.

"Ben and Conner were kind of quiet on that but I had a feeling they had a serious talk with someone." Brent seemed to be pushing past his own issues because he looked up at Garrett and smiled. "So you had fun last night?"

Garrett laughed. "Not *that* much fun but he was so cute. And God, the furniture. It's the stuff from the club but there's more too. He makes custom stuff for people. He's going to show me some pieces he has at his house, after we have dinner."

Brent gave him a look like he could see where that was going. "Dinner at his house?"

"Yes. *He offered*, not that it's your business. I asked him out on a real date but he wanted to cook for me. I couldn't say no to that." Garrett had found that offer entirely too tempting.

"Did he calm down when he realized you were interested in him?"

"Nope, just made the twitchy boy even worse. But now I don't have to sit there and watch him bounce around. I can say or do something to help him relax." Staying professional and keeping his hands to himself had been a lot harder than he'd realized.

There had been so many times in the office he'd wanted to rest his hand on the boy to see if that would help him calm down. Wyatt had probably been trying to push back his natural tendencies around a Dominant as well. It only made him jumpier than usual.

As a more lifestyle-oriented sub attracted to a Dom, he'd probably been afraid he would unintentionally out himself. Garrett still couldn't quite figure out why Wyatt had thought he needed to hide his preferences. It probably didn't even matter at this point.

Just being able to touch Wyatt, to take control of him and the conversation made both of them relax more. "I think we've been fighting our instincts, and that made everything weirder. He's still wiggly but now I don't have to try to treat him like a vanilla guy."

"Sounds like you two hit it off, about time." Then Brent gave a wicked grin. "When you gonna tell Mom?"

"You throw me under the bus and I'll tell her you're lonely. I'll sweetly tell her that you thought she should come back home for a while. She could even stay with you." Two could play that game.

Brent grimaced. "All right. I was just teasing. No need to haul out the big guns."

"Have you heard from her lately?" Their mother was currently touring Italy with some of her friends. At least, Garrett thought that was right. Maybe it was France?

"Entirely too often. You?"

"Same. I thought when she started traveling, she'd find something else to obsess over besides us. I think being gone made it worse." Now when she called it was endless questions on what they were doing. Garrett had hoped the traveling would give her other things to talk about. Instead, it made her more focused on them. Why would she want to talk about what she'd seen when she had children to interrogate?

"Yup. Now she doesn't have anyone to boss around and control on a regular basis. She's going through withdrawal."

"Serves her right for putting together a travel group with only Dominants. I told her she needed to mix it up more."

"You heard her. She was afraid too many of them would get *distracted*." Brent was laughing but only because their mother had been a lot more descriptive in her explanation. Something about wanting to keep them focused on doing stuff outside the bedroom.

When their dad passed, she lost not only her husband of forty years but the only submissive she'd ever had. It hit her hard and for about a year they'd been afraid she was going to follow him. She lost her will to do anything.

Eventually, they'd stepped in and made her see a therapist. She slowly got better and turned her need to control on them. That's when they decided she needed a hobby. A few trips slowly turned into a travel group for Dominants.

They'd all decided she didn't want the temptation of submissives around. She wasn't depressed any longer, but she wasn't ready to admit there was a possibility that she might fall in love again. There were some mixed feelings on that in the family.

Of course, they had mixed feelings on everything.

With Dominants, a submissive, and a switch, along with assorted personality traits, they never saw things the same way. Garrett thought it made their family more interesting. Except when they were driving him crazy. Then he just wanted them to give him some space and let him do his own thing.

That wasn't going to happen.

"It sounds like you like him."

"I think I might. I never let myself really see him."

"Well, you're going to have that chance tonight."

6

WYATT

"So how was your night?" The look on Carter's face when Wyatt walked into the store said he had a good guess how well the evening had gone.

"How did you know?" Wyatt had barely had enough brain cells to get home, much less call anyone and try to explain what happened.

Carter laughed and leaned back against the counter, his long flowery skirt swishing over his black boots. No more almost-masculine. Wyatt was betting Carter's evening hadn't gone nearly as well. "How do you think he found you?"

Um. "I hadn't thought about that." Higher reasoning had been beyond him last night. Just the Dom's presence made all the blood in his body run south.

Shaking his head, Carter laughed again. "He came by the store last night to see if you were still here. He had this look." Carter's smile turned into a mischievous grin. "That man seemed very excited to see you. So I told him you were down at your shop. I'm assuming I did the right thing?"

"Oh, yes! It was *incredible*."

"Tell me all the details." Carter grabbed his mug and went over to the funny little chairs to sit down.

Walking over to relax with him, Wyatt blushed and Carter nearly giggled. "There's nothing like *that* to tell. He was a gentle-man. He asked me out to dinner tonight!"

That had Carter frowning, "Just don't let him take you out for steak." His words came out sarcastic and to Wyatt's ears, sad.

"What happened? Why were you even here last night? When I left, you were walking out the door." Wyatt had stayed complaining and moaning right up until Carter needed to leave for his date. When Garrett stopped by, Carter should have been long gone.

"The *steak dinner* turned out to be the Golden Corral. Even then he was worried I was *overdressed* for the restaurant." Carter made air quotes around overdressed. *Oh.*

"Vanilla guy was *really* vanilla, huh?" That sucked. Wyatt had hoped the guy would end up being more open-minded than that. Not high hopes, but still.

"Interesting is okay at home or in the bedroom, evidently, not out in public." Carter sounded kind of bitter. Wyatt didn't blame him.

"He knew you were more colorful than that. Heck, your profile picture is the one we took with you in that sundress." Carter hadn't lied about anything on his profile. He might have toned down the submissive part to hint at something like a more traditional bottom, but still, the guy had expected *boring*?

"That's what I said. He frowned and said he'd *thought* I knew how to act in public." Carter took a sip of his coffee and smiled at the look on Wyatt's face.

"You've got to be kidding? That's nuts!" Richmond might not be the most progressive place but there had been nothing outra-geous in Carter's outfit last night.

"Nope. So I told him *very* politely where he could stick it.

Then went through the drive thru before coming back here." Carter started to perk up again. "That's when I ran into tall, dark, and naughty, looking for you."

"You should have come to the shop or called me at least. We could have done something together." Wyatt couldn't get past the idea that Carter had been here alone after his disastrous date.

"Sweetie, I was hoping you were doing something much more fun than watching movies with me. And besides, I was terrible company." Then he shook his head teasingly. "I am very disappointed you didn't do anything *interesting* with that man."

"He makes my knees weak just by looking at me. I had tons of fun showing him my shop. When I could actually talk to him. I was a bit wound up. When he asked me out, *you're going to be so proud of me*, I did something completely shocking." Wyatt paused for dramatic effect. "I asked him over to my house instead. I'm going to cook for him tonight."

"Look at you, so take charge you're almost a Dom! I'm surprised you made your mouth work enough to be able to ask him." Carter knew Wyatt well enough to be surprised he'd managed to function. It wasn't mean, just the truth.

Now Wyatt had to blush. His voice dropped like he was going to say something crazy. "I was sitting on his lap and my brain was in complete overload."

Carter started laughing so hard he had to put his coffee down. "I thought you were going to say something naughty. All he had to do was make you sit on his lap and he blew your mind?"

"Yup, he can do it just by looking at me. He makes me crazy. But this time he was holding my hands in one of his so I didn't fidget and he had his other hand on my leg. He was touching me! And not shaking my hand kind of touching. So it is perfectly acceptable to have gone a little nuts." Wyatt knew he was starting to get too excited but he couldn't help it.

"How nuts are you going to go when he wants to play with your *furniture* tonight?" The words weren't dirty but the way Carter said them certainly made them seem that way.

"Do you think he will? I mean, will want to try them out? He said he wanted to go slow but not *too* slow and I was honest about the whole not-just-in-the-bedroom thing. But he also said he wasn't going to go too slow. I think I said that. What do you think he meant?" Wyatt was starting to talk too fast and repeat himself but he couldn't help it. Luckily, Carter interrupted him.

"I think you are going to have a *fabulous* evening but not get completely naked. If you're lucky, he might get you all wound up and not let you come. If you're *really* lucky, he might even say you can't come all next week." It probably sounded like Carter was teasing him but they both knew he was telling the truth.

"*Do you think he knows*?" Wyatt was shocked and slightly scandalized.

"How can he not have guessed that? You're a sub who wants to be controlled in and out of the bedroom. You told him you're looking for a more lifestyle relationship. He had to have guessed that last night. At the very least, he's probably going to connect the dots tonight." Carter smirked a little when he saw Wyatt start to squirm.

"I still don't understand how you can be so shocked and nervous around Doms when you were in a serious relationship with one. You went to that club you're always talking about and did things in public with your previous master."

"That's different. Doing stuff there was up to my master and I just had to behave. Not ask for stuff or start conversations. And he knew how nuts I was. I bounce back between desperate and crazy scandalized constantly. I can't help it." Wyatt shrugged.

Wyatt was starting to wish he hadn't shared so much with

Carter. He'd been feeling better about the date when he hadn't been focused on those kinds of details. "Obsessing over what he knows and what I'm going to have to tell him will make me crazy. No more me talk. We're going to focus on you."

"I don't like the sound of that." Carter looked suspicious. Wyatt always knew he was smart.

"No more vanilla or even vanilla-ish dating sites. We're going to find one that's a better fit if you still insist on those sites. We are also going to make a plan to go visit the club! No excuses this time. Once I find my brain around Garrett, or maybe I'll just email him or something, I'll talk to him about us going up to the club. I think that's something I need to get his permission on, even at this point. Maybe. I'll probably figure that out more tonight. But when that's all organized, we'll make plans. I'm not going to be told no this time." Wyatt tried to give Carter his best I-won't-take-no-for-an-answer look. The kind of firm look you would give a salesman who wouldn't back off.

It must have worked, or maybe Carter was tired of bad dates and guys who were completely wrong for him. "Maybe. We'll have to see how it works out for you and your sexy new Dom."

It might not have been a yes, but that was definitely not a no. Wyatt wasn't surprised though. As much as Carter seemed to dislike the idea of going to the club, the idea of trying to tone things down enough to date normal guys was worse. He should have dragged Carter before, but he'd thought his friend might like having a Dom come with them too.

Wyatt wasn't sure exactly what made Carter nervous about the club. He preferred to go with a group if he was just going to have fun and relax. But even when he'd gone alone to look for something more serious, he'd never had a problem. Ben and Conner made sure the club was a safe space for everyone.

Carter must have had enough of Wyatt's brilliant idea

because he turned the conversation back around again. "So are you going to be okay if he wants to play some later?"

Wyatt thought about it but he wasn't sure how to explain it. His leg started bouncing, and he fought the urge to start pacing around the room. "Yes and no. I'm going to be so wound up, I'm worried about scaring him off. Once there are rules and we've gone over expectations, I'll be much calmer. But right now the unknown makes me want to climb the walls. Can I kneel or do I have to stay in my seat? Because let me tell you that feels really wrong around him. One plate on the table or two? Will my spanking bench in the living room be too much or all right? Should I have a list printed out to show him my limits or do I let him bring that up?"

He slouched down in the chair and took a deep breath. "Once I get past this part, I do calm down. You saw me with Richard a few times. I was nowhere near this scatter-brained."

"You're right. You are much more settled and focused when you're in a good relationship. I want you to be happy. And until I can see you are, I'm going to worry." Carter leaned over and gave Wyatt's leg a squeeze. "I expect juicier details tomorrow! I know you're not working here but I expect a phone call, unless you want me to hunt you down."

"All right. Some details." Maybe. Wyatt could keep things to himself when he needed to but depending on how stressed or nervous he was everything came tumbling out. Tomorrow could go either way. "*What if it goes terribly?*"

Carter gave his leg another squeeze. "The object of your obsession has finally noticed you. The BDSM gods are not going to take this away from you now. Just try to be open with him. Let him know what you're feeling and what would make you happy. Just from the little I saw last night, he wants to make you happy."

That sounded too easy and too perfect. "The BDSM gods have a wicked sense of humor sometimes."

HE MIGHT HAVE BEEN GOING a bit nuts. The food was ready, and he'd managed not to burn anything or forget something. The house was clean. Everything should be ready and he should have been relaxed because there'd been no major issues. But he wasn't.

He still hadn't decided about the furniture. Did it send the wrong signal or the right one to have a spanking bench in the living room? It looked like a nicely carved traditional bench, with a padded seat and back. It was old-fashioned, something that looked almost antique. It just changed into a padded spanking bench. Most people wouldn't even know what it was, but Garrett would.

Wyatt liked the bench. It was one of his favorite pieces, which was the main reason he kept it. That, and he wanted that little reminder about who he was and what he wanted. He'd been without a master for so long and it was comforting.

Maybe that wasn't the right word, but it made him feel better. It was kind of like the people who put up pictures of the nice vacations they wanted to be able to afford. Inspiration and something to work towards. It was just his version of what he wanted to attract from the universe.

He and Richard might not have been the best fit but Wyatt missed it. Having someone around who needed him and who didn't think he was a little odd for wanting a full-time master. He liked kneeling. He liked making someone happy. He got a little thrill from having to ask his master for permission to do something.

When he'd started exploring the scene, he'd figured out pretty quick that just weekend fun in the bedroom wasn't for him. If something felt so right, why would you want to do it once in a while? Why not all the time?

He hadn't expected it to be so hard to find someone who wanted the same things he did. Most men he'd dated in the lifestyle thought a full-time D/s relationship was too hard. Maybe it was because Wyatt wasn't into being anybody's slave.

There weren't a lot of masters who wanted something kind of in the middle. They either saw it as a role that you sometimes played in the bedroom or they wanted a full-on slave. Wyatt loved his work and couldn't imagine giving it up. He also liked talking to his master and didn't want his opinion completely pushed aside the way he'd seen happen to some subs in full-time relationships.

Garrett seemed to understand that. And Wyatt had never heard anything bad about him as a master. Some subs had complained he lived too far away from D.C. but no one said anything about him being too rough or just looking to play without any commitment.

Taking a deep breath, Wyatt walked around the living room one more time. He wasn't going to change anything. Even though it was a rental, he liked the way everything fit together. And he wasn't going to hide pieces of himself from Garrett.

Especially important ones.

But there was still the whole what-to-do-about-dinner thing...Should he do what he wanted or what was probably more socially acceptable? Garrett had wanted to take him out for a traditional date in a restaurant. Did that mean he just wanted a more traditional date here?

One plate or two?

What he wanted was to have one plate so Garrett could feed him while he knelt on the floor. Would that be too much? It was probably borderline but Wyatt wasn't sure. It had been so long since he had someone to kneel for.

It was easy to imagine. His cushion on the floor by Garrett's chair. Waiting for the Dom to feed him. Licking the food from his fingers. Wyatt shook his head to clear his thoughts. This had to stop. He couldn't open the door hard and horny. That was probably not the best first impression.

It would be memorable though.

He still didn't know what to do about the table. He was halfway there but not sure if he should push it. His cushion was sitting in the corner next to a bookshelf that divided the living room and the dining room. It could easily be brought out. There were two place settings on the table, but again, that was easy to fix. But did he want to?

Did he have the nerve to, was the better question.

Probably not.

What he wanted and what he had the nerve to do were two very different things. It had always been like that. When he was on his own, taking that last step to say what he wanted was almost impossible. When he had a Dominant it was completely different. He felt more comfortable and confident knowing he wasn't doing it on his own. Knowing there was someone to help and guide him. A safety net.

He liked rules and liked knowing the best way to make someone happy.

He didn't know what would make Garrett happy. Yet.

Wyatt knew the date wasn't just about Garrett. He wasn't completely fixated on the idea of only pleasing him. It would just be uncomfortable and awkward if Wyatt presumed too much...or not enough. He wanted the evening to be...well, perfect was too much to expect, but he wanted it to go smoothly.

The doorbell rang before he could talk himself into a decision.

"Deep breath. You can do this. You can even do this without looking like a spaz. You know you can." The pep talk didn't help.

7

GARRETT

Wyatt probably didn't realize how loud his little pep talk was.

Garrett stared at the front door, trying not to smile. That might not be the best first impression. What was the boy so worked up about? It could be anything. He didn't know the cute sub well enough yet to understand exactly, but hopefully, he'd be able to guess.

He wanted Wyatt to be relaxed and open tonight. Not worried and second guessing every decision. They both needed to be themselves and see what happened. *Not that he'd been reminding himself that.* No, he was calm and their date was going to go fine.

When Wyatt opened the door, he was *looking* a lot calmer than he'd sounded. But that wasn't saying much. His hands were still twitching, and he was shifting his weight from one foot to the other like he was one worry away from needing to pace around the room.

There was no way the boy was going to have a good evening if Garrett couldn't get him to calm down. Even a little would probably help. However, before he could do anything, Wyatt needed to invite him in. "Hello, Wyatt."

Wyatt blushed, and the wiggling got worse. "Um, I, um, hi."

"Hello. Can I come in?"

"Oh, yeah. I mean, yes, please come in." Blushing, Wyatt stepped back from the door pointing toward the living room. "Come sit down. Dinner's almost done. Well, most of it's done. I have to finish a few things off when we're ready to eat." He must have realized he was starting to ramble because he abruptly closed his mouth and seemed to be trying to take a subtle deep breath.

This was a sub in desperate need of a master.

It was even worse than when he would come into the office. Garrett had wanted to comfort and take charge of the boy before. Now there was nothing to hold him back.

Wyatt closed the door and led him into the house. Garrett watched his lean, lithe body move. He couldn't wait to see the boy naked. Not tonight of course, he wasn't going to rush things. But soon, though. He and Wyatt had been dancing around each other for too long for his control to be that good.

The boy pointed to the couch. Then moved to sit on a chair that was adjacent but Garrett was having none of that. Garrett sat down on the couch, but he wasn't going to sit by himself. "I think this will work out best. You are *very* nervous."

Taking Wyatt's hand, he gave it a little tug. The sub could have easily pulled away, but he blushed and allowed Garrett to steer him into his lap. Once he had the sexy boy settled, he took Wyatt's hands in his, bringing them around to his back.

The change in Wyatt was dramatic and immediate. His breathing evened out and Garrett could feel his muscles relax. Everything about him seemed to calm. He looked down at his lap, then peeked up at Garrett through the longest lashes. Not quite flirting but it made Garrett fight for control of his cock.

The boy was too sweet. Garrett tried not to moan at how perfect it all felt. "This is much better."

Wyatt's cheeks pinked a little, but he nodded.

"If I do something to make you uncomfortable, I expect you to tell me. I know we haven't discussed limits or expectations yet. If I go too fast, then I'm going to require you to tell me. That's our first rule. Is that clear?"

Wyatt seemed to relax even more and this time he didn't just nod. "Yes, Sir."

"Sir is fine for now until we discuss it. Even Garrett is okay, if that's what you'd prefer."

"I...I...um...I'd like to use Sir for now. As long as it's just us, of course."

"That's perfectly acceptable. You may even call me that when my family is around. They're all in the lifestyle as well. I'm not going to brush over the dynamics of our relationship like that unless it's what you want." Garrett was curious to know what Wyatt would say. His wasn't the most conventional family.

"So...Like...So *everyone* in your family is into BDSM?" Wyatt's expression was so cute. The shocked confusion made Garrett want to kiss him.

"Yes. My brothers are all into BDSM. Even my parents were before my father passed. No one has brought anyone serious home yet but they wouldn't expect me to hide it. They also wouldn't expect you to push down your natural inclinations. That's what some of the nervousness in the office was about, right?" Now that he was starting to get a better feel for what Wyatt needed, the idea made sense. If he leaned towards the more lifestyle end of the spectrum, then he had other needs that weren't being met.

Wyatt squirmed a little and looked down at his lap again. He tugged the hand that was still restraining his arms behind his back. But it didn't feel like he was trying to get loose, more like he was testing to make sure Garrett was holding him tight. His words came out low but not nervous. "Yes. I didn't want to look ridiculous but sitting in the chair was hard. It didn't feel right. Not with you there."

Garrett wasn't going to guess what Wyatt meant, even if he thought he had a pretty good idea. "What would have felt better? What did you want to do when you came into the office?"

Wyatt peeked up again and his expression looked a little skeptical. Like he wasn't sure if he should answer the question. Garrett took the hand that had been resting on the couch and moved it to Wyatt's leg, giving him a little squeeze.

"I wanted to kneel." Again, not nervous but quiet and maybe a little curious. He probably wanted to know where the conversation was heading.

Garrett wasn't sure where they were heading. All he knew was that he was finally starting to learn what made Wyatt tick. It was fascinating and Garrett wasn't going to let the conversation drop just yet.

"You wanted to kneel while we were talking?" Garrett tried to sound as neutral as he could. Then he waited for Wyatt's response. He wanted to be perfectly clear. No guessing.

"Yes. Sitting in the chair wasn't comfortable." Then he took another deep breath and continued. "Knowing you were a Dominant and one that I...that I liked made it difficult."

Garrett gave him another little squeeze and tried to be just as honest. "I found those meetings *very* difficult as well. I kept wanting to touch you and help you relax but it didn't seem appropriate at the time. Unlike some people I could name, a certain sexy sub, I had no idea you were into the lifestyle."

He gave Wyatt a little grin when the boy glanced up, blushing again. "There wasn't a good way to bring it up and then it just felt more awkward..." Wyatt shrugged obviously not sure how to explain it.

"A simple, *Ben and Conner recommended you* would have sufficed. I would have gotten the hint and you wouldn't have had to say anything more specific."

Wyatt sighed, then hunched over. "But then you might have mentioned me to them and they might have mentioned that I had a little crush on you and then I would have died right there the next time I came in to pay a bill. It would have all been very messy."

Garrett didn't fight his smile. Wyatt was so cute, even obviously mortified. "Did we meet before? I can't remember talking to you at the club. That's where you saw me, right?"

"We didn't meet exactly. I was with someone else a couple of years ago, when you were introduced to my previous master. You were polite, but we didn't talk. When he left the country, I decided not to follow. I saw you a few times at the club but I didn't go out of my way to get your attention. Then you stopped coming as often. Ben and Conner said that business had picked up so much you were really busy."

"Ah. That makes sense." At least, a little. If the sub was too shy to come up and talk or even to walk by and flirt a little, Garrett might not have noticed. He typically didn't go after subs that didn't seem to be interested.

There also had to be more to the story. Already, he could tell that Wyatt didn't give his submission lightly. If he decided not to move with his previous master, he must have had a good reason. Garrett decided it wasn't something he was going to press right now, but he wasn't going to push it aside completely.

"So Ben and Conner knew that you liked me, huh? They didn't say anything about it." He was going to have a talk with those two.

"Yes, but I begged them not to say anything." Wyatt was still clearly embarrassed at how the conversation was going.

"I wish you would have. I thought you were sweet and cute

the first time you came into the office. You've sorely strained my control over the past year." Garrett decided to test the waters a bit. "At some point, I think you might need to be punished for that."

Watching Wyatt look over to the spanking bench in the corner, Garrett felt his arousal surge. There was no way a sub who had a personal spanking bench would hate it. Wyatt started biting his lip, and they were close enough that Garrett could see his pupils get wider. Someone really liked that idea.

It took Wyatt a minute to be able to respond but finally, he managed a breathy, "Yes, if I was...if I was bad then you'd have to, Sir."

Garrett tightened his grip on the sub and gave him a little wink. "Oh, I think I'll have to. You've given me no choice, boy."

A low moan escaped Wyatt and Garrett felt his legs tighten. Looking down, it was easy to see the sub's erection pushing out against his pants. Wyatt didn't mind that idea at all. Garrett had to remind himself they weren't going to rush things.

A naked spanking over the bench would be rushing things.

However, a clothed spanking over his lap wouldn't be. It was all a matter of perspective.

They both got a small reprieve from the growing sexual tension when a timer started going off in the kitchen. Wyatt blinked a few times then his brain seemed to clear. "Timer...Oh, the timer. I've got to finish the rest of dinner."

Garrett gave the sub one last little squeeze and released his grip on the boy's arms. Taking his hand off Wyatt's leg, Garrett gave him a smile. "I can't wait to see what you've made. I'm starving."

Wyatt gave him a sheepish grin. "Good. I might have made too much."

Helping Wyatt off his lap, Garrett followed him into the kitchen. The wonderful smells were even better in here. It was almost like he was walking into a nice restaurant. Something about the smells made him think of juicy steaks and fried potatoes.

"Smells incredible."

"Thanks. I like to cook."

"I don't mind cooking but I never seem to have enough time during the week. And on the weekend, I usually end up at one of my brothers' houses grilling out or something like that. My mother made sure all of us were functional and could cook, but there are only so many hours in the day." He loved his job but between regular business hours, extra time with clients who couldn't come in during traditional hours, and other assorted meetings with local business groups, his day was sometimes incredibly long.

"I can understand that. With trying to get the furniture for the club done, I haven't had much time either. I'm finally starting to feel like I've got a handle on it, though."

"I hope they haven't been driving themselves crazy trying to get it ready. I've been meaning to take a day off and go up to see the new location. I haven't made the time. They've offered to give me a tour when I finally make it up there. Have you seen it?"

Wyatt nodded as he bustled around the kitchen stirring pots, mixing things in small white bowls, and heating up a heavy skillet. Garrett was curious, but he wasn't going to question the cook. In his family, if you drove the person making dinner nuts, even by asking too many questions, you'd end up getting the burned pieces or the smallest portion. He didn't think Wyatt would do that to him, but he wasn't going to take the chance.

Sub didn't mean pushover.

"It's nice. The same kind of feel as the one in D.C. but more open. They're thinking it will be easier to monitor that way and they're not expecting people outside of politics to be quite so nuts about privacy."

"That sounds good. I'm going to have to head up there and take a look. It will be a nice day trip." The more he thought about it, the better it sounded. "How about we head up there? You can show me around one weekend."

Wyatt's head came up from looking at the pot he'd been stirring. "That sounds like fun."

Buzzing around the kitchen, Wyatt went to the fridge, pulling out a bowl with plastic wrap over the top. Garrett had to fight off the urge to go over and peek but he knew the best idea would be to stay right where he was. The kitchen was cute and well laid out but still small enough that if he got up from the little round table, he'd be in Wyatt's way.

The smells that came from the bowl were incredible. It wasn't until Wyatt grabbed some tongs and started lifting meat out that Garrett realized it was some kind of steak tips. The sizzle as the meat hit the pan made his mouth water.

"You are so much better in the kitchen than I am."

Wyatt blushed and ducked his head down, trying to look busy by the stove. "Thank you. I've probably had more practice is all. I'm sure whatever you made would be wonderful."

"How about I cook next week and we'll see? You may end up having to soothe my bruised ego. As good as that smells, I'm not sure I can compete." He was mostly teasing, but the way Wyatt's whole body perked up made Garrett take notice.

Wyatt obviously wasn't sure what to say because he shook his head and went back to focusing on the food. From what Garrett could see, he thought everything was nearly done. "Did you want me to grab the plates out of the dining room so we can fix them up in here? Less mess and all."

There was the slightest hesitation in Wyatt's voice when he responded. "Sure. That would be easiest. There are a few little things to take out there but at least we won't have to worry about the main items." Garrett wasn't sure what was on the sub's mind but he was clearly missing something.

What could he have missed?

As he walked to the dining room, Garrett played over the conversation in his head. Something about the food or the table. Wyatt had been fine until Garrett had asked about the plates. Had he overstepped his bounds? Walking to the table, Garrett stopped to look. There was something Wyatt needed him to figure out.

The table had an antique feel, but the solid kind, not something flimsy and fancy. Craftsman he thought it was called. There were two place settings at one end with place mats and everything. His mother would be impressed. It was a table meant for guests and nice meals. Garrett thought it was sweet Wyatt had gone to so much effort.

He was going to have to up his game next week or he'd look like a poor excuse for a Dom.

It wasn't until he noticed the small cushion hidden away in a corner that the conversation from the couch came back to him. Now it was starting to make sense. If Wyatt had wanted to kneel in the office instead of sitting, what were the chances he wanted to sit at the table now?

Slim to none probably.

Even if he was okay with the idea of sitting at the table, Garrett couldn't get the image of the sexy sub kneeling while he fed him out of his head. He wouldn't have a cushion if he didn't want to use it. This wasn't a playroom or a club. This was his house. He'd only have things he wanted to use.

Garrett took a second to rearrange the place settings and chairs, before grabbing the plates and walking back into the kitchen. "Here we go."

Wyatt had everything ready when Garrett came back in. Dinner turned out to be steak tips, with homemade golden brown steak fries, and cooked baby carrots in some kind of glaze. As Wyatt plated the food, he looked up at Garrett. "Sir, would you take those little bowls out to the table?"

"Of course." Following the directions, Garrett took several little white bowls filled with different sauces out to the table. There was no way he could compete with homemade steak sauce. And multiple varieties at that. Wyatt followed him out with the plates, loaded with food that looked amazing.

Garrett could see the moment when the sub noticed the changes to the room. His eyes widened, and he seemed to operate by remote as he set the plates on the table. He looked to Garrett, clearly not sure what to do next.

"All right, sweet boy, come kneel down next to me."

"Yes, Sir." Wyatt blushed faintly but by the time he walked around to the cushion he seemed much more focused. He lowered himself gracefully, hands resting behind his back, then looked up to Garrett.

Beautiful.

8

WYATT

W yatt didn't care what had given him away. It was perfect. It was what he'd pictured from the very beginning. Kneeling beside the sexy Dom and just having to focus on him. No worries about making small talk or what Garrett thought of him. When he was kneeling and submitting for his Dom—even if it was just his Dom for the evening—nothing else mattered.

Garrett had moved the plates around so both were in front of him and Wyatt now had plenty of room to kneel beside him. The only thing that would make it better was if he was naked with just a collar on...or maybe a collar and a cock cage. The image made him shiver. He might have had too many fantasies that started just like this.

"Should I ask what you're imagining? If I had to guess, I would have to say it was probably naughty." Garrett's voice came out slightly husky and from Wyatt's position it was easy to see the Dom was turned on.

He thought he might die if Garrett made him tell his fantasy out loud. "Um. Do I have to, Sir?"

Garrett laughed and shook his head. "Not this time. In the future, yes. I would love to know what you were picturing."

That made Wyatt blush, and he ducked his head. "Thank you." He was relieved at the reprieve, but he also didn't miss the way the Dom hinted at other dates.

"You're welcome. And thank you for dinner. This looks amazing. I don't even know where we should start." Garrett picked up his fork and speared a piece of meat. "One fork or two?"

"One." He would have said that even if Garrett was a walking flu virus. Just knowing his mouth was going to touch the same place as the Dom's made him giddy. It was a total fangirl moment again but he couldn't help himself. This scene could have been in any fantasy he'd had since moving there. But this time it was real, not just in his head.

Garrett speared a piece of meat and brought it to Wyatt's mouth. It tasted as good as he'd hoped but he was more worried about what Garrett would think. He didn't have to wait long. As soon as the Dom had fed Wyatt, he took a bite for himself.

"This is wonderful, Wyatt." His hand reached out and ran over Wyatt's head, ruffling his hair in a soothing caress. "You've done an incredible job with dinner. Thank you."

"You're welcome, Sir."

Garrett went back and forth feeding them but eventually, they were both relaxed enough that he put the fork down. Picking up one of the carrots with his fingers, he brought it to Wyatt's mouth. Wyatt couldn't help himself. Gently taking the carrot with his lips and teeth, he sucked in Garrett's fingers, cleaning the sweet glaze off.

He couldn't help the little shiver that raced through him as he ran his tongue around the long digits. Peeking nervously up at Garrett, he was pleased to see how much the Dom liked it.

The arousal in his eyes and the long outline of his cock made it obvious how much he wanted Wyatt.

Releasing Garrett, Wyatt carefully chewed the carrot then gave the Dom a little smile. "Thank you, Sir."

"Cheeky little thing, aren't you?" Garrett didn't seem to mind because the next piece of meat he gave Wyatt was covered in one of the tangy sauces.

He couldn't leave the Dom a sticky mess. A good sub wouldn't do that. So the only thing he could do would be to make sure he thoroughly cleaned him off. The burst of flavor from the sauce and from Garrett made him moan. Licking and sucking his fingers clean, Wyatt tried to let him know just how much he wanted to please the Dom.

They slowly worked their way through dinner, Wyatt taking longer and longer each time to taste not only the food, but the Dom as well. There wasn't a lot of small talk. Garrett just seemed to be enjoying the food and feeding Wyatt. For Wyatt, he was happy with whatever the Dom wanted.

It had been so long since he'd been able to serve anyone like this, if the only thing he did all night was kneel by Garrett's side, it would count as a wonderful date. He didn't understand it when he was younger, but this was where he was happiest. His submission made him feel complete.

When the food was gone, Garrett turned in his chair and looked down at Wyatt. The Dom reached out and ran his fingers through his hair again, smiling. "Let's go sit together on the couch. As incredible as you look kneeling there for me, Sweet, I don't want you to hurt later."

Reaching out to take Wyatt's hands, Garrett helped him up from the floor. Keeping one of Wyatt's hands, Garrett started walking them over to the couch.

"I have some dessert in the kitchen. May I go get it for us?"

The fruit and sauces would hopefully be something else the Dom might feed him.

Garrett squeezed his hand, looking reluctant to let him go. "Yes. I'm curious to see what else you planned."

He fought the urge to squirm and hoped he didn't look ridiculous. "I'll be right back, Sir."

Hurrying to the kitchen, Wyatt was glad he'd already arranged everything earlier. Grabbing the bowl of fruit out of the fridge and the cups of sauce that were warming in the oven, Wyatt put them all on a little tray and carried it out to the living room.

Garrett had moved the side table around to the front of the couch. He gave the couch a pat and smiled at Wyatt. "Come sit with me, Sweet."

The Dom was sitting on one side of the couch and the small area he indicated definitely wasn't enough room for Wyatt to sit by himself. Setting the tray on the table, he squeezed between the two pieces of furniture and looked at Garrett, waiting for instructions.

Taking his hand, Garrett pulled him down so he was sitting with his back against the armrest, his legs lying over the Dom's muscular thighs. Perfect. Wyatt leaned his head against the back of the couch and watched as Garrett looked at the food.

"Fruit and what are these...Ah, let's see. Those look good." He glanced at Wyatt. "Are they too hot to touch?"

"No just warm enough to keep them melted. That one is milk chocolate, the next one is caramel, and the last is white chocolate." Wyatt expected Garrett to pick up one of the pieces of fruit but he took Wyatt's hand instead.

"I need to see which one I like best first."

Wyatt let Garrett bring his hand over to the little bowls. Carefully using one of Wyatt's fingers, Garrett dipped it in the milk chocolate and brought it up to his mouth. It had to be one of the most erotic things Wyatt had ever experienced.

Garrett gently sucked the chocolate off like he was sucking on Wyatt's cock. That was the only comparison Wyatt could make. Running his tongue around the shaking finger, Garrett made sure to get every drop of chocolate he possibly could. Just that alone would have been hot but something about the way Garrett was using his body took his arousal to another level entirely.

It was the same incredible feeling as when he would be used for his Dom's pleasure. Even knowing he wasn't going to be able to come, it still felt naughty and addicting. Being deliciously used and denied. This time he wasn't being denied, he was being used by hopefully the man who would become his Dom. It made his cock throb with every lick.

Continuing with the sauces, Garrett took his time tasting every one and almost ignoring Wyatt. It could have felt impersonal and awkward. But with the sexy man, it just made Wyatt want to throw himself at the Dom and beg to be used even more. By the time Garrett tasted each one twice, Wyatt was a quivering mess ready to explode.

"I think I like the caramel best. Let's see how that tastes on the fruit." Garrett put Wyatt's hand back on his lap and picked up a strawberry. Dipping it, he brought the treat up to Wyatt's mouth.

Sucking the juicy berry into his mouth, Wyatt moaned. The fruit wasn't that good, it was just the combination of everything. Garrett gave Wyatt a wicked grin. "I agree. It's delicious. You're going to have to make me the caramel again. There are so many things I could lick it off of."

Wyatt felt his cock jerk. Precum was leaking out so bad, he was going to have a wet spot on his pants soon. Next time, he was going to wear thicker briefs and not the sexy, thin, silky ones he'd worn, just in case. Wyatt wasn't sure if it was a question or not but all he could do was nod. He'd make as much as the Dom wanted.

"You're such a...good chef." Garrett paused like there were other things he wanted to say. What was the Dom thinking? He was such a needy little slut? Wasn't that true. He was such a good sub? That's what he wanted the sexy man to think.

"Thank you." It came out stuttered and needy but Wyatt couldn't help it. His mind wasn't working.

Garrett picked up a piece of pineapple and dipped it in the chocolate. "How long have you been in the lifestyle?"

He had to think?

"Um...I..." He couldn't focus. Watching Garrett's tongue come out to lick the dripping treat, Wyatt's brain couldn't think of anything else but how incredible...

"Wyatt? Sweet, I asked you a question." There was laughter in his voice but his expression was serious. The man knew exactly what he'd done to Wyatt.

He had to close his eyes so he could think. Watching Garrett, he'd never get his brain to work. "Um...My parents got me an e-reader in high school. I was supposed to use it for reading classics and all these books they thought were so important, but I figured out I could get all kinds of books that were *way* more interesting. When I stumbled across my first gay BDSM book, I was hooked. Just the idea that someone could get that much pleasure from submission blew my mind."

"They didn't look at what you were reading?" Garrett laughed and shook his head.

"Eventually, but by then I was in college and they couldn't figure out what to do. So they went back to pretending I was straight and *normal.* I focused on finding people who were into the same things that I was."

"I'm sorry." Emotion was thick in the Dom's voice and his

hand came up to play with Wyatt's hair again. Wyatt leaned into the touch, wanting to soak up every caress.

"It's okay. We still talk and they've stopped trying to pretend I'm not gay. I can live with them not understanding everything else." He wasn't that upset about it anymore. He'd long since accepted that lots of people, gay and straight, had parents who didn't understand them.

"I can't imagine. I've been lucky enough to have parents who were supportive and probably *too* open. You didn't ask questions in my house, unless you were prepared for a full and descriptive answer. And we learned very early you didn't even knock on my parents' bedroom door if it was closed."

"You mean your parents really were in a Dominant-submissive relationship? I mean, you said everyone in your family but…" Wyatt couldn't wrap his mind around that.

"Yeah, we didn't understand until we were older what made their relationship different. They were just really in love and we knew our mom was more in charge than other people's moms seemed to be." Garrett smiled at the memories.

"I can't imagine that." His parents were so narrow-minded that he couldn't wrap his head around it.

"Once we got older and started reading stuff and figuring out what we liked, it kind of clicked. I think it made things easier for Brent and Bryce…" Garrett's voice trailed off but he kept playing with Wyatt's hair and he had to fight to stay focused.

"What do you mean?" There was something Wyatt was missing.

"They're subs. Well, Brent's a sub and Bryce is a switch. With Grant and me being Doms, without my dad for them to relate to, I think it could have really screwed things up. Teenagers aren't always the most sensitive individuals. If we didn't have my dad as a good example of a strong sub, I think it would have changed our relationships."

Wyatt stared in shock. He couldn't remember seeing Garrett's brothers at the club but he'd imagined them as a bunch of Doms. The picture Garrett was painting was totally different.

The Dom either didn't notice his shock or maybe he was just giving Wyatt time to think things through because he kept going. "Seeing how much my parents loved each other and worked together made things easier. My dad was the man in charge at work and my mom did everything she could to support the business. It let us see that being a man wasn't about being macho and shit like that. I think we all turned out better because of them. Even if it was an awkward couple of months after Grant came out and everything else came out with him."

"Sounds like there's a story there." That was probably an understatement but Wyatt was still in shock. He'd felt so weird growing up. He couldn't imagine how it would have felt to have had a role model who understood.

Garrett laughed and seemed to put the memories away enough to focus on dessert again. Taking another piece of fruit he dipped it in the white chocolate and brought it up to Wyatt's lips. "Absolutely. But enough about me. I think I was trying to learn more about you until you distracted me. Very naughty."

He almost choked on the berry he was swallowing. Just the way Garrett said "naughty" made his cock jerk in his pants again. Did he have any idea what he was doing to him? Glancing up at Garrett and seeing that sexy smirk, it was easy to see the Dom knew exactly what he was doing to Wyatt.

"I'm sorry for distracting you, Sir." He fought to sit still but the little shivers of need that were racing through him weren't helping.

Ignoring the dessert, Garrett left one hand playing with Wyatt's hair and used the other to tease his legs. Running his hand up and down from Wyatt's shins to his thigh, he was clearly enjoying what he was doing. Wyatt didn't even realize he was starting to wiggle until Garrett's hand tightened and he stilled. "Hands behind your back, Sweet. That's better."

Even though he wasn't held down or kneeling, the Dom pinned him in place with just his expression and voice. Wyatt's cock was leaking so much his boxers were wet and this would only make things worse.

"Now, how did you start making furniture?" Garrett smiled at Wyatt's confusion.

"What?"

"Is that any way to talk to me?"

"I'm sorry, Sir. Um, I...I don't understand, Sir." That earned Wyatt another caress of Garrett's hand through his hair, this time dipping down the side of his head to tease around his ear. He'd never realized how much of an erogenous zone his head was.

"I want to know how you got started with your furniture. You're very good. It isn't often these days you see someone who is such a talented craftsman, especially someone so young." Garrett seemed so sincere that Wyatt knew he was blushing.

"Um...shop class to start. My dad thought it was manly but what he didn't realize was that my *manly, macho* shop teacher was in a long-term relationship with another guy. They weren't what you would call out and proud, but I guess he could see how confused I was because he casually brought up their relationship one day after school. It was some place I fit in, even though I wasn't out yet." Wyatt tilted his head and tried to push closer to Garrett's touch. He sighed when Garrett kept it up, it felt incredible.

"He had to know, but he never said anything. He let me take as many classes as I could get away with and showed me all kinds of things. He even worked with me after school on tons of stuff. His partner would come in and hang out too sometimes. They were my first exposure to a real loving gay relationship. I got a degree in graphic design but I spent more time at the local art center taking more woodshop classes than I did on my major." He moaned and fought to stay still as Garrett's hand wandered temptingly close to his cock.

Just imagining how it would feel completely broke his concentration and Garrett had to prompt him again to keep talking. He didn't know how he was supposed to keep going when the sexy Dom was driving him crazy with those teasing touches. Garrett wasn't going to let that be an excuse though so Wyatt tried to remember where he left off.

"I...um...Oh, the art center. At the same time as I was getting better with building furniture and stuff, I was also starting to explore the scene. Eventually, I realized that a lot of the common pieces people wanted to own, but were too shy to have in their house, could look like something simple."

"Like the spanking bench that looks like an actual bench." Garrett's voice was rough and his fingers were getting even closer to Wyatt's hard, leaking cock.

There was no way Garrett could miss the wet spot that was forming on his pants. Wyatt knew he'd be embarrassed later but at that moment, all he wanted to do was beg for more. "Yes. I like making things like that. Pieces that look innocent but..."

"But that are really very naughty. Kind of like you. You seem so innocent and sweet but you're a naughty sub, aren't you?"

9

GARRETT

His little sub was so excited he was shaking. Pupils blown wide and a cock so hard he was tenting the front of his pants, it was impossible to miss. Every little touch had him nearly begging for more. It was in the way he leaned into Garrett's touch and the shivers that raced through making his muscles clench and strain.

A spanking was obviously next on the agenda. But what should he do about how turned on his boy was? And he was his. It didn't matter if this was technically only their first date. Wyatt was his.

If Wyatt had wanted to keep their playing just in the bedroom, Garrett knew he wouldn't mind pushing things far enough tonight that Wyatt got to come—but they weren't going to keep things just in the bedroom. That meant the rules weren't quite the same. Wyatt needed to be kept on his toes and he seemed to need the constant reminder of his submission to be centered.

Right now, though, letting him orgasm wouldn't do that.

"I think it's time for a naughty sub to be punished." Garrett knew his words came out deep and thick with arousal, but he didn't mind his boy knowing how turned on he'd gotten his master.

Wyatt gave him another sexy, wide-eyed look and slowly nodded. Garrett might have been worried that the hesitation meant the sub wanted to say no, but his labored breathing and little moan made it obvious how much he wanted it.

"Red, yellow, green for right now, Sweet. Do you understand? We'll go over safe words and put together a contract soon but for right now, red to stop." Garrett watched as Wyatt nibbled on his lip but nodded. "Words. What did I say?"

Wyatt shivered again with Garrett's words, but he managed to talk this time. "Red to stop, yellow to slow down...spanking, because I'm a naughty sub." The words came out breathy and excited, like he couldn't believe it was happening.

"Good boy. All right, stand up."

His little sub climbed off to stand on shaky legs. It was obvious there was nothing else on his mind. Garrett pushed the little table with their dessert out of the way and scooted down the couch. When there was enough room for Wyatt to stretch out over his legs, Garrett reached out and took his hand.

"Wyatt, look at me." He waited until the sweet sub was focused before he continued. "You may not come. The next time you get to come will be by my hand. However, we're going to take things slow. That means we're going to get to know each other more before I strip you down, touch you, and watch your pleasure. Do you understand?"

The calm dirty talk evidently did it for the boy because he gave a low groan and his hips thrust out, unconsciously drawing attention to how hard he was. So sexy. "Yes, Sir. No—no coming. No coming until you give permission."

Then his eyes cleared a little, and he spoke again. "That means...that means I'm yours? That you're mine? My Dom...My Master?"

"Yes. You're mine, sweet boy. We'll talk about it in more detail later and we're still going to spend a lot of time getting to know each other better but I'm *not* letting you go." To some people the words might have been too much, too controlling, but to Wyatt, they seemed to make him melt. The pretty little sub's eyes teared up, and he nodded like he couldn't agree enough.

"All right, over my lap. I think someone's overdue for a spanking." Garrett watched as a blush crept up Wyatt's face but the boy didn't deny the truth of the words.

If he'd been without a Dominant for well over a year, there was no telling how long it had been since he'd given himself to someone like this. His sweet sub was starved for the kind of touch and attention he really needed. Garrett hated it had taken him so long to see what was right in front of his face.

He wasn't going to waste any more time though.

With quivering muscles and unsteady legs, the sweet boy laid himself over Garrett's lap. Stretched out, offering himself up for his master, Wyatt looked incredible. He'd look even better naked, but Garrett wasn't going to rush things. No matter how much he wanted to.

"The next time I spank you, I'm going to get you naked for me. Then I'm going to bend you over the spanking bench, so I can see you and touch you everywhere while I make your ass nice and red." Garrett was starting to understand just how much his boy liked hearing his master's fantasies. Wyatt reacted just like Garrett had hoped.

Beautifully.

He moaned. It seemed to take all his willpower to keep his body still. It was so easy to see how much he wanted to thrust himself against Garrett's legs. The hard cock, which had been clearly outlined in his pants, was now pressed against Garrett's lap.

"Remember. You may not orgasm. That means no humping

your cock against my leg and if you get close, you have to tell me." Letting his hand gently come down to rest on his boy's ass, he could feel the excitement that radiated from him. He could even feel the moan that tore through Wyatt as the sub struggled not to move. "Do you understand?"

Wyatt managed a strangled, "Yes, Master."

Garrett squeezed his ass and started playing with the boy's sexy body. "We're doing this because you were *naughty*. You need to be *spanked*, not *pleasured*."

They both knew this really was about the pleasure, bonding, and shared fantasy. It didn't mean the fantasy of punishing his naughty boy wasn't fun, though. He didn't know how much of a pain slut his little sub was but Garrett was going to find out when they went over limits next week. This time he would keep it gentle and be careful not to push things too far. He didn't want the boy to come, and he didn't want to scare him either. It was going to be a balancing act.

"Please...please...Master...I...I was naughty...and I need to be punished." Wyatt's sweet pleas were incredible. Filled with need and so ready to taste the sweet pain again.

Garrett squeezed his ass and kept up the slow torture. Building the anticipation was as much fun as the spanking itself. "You need to learn your lesson. That's why you're draped over my lap with your ass offered up for me. We're going to make sure you're a good sub for your master. Are you going to be good for me, Sweet?"

Every muscle tightened and Wyatt seemed to be holding his breath, but he finally got enough control to answer. "Yes, Master. I'm going to be good."

So damned sexy.

"That's a good boy." His sweet sub moaned and the little shivers had him almost dancing on Garrett's lap. He gave the boy's ass another squeeze and let his thumb trace along the seam of his cheeks. Teasing and hinting at what was to come. "Needy little slut, aren't you? My needy slut."

Garrett wasn't sure if he'd pushed the words too far but he shouldn't have worried. Wyatt shook even harder, and it seemed to take all his strength to hold back the pleasure. There was no way the naughty sub was going to be able to hold it back.

It looked like Garrett was going to have the perfect excuse to punish the boy next week too.

Before Wyatt could get himself under control, Garrett lifted his hand and brought it down on the boy's ass. Wyatt's cry of pleasure and pain echoed around the room. With the clothes to protect his skin, it probably hadn't even marked him but just looking at his reaction was enough for Garrett.

Arching up into Garrett's touch, Wyatt did his best to be good. It was going to be a losing battle. Bringing his hand down again, Garrett alternated between each cheek. He watched Wyatt dance and writhe, desperate to obey but drowning in the pleasure.

It had just been too long since the sweet sub had felt the beautiful mix of pain and pleasure. As Garrett brought his hand down over and over, he started teasing the boy's imagination with his words again. That proved just as erotic to the sub as the spanking.

When Garrett told him how pretty he would look naked and in his collar with his ass nice and red, the boy whined and clenched. When Garrett told him that next time they had dinner together he wanted his sexy sub to be kneeling naked on the floor, the boy pleaded and shook. When Garrett went into crazy dirty details about how incredible the sub would look in a cock cage and plug, he came.

Shouts of pleasure and endless waves of desire seemed to crash over him. His orgasm went on and on while Garrett

continued to give him all the painful pleasure he'd been missing. Finally, he calmed and sagged down on the couch.

Things may have gotten slightly out of hand. But he didn't
regret a minute of it. This might not technically be going slow
but it wasn't as much as he'd wanted to do to the boy so it was
still in the spirit of it. Running his hands over the boy's ass and
legs, Garrett watched as Wyatt slowly started to come back
to him.

"So beautiful. You took your spanking so well, sweet boy."
Then he let his need show in his voice as he kept up the gentle
caresses. "It's very disappointing that you were naughty and
came without permission. I guess this means you're going to
need to be punished again next week as well."

They both knew Garrett wasn't upset by that. Wyatt turned
his head and gave Garrett a cheeky little grin. "I'm sorry, Master.
I'll do better next time. I promise."

"I hope so. We'll just have to keep going until you learn to be
good during your spankings. It might take us a very long time."
Garrett carefully kneaded the boy's high, tight ass. "I have a
feeling you're probably going to be very naughty and
come again."

Wyatt blushed and looked away but didn't deny it. Garrett
couldn't wait to get the boy naked and displayed for his master.
He was going to look so incredible. So sexy. "Come here,
sweet boy."

Helping him to roll over, Garrett pulled the sub into his
arms. Wyatt laid his head on Garrett's chest and sank into his
master's embrace. There was no trace of the bouncy out-of-
control sub. This was a submissive who was centered and
perfectly content.

∽

THE PHONE RANG as Garrett was stumbling in the back door, bogged down under the weight of grocery bags and laptop. Cursing under his breath, he struggled to put the bags down and answer the beeping that was starting to drive him crazy.

The goal had been to be home and relaxed before the call came in. However, a late meeting and an insane trip to the grocery store ruined that plan. Finally untangling himself from the plastic bags that worked more like handcuffs than help, he swiped his finger across the screen. He couldn't help the smile that spread across his face. He might be frustrated, but this was going to be the highlight of his day.

"Hello, Sweet. How was your day?" After their sexy, incredible date last weekend, Garrett's second rule had been that Wyatt needed to call him at eight o'clock every night. Yes, he wanted to get to know his funny sub, but he had a naughtier motivation.

"It was good. I was at the store this morning but I got a lot done on the next pieces for the club. They're turning out even better than I'd hoped. I think Ben and Conner are going to be really pleased." Shy excitement was clear in his voice. Wyatt was having a hard time talking about his work with someone new.

He was also a bit embarrassed and more than a little turned on about what was going to be the next part of their conversation. "Were you careful in the shop?"

"Yes, Master. I locked the doors and didn't stay too late." His voice earnest, it was obvious he wanted to please Garrett.

"Very good." Garrett leaned against the counter and relaxed. Now the fun part. "Did you behave yourself?"

There was the slightest hesitation, need was starting to thread through his words. "Yes. I was good."

"You didn't play with your cock? You followed directions and left it alone? I know you probably woke up hard and needy this morning. Didn't you?" This was *definitely* the best part of his day.

They might not know each other well enough to jump into a full-time D/s relationship too soon but that didn't mean Garrett wasn't going to try to give the boy what he needed. To start, that meant evening calls to explain what he'd done that day and confirming he'd left his hard on alone. Of course, that made Wyatt's *situation* even more *frustrating* but the sexy sub seemed to love the torturous denial.

"I didn't touch it, Master. I...I woke up hard, but I left it alone." There was a hint of embarrassment in his voice but Garrett knew he was also hard as a rock.

"What were you dreaming about that made you so hard?" Garrett had to reach down and adjust his own cock that was starting to harden.

Wyatt gave a little groan. "I was dreaming about this weekend...and what you said about...about me needing to be punished again."

"So you were fantasizing about being naked for me? Being bent over the spanking bench? How it would feel when my hand came down on your naked ass? Oh, someone was a *naughty boy*. Are you supposed to be getting hard thinking about *punishments*?" If he weren't in the kitchen, Garrett would have had his cock out, stroking it off to the pictures in his head and the breathy sounds of Wyatt's need.

"I'm sorry, Master." He sounded sorrier that he was turned on and couldn't come, but Garrett wasn't going to complain. He wanted the sexy sub needy and focused on their plans for the weekend.

"Good boy." Time to distract them both, he had groceries to put away. "Tell me more about your day? Did you have fun at the shop?"

Wyatt gave a frustrated huff, but he didn't complain. "Yes. Kind of. Carter was in the shop and normally we have fun. Even moving stock around and talking with boring people is entertaining, but he's been frustrated lately."

"Still upset about that bad date?" Garrett pushed off the counter and turned around to start putting groceries away.

"That's probably part of it but I think it's more like he's just frustrated with everything. I wish there was something I could do to help."

"Did you still want to take him up to the club sometime? We could go as a group. That way, he wouldn't feel like he was doing it alone." Putting the vegetables away, Garrett had a nagging feeling that he forgot something.

"Yes! I think it would be perfect for him. He needs a good guy. Ideally, a good Dominant but at this point, I think he'd take someone who wasn't much of a Dom but was open-minded." Wyatt sighed. Garrett could hear how worried Wyatt was for his friend.

"I'd say we should go up this weekend but we've got a family barbecue and that's kind of mandatory. Are you going to help me figure out a dessert to bring over?"

"Me?" Wyatt's shock was almost comical.

"Yes. How else can I introduce my boy to my family?" That's what he'd forgotten, the barbecue.

"*Oh.*"

Garrett tried not to laugh, but the utter horror in that one word was obvious.

"It's not funny. What if they hate me?"

"They don't hate you. They've all met you and thought you were cute and funny."

"*They have*?"

"Yes. Most of the time when you came in to *pay your bills* there were other people in the office, right? Brent is constantly in and out and Grant, Bryce, and I have meetings in my office several times a week. My conference room is nicer than theirs."

Yeah, he might have gotten a kick out of that but it drove the other two nuts so he had to mention it on a regular basis.

"So they all saw me? Like saw me all...you know...and bouncy...and...Oh dear." Wyatt sounded like he'd rather hide under the bed than come to eat with them.

"You will go, Sweet. There will be no emergency antique problem or anything else you might come up with. We just have to figure out dessert and show up at one on Saturday. Then we can head back to your house. Because if my memory is right, we have plans for that evening, don't we." Time to distract his boy.

"Yes." His voice came out sexy and needy.

"What are we going to do? I want you to tell me in detail while I relax, sweet sub."

There was a shocked gasp. "Master!"

"Oh yes, *graphic* detail, boy."

Looked like his evening was going to end on a high note.

10

WYATT

"Are you sure you don't need more help today?" There was an edge of panic in Wyatt's voice but he was trying to hide it. "I don't want to leave you in the lurch."

Carter gave him this look like he wasn't going to fall for that line of shit. "It's Wednesday evening. Try again. There's nobody here. Even I never stay late on Wednesdays."

Wyatt sighed and tried to look as pathetic as possible so Carter would feel sorry and help him. His friend snorted and shook his head. "I'm not going to save you from the *big bad master* who's making you do something terrible."

"I don't want to go."

"Why? You've been to his office tons. Like more than anyone else he deals with." Carter laughed and leaned over on the counter propping his head in his hands. "What makes this time different?"

It should have been obvious, but Wyatt was willing to explain it anyway. "Because now they *know*. I don't *know* how much they do—but they do!"

"*Darlin'*..." Carter said in a sickeningly sweet fake Southern accent. "You need to calm down. Because that didn't make as much sense as you thought it did. Now, more than likely, they already thought you were kinda odd. *Now it just makes sense.* You're going to be calmer because you won't have to hide who you are. They're going to love you."

"You think?"

"Of course. They were nice to you before, right? Even when you were jumpy and shyly stalking their boss?"

"I wasn't stalking him!"

"Potato...Patato...The important thing is that they liked you enough not to make you feel weird. What makes you think this will change anything? From what you said, everyone in the family is on the more *unique* side of the spectrum. What makes you think the employees and everyone else are going to be that normal? *Like attracts like*...you're going to fit right in." Carter nodded like the discussion was over. He was right, and that was all there was to it.

"How am I supposed to act? I'm not going in there to pay my bill. I mean, I've got the regular part...I walk in, say hi, ask for...*Who do I ask for*?" Wyatt tried to take a deep breath. It didn't seem to help. "Do I ask for Garrett or for Master or Sir?"

"What did he say?" Carter seemed to think this part was obvious too.

"We didn't talk about the office. We talked about the barbecue and being around his family." This discussion wasn't making Wyatt feel any better. It was, however, killing time, so he didn't have to go.

Carter sighed again. "What did he say about *that* then?"

"Well...Garrett said it was up to me how to act and what to call him."

"What do you mean?" Carter looked like he wasn't quite getting what Wyatt was trying to say.

"If I want to call him Garrett, Sir, or Master…and if I want to kneel or use a chair. That kind of stuff."

"*Wow*. I know you were saying how open his family was but I wasn't expecting that."

"Me neither. I don't know what I want to do."

"What have you always wanted to do before?" They both knew the answer to this already, but it looked like Carter was trying to humor him. "What would have made you calm down and be more comfortable with Garrett?"

"To kneel and let him be in charge." It came out slightly whiny and dejected. He was going to end up looking even more ridiculous than he had before. In the past, he'd thought he'd been subtle, evidently not.

"I don't see the problem then. You are going to be much calmer when you're kneeling and not trying to ignore what you need. Show them that. Show them your confident sub side. The side that kneels in the club perfectly happy at his master's feet. They've only seen the 'I'm–trying–to–act–vanilla–and–it–isn't–working' side. It's not like you're going to be naked or something. As long as it's reasonably private in the office, do what makes you happy."

"Do you think it's that simple?"

"Yes. You're over-thinking this. And I get why. Your family sucks when it comes to accepting you. It doesn't sound like his family is the same way. From what you've said, it seems like they won't mind." Carter walked around, coming up beside Wyatt. Giving him a quick hug, Carter shrugged. "As long as Garrett doesn't mind, and I know I've already said this, *do what makes you happy*."

"It's just, I know how to behave in the club and I know what I like at home. I don't know how to act other places with him. I never had to go through this with Richard." Saying that made Wyatt think.

Richard had never brought him home to meet his family or took him out in public as his sub anywhere besides the club. Even there, they'd been cautious and hadn't played much. When they went out, it was as regular boyfriends. Wyatt hadn't called him anything besides Richard when they were out in public. He was only Master at home or in the club, that was it. It seemed reasonable at the time when Richard had explained it.

Wyatt couldn't figure out how he felt about it all. On one hand, it made him really think about his previous Dominant. He hadn't thought Richard had been ashamed of the dynamics in their relationship but maybe he'd missed it. On the other hand, the idea of everyone *knowing* was giving him hives.

Was there a middle ground?

Did he even want one?

If they already knew he was a submissive and Garrett was a Dominant, was there any reason to pretend to be vanilla? He would have been more comfortable in the office if he could have knelt and related to Garrett in the context of the lifestyle. Even if they'd never moved past a business relationship, it would have made him less nuts.

Once he'd gotten out of his parents' house, he'd never hidden his *sexual preference* in the closet. However, he also hadn't gone out of his way to show people he was any more *different*. These weren't just people, though. These were Garrett's family and co-workers. Wyatt didn't know if that made it better or worse.

"*Richard was a dick*. You were starting to realize that. Otherwise, you would have gone with him. And don't even open your mouth, we both know I'm right." Carter gave him this look like he wasn't going to take any bull about it.

Wyatt decided to ignore the comment completely.

"What would you do if you knew, *like alternative reality kind of thing*, you knew everyone wouldn't care and was entirely open to whatever you did? You walk in there in some kind of naughty French maid costume and they wouldn't even think it was odd at all. What would you do then?"

It should have been harder to answer but Wyatt knew exactly how that would go. Even though the maid's outfit was probably more Carter's fantasy than his. "I'd walk in. Say hi, that kind of stuff. Then I'd ask if Master was busy. When I got in his office, I'd kneel and then we'd talk."

"So do it."

"*No!*"

"He likes you...head-over-heels kind of likes you. He's not going to get upset. Now you have to get going or you're going to be late."

Something on Wyatt's face must have given him away because Carter snorted again. "Didn't think I knew you were stalling, huh? Go."

Wyatt was unceremoniously marched to the door. "But..."

"Nope. Go. Talk about your list with your master and have a fun evening. Don't overthink it." Carter was firm and strangely cheerful. He looked like he enjoyed making Wyatt nuts.

Wyatt wouldn't have been nearly as embarrassed, except Mrs. Jenkins chose that moment to walk up to the door. She didn't even pause. She just gave them a sweet smile and inclined her head slightly. "So you have a new beau. That's wonderful, dear. You've been alone since you moved here, and we were starting to get worried."

"We?"

"Oh, the ladies I have tea with. They find you two boys...*sweet*." She said it innocently but Wyatt had a feeling she didn't mean exactly what she'd said.

"Um, thank you?" Now he really had to go. He had no idea how much she'd heard and he wasn't going to stay and figure it out. Carter could tell him later if he needed to duck under the counter and hide the next time she came in.

Even considering what those naughty little old ladies could be saying about them was going to make his hives worse. "I have to run but good seeing you, ma'am."

Then he ran—well, walked very quickly.

As he got in his car, he heard Mrs. Jenkins talking to Carter. "He has such good manners. Now it makes sense. This day and age most young men are so rude."

For the love of...

Wyatt had to take a deep breath. He'd worry about her later. For now, he had to focus his panic on going to Master's work. That was enough to concentrate on. He'd figure out the rest later.

He was never going to be able to look her in the eyes again.

WYATT STILL WASN'T sure what he was going to do as he walked up the front steps to Garrett's office. Normally, he got butterflies because he was so excited at the idea that he would even catch a glimpse of the Dom. This time, the butterflies had changed into man-eating vampire bats determined to eat their way out of his stomach.

Opening the door, he was still debating the best option when the wind came out of his sails completely. Master was standing right there by the receptionist's desk waiting for him. Thank goodness.

"Hi." Hopefully he didn't look too excited, but he'd never been so glad to see the Dom.

"Hello, Sweet. Did you have a good day?" Garrett smiled and took Wyatt's right hand, pulling him close.

"Yes. The store was busy earlier but things slowed down in

the afternoon. We were able to get some of the new inventory sorted out." This was so much less stressful than he'd feared, Wyatt didn't know what to do.

"That's wonderful." Garrett leaned down a little and gave Wyatt's forehead a kiss. "Melissa? If you could take a message if someone calls for me. I'll get back to them later if it's important. If it's not, just tell them I'll call back tomorrow." Then he turned back to Wyatt. "You ready for our discussion, Sweet?"

Wyatt fought the urge to blush. "Yes..."

Garrett gave him a tender smile and nodded. Wyatt still wasn't sure about it but Master said it was okay, so he settled with. "Yes, Sir."

That earned him another kiss on his forehead.

"Don't let Melissa's vanilla looks fool you. We've seen what's on her Kindle. She's got more dirty books than I've ever seen." Then Garrett looked over at her and gave her a wink. "She claims to be innocent but we're not buying it."

Melissa laughed and went back to typing something on her computer. "I'm more innocent than the rest of you, that's all that counts. Besides, you should have never peeked."

Garrett shrugged not looking repentant at all. "You said you were reading Gone With The Wind. For six months. It was like waving a red flag in front of a bull."

She shook her head and ignored the teasing. "Some of us have to work and can't quit early to play with our new...boyfriend."

That made Wyatt blush, and he fought the urge to pace. Garrett must have sensed something was off. He wrapped one hand around Wyatt's waist and discreet brought Wyatt's opposite hand behind his back.

Feeling his master's tight hold centered Wyatt, the urge to wiggle and fidget faded. He leaned his head against Garrett's shoulder and waited for instructions. Master was in charge and all Wyatt had to do was relax.

"Perks of being the boss. Come on, Sweet. Let's head back to my office. I have a present to show you."

As they walked into Garrett's office, Melissa called back before they could close the door. "Don't let him take all the credit. It was Brent's idea, and I picked out the color. Hope you like it."

Her innocent comments had the bats doing circles again. Garrett's pleased expression made Wyatt wary as well. "*Present*?"

"I think you'll like it. And she only picked out the color because I had so many late meetings this week I couldn't get away early enough to surprise you. This is the first day I'll get off at a reasonable time." The Dom was so excited Wyatt wasn't sure what the present could be.

Led around the desk by Master, Wyatt looked in shock.

Sitting on the floor, tucked discreetly behind Garrett's desk was a small cushion, almost the same brown color as the hardwood floors but with some kind of striped pattern. Wyatt wasn't sure what to say.

It was what he'd wanted, what he'd fantasized about if he was honest. He couldn't get over how normal everyone was treating it. Garrett must have guessed something about what was going through his head, because his master sat down and pulled Wyatt onto his lap.

"We're discreet in the community, my sweet, but we've never hid who we were from our friends. It would be too difficult to constantly be worrying about how something would come across or if it gave too much away." Running his hands over Wyatt's legs soothingly, his master waited.

"Everyone in the office?"

"In some way or another. I almost didn't hire Melissa because she looked so vanilla. I was worried she wouldn't fit in. It wasn't until the end of the interview she said she wrote romance as a hobby. She wanted to make sure it wouldn't be an issue. Something about the way she said it made me sit up and take notice. So, I asked a few more questions. More than was probably reasonable. But it turned out she wrote BDSM romance novels." Garrett laughed and shook his head. "I decided she'd probably fit in."

"I can't believe it."

"Right?"

"Then her Kindle…"

"Oh, it's full of all kinds of dirty books. When she'd accidentally left it in the break room one day, Calen 'borrowed' it to see if he could figure out her pen name." Garrett made that sound entirely too reasonable. "He gets antsy on Fridays."

There was definitely more to that story.

Garrett turned his sexy smile back on Wyatt. "Would you like to try out your cushion?"

"Yes." He'd thought about something like it for so long that he was curious to see how it would feel. Climbing off Garrett's lap, Wyatt waited while his master arranged the little pillow. It looked like it was part of an outdoor furniture set.

Garrett positioned it between his feet. Wyatt wouldn't be squished against the desk but it gave him some privacy just in case. His master smiled. "There we go."

Wyatt knelt down and positioned himself the best he could. It was a little awkward because it was higher than what he was used to. Eventually, he made it work and felt like he looked presentable enough. Glancing up at Master, as he tucked his hands behind his back, he was relieved to see how pleased he looked.

"Beautiful, my sweet."

"Thank you, Master."

"Are you ready to discuss limits? Then, I'm going to take you out to dinner."

This was more familiar ground. Even being in Master's office and still unsure about how to act, he knew what to do now. "Yes, Master."

11

GARRETT

Garrett was afraid it was going to be Wyatt calling to cancel when the phone chimed on Saturday. He relaxed when he saw it was Brent. "Hey. Everything still on for one o'clock?"

"Yeah. I wanted to make sure you had dessert?" Brent tried to sound like he was teasing, but it was clear he was concerned.

"I only forgot it once!"

"You forgot it once and then brought *boxed donuts* the next time."

"Those donuts were not boxed." A couple of screw ups and no one ever let you live it down. "Stop giving me dessert then."

"You can't be trusted with something more important!"

"Bull shit."

"Are you saying you have dessert all ready and it's not something weird like donuts?"

"Yes." Ha. Well, he didn't have it ready, but Wyatt did. Wyatt might not have trusted him either. Oh, it was all very carefully worded. However, the reality was Wyatt wanted to be guaranteed to make a good first impression on Garrett's family.

"A real dessert?" Brent was clearly skeptical.

"Yes!" This was starting to get ridiculous.

"Wyatt made it, huh?"

"My boy, my dessert. Unless you want me to eat all the coconut, caramel covered brownies on my own? If you're not careful, I'm going to bring something crazy just to make you nuts." He'd do it too. "Remember the M&M's?"

"Fine. That wasn't what I was calling about anyway." Brent's voice took on a more business-like tone.

"Nope. Unless it's an emergency with one of our insureds, I'm not talking about work. I'm going to head over in a few minutes and pick up Wyatt and Carter. That's it. This is a full day off. I didn't even bring any work home."

"It will only take—"

"No. I'm–taking–the–day–off!" He enunciated it clearly and firmly. This was getting absurd. The guy needed a boyfriend, Dom, or even a good weekend fling. He was working entirely too hard.

"Fine." Brent's voice was more tired than it should be.

And he'd given up too fast. Especially for their family. "You need a vacation or to get laid. Pick one but do something besides work."

"I'm fine."

No one who ever said those words was actually fine. Even Garrett knew that. "*Sure.* Maybe we should give Mom a call and see if she's having fun. She might be ready to come—"

"I will schedule some time off! You call her and I'll tell her about Wyatt. I might even mention I hear wedding bells and a collaring ceremony."

That was just mean.

It didn't mean he was wrong though. Besides, Garrett had that covered. "I already told her, genius." He knew a secret like that was perfect blackmail material so he'd tackled that conversation right away.

And luckily, she was only half-way through with her current trip. There was no way to cancel and come home early without inconveniencing too many people. He'd promised to send pictures and had to agree to give her Wyatt's email address. He still hadn't told Wyatt about that part yet. He figured he needed to get his sub in the right frame of mind before he sprung that on him.

His sweet sub was a *little* nervous right now.

Brent made a frustrated huff as the wind came out of his sails. "I'll look at the calendar on Monday and schedule some time off."

Ha! Victory.

"We'll see you in a little while." A little smirk in his voice, Garrett really did have to go. He was due to pick up Wyatt and his friend in a few minutes.

For the past two days, their evening phone calls had been filled with more worries and less flirting. Garrett didn't mind more real conversations with his boy. However, he was starting to get concerned about how nervous Wyatt was. Inviting Carter seemed to have helped somewhat.

Maybe.

According to Wyatt, Carter was concerned about what to wear and how to act around the rest of the family. It was distracting Wyatt from his own fears, but now Garrett had two worried subs on his hands. Which was one more than he was prepared to deal with.

He'd said repeatedly Carter should wear whatever he was comfortable with, but neither sub had absorbed it. Finally, when they were talking last night, Garrett had tried to take a different approach.

He'd interrupted the stream of worries with a question. "What do you think he should wear? If you guys were just doing something fun and there was nothing to worry over, what's your favorite thing?"

Garrett was already well aware that Carter was more flexible in how he dressed. The rest of the family wasn't going to care, but there had been no way to make the subs believe it. Wyatt had paused for a minute and then spoke hesitantly. "Let me show you. I have a picture on my phone. This is my favorite outfit. I think he looks great in it."

The picture had been some kind of a simple sundress. Wyatt had been right. Even Garrett, whose fashion sense was limited to suits, could see that Carter had felt fabulous in the dress and it suited his frame. To Garrett, that made the decision simple. "Okay. Tell him to wear that then."

Wyatt had been uneasy, but Garrett had tried to soothe his nerves. "Would I tell you to do anything that would make things harder on you?"

His sexy sub had found that terribly funny, but it seemed to stop the worries.

"You told everybody to be nice to Carter and not mention the clothing, right? I want Wyatt's friend to be comfortable." He might be starting to obsess like Wyatt but he wanted this to go smoothly.

"Yes. Message sent and received. We want to make a good impression on Wyatt. We can behave. We just choose not to when it's only us. Company manners this time."

"Or I'll tell Mom."

"Still fighting dirty, I see."

"Yup."

"I'll pass the message on."

"Thanks. All right, I have to go, time to go pick up Wyatt."

"See you. Don't forget dessert!"

Garrett hung up on him. The donuts hadn't been that bad. That bakery was good and considering he'd gone in there at the last minute, he'd been glad they had anything he could bring. Grabbing his keys and phone, Garrett headed for the door. Fingers crossed Wyatt was calm and ready to have a fun afternoon hanging out with everyone.

EVIDENTLY, crossing your fingers didn't help once you got to be an adult.

His sweet sub was bouncing off the walls. Carter seemed cautiously resigned. Garrett thought he looked good, and that they were both worrying too much. There wasn't anything he could do about Carter's emotions but Wyatt was another story.

He hadn't been in the house five minutes and he knew he had to help Wyatt relax. Wyatt was doing some last-minute fussing over the brownies and kept saying he was almost ready. He looked ready. Garrett was convinced it was a delaying tactic.

"Wyatt." That one word stopped his sweet sub in his tracks.

Reaching out to restack the brownies again, he froze. "Yes, Master?"

Carter was leaning against the counter, watching them. Garrett wasn't concerned about the other man. Wyatt had already said he hadn't hidden anything from his friend.

"We are going to *talk*. We can do it in here or we can have some privacy. Which would you prefer?" Garrett could see that Wyatt understood they were going to probably do more than talk right away.

His boy sighed. "Private." Then he turned to Carter. "We'll be right back."

Wyatt took Garrett's hand and led him back through the house to his bedroom. It was the first time Garrett had seen Wyatt's room, but he didn't have time to look around. His sub needed his attention, and they needed to leave soon.

There were only two places to sit, the bed and a small side chair. Garrett thought the chair was a safer option. Temptation and all. Sitting down, he spoke to Wyatt. "Come kneel, Sweet. I want to talk to you."

Wyatt slowly walked over and knelt, presenting beautifully for his master. "Yes, Master?"

Garrett watched as Wyatt took a deep breath and settled into his submission. It was like a warm blanket wrapping around his boy. Something that made him feel secure. Posture straight and legs spread, Garrett watched as his shoulders lowered and the stress melted away. It wasn't perfect, but it was a long way from his behavior in the kitchen.

What to do?

If they'd still been in the kitchen then this discussion would have been different but now he had more options. "I know there is nothing I can say that will take all your worries away. You just need to *see* that they're going to love you. However, I am worried that you're going to make yourself sick. You look more nervous than when you used to come into the office. That can't continue."

Wyatt needed something else to focus on that would keep pulling his mind back from his worries. "Where are your toys?"

"*Master*?" The rising blush on Wyatt's face made it clear he'd hoped he hadn't heard Garrett right.

"Toys, Sweet. Where are they?" Wyatt was a sub who'd been alone too long. He had toys. Lots of them more than likely.

Looking down at the floor, the cute sub mumbled, "Bottom drawer of my dresser, Master."

Standing, Garrett walked over to the dresser and crouched

down to see what fun things his boy had. Perfect. It was no wonder he'd been embarrassed. His boy had fun things in all shapes and sizes. Plugs, cock rings, massagers, and even several types of cuffs were mixed in with different impact toys.

Picking out a small slim plug, lube, and a flexible cock ring that looked like it wouldn't cause a problem for his boy to wear for a couple of hours, he went back over to his kneeling sub. Wyatt still wasn't looking at him but that was okay. He liked how cute he looked when he was all bashful. "I have a cock ring you will wear while soft. You have two options. You may go in the bathroom and put it on yourself or I will do it for you. Which would you prefer?"

That had the sexy sub curious. His head came up, and he looked at what Garrett was holding. "Um. I...I pick?"

"Yes, Sweet. Do you want me to put it on you or do you want privacy? This is not a discussion on *if* you will wear it...we are simply discussing privacy."

Garrett watched as Wyatt swallowed and seemed to consider the options. Once he'd made the decision, he looked even calmer. "You, Master. Would you put it on me?"

"Of course. Stand up."

Still with that incredible grace, Wyatt rose and took a step closer to Garrett. Placing his arms behind his back, he waited to see what Garrett would say. The change was startling. Gone was the worried, almost frantic behavior. His sexy sub was now centered and focused.

Garrett made quick work of opening Wyatt's jeans and letting them slide to the floor. He made no move to hide how sexy he found his boy. If he hadn't wanted the sub soft, he would have done more than just admire him.

Wyatt was wearing the tiniest pair of boxer briefs that Garrett had ever seen outside the club. They cupped his package beautifully, but they were tiny enough that his dick poked out the top, giving Garrett all kinds of sexy ideas. Reaching out, he slid the briefs over Wyatt's hardening length. That wouldn't do. Taking the base of Wyatt's cock tightly in his hand, he kept the boy from getting any more erect.

"You're beautiful, Sweet. However, I can't have your cock hard right now." For many subs, a little bit of pain would soften their erections. However, from the way his boy took to his spanking, Garrett wasn't going to bet on that working. "I need you to focus on something else for a minute. I want your pretty cock soft today. We'll play with the ring while you're hard another day."

"Yes, Master." Wyatt took a deep breath and closed his eyes. Garrett wasn't sure what he was thinking of, but he quietly waited for the sub to do his best to bring his half-hard erection under control. It took a little while, but eventually, the boy's cock was soft enough that Garrett was satisfied.

Quickly slipping the cock ring over him, Garrett had the boy wrapped up beautifully in seconds. Now that they weren't going to have to worry about Wyatt's erection any longer, Garrett didn't fight his need to touch the sub. "Good boy. You did very well. I think you're going to deserve a reward later."

Wyatt shivered and opened his eyes. "Thank you, Master."

Garrett loved the feel of a sub's trapped cock. Something about denying the boy not only permission to come but the ability to become hard was incredibly erotic. Even soft, Wyatt wasn't small, and that just made it sexier. "You're stunning like this, Sweet. We're going to have to keep you like this more often."

Another shiver rolled through Wyatt and he licked his lips.

"I like seeing you confined. Knowing you can't even get hard without my permission is addicting." Teasing Wyatt's flaccid length between his fingers, he could see the sub's growing arousal even though his cock couldn't react. It was going to be a long day for the boy. It should keep his mind off his worries though.

With one last gentle caress, he gave the boy's soft dick a pat. "Very good. Now as long as you haven't changed your mind about privacy, turn around for me. We're not done quite yet."

Wyatt nodded and shuffled around, looking so cute with his pants still down around his ankles. The boy's ass was a work of art. High and full, with perfectly split cheeks that let his little hole peek out as he moved. Cupping the boy's bottom, Garrett gave it a squeeze. "Oh yes. We are going to be keeping you naked as much as I can, Sweet. Now open up your legs and bend over. I need your pretty little hole. We're going to keep you nice and distracted today."

He could already hear the strain in the sub's voice as he answered. "Yes, Master. Thank you." Wyatt spread his legs as much as his pants would allow and bent over.

So damned sexy.

Lubing up two fingers, Garrett kept one hand on Wyatt's lower back, trying to keep him steady. Yes, the bed or even over his lap would be easier for the boy, but this would make him feel deliciously submissive. Bending over and presenting himself like this to his master in a way that would make him feel almost used.

"So sexy. And such a good boy." Garrett let one finger tease his boy's tight entrance. His little pucker twitched and a sexy moan escaped his boy. "That's it. Let me hear how much you want this. How much you want to be on display for your master. How much you want to please me. How much you want to be used."

Needy little sounds escaped his sweet sub and Garrett relished the sexy noises. However, this was just the starting point. His boy was going to be desperate by the time the day was over. Carefully sliding one finger in, Garrett started opening the boy and carefully working the lube around. Even if the plug was small, Wyatt would be wearing it for a while and he wanted the sub comfortable.

Maybe comfortable wasn't the right word, but he didn't want Wyatt to be sore by the end of the day. He had plans for the evening that didn't include a sub too tender to play. When he was accepting one finger easily, Garrett added the second. Carefully working to stretch his sub just enough for the plug, Garrett watched as the boy fought to stay still. It was getting much more difficult for the sexy sub.

However, Garrett wasn't trying to get him too turned on. So he slowly removed his fingers and brought the plug up to his boy's stretched hole. He gently pressed the slim toy and watched as Wyatt's body stretched around it seductively.

Once it was seated, he gave the sub's sexy bottom another pat. "Wait just like this. I'm going to clean up but I don't want you to move. I like seeing you like this."

Wyatt let out another little moan but nodded. "Yes, Sir."

"Good boy."

Walking into the adjoining bathroom, Garrett quickly washed his hands and came back out to his boy. Oh yes. He was going to keep the boy as naked as possible. He looked incredible.

"You've done such a good job. Stand up now and we'll get you dressed again. We need to head out so we're not late."

Wyatt straightened up and waited for instructions. Perfect sub. "You may get dressed, Sweet."

Pulling his pants up, Wyatt wiggled a little and Garrett could see he was struggling to ignore the plug in his ass. Garrett didn't plan on letting him get too used to it but the sub could try. When he was dressed again, Garrett had him do a little turn to make sure his toys weren't visible.

"There we go. No one will know but us how sexy you look under your clothes."

Wyatt wasn't embarrassed, but he looked relieved no one would see. Almost too relieved. Maybe it was just that he was nervous about meeting Garrett's family but he was starting to think it might be something else. Wyatt had mentioned the club before but maybe that had been the only place outside his home that he'd played.

The problem would have to wait for another time. They had places to be.

"All right. Let's go. I think we've kept your friend waiting long enough." Garrett took Wyatt's hand and led them back out to the kitchen where Carter was waiting, trying to look very nonchalant.

Carter looked up and gave Wyatt a look, only relaxing when his boy smiled and gave him a wink. Cheeky little thing. Grabbing up the brownies, Garrett looked around the kitchen. "Do we need anything else?"

"No, I don't think so, Master."

Carter chimed in. "Are you sure I don't need to bring anything? I feel weird going with nothing."

"No, don't worry about it. There's a list and everyone is assigned something to bring. If you enjoy yourself and want to keep coming, then they'll put you on the list too. Otherwise, relax and have fun. There's always plenty of food." There were usually tons of leftovers. Some weeks, depending on what was on the menu, Garrett had leftovers for days.

He leaned over and gave Wyatt a quick kiss on the cheek. "If they eat all this you'll make me another, right? This will be the best dessert ever."

Wyatt laughed and shook his head. "What did you bring last time you got dessert?"

Garrett knew he looked sheepish. "That's not the point. I just want to make sure I get some."

"I think that is the point but I'll let you get away with it for now. If I end up having to make another one, you're going to have to fess up." Wyatt gave him a wicked grin. "I bet one of your brothers would tell me if I asked."

"You cheat as bad as the rest of the family. You're going to fit right in."

G arrett might have had a good idea.

When it became clear what he was going to do, Wyatt had been skeptical that it would work...and turned on and slightly embarrassed and then really turned on. It turned out Garrett's idea might not have been that crazy after all. Wyatt was definitely more relaxed and felt more like he usually did when he was kneeling for his Dominant.

This time, it was just without the kneeling or the obvious submission.

At least, he hadn't knelt *yet*. The fact that they'd only been there about thirty seconds may have had something to do with it. Walking around to the back of the large ranch home, the weight of the plug and the comforting hug of the cock ring kept him from panicking.

He could do this. They'd always been very nice, even if he hadn't realized he'd met them before.

Thankfully, it wasn't that big of a deal when they came around the back. Garrett took a minute and pointed out everyone to them. That was when it hit him that he *had* met everyone. Brent was the man who'd answered a hypothetical claims question. Bryce had been a teasing funny guy who'd been driving the receptionist crazy one day. And Grant had been the large brooding man who Wyatt had seen coming out of Garrett's office.

Brent and a few other people raised their hands and called out a quick hello. Grant shook his head and made a big deal of looking at his watch. "We were starting to think you'd run off with the dessert."

"Don't be an ass. At least try to make a good impression. Mom wouldn't be pleased to hear you tried to run off Wyatt and his friend. She's excited to hear I'm finally settling down."

Wyatt hadn't heard that smirking, I'm–better–than–you–are voice before from Garrett. It was eye opening. To him, Garrett had always been the sexy, out-of-reach Dom, but he was starting to see a different side. One that liked making his brothers nuts. It was cute.

"Now who's being an ass? Mom would have my hide!" Grant threw what looked like a roll at Garrett, just missing him. Unfortunately, it bounced off Carter instead, who stood there shocked.

Neither Wyatt nor Carter knew what to do. Their families weren't like this at all.

"Shit! I'm sorry." Grant's words had everyone in the backyard looking in their direction.

"Are you okay?" Garrett turned towards Carter and tried to see if he was hurt.

Carter laughed, then tried to reassure him. "It was a roll, not something dangerous. I'm fine."

"Way to make a good impression, jackass," Garrett growled at Grant.

"I'm sorry. I didn't mean to hit you. I was aiming for that tattle-tale over there." He tilted his head in Garrett's direction but seemed to be refusing to talk to him. "Are you sure you're okay? I didn't mean to hit you."

Carter blushed and looked down at the ground, mumbling something Wyatt couldn't hear. Grant evidently heard him though because his head came back and he laughed. Carter's blush went into overdrive and he looked mortified. This time Wyatt heard his words. "Where's a rock when you need to crawl under something?"

Grant laughed even harder. Garrett was looking at his brother like he'd never seen him before. Wyatt was missing something.

Grant managed to get ahold of himself and stopped laughing. He held out his arm like someone from one of those old timey movies, where men wore suits and were very suave. "May I show you where the drinks are located?"

Carter looked like he wasn't sure if Grant was being serious, but when he made up his mind he just smiled and nodded. "Thank you, Sir."

As they moved away from Wyatt and Garrett, Grant leaned down and whispered something to Carter. Whatever it was had Wyatt's friend blushing again but this time it looked more like flirting than embarrassment. Very interesting.

"I'll be damned."

"So that's not normal for Grant?"

"Nope. Not normal at all. Very curious." Garrett shook his head. "All right, let's go set these down then I'll introduce you to everyone." Then his voice dropped to a husky whisper. "Later, I have to check to make sure your toys aren't hurting you."

It wasn't a question so Wyatt gave the naughty man a little smile. "I understand, Master."

Wyatt had never worn any toys out in public. The idea was... shocking. Yes, he knew other subs who wore things like cock rings and even full cages all the time but Richard had never made him do anything like that. And it would have never occurred to Wyatt to decide to do something like that on his own. Sure he liked his toys when he was alone, but that was at home with the door locked.

Not out in public.

Master had just seemed so...decisive about it earlier. He knew what he was going to do to help pull Wyatt back from the edge of panic and it worked. He felt centered and calm, like he did when they were at home together or even talking on the phone.

Part of his worries had been because he wasn't sure how Garrett was going to act when they were out in public. Wyatt knew Garrett had said he wasn't going to hide who they were, and the office had given some strength to his statement, but it was still a lot to take in.

There was no more time to worry about it, though.

As they moved over to the table where the food was laid out, Brent came over. "You actually brought something real this time. I'm impressed." Then he grinned and looked at Wyatt. "Thank you for making something, because we all know he didn't go to this kind of effort for us."

"My boy, my dessert. I told you that earlier. I get to claim credit too." It came out very dry and matter of fact but there was laughter in Garrett's eyes.

Wyatt couldn't control the blush that crept over his face. He wasn't sure how to respond. He loved the possessive sound in his master's voice but it was a lot more open than he was used to. He looked at Brent and finally decided on a short, "Thank you."

Brent couldn't seem to help poking at Garrett. "See, even he agrees. It was his dessert."

Wyatt had to fight off a smile. Was this what he'd missed by being an only child? Suddenly he was much more thankful for his lack of siblings. Garrett looked at him with this stern sexy look.

"Were you agreeing with him? Hmm, I'm not sure that's a

good idea, Sweet." The growl in Garrett's voice made Wyatt shiver.

"No, Sir. I was just being polite." Wyatt desperately wanted to know the punishment for agreeing with Garrett's brother but it didn't seem like the best time for that. The audience, and all.

"Good boy." Garrett took a step closer.

Wyatt wasn't sure what would have happened but Brent piped up before his master could close the distance. "Get a room, you two."

Coughing and choking in surprise, Wyatt couldn't decide where to look. There were just too many people. He finally decided on making a thorough study of Master's shirt.

"Where are your manners? You're not supposed to embarrass him the first time I bring him over. Good first impression, remember?" His master's voice was filled with frustration.

"What? I'm behaving. You should have been here earlier when Grant and Bryce were arguing about the salad. Some of the shit they said made *me* blush."

Even Wyatt could see the deflection to another sibling but Garrett fell for it. "Why were they fighting over it?"

"I don't know. Something about Bryce bringing the wrong one. Grant was growling about wanting the other dressing and Bryce exploded. Bryce just told him if he wanted someone to boss around and drive crazy he should go get laid, not take it out on him. Then Grant went off, and it got colorful." Brent smirked and glanced over at Wyatt before going into more detail on the crazy insults. "Bryce is a switch, so it makes it so much easier to fight with him. You can go either way, all the insults work."

Wyatt couldn't think of a polite response to that. He wondered if it was rude to think they were strange.

Probably.

Maybe it wasn't that they were strange...they were just completely unlike anything he was used to. His family ignored the fact that he was gay as much as they could. The fact that he was submissive was hidden so deep you'd need a treasure map to find it. He couldn't imagine anyone in his family telling him to go get a Dom and blow some steam off because he was an ass.

It felt like he was watching some kind of reality TV show.

"Um, okay." He still wasn't sure if a response was required but he didn't want to be rude.

Garrett laughed and shook his head at Brent. "Troublemaker." Then he turned to Wyatt and gave him a quick kiss on the cheek. "Come on. Let's go say hi to everyone else."

Garrett walked them around the spacious backyard. There weren't that many people, Garrett's brothers and some people from work primarily. It was nice. He already knew more people than he expected and no one was surprised at his relationship with Garrett even though they kept things pretty vanilla. Well, vanilla with some sprinkles maybe. But overall, not outrageous.

The whole being open thing was still weird but after a while it didn't feel as wrong.

He didn't have to constantly watch what he said about Garrett or how he responded. If he said "Sir" or "Master" instead of just Garrett no one blinked. If he responded to a question by saying he would let Garrett make that decision, no one thought it was weird. They expected it or at least understood how the dynamics probably worked in their relationship.

So maybe being accepted *was* weird.

It was a kind of weird he could get used to, though.

It was a kind of weird he hadn't realized he'd been missing.

The food was good, and it was an insane relief to see that everyone loved his brownies...their brownies. Garrett was still saying he got credit too. There was definitely a story behind it. Wyatt thought he would have to corner one of his master's brothers to get the scoop.

Not that Master was going to let him out of his sight that long.

Garrett had stuck by Wyatt's side all afternoon. His master hadn't gotten more than five feet from him and as much as it probably looked like Garrett was hovering, Wyatt appreciated it. It was another constant reminder that his master was there to take care of him.

Of course, sometimes *taking care of him* was a little literal.

After they'd eaten and were helping to clean up, Garrett leaned close and discreetly whispered in Wyatt's ear. "Let's head back to the bathroom, Sweet. I want to check on you."

Wyatt nodded and tried not to stand out as they made their way through the kitchen and living room to the back of the house. He wasn't sure what to expect, so he tried to simply follow Master's direction. The silent reminder to himself that his master was in charge soothed some of his nerves.

Walking into what seemed to be a guestroom, Garrett led him into a spacious bathroom. "I'll wait outside while you use the restroom. Then we're going to take a look at you."

Thankful that he had privacy, Wyatt quickly handled his needs and washed his hands. When he was ready, he opened the door and waited for his master's instructions.

Garrett walked in, and after locking the door, went over to sit on the edge of the tub. "Come here, boy. I want to see how you're doing. I don't want you sore, remember."

It wasn't a question, but as Wyatt walked over to him, he nodded. "Yes, Sir."

He still couldn't believe it was real. Standing there with Garrett as his master, while the sexy Dom took off his pants. If Wyatt was the swooning type, this would definitely do it. Master was obviously as turned on as he was, judging by the tenting in his pants. If Wyatt's cock wasn't restrained, it would have been hard too.

The fact that his master had him walking around with a cock ring on and a plug up his ass was still crazy hot. The plug wasn't big enough to make it too difficult. It was just a constant reminder of his master's control. That was hot too.

Master reached out to unbutton Wyatt's pants, letting them slide to the floor. Master gave him the same hungry look he had earlier as he eyed Wyatt's underwear. Sexy underwear got his master going. Good. Wyatt was going to have a wonderful time finding new ones to tempt him with.

Sliding his hands up Wyatt's legs, Garrett cupped his ass, letting his fingers caress the edge of the material. Wyatt wanted to shove his ass back and beg Garrett to touch him harder, but he knew he shouldn't.

The wait made him crazy but eventually, with slow, deliberate movements, the sexy Dom slid the tiny, tight briefs down to Wyatt's thighs. Half-naked, with his ass hanging out, he felt deliciously naughty. He wanted to spread himself out over Garrett's lap and plead for a spanking. He couldn't do that either.

Crazy frustrating and incredibly arousing.

Garrett trailed his hands up Wyatt's legs and around to his cock. The look on his face made it clear Garrett knew how wound up he was making him. Having Garrett inspect him shouldn't have been that sexy. It was like his body truly belonged to his master.

Insanely hot.

It could have been a fantasy he jerked off to a thousand times. A master inspecting his property before he uses it. Thank goodness, Garrett couldn't see the dirty thoughts running through his head. His master would think he was probably a little unbalanced.

"Oh, the naughty thought running through your head." Garrett's deep voice pulled Wyatt back from his fantasy.

"Um, Master?"

"One of these days, Sweet, you're going to kneel down in front of me and tell me about those naughty fantasies." Garrett's hand gently rubbed Wyatt's not so happy cock. The tender touch was making it hard to focus.

The image made Wyatt's knees weak.

Maybe in panic, maybe in need...it was hard to be sure which.

"Um, yes, Master?" Wyatt didn't mean for it to come out as a question. He would never voluntarily do something like that on his own, it was hard enough to tell a guy he wanted a full-time Dom. Sharing the crazy fantasies that ran through his head would be...He couldn't even describe it.

"Yes, Sweet. I want to know every sexy, dirty thought that runs through your head." Garrett looked down at Wyatt's soft length. "Not right now, though. I want to be able to see how hard they make you."

Saved for now...but probably not for long.

Master gave Wyatt's cock a pat. "All right. Turn around so I can check on your plug."

Nothing to think about or even worry over. He just had to follow directions. That thought always made things easier. It wasn't his dirty desires, it was what his master wanted. At some point, Wyatt knew he was going to have to work on that but for now, it made him feel calmer.

Turning slowly, trying not to trip on his pants, Wyatt leaned over and bared himself for his master. It felt incredible. Pleasing Garrett, obeying him, letting his master see his body...use him... Shivers raced through him. He couldn't wait to get home.

Master hadn't said anything specific but Wyatt knew they'd do something—Please, God, they had to do something.

A light smack echoed through the room as Garrett gave his ass a pop. "Reach back and open yourself for me."

Could you die from arousal?

Reaching back, he grabbed his cheeks and pulled, showing Garrett everything.

"Very good."

Wyatt heard packaging rattling, and he fought the urge to look behind him. If Master wanted him to know he'd tell him. The waiting cranked his desire even higher. Garrett had to know what he was doing to him. The steady pull of the plug made Wyatt gasp. Was Master taking it out? As unsure as Wyatt had been about the idea earlier, he couldn't imagine not having it in.

"We're going to make sure you're not too sore later. I'm going to put more lube on this and then we'll be all set." Garrett's deep voice was rough with desire. Please let that mean his master was going to use him later. Wyatt needed to come.

The plug came out making a noise that had Wyatt blushing. Garrett just ignored it. When Garrett's slick fingers carefully entered Wyatt, he thought he'd lose it. The image of humping back on Master's fingers and already overwhelming pleasure made Wyatt moan.

"That's my sexy boy. You're so needy, aren't you? I can't wait to get you home." Garrett didn't say exactly what he'd do, that made Wyatt even crazier.

Thankfully, Garrett didn't torture him too long.

Even though Wyatt hated to lose the incredible sensations, he wouldn't be able to function around everyone else if Master didn't stop. Pushing the plug back into place, Garrett gave Wyatt's ass a gentle slap and started pulling up his briefs. Just the act of Garrett dressing him was embarrassingly hot. It made him feel even more exposed.

"Okay. Straighten up and turn back around this way. We need to get you dressed." Garrett might have been matter of fact, almost stern, but the erection straining his pants let Wyatt know he wasn't as detached as he was trying to appear.

What he wanted to do was to kneel down and beg to relieve his master. This wasn't the place for that, though. And they'd already been gone too long. Someone was going to notice if they were gone even longer.

Straightening Wyatt's clothing, Master smiled up at him. "Oh, the things I want to do to you, Sweet."

Yes!

13

GARRETT

"What did you think about the sparks between Grant and Carter? That wasn't my imagination was it?" Wyatt looked over to Garrett as they were walking in the door to the sub's house.

"No. Definitely not. I've never seen Grant that taken with someone right off the bat." Garrett had been incredibly surprised to see how easily his gruff brother had charmed Wyatt's friend. Garrett shut the door and locked it. He had plans that didn't involve interruptions.

"What kind of guy does Grant usually date?" Wyatt didn't seem to want to let the topic drop.

It was easy for Garrett to see he was concerned for his friend. "You are going to talk to Carter tomorrow. Sometime when I'm not around. That way, you two can have some privacy and he can tell you what he thought and what they discussed. Then, I think you will feel better. For now, we are going to leave the topic at the door and simply focus on us. Are we clear, boy?"

Wyatt got a surprised look and glanced around, finally understanding they were home. He blushed then nodded. "Yes, Master."

Garrett could see that his boy was connecting the dots now. How to start things off...

He took Wyatt's hand and tugged him close, pressing the sub against his body. Giving into temptation, Garrett gave his boy a long, slow kiss. Unwilling to get completely sidetracked from his plans, no matter how tasty his boy was, Garrett pulled back. "We are going to go into the living room. You're going to strip down to that sexy underwear and kneel on your cushion for me. When you're ready, we're going to talk and I'll explain how the rest of our evening will work."

There was no question and nothing to debate. Just the way Wyatt wanted it. He didn't want discussions on what the scene might entail. He didn't want to keep things mainstream and sneak off to the bedroom later. He wanted to belong to his master, and Garrett thought, to be used for his master's pleasure.

That was the part Garrett had a few questions on.

Just to make sure they were on the same page. Then he'd give his sub what he needed.

"Go on then. Go get ready."

Wyatt took a step back and gave Garrett a peaceful smile. "Yes, Master."

Once he'd walked into the living room and Garrett could hear the rustle of clothes, he leaned back against the door and took a deep breath. Wyatt might have been the one with the toys on but Garrett had been hard for hours thinking about it. The image of his boy bent over with the plug sliding in his ass was incredibly erotic.

Their evening was a long way from over too. It was going to be quite a while before he would get any relief. He could wait. It was going to be worth it to play with his boy. Getting himself under control, he pushed off the door and walked into the living room.

Stunning.

His sweet sub was kneeling by the couch, head bowed, arms behind his back, and those sexy briefs cupping every curve. Now that he was kneeling, the underwear was so tiny a good length of his ass showed as he knelt.

"Very good, Sweet." Walking over to the couch, Garrett could see Wyatt relax with the words. Wyatt obviously loved knowing he'd pleased his master.

Relaxing on the couch, Garrett spread his legs and motioned Wyatt closer. "Right over here where I can touch you. Perfect."

When the sub was in front of him, Garrett reached out so he could caress Wyatt's hair. He would never get enough of his sweet, sexy sub. "This came up a little when we were talking about limits, but I want to make sure I understand what you like before we continue."

Wyatt looked up and Garrett could see the wheels turning in his head. Finally, he gave a simple response. "I'll do my best to answer you, Sir."

"I know you will. Even if this is hard, I need you to tell me the truth. I want to make sure we both understand what you like. Not just your limits." Garrett paused for a moment to let that sink in. Wyatt waited, beautifully presented between Garrett's legs. "I know you like to serve, Sweet. I know you want to completely belong to your master. Having someone who sets boundaries for you and gives you the structure you crave makes you feel safe. I need to understand how you feel about not just serving your master, but being used by your master."

The way Wyatt's face pinked up and his struggle to maintain eye contact let Garrett know he was on the right track. "When you picture our relationship, Sweet, do you see me walking in and you coming over to kneel for me or do you picture me walking in and using you for my pleasure? Do you fantasize about me coming and telling you to kneel and suck me off? Do you fantasize about your cock being caged and having your master fuck your tight little hole even though you don't get to come, just because that's what your master wants?"

With his flushed cheeks and the way he was nibbling on his bottom lip, Garrett thought he had a pretty good idea where his boy's fantasies lay. He had to be sure though. He didn't want to misunderstand things and cause problems in their relationship. He'd never had a full-time sub before and he wasn't going to try to guess what was on the sub's mind.

It took several long moments for Wyatt to respond. He may have been stunned by the question or he might not have known how to answer, but eventually, he seemed to get his thoughts in order. Not that Garrett minded if he took even longer. Watching the sweet sub kneel at his feet, nearly naked and wanting to serve, Garrett had an incredible view to keep him occupied.

Wyatt had to clear his throat several times before he could answer. It finally came out in an almost hesitant voice. "I...I like both. Sometimes the first but a lot of times the second." Then he paused. Garrett wanted more information though, so he waited. Wyatt must have realized it wasn't quite enough, so he kept going, this time more embarrassed. "I liked the way you made me bend over while you plugged me. I like the idea of you using me. Just not all the time, you know, but sometimes. And it was...you know..."

It looked like they were coming to the end of what Wyatt could share at that point. That was okay, Garrett was starting to get the picture. "Was it something like that you were fantasizing about in the bathroom earlier?"

The boy had loved it when Garrett had taken a very no-nonsense attitude when he'd been checking the plug. The more detached he'd acted, the more turned on his boy got. Wyatt might not like the idea of admitting he wanted to be used and maybe slightly objectified, but it certainly excited him.

At some point, he'd have to see Wyatt's thoughts on humiliation play, but not yet. Later, when Wyatt was more confident about sharing and when Garrett was more confident he could read the sweet sub well enough.

Wyatt managed a little nod before looking down at the floor. "Yes, Master."

"Thank you for letting me know." Now, on to the fun part of their evening. "Stand up. It's time for those briefs to come off." Wyatt rose, so graceful it still awed Garrett. Standing quietly with his hands behind his back, he waited for the next instructions.

Reaching out, Garrett fingered the edge of the fabric, loving the little shivers that raced through Wyatt. Sliding the underwear down Wyatt's legs, Garrett watched as he stepped out of them and stood naked for his master.

So incredibly sexy.

Mentally crossing his fingers that he understood Wyatt's needs, Garrett let his hands trail back up the sub's legs to his still trapped cock. Casually rolling the sleeping length between his fingers, he looked up at Wyatt. "I like knowing that not only your orgasms belong to me but even your erections."

His boy obviously liked it too. He started breathing faster and Garrett could see him biting back a moan. "You like it too or you wouldn't have so many cock cages and sexy rings. You like knowing you belong to me completely, that you can't even get hard without my permission." He stated it like a fact, no question, just telling the boy that he understood his secret. Something about his matter-of-fact tone when talking about desires made Wyatt even more aroused.

"You're going to stay like this for a while. If you're very good, I might let you come. Of course, I might not. I might bend you over the couch," he let his fingers wander down under Wyatt's cock to tease at the edge of his tight pucker, "and then I'll fuck your ass until I come. You'd still be horny and needy but with your cock restrained like this, you can't even get hard."

Oh, that just did it for the boy. Something about the fantasy or the dirty talk took him from aroused to desperately wanting in seconds. A little moan escaped, and he spoke out before he could catch himself. "Please, Master."

Deliberately misunderstanding, Garrett gave him a wicked smile, before coming back up to play with the boy's flaccid dick. Garrett wasn't going to let him forget he was trapped and at his master's mercy. "You want me to leave your cock nice and confined, so I can fuck you without you being able to come? I might do that then since you want it so much you're begging for it. Naughty little sub for begging. We might have to punish you for that. Later, though. Right now, I have something else in mind."

Another little groan escaped his needy boy. Muscles clenched, it was clear he was fighting to stay still. So turned on and so sexy. "Kneel." Nice master was gone...his boy wanted something firmer right then.

Reaching for his pants, he made a show of slowly unbuttoning them and sliding the zipper down. "You're going to snuggle right up close and I'm going to use that sexy mouth of yours to keep my cock warm. You don't get to suck and you're not even supposed to get me hard. I'm going to use you as my naked little cock warmer while I watch TV. Do you understand?"

The broken moan that escaped the sub had Garrett's cock fighting to get hard. So damned hot. His boy's eyes glazed over and he leaned forward. "Yes, Master. I'm just your naked little cock warmer."

Pushing his boxers down and easing his cock out of his pants, Garrett watched as Wyatt followed every movement with his hungry eyes. If his reaction was any clue, this was right out of one of his boy's dirty fantasies. Perfect.

Reaching out to guide Wyatt's mouth closer, Garrett wrapped one hand around the boy's head. Controlling his movements, making sure the boy knew who was in charge, Garrett slowly lined the boy up with his cock. "Open, boy."

Even without touching him, Garrett would have been able to see the shiver that raced through him. Wyatt braced his chest against the couch and opened his mouth, waiting for Garrett to move him. Such beautiful submission, complete and unwavering. Funneling his thickening cock into the boy, he brought the sub's head down to rest against his thigh.

"Just like that. All you're going to do is hold my cock in your hot little mouth." Watching the sub shiver again as the dirty words rolled through him let Garrett know he was pushing all the boy's buttons.

Wyatt curled into Garrett's legs, letting his head relax on Garrett's lap. Closing his eyes, he lay there quietly. His mouth was warm and the way his tongue caressed the cock that filled his mouth made Garrett want to moan. It was all he could do to fill his mind with other things, keeping his cock from getting fully erect.

Reaching for the remote, he turned on the TV, searching for something to occupy his thoughts. Running his hand through his sub's silky hair, already addicted to the feel, he tried to relax and ignore the sexy naked sub at his feet.

It was nearly impossible.

Wyatt's occasional little suck on his dick was incredible. If the boy kept that up he'd come entirely too soon. "Little cock warmers do not get to suck their master's dick. Be good. I'll use your mouth another time if you behave."

Garrett's mind was working overtime trying to make sure he said everything right. His first thoughts were always too nice for this type of scene. *If you'd like to suck me* instead of *I'll use your mouth*...The end result would be the same, a blow job for him, but the meaning and the physical reaction the words invoked would be strikingly different.

There would be other times where gentler domination would be the mainstay of their relationship but evidently, his boy liked a dirtier Dom on occasion. It would be fun keeping his boy on his toes. Garrett would have to plan things out carefully so that Wyatt would never be able to anticipate the naughty side coming out.

Wyatt made a little noise Garrett interpreted to mean he was sorry. "That's all right. You'll get lots of practice being a good little cock warmer."

They didn't sit there for long, just enough time for Garrett to finish the local news and for Wyatt to sink into the feeling of being used. It wasn't long before his boy's breathing evened out and he relaxed even more. He wasn't asleep, just drifting towards subspace.

He didn't want his boy to get too far gone.

When the news was over, Garrett turned off the television. He couldn't wait any longer to touch his sweet sub. "You were a very good warmer for your master, but now I want to play with my sub. Stand up."

Garrett watched, trying not to smile, as Wyatt blinked up at him in confusion. Haze clearing, he finally understood and released Garrett's cock to stand up. As his boy rose, so did Garrett. Wyatt didn't look terribly steady on his feet. He hadn't been kneeling long but he might have been deeper into subspace than Garrett had realized.

Taking his boy in his arms, Garrett let his hands wander down Wyatt's back to his high, beautiful, filled ass. "I think I'm going to play with this little toy." He squeezed his cheeks and gave Wyatt a kiss on his forehead. "Time to take this into the bedroom, I think. More room to stretch you out and have fun."

Wyatt shivered and swallowed a few times before he could talk. "Yes, Master."

Keeping Wyatt close, he didn't want his boy to fall, Garrett led them into the bedroom. Taking more time to look around, Garrett was pleased to see his boy's bed had a high headboard with a metal frame. Perfect for grabbing onto or for tying a boy to.

He gave Wyatt's ass a pat. "Does my sub like to be tied to the bed? I can't think of a reason to have a bed like that unless it's to tie a sexy sub to."

Wyatt blushed but nodded. "Yes...I...I even have things in the drawer if you need them."

"Things to tie you up with, Sweet?"

"Yes, Master." His voice was thick and filled with need.

"I'll have to look through your treasures another time then. Right now, I want my sexy boy spread out so I can play." Then he reached around and gave Wyatt's still bound cock a slow stroke. "This will help make sure you're not focused on your own wants. Your body is just for my pleasure right now, isn't it?"

Taking a ragged breath, Wyatt managed a reply, but it was needy and slightly embarrassed. "Yes, Master."

"Good little sub. Up you go on the bed. On all fours, that's right. I want your head on the bed and your ass in the air. Very pretty. I want to be able to use my toy." Little shivers were dancing around in Wyatt's body and his ass kept jerking, desperate for attention.

He was trying so hard to behave. It was only going to get harder.

14

WYATT

Wyatt heard the crinkle of packaging from somewhere behind him and he knew what it was. The sound was unmistakable. More of the little lube packets from his drawer. How many had his master grabbed before? Had he been planning naughty things all day? He felt Garrett's hands run up his legs and over his ass. He had to fight to stay still. Every muscle in him was tight with anticipation.

"I think this sexy bottom needs some color." His master's words sent shivers through him.

Trying not to sound like he was arguing with his master, he had to make sure he hadn't done anything wrong. At least, not actually wrong. *Playing* the naughty boy was fun. "Was I bad, Master?"

"No, Sweet. I'm just playing with this sexy bottom and it looks so cute when it's pink from my hand." Again, very matter-of-fact, just describing how he'd play with his toy.

Another little moan escaped Wyatt and his legs quivered. They weren't playing he'd misbehaved. He hadn't been bad.

Master just wanted to spank him. It was so hot Wyatt almost couldn't form a sentence. "I understand, Master."

Pop! It wasn't hard, but it made Wyatt jerk and a breathy hiss escape. Even his cock twitched as he thrust his hips up. He couldn't help it. The idea that Garrett was only doing this because he found reddening Wyatt's ass arousing made this spanking even hotter than they usually were.

"Naughty boy. Stay still. This isn't about you. This is about my pleasure, isn't it?" The constant reminder that he was just a toy for Garrett to play with was short-circuiting his brain. No one had ever treated him like this. Using him...using his submission for their pleasure...If it weren't for the cock ring, Wyatt would have exploded.

"Yes, Master." He tried for more but his mind wouldn't work.

This had been his fantasy for so long. It was perfect.

And the best thing was, he hadn't had to ask for it. Garrett had known. Wyatt felt like the center of Garrett's world. Every little thing about his master seemed to be constantly focused on him. From the phone calls to their first dinner together, he'd never had to worry that Garrett's mind was somewhere else. He'd never felt ignored or too needy.

Master was incredible.

The heat raining down on his ass had pleasure rolling through his body. Knowing he wasn't *supposed* to be enjoying it made the already erotic play even better. Even though the slaps weren't hard they combined to make his cheeks warm, and he knew he'd be beautifully red.

Wyatt couldn't help but hope Garrett found it so appealing that he'd make Wyatt stay naked for him to look at. For him to touch...For him to tease...For him to use again. The fantasies had him fighting subspace. He wanted to sink into the pleasure and the pain.

When the draw of subspace was getting too strong, Garrett

changed things again.

There was more time between each swat. In those precious seconds where the pain was flowing through him, Master started teasing the plug. Pulling it out, then pushing it back again...then swat. The rhythm had him breathless.

Out

In

Pop

Out

In

Pop

He tried, he really did. It was too hard. "Please, Master! Please!" He couldn't say what he was begging for. He needed something...Something more.

"Naughty boy." This time Master's hand came down right on his plugged hole, shoving the toy into his prostate.

It was incredible. Almost too much, but not enough.

Garrett's hand slid down Wyatt's crack to tease at his balls and desperate cock. Wyatt loved having his body restrained for his master's pleasure but he wanted to come. Not as much as he wanted to please Garrett though. Was Master going to leave him soft and deny him an orgasm? Would that make him happy?

The threat of denial hanging in his mind made him even more desperate.

"I'm sorry, Master. I'll be good." Wyatt would be good for Master even if it killed him.

Then Master made it even harder.

Feeling the plug slide out of his ass, Wyatt almost cried out at the empty feeling. He'd been filled for so long, he wanted it back. The press of Garrett's fingers caressing the sensitive edge of his hole made him hold his breath. He wanted to beg but he couldn't. The desperate words ran through his head even though he couldn't say them out loud. He needed more.

The incredible feeling of Garrett's thick fingers entering him tore a moan from him. Deep and guttural it seemed to rattle around in his chest before escaping. "Please...please...please... I'll be good...Please...It's so hard...Please, Master. I don't want to be bad."

He couldn't do it.

It felt like he'd been good for so long.

Garrett's wicked chuckle was like lightning shooting off in Wyatt's body. "Does my little toy want more? This was supposed to be about my pleasure. If I stop playing and give you what you want, you're going to be punished later. Is that what you want? Pleasure now, even if you have to pay for it later?"

"Yes! Anything!" He'd take anything. It didn't matter the cost.

"I'm going to have so much fun punishing you later, Sweet." Naughty pleasure dripped from Garrett's voice. Wyatt knew his master was going to be thinking up all kinds of crazy things he would do to his sub.

Wyatt couldn't wait.

"Yes, Master. Please!"

"Very good, Sweet." Then the two thick fingers entered him and Wyatt would have sworn he felt them all the way to his throat. Yes, this was so much better than the hard plug. Master's finger touched everywhere making him feel taken.

Garrett fucked him slowly and soon left him wanting more. But before he could even beg, Master changed things up again. "Fuck yourself back on my fingers. If this isn't about my pleasure anymore, then I shouldn't be doing all the work. Give me a show, Sweet."

Wyatt thrust back and crazy needy sounds burst out of him. Whimpers and groans escaped as he rolled his hips, working his sexy Dom's fingers. Squeezing down, he tried to pull them even deeper into his body.

"Such a needy little sub. You want to be filled, don't you? You

want something long and thick in that hot little hole. Dirty boy."
The naughty words teased at Wyatt's senses pushing him higher.
Closing his eyes, trying to block everything out, Wyatt's whole
focus was on that one small part of his body that was receiving
his master's touch. Riots could have been happening in the
street and he wouldn't have heard.

The delicious penetration was the only thing that was
important.

For a split second, the incredible feeling was gone, and he
was empty again. Then with one thrust, before he could even cry
out, he was filled. Master's long cock slammed into him on one
long push. Wyatt's head came off the bed and all he could do
was cry out.

The pleasure was staggering.

Thrust after thrust, Garrett rode him hard, the occasional
slap to his ass only ratcheting his pleasure even higher. Every
slide of his hard cock, rubbed over Wyatt's prostate making him
nearly crazy. He wanted to come, but he hadn't been given
permission and he was still trapped in the incredibly frustrating,
hot, sexy cock ring.

Was he even going to be allowed to come?

Was the maddening pleasure the only thing he would be
permitted?

Garrett pulled him up until he was kneeling on the bed, held
in his master's arms. The new position had his sore ass rubbing
against Garrett's body. The sweet pain was like a spice that made
the meal perfect.

One hand wrapped around his chest, pressing him tight
against Garrett, the other hand slid down to grab his cock. Even
though it was confined in the cock ring, it was still incredibly
sensitive. The rough handling had little mewling sounds
escaping.

"My boy's got such a pretty soft cock. It's too bad you can't get hard. You won't get to feel that heavy ache as your cock fills. You won't get to feel the incredible pleasure that's so good it almost hurts. I bet you'd like to get hard, wouldn't you?" Garrett's words were dark and filled with wicked pleasure. His master loved making him crazy.

But he knew what his master wanted.

"Please let me come, Master. Please let me get hard. I'll be good. I'll do anything!"

"Are you sure you'll do *anything* for me, Sweet?" Garrett's need came through in every word. His master wasn't going to last much longer. Wyatt just knew it.

"Anything, Master!" Wyatt would promise him the moon as long as he got to come.

The hand that had been playing with his cock stilled and for a moment Wyatt thought he was going to be denied. Then he felt Garrett's hand on the toy and he started shaking. The rush of pleasure that flooded him as he realized Master was going to take off the cock ring was amazing.

As the ring came off, his dick filled so fast he swore the room started to move. It was a rush like no other. Garrett kept tugging on his cock. Jerking him off and roughly handling his sensitive length. Wyatt couldn't have asked for anything else. It was perfect.

The only thing that would have made it better—

"Come. Show your master how much you wanted this. Come!" Garrett's voice was deep and gravelly.

Wyatt had to obey. There was nothing else he could do.

He couldn't ever remember an orgasm that ripped through him like that one. Shaking and shouting, cum burst out of his body covering the bed in long ropes. As the pleasure shot through him, he felt Garrett stiffen behind him and his cock jerk inside Wyatt. Knowing Master was coming too kept the pleasure going longer.

When his vision was starting to gray out, and the pleasure was fading, Garrett lowered him to the bed and pulled out slowly. Wyatt instantly missed the closeness. Garrett took care of the condom and was back quickly, wrapping himself around Wyatt. That would have to do. But having Garrett inside of him was better.

As sleep started to claim him, he heard Garrett's deep voice, speaking low. "Sweet? Do you remember promising me anything to get to come? Anything I wanted if I would just take off the ring and let you get hard?"

Wyatt knew he was blushing, but he answered anyway. "Yes, Master."

"You know I'm going to make you keep your word, don't you?"

"Yes, Master. I meant it. Anything you wanted. Thank you for letting me come. I know you didn't have to." Wyatt knew some people wouldn't understand but his pleasure had been up to his master. Garrett had chosen to let Wyatt come. He'd give his master his pleasure and his body.

"You're my *anything,* Sweet."

Wyatt didn't understand, the lure of sleep was making things foggy. "Master?"

"You're my *anything.* I'm keeping *you* as my payment for your pleasure, my sweet sub."

Warmth flooded Wyatt, and he knew his smile was goofy and filled with surprise. Some people wouldn't understand, but they were the most beautiful words he'd ever heard. "Yes, Master. Thank you."

"Love you, my sweet boy."

"I love you, Master."

"*All mine.*" Garrett's low words, growled out, staking his claim, followed Wyatt into his dreams. His master's love wrapped around him as tightly as his arms were.

BRENT

FIRST EDITION JULY, 2017

1

CALEN

"What the hell, Calen? Are you drunk? It's not even eight o'clock in the morning!" Garrett's angry words echoed off the office walls as Calen walked in.

Why couldn't Garrett have gotten in late? He had a new sub and a wonderful relationship. Surely there was something else he could have been doing this morning. But no, he had to be waiting right there at the front desk on the very morning when what Calen needed more than anything else was coffee and some space.

Melissa looked back and forth at the two men, then shook her head before focusing on her computer looking like she'd rather be anywhere else. The office was usually fairly calm. They all did their best to keep things businesslike and push their more aggressive tendencies to the side. Melissa seemed to understand this wasn't going to be the most civil discussion.

Not that Calen felt like arguing this morning. He was tired. Fighting with Garrett was the last thing he wanted. Why couldn't Garrett figure out that he simply needed to back off?

"I'm not drinking at breakfast!" Technically, that wasn't a lie.

He was still hungover from the night before but nowhere near the legal limit. He'd been too frustrated for moderation. The weekend had been a total fuck up. And his morning hadn't started any better.

"We need to talk." Garrett's firm words had a final ring to them. Turning his back to Calen, Garrett almost marched back to his office, clearly expecting Calen to follow.

Why did he work for a Dom who was his best friend again?

Trying to remember that it usually seemed more like he was working *with* Garrett than for him, Calen sighed. He liked insurance. He liked knowing that he was making a difference. Guiding people to the best choices to help protect themselves felt right. He always thought it was the Dom in him wanting to make sure people were getting what they needed.

When Garrett's father died, he'd been lost. Stepping in to help was instinctive. He'd been working in corporate sales for a large national finance company and while he'd been doing well monetarily, he'd hated how impersonal it was.

Garrett needed someone he could trust to help get the office organized. Calen needed to fix things, so it had been a perfect fit. Some people didn't understand how he could work for Garrett. They'd seen it as a step back in his career and thought he was crazy for working for another Dom. It might not pay as much but the flexibility and family he'd gained more than made up for any occasional frustrations.

This was going to be one of those occasional frustrations.

Calen shook his head and winced as his brains rattled around. He should have at least taken the time to grab some aspirin or something. "Can I grab a coffee first before you chew me out?"

"No!"

He shouldn't have to listen to Garrett lose his mind without caffeine first. Maybe several cups. Calen's alarm hadn't gone off this morning, or at least he couldn't remember it going off. He also hadn't had time to stop anywhere without being late. He was cutting it close already with only minutes to spare before the doors officially opened.

Taking his time walking to Garrett's office, he tried to think of what to say. There was no way he was going to tell his friend the truth. Admitting to another Dom that he'd gone to the club but hadn't found a single sub he wanted to play with was not going to happen. He wasn't embarrassed about not doing anything, it wasn't like he was a slut, but it would open up a can of worms he wasn't ready to deal with.

Garrett's first instincts would be to ask what was going on so he could to try to help, and that was the last thing Calen wanted. He just needed to put everything out of his mind. Calen had hoped jumping into work would help distract him. But having to listen to Garrett wasn't going to let him ignore his problems.

He'd gone up to the club Sunday evening with every intention of having fun. Possibly a scene, maybe just getting to know someone, but when he'd gotten there everything felt wrong. Being by himself was weird. The subs were all wrong. Even the club seemed empty without *him* there.

Calen knew he was a pathetic excuse for a Dom but he couldn't help it.

He never thought he'd be the type to fall for a sub who didn't want him.

Garrett was leaning against the desk as Calen walked in, shutting the door behind himself. Concern was clearly written all over Garrett's face. "What the hell is going on? I've tried ignoring it and giving you some space. I've even tried talking to you about whatever is making you so crazy lately but it hasn't helped. This has to stop, Calen."

"I'm not drinking before work. I just—"

"Yeah, you didn't sleep well. Being hungover will do that to someone. And for you to still be this fucked up, you must have had a hell of a lot to drink last night. What is going on? I'm asking as your friend, Calen, not as your boss." Garrett's tone started out mocking and sarcastic but by the end, Calen could hear the sincere worry in his voice.

Fuck. He couldn't talk about this.

"I'm fine. I went up to the club last night and stayed up too late. It's been a while since I went and I lost track of time." That was *almost* the truth. Well, it had part of the truth in it. He'd just left the part out where he'd gone home early and drunk himself into oblivion.

He hadn't intended on getting wasted but when he thought about *him,* he didn't always make the best decisions. Calen knew things had been unraveling for months, ever since *that night*, but he couldn't figure out what to do. How do you get over someone when you have to see them almost every day?

He'd known Brent for years but it had only taken one night to change everything. One innocent suggestion...that's all it took for everything to unravel.

"This can't continue. Even if you're sober, you look like shit and the customers are going to think something's wrong. Relaxing things Friday afternoon is one thing, but this is Monday." Garrett's body language made it clear he was waiting for a good answer, but Calen didn't have one.

Shrugging, Calen leaned back against the door and tried to appear calm. He was at a complete loss. He wasn't going to tell Garrett the truth and outright lying to him felt wrong. With no idea what to say, he stayed silent.

Garrett's frustration was clear in his sigh. "Calen. You've been unhappy for months. I can't remember when you weren't sarcastic and frustrated. This isn't you. What's going on?"

"Nothing's going on. I'm fine."

Garrett looked at him and it felt like the other Dom was

trying to see inside his head. There was no way he would guess the problem. It had taken Calen a long time to admit it to himself.

"Nothing? You're going to stand there pretending everything is fine?" Disbelief threaded its way through Garrett's voice and Calen knew he was barely holding back a sarcastic remark.

"Everything *is* fine." Maybe if he said it enough, it would sound believable.

"If that's the only thing you have to say then I think you need a vacation. You haven't taken time off in months, if not longer, and if you're so stressed that you're not sleeping well then you are going to take a break. Maybe some time off will help you work out whatever you're struggling with."

"What! I don't need time off!" More time to think was the last thing he needed. Keeping his mind occupied with work gave him a break from real life. Besides, he had several big policies he was working on for a local small business that was starting to offer benefits for its employees.

"Not negotiable. I'll handle anything you're working on. You're going to take a week off. If that's not long enough for you to figure out what the problem is, we'll work out more time. I need you here and lately you've been somewhere else. Get your shit figured out, if you don't want to talk about it with me."

Calen thought he could hear a thread of hurt in his friend's voice. "Hey, that's not—"

"Save the bullshit for someone else. I can't make you tell me what's going on, but you can't go on like this and we both know it. Besides, if you really didn't need the time off, you'd be putting up a lot bigger fight. God, between you and Brent I'm going to go crazy."

"What about Brent?" Yeah, like that wasn't going to give him away. Maybe Garrett would think it was his way of deflecting the comment about the time off. Because that was bullshit.

Luckily, Garrett didn't think anything of it. "He's been nearly as crabby as you lately. I made him take some time off work, too." Garrett gave Calen a wicked grin. "I threatened to sick Mom on him if he didn't figure his shit out. Maybe I should make the same deal with you."

"Hey, that's playing dirty." While the thought of Garrett's mother hovering over him made him nuts, Calen hoped the teasing meant they were done with the soul searching bonding moment but no such luck.

Getting serious again, Garrett gave Calen a pointed look. "I'm not even going to ask you if it's about work because I know you'd tell me if something here was wrong. Whatever personal shit you have going on, it's making you crazy. I'm here if you need to talk. As long as it's not at work. You're banished for seven days."

"So I'm grounded, Dad?" Calen couldn't resist a grin. Garrett was hilarious when he pulled his "mother hen" routine. And maybe if Calen could lighten things up, Garrett would back off with the questions.

"Yes. Grounded from work for being insane. You can come back when you've handled the problem. Or are ready to *talk* about it!" Garrett shook his head and took a deep breath. "Go home and get more sleep. If you're bored, give Brent a call later. He'll probably be climbing the walls by the afternoon. He's more of a workaholic than you are."

Trying to keep his face blank, Calen inwardly groaned. Yeah, calling the object of all his craziness would not make things better. "Sure."

"You two are going to be the death of me. Go home." Then Garrett pushed off his desk and came over to look into Calen's eyes. "You're my best friend."

"Mushy dork. Having a full-time sub is making you all lovey-dovey."

Garrett realized he was trying to deflect but luckily he didn't say anything, letting him get away with it for the time being. "Damn right."

Calen was glad the two men had stopped circling around each other and finally admitted what they wanted. Garrett said over and over that they were taking things slowly but Calen knew it was only a matter of time before they had a collaring ceremony and were living together.

Irritated with how the conversation had gone, escape seemed like the best option. Before he said something he'd regret—like actually talk about what was wrong. Calen reached out and gave Garrett's shoulder a squeeze and moved away from the door. "I'm heading back to bed. I'll talk to you later."

Garrett's expression was full of frustration but he seemed to accept that he wasn't going to find out anything else right then. "Good. Have some fun and don't forget to call Brent. He seems like he could use a distraction."

Great. Just great. "Sure."

He had a week off and instructions to spend time with the man who didn't want him. Perfect.

It took him a long nap and two strong cups of coffee before he fully processed what his friend had said. *Brent was miserable.*

That didn't exactly make him happy—but it did make him think.

Brent was usually even-tempered and had a way of organizing everyone without being obnoxious. He was the king of getting meetings back on track and keeping his brothers in line. For him to be considered cranky it had to be something serious. Calen couldn't remember anything flustering him. If he was upset or even distracted enough to make his brothers worry, it was important.

Would it be too much to hope that he'd been remembering that night as well?

Did he even want Brent to be thinking of it?

Calen might be obsessing over what happened and how things changed in his mind but he couldn't decide if he was ready to deal with the consequences. Was he ready to open himself up? Those were a damned good questions that he didn't have any kind of answer for. Calen got up from his chair and started pacing around the living room, trying to sort through his emotions logically.

Too much caffeine and not enough exercise, probably. Nothing to do with his nerves.

His living room was mostly empty so there wasn't much furniture to dodge as he went back and forth across it. Moving around was better than sitting. He always thought clearer when he was active. A run would be the perfect solution.

Instead of turning around when he hit the end of the living room, he veered off towards his bedroom. When he'd first bought his condo, he thought it would be short term, so he'd gotten something small that would have good resale potential. But now that he'd been living there for several years, it didn't seem so temporary anymore.

Digging through his dresser to find his workout pants, he once again kicked himself for not buying something that had enough room for a home gym. A run would do but a good workout sounded even better. He just didn't have the patience right now to drive over to the gym. All his thoughts were on the magnetic sub that was pulling at him.

Brent wasn't a sub who wanted a temporary Dom for the weekend. He'd always been honest that he wanted more than that. He'd mentioned boyfriends and Dom's in the past but it was never casual. He was always incredibly clear that he was getting to know them so see if they would work long-term.

Calen was possessive enough that long-term didn't scare him.

Sure, he'd had mostly short-term relationships and contracts but that was because he hadn't found the right sub yet. Yeah, it sounded like total bullshit and with most guys he'd think they were giving them a line of crap, but it was true. Most subs he'd met had very clear ideas of what a Dom should be like. He fit their image as long as they didn't look too deep.

Not that he was encouraging them.

Tossing his workout clothes on the bed, he started stripping down. Catching his reflection in the mirror he had to admit he looked the part of a Dom. Even with a desk job, he'd kept in shape. He might not be twenty-one any longer but he still looked good. His short dark hair, cut tight to his head, wasn't showing any grays, and neither were the finer ones that sprinkled his chest. At just over six foot, with a broad frame, subs never complained about his appearance. But he wasn't sure they would accept what he wanted in the bedroom.

As soon as they would start discussing limits and preferences it was clear with most guys they wouldn't be a long-term match. So he was careful not to promise them anything. Maybe it was a little underhanded, but putting himself out there to be judged when he and the sub weren't looking for the same things didn't make sense.

It had given him a bit of a reputation as a player but he wasn't concerned. Subs understood they could trust him to stay in their limits and to make sure everyone had a good time. They knew he wasn't one of those Doms who left right after a scene or was only there for the hookup. He also never promised anything he wasn't going to deliver.

If they never realized he didn't share much about his own

preferences, he didn't point it out. He discussed their limits carefully and asked clear questions, but he didn't overshare. Once a sub made it clear that they expected there to be clear cut roles in the bedroom, Calen knew sharing wasn't a good idea.

Who wanted a Dom that didn't prefer to top?

Nobody.

2

BRENT

"You ready to talk about what's going on? Or are we pretending you're hanging out here because you love my decorating skills?" Bryce's questions dragged Brent's mind away from his daydream.

"What?"

"Why are you here? I know you're supposed to have the week off. Garrett sent that email out first thing this morning. So why aren't you out having fun?" Brent was hoping that if he feigned ignorance Bryce would've left it alone but evidently it wasn't his lucky day.

Some days he loved sharing the building with Bryce but this wasn't one of them. At least, that's what he was going to tell himself. Brent ignored the fact that he'd wandered into Bryce's office instead of going home.

"I had a few things that I needed to give Hudson before I could go on vacation." Hudson was Brent's assistant. But he did far more than answer the phone. He helped Brent manage the claims and inspections that needed to be done for any of the offices.

They didn't have enough claims to keep him doing that

exclusively, so he also handled any inspections on properties or for business policies. It kept him from the sales aspect of the business, because he was terrible at that, and allowed him to work on the parts he excelled at.

It also kept his brothers from having to do any of them. They hated the paperwork and how time-consuming it was. So it worked out well for everyone. Things were actually slow enough that unless something unexpected weather related happened, Hudson could keep up with things without putting them too far behind.

Not that he wanted a vacation.

Who wanted extra time to play guessing games? A vacation would only give his brain more time to race. Did Calen like him? Was it just his imagination? Was Calen waiting for him to say something? Was he an idiot who needed to get his mind off the Dom who didn't seem to want him?

Yes. That one was easy to answer.

"You could have called him and we both know it. There's something on your mind lately. Garrett was hoping time off would help you figure shit out but I think you need to talk more. You've been working longer hours lately and you're not happy. What gives?" Bryce leaned back in his chair and looked at Brent.

Bryce had too much patience for Brent to wait him out, so it was either talk or make an excuse and head home. They were both terrible options.

"I don't know."

They both knew that was a lie. Bryce lifted one eyebrow and tilted his head, giving Brent a look like he was being ridiculous.

"I met someone. Well, I think I did. It's complicated."

"I take it this isn't the online guy?"

"God, no. This one's real and not nuts." Brent snorted and reached for his coffee, pushing away the lingering frustration over how that had ended. Taking a sip, he tried to figure out what to say. "I'm not sure if I read the signals right or not. I'm having a difficult time telling. Most Doms want to be the one to make the move but with this guy, I can't tell. And now I'm at the point where I'm probably sending out mixed signals because I'm so confused."

"So let me see if I have this right. You met someone in the lifestyle and for whatever reason when you guys noticed each other neither of you actually made a move. Now you don't know what to do. Right?" Bryce leaned forward, resting his elbows on his desk.

"Yes."

"When you first thought something clicked with this mysterious Dom, because don't think I didn't notice you didn't give his name, you felt like there was something special but you didn't say anything? You're not usually that...passive." Bryce looked confused.

He was right. Brent usually took a more aggressive role in letting a Dom know he was interested. But this was different. If it had been anyone else but Calen, Brent might have said something. Calen was like part of the family, which meant Brent had always put him in the off-limits category.

Everything changed the last time they were all at the club together.

They'd gone up as a big group and it had been a lot of fun. However, gradually people had wandered off. Garrett seemed frustrated and had gone home early. Several of their other friends had roamed away to play in the private rooms. Even Grant and Bryce had found someone to play with. Eventually, only Calen and he were left.

He'd been honest with his brothers that he wasn't going to stay late and had told them all to go have fun. But when he was finally alone with Calen, he'd found that he hadn't wanted to leave. There had been something pulling at him to stay. Calen hadn't seemed to mind that it was just the two of them either so Brent hadn't hurried to leave.

It probably should have felt awkward, but it hadn't. Even dressed for the club, he'd always been comfortable with Calen. The fact that he'd been shirtless, barefoot, and only wearing slacks and cuffs on his wrists wasn't important. He wouldn't have even thought twice about it if people had left them alone.

Maybe it was because he wasn't wearing a collar or maybe it was because Calen didn't seem to be his Dom, but every time he turned around someone else was coming up to him. Offers from a soda at the bar to invitations to the playrooms were constant, but he didn't want any of the other Doms. He'd wanted to hang out with Calen.

Eventually, they'd both gotten so frustrated at the interruptions that Calen had asked if Brent wanted to kneel down beside him to at least give the impression that they were together. That got Brent thinking, but he chalked it up to an overactive imagination. He knew Calen couldn't have been hinting at anything.

When he'd gotten up from the chair and took those short steps over to the couch where Calen was sitting, something changed. It could have been the way Calen watched him, the predatory look that flashed in his eyes, but suddenly it wasn't the same. He wasn't only Calen, the friend and coworker...he was Calen the Dom.

By the time he'd knelt at Calen's feet, he'd known he wasn't going to see the man the same way again. They still talked about the same things...work, sports, movies...whatever came up. But the act of kneeling made his mind look at their interaction differently.

Was Calen looking at his chest?

Did Calen's gaze linger on his neck too long?

Was it just the lights or was that a spark of interest in his eyes?

Once he was kneeling, the number of people who came up to them slowed down but some stubborn morons still couldn't take a hint. When one particularly dense older gentleman wouldn't stop watching Brent, Calen had brought his hand up to rest on Brent's neck. He let his fingers caress Brent softly before giving the other wannabe Dom a glare that blatantly said back off.

Even when the touch was no longer necessary, Calen had let his hand rest on Brent's shoulder. His fingers stroked Brent's skin sending shivers down his spine. It took all his strength not to move. He wasn't sure if it was an unconscious gesture on the Dom's part or if he was doing it on purpose. But Brent had no desire to chase him away, so he did his best to stay still and not draw attention to it.

Had Calen been looking for a signal from Brent?

Did the Dom even realize what he'd been doing?

Brent had a thousand unanswered question and no way to find out the answers without letting Calen know he was interested. He couldn't figure out if the risk was worth the reward. He wanted a long term relationship. Did Calen?

He'd never let things get too serious with any one sub but he'd also mentioned settling down, eventually. Was he looking for something specific in a sub and hadn't found it, or was he not ready in general?

"You're not listening to anything I'm saying, are you?"

He almost dropped his coffee cup when Bryce's voice came out of nowhere. "Huh?"

"If you're going to ignore me, go home and drink your own coffee." Bryce frowned at him, shaking his head.

"Sorry, you got me thinking."

"About what or should I say whom?" Bryce stubbornly wouldn't give up and let it drop.

Did he want to share? If he was being honest...probably. He

wasn't going to get anywhere trying to figure things out on his own.

"I'm not sure if it's all in my head." He let his head fall back, staring up at the ceiling, and sighed. "I'm not the kind of sub he usually goes for."

Bryce paused for a moment, then cleared his throat. "What's his usual type?"

"I don't know...I guess if I had to say...maybe twinks. But I'm not sure if that's on purpose or not." The club had a lot of single twinks lately so there was no way to tell if that's what Calen preferred. "I don't really look like a sub."

Not that Brent minded how he looked at all. It wasn't that he looked like a gorilla or something, he just didn't come across as what most guys thought a sub should look like. When you combined that with his desire for more than a Saturday night kind of Dom, it was hard to meet someone.

He wasn't looking for something completely lifestyle but he also didn't want to pretend to be vanilla during the week. Brent had met plenty of men who wanted to have a regular relationship most of the time and only play at the club occasionally. That wasn't for him.

Life would be so much easier if he was a twink who was a complete bottom type of sub. Being complicated sucked.

"Did you get the feeling it mattered?" Bryce's voice pulled Brent back to the conversation again.

"Huh?" He looked at Bryce's frustrated expression before sinking down in the chair and letting his head fall back again. Bryce really did have the best chairs. Garrett was ridiculously proud of his conference room but the care that Bryce had put into picking out the furniture in his office put the rest of them to shame.

No simple fabric covered chairs for his customers' asses. No. He had soft leather with so much padding Brent thought someone could bounce on them. And Bryce hadn't stopped there. The wood in his desk was a warm, rich color that didn't scream expensive but it looked solid and well put together. His office didn't look like it cost a fortune, but it radiated a confident dependability that Brent loved.

"Lord, nut, you're going to drive me crazy." Bryce took a deep breath before he continued. "I was responding to your comment about looks. When you guys were starting to hit it off, did it seem to matter to him what you looked like? Was he checking you out?"

"Possibly. I didn't even think about the kind of guy he usually goes for until later. At the time, it felt like he was into me. But now...I don't know." When he'd been kneeling there, he'd been so focused on Calen's touch that he might have missed a look one way or the other.

"Who are we talking about? No more hinting. We're not teenagers talking about your first crush. I'll keep my mouth shut."

Time to put up or shut up.

"Calen."

He waited, still not looking at Bryce but there was no response. Finally, he tilted his head up and peeked at his brother. Bryce had a smile from ear to ear. A big shit-eating grin that made Brent want to throw something at him. "*What*?"

Was he not going to say anything?

"Grant owes me twenty bucks." Bryce smirked, looking one step away from doing a happy dance.

That was not what he'd been expecting. "You're gambling on my love life?"

Not that a seemingly one-sided crush added up to a love life, but still.

"Hell yes. Especially when you were both crazy and bitchy lately. He's been drinking like a fish and you've been working such long hours I was going to put a bed in your office. It had to be something like that. It was the only thing that made sense. Grant guessed that you two were mad at each other and I don't even think Garrett realized anything was off. He's totally oblivious when it comes to shit like that."

That made Brent laugh, Garrett never even noticed that a sub was into him until they were literally throwing themselves into his lap. "So you don't think I'm crazy?"

"No, you two would be good together. And with the way he's been acting lately, it wouldn't surprise me at all he was interested in you. What are you going to do about it?"

"I don't know. He hasn't said anything that makes me sure either way. It would make things awkward if I misread his signals and said something. But he could be simply waiting for me to show him I'm interested. With him working for Garrett, it might be weird for him." There were too many possibilities for Brent to list them all.

"You should go for it. He's clearly distracted by something. Give him a call and see what happens."

"Just ask him?" He sounded horrified but he couldn't help it. Brent was take charge, but that seemed too risky—like he was asking to get shot down or something.

Bryce laughed. "Text him or something and sympathize with him for having enforced time off this week as well. See if he wants to hang out. That might give him an opening to take things up a notch."

"What do you mean he has time off too?"

"You didn't see Garrett's email? I got it right before you came in. Reading between the lines, it looked like Calen came in this morning looking rough enough that Garrett made him take a vacation. You're both in the same boat. I thought it was interesting."

Brent had to admit it sounded...curious.

"Maybe I will."

"Good. Now get out of my office. I have a meeting in a few minutes." The words were bossy and there was nothing special about them. They shouldn't have caught Brent's attention, but they did.

"Who's coming in?"

Bryce looked down at his desk and shuffled papers around. *Interesting.* "Oliver Stanton."

"That name's familiar but I can't place him. Has he been insured here long?" Brent dealt with the insureds at all the offices so he couldn't be sure, but he was pretty good with names.

"No. He and his partner are fairly new."

The tone in Bryce's voice said he was hiding something. "Do we know them from somewhere else? I know the name but I can't think of a claim it's related to."

A barely audible sigh escaped Bryce. "They're from the club. When they realized we handled insurance, they decided to move everything over."

That should have made his brother happy. The insureds they'd meet through the club were some of their best customers. Open and honest about what they were looking for and they were easy to deal with because you didn't have to worry about how something sounded. What was Bryce worried about?

"Everything okay with them?"

To Brent's astonishment, Bryce blushed. "Yes. It should be pretty straight forward."

Oh, there was a story. But it didn't seem like he was ready to talk about it, so Brent stood up and ignored Bryce's fidgeting. "All right, I'm out of here before Garrett figures out I came in today."

Bryce looked relieved that Brent was going to let everything drop. "Yup. If he finds out, you're toast. He said he'd call mom. And she'd love to know what was going on with you two."

"I'm leaving." He shook his head and frowned at Bryce, drawing out the words like he was shocked. "No need to resort to threats."

Laughing, Bryce called out as Brent strode out of the office. "Have fun with Calen."

He always had a good time with Calen. But this time, he wasn't sure what kind of fun to hope for.

3

CALEN

The beep of Calen's phone signaling an incoming text was the first thing he heard when he walked in through the back door. He'd definitely been doing too much drinking and not enough running lately because his usual route had been a lot more difficult than it typically was. Grabbing a bottle of water out of the fridge, he walked over to the phone.

Sliding his finger across the screen, he was shocked to see Brent's name pop up. He probably shouldn't have been surprised. Brent was off work too this week, but he was the last person Calen expected.

There were always group texts going between Garrett and his brothers and somehow Calen always got included in them. But he couldn't remember the last time Brent had texted only him. Refusing to be a wimp, he tapped the message.

Hey heard you were banished too. Dinner later?

It was interesting. Dinner. Not a casual invite to go hang out or do something. Not a message about barbecuing something. An invitation to dinner. Calen knew he probably shouldn't read too much into it, but something about the message made him hesitate.

Normally, he would have made some kind of teasing response about grabbing a pizza, because Brent couldn't cook *anything*. But that didn't seem like a good idea this time. He was overthinking it, but it felt like Brent was putting himself out there to see what Calen would say.

He was second-guessing this too much. It was only a text, damn it.

Sure...Want me to bring anything... Time?

Brent's quick response made him smile.

Food? Unless you want me to burn something.

Maybe he was pushing his luck but he couldn't help it.

Ask me out and expect me to bring dinner...what kind of date are you...lol

He'd finished his bottle of water and was heating up some leftovers for a late lunch when Brent finally responded. Five minutes was a long time for a guy to reply when he was right by his phone. Not that Calen was keeping track of the time.

What can I say I'm high maintenance.

Now that was an interesting response.

Not denying the possibility of a date but teasing enough that it could be passed off as joking around. Was he trying to be funny? Was it something more? The Dom in him, the part he'd done his best to push away for months, was insisting it was the sub's way of showing interest.

He never used to doubt himself like this. It was time to stop.

Hell. What was the worst thing that could happen? Brent saying Calen misunderstood things, and they both felt awkward for a little while. That was better than what he was dealing with now. He'd worry about the other issues later. Right then, the only thing he was going to focus on was figuring out if Brent felt the same way about him.

It was like high school all over again. Only instead of notes in class, it was vague texts. Might as well push his luck.

I don't mind high maintenance...just might have to make it worth my while to put up with it

There was another long pause while he finished his reheated stirfry, and this time he had to grin. It was so easy to picture Brent hunched over his phone trying to figure out what Calen meant. Brent's eventual reply had a teasing tone to it as well.

Dessert huh? That seems fair ;-)

The little winking face made Calen laugh. Oh yeah, just silly enough that Brent could pretend to be teasing later, hamming things up and playing along but still sexy enough that he might be serious. Time to kick it up a notch.

Not exactly what I was thinking...guess it depends on your definition of dessert

There was another long pause and Calen was imagining Brent blushing, trying to decide how to reply. He kept an eye on the phone as he cleaned up his lunch and started poking around the cabinets. He wasn't sure what to make for dinner. He'd been planning on something simple or possibly going out, but now he needed to impress Brent.

Brent did pretty good at the grill but cooking wasn't something that came naturally to him. When they had the weekend barbecues, Brent either manned the grill or put together a salad, so impressing the sub with a real meal wouldn't be too hard. Looking in the fridge, Calen realized he had everything for lasagna. That was definitely a date meal.

Glancing over at the clock on the stove, he saw that he had a couple of hours before Brent would probably want to meet. As long as he got started now, there would be enough time. He'd already gotten the water boiling for the pasta when his phone chimed.

Maybe I should let you decide on dessert...since you're the Dom and all ;-)

There was that ridiculous wink again. They were going to have to have a discussion on how grown men texted. Trying not to second-guess himself, he responded back flirtatiously, like he would if it were any other man he was interested in.

I'll take charge of anything you like...dessert's a good first step

There was another pause from Brent. This time long enough that the timer for the pasta was going off as his phone chimed. When he had the noodles drained, he went over to the phone.

6 okay?

Was he ignoring the flirting or did he not know how to respond? Maybe a little of both. He was probably unsure exactly how Calen meant it too.

Great...got dinner planned...if you have salad or something like that it would be good...

He was going to leave it there and not push Brent too far, but Calen didn't want there to be any doubt that he wasn't simply goofing off.

Don't forget I'm in charge of dessert

This time it only took seconds for Brent to respond.

There's no way I'm going to forget.

Calen couldn't decide if he'd scared Brent or if he was overwhelmed. He'd find out later. Hopefully, his pushing hadn't backfired. But Brent had clearly been flirting back. His nerves might be going all kind of crazy but he hadn't been passive in their conversation. Calen grinned; the evening would be interesting.

IF ANYONE WAS WATCHING, it probably looked like he was moving, but at least Brent would be well fed.

He figured just in case Brent was expecting him to show up with an actual dessert, he'd better have one. So he'd whipped up some brownies. Worst case scenario, they'd be good comfort food. And best case, they'd be fun to eat with his fingers.

Calen figured he could probably get Brent to react beautifully if he worked it right.

He was going to have to pay attention to figure out what made Brent react though. Calen had spent so long trying not to notice the people he worked with, he wasn't sure what Brent's preferences were.

Sure, they'd gone to the club with the same people. But when you were in a group of Doms and subs who were mostly related, you had to be more careful. He'd done his best not to pay attention to anything the other guys were doing.

If he happened to see one of his friends in a more intimate situation or even something that looked personal, he'd walk away. And with Brent looking for a more serious long-term relationship, Calen hadn't even seen him flirt with that many men at the club.

Parking his car in front of Brent's house, Calen walked around to the passenger side to grab the food. As he tried to figure out a way to carry the lasagna and the brownies without dropping them, he heard the door to the house open.

"Need any help? Since you cooked, so the least I could do was help carry it in."

"I was going to have you work off your debt another way—but I guess this is a start." Calen's dirty mind was working overtime. He hoped he hadn't pushed his luck.

As he stood up and turned around to hand Brent the heavy casserole dish, he caught a little grin and the faint blush that was tinting Brent's cheeks. Knowing that Brent wasn't immune to his teasing eased some of his worries. If he could make Brent blush, there was a good chance that the sub didn't just think of him as a co-worker.

Brent cleared his throat and glanced at the dish. "Smells good."

"Thank." Picking up the plate of brownies, he shut the door and locked the car.

Brent gave the brownies a curious look. The fact that Calen showed up with dessert seemed to have thrown him. Not wanting Brent to get the wrong idea, he waited until Brent looked up to speak. He did his best to make sure Brent could see the desire in his eyes and gave him a wicked grin. "I figured this would be a good start to dessert. First course maybe—we'll figure out what else should go with it."

Bingo.

Brent's blush flared back to life, obvious and bright. Then he looked away. He swallowed several times and Calen could tell he was trying not to react, but it wasn't working. Calen was glad Brent couldn't hide his reactions. It made him feel more confident about his own decisions.

"Come on. Let's get the food inside before it gets cold. Right now, it's hot and should be delicious." Calen let his voice drop lower, watching as a little shiver raced through Brent.

Calen knew he must have been too obvious because Brent gave him a frustrated look and shook his head.

"*Calen.*"

Calen pretended innocence, but he knew it wasn't believable. "Yes?"

"Are you going to do that all night?"

"Oh yeah. Now that I've seen your blush, how could I not?"

"You're going to make me crazy." There was a feigned frustration in Brent's voice, but the look on his face made it clear that Brent didn't mind Calen's teasing.

"You are going to love the way I make you crazy." Calen let

his desire for Brent fill his eyes and was rewarded with another cute blush.

Watching the man who was always so put together and in charge react was addicting. Calen couldn't wait to see how far down that blush went and how much more flustered he could make his friend.

Brent simply shook his head at Calen again, then turned to walk back towards the house. Now that he didn't have to pretend to be immune to the sexy man, Calen enjoyed the view as Brent walked away. The man had the most incredible ass.

He must have realized Calen wasn't following because Brent turned back, a questioning look on his face. "You forget something?"

Calen gave him a naughty smile. "Nope. Just enjoying the view."

Brent didn't seem sure what to say as he turned back to the house and kept walking. It was going to take some time to work out their new dynamics but Calen wasn't worried. Some people might think going from friends to lovers would be hard but it didn't seem that way.

The constant questioning about how Brent felt was the most difficult part. Now that he knew the interest wasn't one-sided, he wasn't going to let anything scare him away. Not even his own fears about what Brent would say. This was his friend. He trusted Brent.

Pushing away his worries, Calen started walking up to the door. Brent had a cute little cottage-style house that fit him perfectly. It was warm without being fussy and more like a real home than Calen's place.

Closing the door, he made his way back to the kitchen. If this counted as a first date, it was going to be the most comfortable he'd ever felt on one. Brent's place was like a second home to him and knowing they were going to hang out was relaxing.

Sure, things would hopefully get more interesting as the night went on, but if all they did was hang out and talk, it would be the best time he'd had recently.

Putting the brownies down on the counter, he started getting plates out and setting the table. Brent laughed and walked over to the fridge. When he brought out the salad, Calen couldn't help but tease. Leaning over to look into the bowl, he gave Brent a concerned look. "Did you burn it?"

"That was one time! And it wasn't burned. It was supposed to be a charred salad!" Stomping over to the table, he set the bowl down hard.

Laughing, Calen came up behind him, pressing close. "I liked your salad." Leaning next to Brent's ear, he whispered low. "I like everything you make."

Feeling the shiver that raced through the sexy sub had his own need rising. Why hadn't he seen this before?

Brent's breathless reply had Calen even harder. "Thank you."

Wrapping his arms around Brent, only so he could put the silverware on the table, of course, Calen let Brent hear his desire, dropping his voice and letting the heat flow through his words. "So polite. I can't wait to see what else you'll thank me for tonight."

Brent tried to hide his low moan, but didn't do a great job of it. Calen couldn't decide if it was on purpose or if Brent was that affected. "Calen. I can't think…"

"I don't want you to. I have a feeling we've both been doing too much of that lately. You are going to relax tonight. We'll think and talk tomorrow. Can you do that for me?" Even to Calen, his voice sounded gravelly and rough. Not that he was trying to disguise his desire.

No, he wanted his intentions to be crystal clear.

Hesitantly, Brent leaned back until he was relaxing in Calen's arms, not just standing awkwardly. "So this is...you want to...I mean, this is a real date?"

Calen tried not to smile as Brent stumbled through his question. "A very real first date. Is that okay with you? I've been thinking about you lately."

Brent nodded. "Ever since that night."

"That night...God, seeing you like that." Calen let his lips graze Brent's ear as he whispered. "You were so sexy. Kneeling there, with your chest bare, legs spread...you didn't even realize how incredible you looked."

Brent didn't even try to hide his moan that time. "I never really thought about you as a Dom before. You were always my friend but something about that..."

Calen finished the sentence for him. "Was perfect."

His sexy sub nodded. "Perfect."

"You're my friend, but I'm hoping you want more. I would love to have you kneel for me again."

Brent didn't even pause to think. "Yes. Again. More."

Calen chuckled, making Brent shiver again. "Anything you want."

"Anything?" Brent's voice was higher pitched than normal. Calen could see he was struggling to think.

So of course, Calen had to push him even further. Tilting his hips so that his cock would graze Brent's ass, he flicked his tongue around the sensitive shell of Brent's ear. "*Anything.*"

Brent tilted his head, giving Calen better access, and whimpered. It was the sexiest sound, needy and pleading. Calen let his teeth graze Brent's ear, biting down gently. "I can't wait to hear what you're imagining. Such a sexy submissive has to have naughty fantasies. But right now, dinner is getting cold."

Biting down again, to hear the beautiful music of his moan, Calen chuckled and rubbed his cock against Brent's sexy ass one last time before stepping away. "Food. Remember?"

"Yes, dinner. Food. You brought food." Brent straightened up and took a deep breath. Looking around confusedly, he questioned, "What was I doing?"

Calen laughed and gave Brent's bottom a swat just to watch him jump and blush. "You were sitting down. I'll get everything ready."

With a sexy smile, Brent went around the table to sit down. "Yes, Sir."

Walking over to the fridge to grab some bottles of water, Calen gave Brent a smile. "I like how that sounds coming from you."

"I thought it would feel weirder." Brent looked like his brain was starting to clear. "But it didn't. Why is that? I mean, I've always thought you were attractive, but you were just part of our group ever since you met Garrett."

Calen shrugged. "Maybe we weren't ready to see anything before. I guess, to me, you were my friend and you don't notice friends that way. Maybe it would have happened sooner but I've never seen you kneel for someone else. When I saw anybody in the group at the club with a Dom or sub, I've always tried to give them their space. Seeing you kneeling for me, even though we weren't in a scene and it was just to get people to leave us alone, it flipped some kind of switch in me."

"Me too. It seemed odd for a minute but once I was in front of you like that..." he paused. "I guess it just felt right."

Calen nodded as he set the bottles down on the table. "What do you think your brothers will say?" Besides his preferences, that was his other big worry. Would everyone else be shocked?

Brent laughed, "Evidently, Bryce and Grant already figured it out. They were betting on us getting together."

Sitting down beside Brent at the table, Calen could only shake his head. He should have expected that. "Garrett's going to be surprised."

"He's always oblivious, but he'll be okay with it. He wants both of us to be happy." Then Brent gave Calen a teasing look. "And he'll support anything that keeps you sober at work."

"Naughty boys get punished. Don't forget that." Calen gave a shrug. "I've been distracted lately."

"Distracted, huh?"

"Oh yes. By a naughty sub who was hiding what he was thinking."

Reaching out to start serving the pasta, Brent tried to hide his smile. "That's a very naughty sub. But maybe he should get a break because the Dom in question was just as hard to read?"

Giving Brent an exaggerated frown, Calen wagged his finger at the sub and said in his best deadpan voice, "Oh no. Doms are perfect. It's the naughty sub who needs to be punished."

That had Brent nearly rolling off his chair with laughter. When he caught his breath, his eyes were still dancing with suppressed humor. "I forgot that rule."

Calen lifted one eyebrow and gave him a serious expression. "It's an important rule to remember."

"Yes, Sir. I won't forget again."

"Very good. Now eat your dinner. I'm anxious for dessert."

Brent's grin turned wicked. Calen thought his sub was looking forward to it as well.

"Yes, Sir."

4

BRENT

I t was the weirdest first date ever. At least, he was pretty sure it was a date. It was probably a date if the flirting and teasing were any indication. Brent kept thinking that it should be harder or stranger but it wasn't. When Calen turned that deep sexy voice on him it was easy to see that he was a Dom but other times it was harder to see.

Calen was funny and kept things relaxed, not listing out rules or expectations like so many men Brent had dated. Brent didn't just want to keep the domination in the bedroom but this was nice. It was almost as if they were hanging out like they would normally but it was more.

It was easier than he expected.

When he'd texted Calen earlier, he'd been hoping for a way to bring up their evening at the club. The way Calen turned things around, making it naughty and funny, had Brent reeling. There had been too many times when he'd simply stared at the phone, not sure how to reply.

He'd been so worried that everything he was feeling was one-sided. It was such an incredible relief to realize how wrong he'd been. But he wasn't sure what to do next. Let Calen decide how things should go? Which was really tempting. Or take charge and insist they talk first?

The problem was, his brain was saying one thing but everything else in him wanted another. If he looked at it the same way he would work, he could take charge, but it wasn't what came naturally to him in a relationship. He was halfway through dinner when he decided to shove his brain out the window and go with his gut. He'd let Calen steer things and see where it led them. It was what he'd wanted from the beginning, anyway.

Evidently, Calen needed a little nudge to get things moving in the right direction.

Brent thought it was sweet that Calen had been as nervous as he had been. It showed a vulnerability that Brent hadn't been expecting. Calen was always a little out there, a little loud, and never quite followed the typical Dom stereotypes, but this was a side Brent had never seen.

He liked it.

When they were both stuffed from too much food, Calen glanced over at Brent, looking relaxed and happy. "How about we put on that new spy movie after we get this cleaned up?"

"Sounds good. Should we take dessert out there?"

Brent meant it innocently but Calen's thoughts were in another direction entirely. "Oh, dessert's still on the table. You don't get to decide when, though, naughty sub."

He knew his cheeks went so red he probably looked like he was on fire but he couldn't help it. The wicked look on Calen's face didn't help any. He was clearly picturing what he wanted for dessert and it made Brent extremely curious. "I'm sorry?"

He wasn't sure if an apology to the Dom was the right response but it was all his brain could come up with at first. Then, once he pushed back his surprise, he decided he could tease just as well as Calen could. Looking down at the table, he peeked up through his lashes and bit his lip seductively. "I'll try not to be naughty, Sir."

Calen laughed but Brent knew he'd gotten his friend back when he reached down and adjusted his cock. "Come on. You do that innocent slut act too well."

Brent smirked and got up from the table to put the food away. If he leaned over too many times or brushed up against Calen too often, he could blame it on the small kitchen. Calen's frustrated growls had Brent trying to not smile. Teasing a Dom had never been his thing, but with Calen, it felt like a natural extension of their friendship.

When they had everything cleaned up, and a plate of brownies ready, Calen casually took his hand and started walking them to the living room. It was nice. They'd been hanging out and working together for years but Brent couldn't remember Calen ever touching him like that.

Calen sat first, taking the plate from Brent and putting it on the side table. Then to Brent's surprise, his friend stretched out on the couch and pulled Brent to lie down in front of him. It was definitely not how they usually watched TV together but it felt right.

Brent was grateful he'd bought a deep enough couch that he wasn't hanging off the edge. He felt secure and comfortable. At least his body did, but his mind was still racing, not sure where things were going. His body loved the heat that radiated from his friend and how comfortable it was. Well, mostly comfortable.

The fact that Calen's rigid cock was pressed against his ass was...different. Not bad, but every time it became obvious he turned Calen on, it was a shock. He'd spent weeks trying to figure out how Calen felt and now the truth of Calen's desire was firm and hard behind him.

Different wasn't bad though, and it wasn't something he was

going to let scare him away. Pressing his body back into Calen's, Brent rested his head on Calen's arm. Maybe it felt so right because he'd imagined it so many times. Brent thought it couldn't get more perfect. He was wrong.

Brent was starting to realize that Calen could always take something good and make it even better.

Once Calen had the movie going, he tossed the remote on the side table. Taking Brent's hand in his, Calen positioned one of Brent's arms so it extended down his side and then did the same to his other arm so that it was stretched out on the couch. Brent wasn't sure what to make of it at first.

"You're going to keep your arms right there for me." Calen's words were low and rough, sending shivers down Brent's spine, right to his cock. "I want to be able to have my dessert anytime I want it. Do you understand?"

Brent could tell by the change in Calen's tone that the Dom was asking more than if he grasped the order. He was trying to make sure Brent was okay with what they were doing. Brent wasn't sure what they were doing, but he was willing to take the chance and let Calen lead them. And if he was honest, he found the idea of being on display and available for the Dom arousing.

"Yes, Sir."

Calen made a deep rumbling noise, and he draped his left arm over Brent's chest, letting his hand rest right under Brent's nipples. Saying it was distracting would have been an understatement. As the movie started, all he could focus on was the fact that he was wrapped in Calen's arms and he'd given the Dom permission to touch him.

Would he do it?

Was he going to tease Brent with the possibility of it but not do it? Brent could easily see Calen doing something like that because it would make Brent nuts. The not knowing was always the hardest part of submitting. Having a Dom who understood him so well was going to come with some unique problems.

"Watch the movie. I can hear your brain going from here."

Brent huffed. "I can't help it."

"Try. If you're this fidgety and naughty through the whole movie, you're not going to get dessert." Then Calen moved his hand up to trace Brent's lips with one finger. "I'm sure I can figure out something that I'd like for dessert, even if you can't have any."

When Calen's finger breached Brent's mouth, he thought he would come right then.

"Suck. Show me what a good little cocksucker you can be. Don't forget, I know you. You're buttoned up at work and always in control, but what you really want is to be taken."

Brent moaned. Calen's dirty words released the gates that always sent Brent's submission flooding through him. He had to keep such a tight rein on it at work that he couldn't always let go easily. But once in a while, it only took something small to unlock the need. Sucking Calen's finger deep, Brent did his best to show his Dom how good he could be.

"Oh, I knew you'd like that. If you're very good, maybe I'll let you show me how you can suck on other things later." Sliding his finger out of Brent's mouth, Calen traced Brent's lips one more time before moving his hand back down to Brent's chest. "No more distracting me. Watch the movie."

Brent tried, he really did. But Calen made it nearly impossible. At first, it wasn't too difficult. He was warm and comfortable wrapped in Calen's arms, and even though he was aroused it was still at the point where he could push it away and ignore it.

Calen didn't let him ignore it for long. He waited until Brent was relaxed and into the movie, then he started letting his fingers trace patterns and circles on Brent's chest. Getting closer to Brent's sensitive nubs before moving his fingers away, Calen seemed to be oblivious to Brent's rising need.

Not that Brent believed that for one second.

When Brent would move or a needy sound escaped, Calen's hand would still, and he'd growl out the order again, telling Brent he had to watch the movie. It was enough to make him crazy. Knowing he was so close to feeling Calen's touch for the first time. Having the incredible sensation of being wrapped in Calen's arms but not being allowed to move. Just knowing it was his friend and now hopefully his lover.

It was adding up to make Brent insane.

And Calen was thoroughly enjoying pushing his buttons. Brent would freely admit he hadn't had that many Doms. But Calen was the first who seemed to get a thrill out of not only the domination but also making Brent nuts. Maybe it was because they'd been friends for so long but Brent thought it was probably just Calen's personality coming through.

When Calen's fingers caressed one nipple for the first time, Brent thought he might fly right off the couch. Even through the soft cotton of Brent's T-shirt it felt incredible.

"Stay still. You're not following directions very well, are you? Bad little subbie." Then Calen made it impossible to behave when he gave one of Brent's nipples a pinch. It wasn't hard, but it was enough to send sparks of desire straight down to his cock.

"Please." Brent didn't even know what he was asking for. It just popped out.

It earned him another pinch, this time to his other nipple. Brent couldn't decide if it was a punishment for begging or if it was a treat because Calen loved seeing how turned on he was. He was good either way as long as Calen would keep doing it.

"What are you supposed to be doing, subbie?" Calen pinched his tender nub again, making Brent gasp and shiver.

"The movie...being good...watching the movie..." Brent was

having a hard time focusing enough to form a sentence. All his concentration was focused on staying still and trying to follow directions.

"Then be good and do what you're told."

Brent moaned and tried not to thrust his chest towards Calen's teasing fingers. "Yes, Sir."

Calen only made it more difficult. When Brent's nipples were so sensitive that even his shirt was making him crazy, Calen turned his sights on teasing other parts of Brent's body. Brent didn't even try to follow the movie once Calen's fingers started trailing down his chest, tracing those same lazy circles and patterns again.

It was clear, this time, Calen's goal was much lower on Brent's body.

Just imagining Calen's touch on his cock made it hard to breathe. Staying still was impossible. But every time he moved and shook, Calen's hand would freeze. Then Brent would get the same lecture about being good and following directions.

It was almost perfect.

The only thing that could have made it better was if Brent had been smarter. He'd worn jeans. It hadn't occurred to him that they would actually play. Sure, Calen's flirting had certainly made it seem like he was interested but Brent kept talking himself out of believing it.

He was an idiot.

He was so hard his cock was pressed against the zipper and even with boxers on, he could feel the metal pressing into his skin. It was just enough pain to make him even harder, but trapped in the denim, there was nowhere for his cock to expand.

Calen's finger kept getting closer to his pants then moving away. Calen must have traced the path between the clasp on Brent's pants and back to his belly button dozens of times before he finally let his hand slide over the front of Brent's jeans.

Palming Brent's cock, Calen chuckled low, making his dick jump. "It looks like my little subbie wants to be touched. Does my little sub want more? Do you want me to play with your cock?"

It was some kind of trick question. Knowing Calen, it had to be.

"Whatever you want, Sir. What...whatever...Sir!" Calen's hand tightened on Brent's erection making it impossible to get the words out. For fuck's sake, why did he wear jeans?

"I'm ready for my dessert. But you have to guess what I want, subbie." Calen's sexy, wicked tone made Brent want to promise the Dom anything. "Do you think I want to see my sexy sub on his knees using that cock-sucking mouth? Or do you think I want to touch you and watch you come?"

He had to choose?

Calen was trying to kill him.

The hand gripping his arousal tightened again, sending waves of pleasure through Brent. The dirty images and fantasies Calen's words put in his mind didn't help either. Kneeling before him, taking Calen's cock in his mouth sounded incredible. But the idea that Calen might strip him naked and play with his body made his dick throb.

It was an impossible choice. Two perfect options. That's when he knew the answer. He'd forgotten the most important thing. This was Calen, not just any Dom.

"Neither, Sir." Brent paused; trying to get the words out was harder than he'd imagined. It just felt so good. "You want to tease me. That's your dessert. *Making me fucking crazy!*"

That last part might have come out louder and more frustrated than he'd intended, but the wicked laugh that escaped Calen made Brent want to throw something at him. Or bite him. Or lick him. That thought had Brent's mind wandering to incredible places, but it wasn't going to help him concentrate.

"I think you've forgotten your manners, subbie. But I'm going to forgive you this time because you guessed right. This is the perfect treat. Watching you come unglued while I touch you and play with you. This is perfect. Now, watch the movie while I have my dessert." Then Calen went back to focusing on the movie while he alternated between playing with Brent's cock and teasing his nipples.

He still had his clothes on, and it wasn't even a full scene, but Brent was ready to climb the walls. Was this all they were going to do? Brent knew they had a lot of talking to do but it couldn't be all that was going to happen.

It was.

As the movie continued, Calen pulled and twisted his nipples. When they were almost too sensitive Calen would move his hand down to trace along Brent's hard cock or rub little circles over the head of his dick, making his whole body shake.

Brent didn't even realize it when the movie ended. He was so lost in the constant stimulation, he'd long forgotten about the movie. When Calen started sitting up and pulling away, Brent thought he might cry...or start cursing...it was a toss-up.

But Calen didn't go far. He rolled Brent, so he was flat on his back, then Calen laid down to cover him with his body. Calen's grin was wicked and filled with a dark humor. "Did you like the movie?"

The movie? He wanted to talk about the movie?

"Sure, it was good. Loved the ending." Who the fuck cared? All Brent could focus on was the way Calen's cock pressed up between his legs. Why did they still have their clothes on?

Calen laughed. "The ending sucked. It was a cliffhanger where you don't even know if the guy is alive or dead. Were you distracted, subbie?"

"God, yes. I have no idea what happened." All he cared

about was getting more from Calen. Anything. "You've been making me crazy. Please, Calen."

"I was having my dessert. Now it's time for one last bite." Then to Brent's utter shock and pure frustration, Calen leaned down to kiss him.

It was sweet and tender. Calen gently worked Brent's mouth like he was making love to it, not just kissing him. Teasing little bites and licks. Sucking Brent's bottom lip into his mouth. Letting his tongue slowly slide against Brent's.

It was beautiful torture.

When Calen finally pulled away, the laughter was still in his eyes but this time there was something else there as well. Brent knew what he wanted to call it but he wasn't ready to even think the word.

"Dessert was perfect." Calen rolled his hips pressing his cock harder against Brent, making him gasp. "Are you ready for the brownies? I think we forgot them."

Brownies? The man was going to talk to him about food? "Damn it, Calen!"

5

CALEN

"Such a naughty subbie. Demanding and bossy. I don't know what I'm going to do with you." Calen didn't even try to hide his smile as Brent's frustration mounted. He might be a Dom, but something about making Brent break that iron control and lose it was just as desirable as watching him surrender.

And no matter what Brent thought, he hadn't surrendered to Calen yet.

He was letting Calen call the shots, but he wasn't ready to submit completely. Calen hadn't earned that yet. He was patient though. They'd get there. Sooner rather than later, if they could talk about some of the things that were standing between them.

Leaning down again, he gave Brent's frowning lips another kiss. "We'll do more when you're ready. You don't trust me yet."

That statement made Brent jerk. "I—"

He shook his head. "No, you don't. Not yet. And there's nothing wrong with that. You trust me as your friend and as a co-worker but not as a lover and certainly not as a Dom. Once we're there, then we'll do more. This has all happened pretty fast. Sure, we've spent the last couple of weeks driving ourselves crazy but this part..." He stole another quick kiss. "This part is new."

Brent was still frowning but this time it was clear it wasn't in sexual frustration. "I don't know what to say. Part of me gets what you're saying, but a bigger part is calling bullshit. I'm not sure what we're doing yet but I know you. I trust you, Calen."

"Humor me. I'm not going to say something crazy like *we're going to take it slow*." That brought a smile to Brent's face and Calen could see he was trying not to laugh. They'd seen how well that vow had worked for Garrett. "I want to talk about where this is going and about the lifestyle preferences we have before we jump into things. I will not make love to you or do anything close until I know more about what you want. Limits, needs, desires...everything."

And he wasn't going to let them get any deeper until he was convinced he wouldn't scare Brent off.

His frown had faded but Brent still didn't look happy. "I feel like you're only telling me part of what's on your mind. I agree with everything you've said, don't get me wrong. I know we need to talk but you're forgetting I know you as well as you know me. You're leaving something out."

Then Brent surprised him by lifting his head and wrapping his arms around Calen before giving him a quick kiss. Then he relaxed back on the couch, still keeping a tight grip on Calen. "Want to tell me what's bugging you? What made you afraid to talk to me after the club? I've seen you flirt with subs and you're generally not indecisive. Something held you back, and it wasn't because we were friends."

Calen wasn't ready for this conversation.

He should have known that Brent would see through him. But he thought he'd have more time before he had to talk about it. Time to psych himself up, maybe. Time to have a few beers before he texted it to Brent, so he didn't have to look him in the face.

The little voice in the back of his head was going crazy telling him to man up. He wasn't a wuss. Brent wasn't like—No, he wasn't even going to go there. That was a long time ago. Looking into Brent's face, Calen had to take a deep breath.

If he blew off Brent's concerns now, he would ruin everything. Brent might never forgive him and even if he did, it would always be there between them. Brent would never give his submission to someone he didn't trust...to someone who would lie to him.

"All right. I'll tell you what was making me nuts, but I can't do it here. Let's go on a walk." It wouldn't be a run, but at least he would be moving. And he wouldn't have to look at Brent while he talked. It might make him a coward, but he didn't think he'd be able to do it and watch his friend's reaction.

The last time, he hadn't been prepared for things to go bad and it had knocked him for a loop.

Giving Calen a strained smile, Brent nodded. "That sounds good. The park is right around the corner and it's well-lit enough that it isn't a bad place to walk after dark."

Reluctant to move, Calen finally climbed off Brent and reached out to help him up. "I'll go put on my shoes and meet you at the door, okay?"

Brent leaned close and gave Calen another kiss. "Sounds good."

As Brent walked towards the back of the house where his bedroom was, Calen forced himself to move to the front door. He trusted Brent. Even if it was a deal-breaker, they'd still be friends. It wasn't like Calen was so far gone that being friends would be settling. It wasn't like he was so into Brent that it would be miserable to be around him, and yet not be able to have him.

Sure.

Maybe he'd been going slowly, but by the time he got to the front door Brent was already coming down the hall. Shaking his head, he tried to lighten the mood. "Come on slow poke. Shoes on."

With Brent standing there watching, Calen knew he had to at least appear more functional. Trying to push away his worries, he gave Brent a grin. "I got distracted thinking about what you might be doing back there."

Brent shook his head like he wasn't buying that line of bullshit. Calen didn't blame him.

Within minutes, Calen had his shoes on and they were out the door. Brent lived in a trendy part of town with a mix of people so Calen didn't even hesitate to grab his hand as they walked down the street. Brent took it easy on him and they walked for a while in silence, enjoying the evening.

Brent's voice broke the quiet. "Back at the club, I thought it would be weird to kneel for you, even pretending."

"Me too, but it wasn't." That was an easy place to start. "I was prepared for it to be awkward. But I was having a good time talking to you and wanted everyone to leave us alone."

Brent squeezed his hand and made a noise like he agreed. "I pictured us laughing about it and treating it like it was some kind of gag, but it was completely different than I expected."

"I never let myself think of you like that. You were a friend and co-worker, not someone to ogle or flirt with. It was the first time I really let myself see all of you." They were still in the comfortable portion of the conversation but Calen knew the hard part was coming soon.

"Me too. I'd put you in that category of people who are friends and nothing more. I guess it was because you were Garrett's friend first and then started working with him." Brent was quiet for about half a block before he started talking again.

Calen looked at the houses and listened to the sounds of the night as Brent collected his thoughts. He wasn't in any hurry to get to the more difficult parts of the discussion. Finally, Brent spoke again, softly and deliberately, like he was carefully measuring his words. "I liked how it felt to kneel for you. You were still my friend, but there was more. I've never had a relationship start like that. I'm a little wary of where this is going, but I do trust you. But I'm not sure what you want."

That was easy for Calen to answer. He didn't even have to pause. "I want a relationship with you. I've spent a lot of time thinking about things since that night. It might seem like this is going fast, but taking our friendship this direction feels right."

"Then what's been holding you back?"

That was the million dollar question.

"I like being a Dom. I've always liked being in control in the bedroom and even outside of it when my sub needed more. I love that look in a submissive's eyes when they're completely gone and are flying. Even something as simple as hanging out with you at the club that night when you were kneeling there was perfect." That was all true, but Calen knew he owed it to Brent to be completely honest.

Brent seemed to understand there was more coming because he let them walk in silence as they entered the park. It was small, but there were lighted paths that wound through the trees, and Calen could hear people talking and laughing. All he wanted to do was to keep walking in silence but he forced himself to keep going.

"Every Dom likes different things, just like every sub does. That's why you discuss limits and see where your kinks are compatible. Mine don't always align well with most submissives. I've tried dating more traditional guys, but that never works out. They understand some things but my need to dominate makes them uncomfortable." Calen paused, trying to figure out how to explain things, but he must have been quiet for longer than he thought because, after a little while, Brent squeezed his hand and interrupted his circling thoughts.

"So something about what you like is more aligned with vanilla guys but you still want a D/s relationship. Do I have that right?" Brent's voice was even and cautious but Calen knew he had to be going crazy inside.

"Yes."

"Are you comfortable telling me what it is? I'm pretty open-minded."

There had to be a thousand strange things bouncing around in Brent's head. He was probably worried that Calen wanted something completely off the walls. It wasn't that crazy. It just wasn't that usual for a Dom.

He trusted Brent. He had to remember that.

"Yes." Then he took a deep breath and reminded himself it wasn't like he was confessing something weird. He was overreacting. Hopefully. But he'd thought he was worrying over nothing the last time he'd had this conversation too. "I like topping during heavy scenes but most of the time I prefer to be the receptive partner. I'm still the Dom and still in control but I like bottoming more."

It shouldn't be that difficult to say. Men had this conversation all the time. But something about the BDSM scene made people assume that to be a Dom you had to top. Like the two things automatically went together. They didn't.

Brent stopped walking for a heartbeat, but before Calen had to stop, he was walking again. He was so quiet Calen wanted to glance and see how he was taking it, but he wasn't sure he wanted to know. Some Dom he was. When Brent spoke, his voice was even and unemotional. "I'm betting someone you told had a very unpleasant reaction."

"That's an understatement." Calen knew it came out

sarcastic but he couldn't help it. But Brent's words gave him enough confidence to finally look at him.

His friend was watching him and had an expression Calen couldn't define. Happy wasn't the right word, but it was an open, pleasant expression. "I have no problems with that at all. I've always been versatile and the idea of bottoming forever was frustrating. The whole 'Doms don't bottom' mentality is stupid. Hello, prostate, duh. It feels good as long as you do it right."

Calen wasn't sure what to say. He'd been prepared for more of a reaction. "Yup."

Brent laughed and shook his head. "Some subs are as bad as Doms when it comes to that idea. I've met a few who were convinced you weren't a sub if you wanted to top."

Calen nodded. Giving Brent's hand a squeeze, he knew it was time to finish the discussion. Brent had already guessed part of it, anyway. "I'd been in the scene a few years when I met Clark. I thought things were going well. We'd started to click and while we were still learning about each other, he seemed nice. And he was submissive but not so much so that I expected him to have an issue with what I wanted. When I told him, he was surprised. Dom meant top to him and we'll just say the discussion didn't go well."

That was an understatement.

To Clark, the idea that Calen wanted to bottom meant he wasn't a real Dom. Clark had accused him of simply playing the role of a Dom and had actually asked him if he didn't want to admit he was a sub. When Calen denied it and tried to explain, Clark had gone off on him, telling him that he was ashamed to admit who he really was. Calen hadn't been able to make him understand that to him, the two things were *very* different. One was a physical preference and one was who he was inside.

"I'm sorry about that, Calen."

Calen shrugged, not sure what to say. "It was a long time ago."

"That's why you were so hesitant to take things further after the club. I can understand why you'd be worried. They're separate things to me though."

"You seemed reluctant to push things too." Calen looked over at Brent, more confident now that he knew his friend wasn't going to walk away.

"I've had terrible luck. It's made me a bit gun-shy. If there's a dick in a hundred miles, I've dated him or at least talked to him. And with the occasional nice guys, we aren't looking for the same thing. I loving being able to give up control in the bedroom, and I'm really more of a lifestyle sub in that respect, but I have no desire to even be in charge once in a while. But that's scared off some Doms because they either wanted complete submission all the time or to only play occasionally. I don't fit neatly into what they expect. So I can understand where you're coming from."

"And it was probably hard to read me." Calen knew he hadn't made it easy for Brent to see what he'd been thinking.

Brent laughed. "Oh yeah. You always said you were looking for something serious when it came up in the past but you never dated anyone for long. I wasn't sure what was going on."

"Are you sure about what's going on now?"

"I think so. What about you?"

Calen let Brent see all the wicked thoughts that were going through his mind. "I'm very sure."

Shaking his head, Brent smiled. "You're going to turn into one of those dirty old men one day."

Calen laughed. "Are you sure I'm not there yet? I could chase you around your desk at work trying to pinch your butt and making dirty jokes."

"You might be right. I'm not going to encourage that at all.

Come on. You ready to head back to my place? You owe me another movie and one of those brownies."

"Brownies, yes, but why do I owe you another movie?"

"I missed that spy movie entirely. I have no idea what happened. This time, you're going to keep your hands to yourself and I will pick the movie."

"Bossy little subbie." But he smiled, letting Brent know he didn't have a problem with the plan. Cuddling up to Brent sounded perfect, even if he had to keep his hands to himself.

"And don't forget it."

"I can already see I'm going to have to get creative with your punishments." Calen watched as a shiver raced down Brent's spine. "And isn't that telling, subbie. I think we need to talk about limits tonight too."

Brent was biting his lip and looking forward, avoiding Calen's eyes. "Do not make me hard. No more talk of that in public. You're going to get us arrested."

"Oh, someone likes punishments."

"*Calen!*" Brent's frustration was clear.

"What kind of punishments? Does my subbie like to be spanked?" Calen wasn't going to let Brent put him off. This conversation was much more fun than the one they'd been having, and he figured he deserved a reward. Making Brent nuts would be the perfect way to treat himself.

"*Calen!*"

He wondered how far he could push Brent before he either fessed up to what he liked or he got frustrated enough that Calen would get to punish him. Tonight looked like it was going to be better than he expected.

6

BRENT

Staring up at the ceiling of his bedroom, Brent couldn't decide if getting out of bed was a good idea. If he had to take a week off from work, he thought he might as well enjoy it. Maybe he'd go to the gym later. Maybe he wouldn't go at all. He'd stayed up late and didn't need to be up at the crack of dawn, anyway. Damn internal clock.

Rolling to his side and pulling the covers over his head, he smiled at the memory of why he was up so late. Calen. He couldn't believe how much had changed between them so quickly. They might not have technically had the "we're in a relationship talk" or the "I'm your Dom declaration" but Brent knew those were going to be right around the corner.

Besides, it had been pretty much implied already.

He'd had a hard time seeing himself getting serious with the Doms he'd dated in the past. They'd always seemed a little-one dimensional but Calen was so much more than that. The man was like the full package. A real man with flaws, desires, and fears, but also sexy, dominant, and had a wicked sense of humor. Perfect.

Brent knew that Calen would keep him on his toes.

He would end up crazy frustrated at times, but even though Calen drew him in like a moth to a flame, Brent had a feeling he wasn't going to get burned. No, Calen might make him nuts but he wasn't setting out to hurt Brent. Their conversation yesterday proved that.

Just the expression on Calen's face had let Brent know something serious was coming, but the talk hadn't been anything like what he was picturing. He'd flashed through all kinds of terrible options but hearing that it was about Calen's desire to bottom wasn't what he'd imagined.

Part of him had been relieved it wasn't something that would have been more difficult to deal with, but the bigger piece had hurt for Calen. Brent didn't think it was that big of a deal, but along the way, subs had done a number on the sexy Dom.

He'd seen it himself in the clubs. Submissives who were unsure of what to say and what a Dom might want went overboard in trying to reassure the Dom that all they wanted was to bottom. Brent liked both. Sure, he'd bottomed when he was with a Dom but—

Had he done the same thing? Had he assumed that he was supposed to bottom...that bottoming meant submission? Pushing the covers off his head, he gave up the pretense of going back to sleep. He liked topping. He'd only done it with the vanilla guys that he'd tried to date, but that didn't have to mean anything...did it?

Brent wanted to say that it didn't, but he wasn't so confident anymore.

Bottoming didn't mean submission to him. He'd dated enough guys outside the scene to realize that. But did he associate topping with being the dominant partner? Maybe. Not liking how that felt, he climbed out of bed and headed for the bathroom.

As he finished his morning routine and washed his hands,

Brent stared in the mirror. If Calen wanted to bottom, Brent didn't have a problem with that. He had a feeling Calen would figure out a way to take him right to the edge of insanity before he let Brent come, no matter how they were having sex.

Hell, he'd had scenes where no one had any kind of penetrative sex and they'd been hot. He was worrying over nothing. Shaking his head at his reflection, he said, "You are just trying to find something to worry about."

Maybe the gym was a good idea.

Coffee first, though. That was a must. Heading to the kitchen, he'd barely gotten the coffee started when he heard a notification go off on his phone. "Who's texting at six-thirty in the morning when I don't have to work?"

After making sure the coffee pot was filling, Brent headed back to his bedroom. He was in the middle of plotting all kinds of evil payback for whichever brother thought it was funny to wake him up when he picked up his cell. Shaking his head, he had to laugh. Calen.

U up?

What was he doing up this early?

Yes what's up?

Was his brain going ninety miles an hour like Brent's was this morning?

Always up early…brain doesn't know how to sleep in

Wandering back to the kitchen, Brent was happy to see the coffee ready. Setting his phone down, he doctored it up and went over to the table. Grabbing his phone, he texted Calen a picture of his coffee.

I'm no better. What are you doing today?

They belonged to the same gym. Maybe Calen wanted to come with him?

Nothing

Within seconds another text came in.

stupid auto-correct I had that spelled all funny on purpose

Shaking his head, Brent could only imagine what Calen's dirty mind had done to that word.

Dirty Dom. I thought about heading to the gym want to go?

Taking a sip of his coffee, Brent tried not to stare at his phone. Thankfully, Calen responded right away.

Sure...what time...not too soon...I need to put on clothes

The devil face with the horns that followed the text had a lecherous look. But maybe it was his imagination. Not sure what to say, he ignored the hint that Calen might be naked.

About an hour?

He had to laugh at Calen's response.

No fun...I gave you a good opening for naked talk...might have to punish you later

Calen was definitely a morning person. Brent was having a hard time pushing away the image of an aroused Calen lying on his bed naked. He shouldn't encourage Calen but it was almost impossible not to.

How are you going to punish me?

Did he want to sext with Calen? Maybe.

There's my dirty little subbie...Not going to tell u...it's a surprise... think I need to remind u of who's in control though

That was mean, but it was typically Calen. Tease and flirt then make Brent nuts. He thought he might as well play along.

When will this punishment take place?

It took Calen a second to respond but Brent wasn't worried.

Bring clothes to the gym...we'll get breakfast after...talk limits... then punish later

Then another one of those naughty smiley faces. This time with an angel whose halo was crooked. Where did Calen find those things?

Breakfast and talk sounds good.

He laughed at Calen's response.

Dirty subbie thinks punishment sounds good too...can't hide that from me

Finishing up his coffee, Brent picked up his phone again.

No idea what you're talking about.

Laughing, Brent rinsed out his cup and grabbed his phone before heading back to the bedroom. As he started getting ready for the gym, his phone beeped signaling another text.

I know u too well...that innocent act is bullshit...got to be punished now for lying...naughty subbie

Brent couldn't help but picture all the things that Calen might do to him. The man had a wicked sense of humor and an incredibly dirty mind, it could be anything. Hell, it could even be something simple just to make Brent overthink it and drive himself nuts.

Yes, Sir. I'm sorry I was bad. Are you going to have to spank me? Bend me over your lap and punish me?

Two could play this game, Brent smirked.

Don't think that would be a punishment for u subbie...I think u'd like that...maybe if u r good then u can beg for one...

Brent couldn't wait to figure out where Calen was getting the naughty emoji's from. His phone certainly didn't come with anything like what Calen had. This time he'd sent Brent a picture of a little bottom that looked like it had been spanked. It was waving back and forth like someone was bent over mooning him.

Where did you get those from? My phone did not come with BDSM emojis.

Calen just sent back another cartoon image of a smiley face laughing before texting another note.

See u at the gym subbie

Shaking his head, Brent's only thought was that Calen was going to drive him crazy. He just hoped Calen could behave while they were there. Brent was out, and he'd never had any issues working out, but Calen always pushed the limits. Brent knew that all he could do was keep his fingers crossed. Hopefully, Calen would remember that Brent needed to keep a low profile when it came to the lifestyle.

BRENT WAS SURPRISED at how well Calen was behaving himself. Aside from a few teasing looks and flirting comments, the Dom had been surprisingly tame. It made Brent slightly paranoid. Calen had to be plotting something. Anytime he controlled himself this well, it was usually because he was planning something. The calm before the storm.

What was he up to?

They'd arrived at the gym as the morning rush was starting to subside. Once they'd started running on the treadmill, there were only a handful of people still there. Most of them seemed to be the mom crowd.

Brent didn't care who was in the gym, but it made working out go faster since there wasn't a line on any of the weights and machines he usually used. By the time they'd finished working out, he was starving and relieved that Calen had behaved himself.

He hadn't even needed the compression shorts he'd worn under his regular workout shorts.

Unsure of Calen's plans, Brent had decided that making sure he wouldn't get thrown out of the gym for being indecent would probably be a good idea. As they headed for the locker room, Brent started to relax and turn his thoughts to food.

He should have known better.

Walking down the hallway that led to the bathrooms, they turned a corner so that they were no longer visible to anyone in the gym. That's when Calen struck. He gripped Brent's shoulder and pushed him so that he was sandwiched between the wall and an incredibly turned on Dom. Calen's erection was pressed tightly against his own growing arousal, making it clear his Dom didn't want to just talk.

"Calen! Someone's going to see."

"We're the only men in here, aside from the old guy working at the desk. Now behave, subbie."

The growl in Calen's voice and the desire radiating from him had Brent fully hard in seconds. "What—"

"No. My turn. I have one question for you. Are you mine? I know we haven't gone through lists or safewords yet, but are you my submissive or do you need more time?" Calen pressed his body even tighter against Brent's and whispered in his ear. "I'm not giving up no matter what you say, subbie. You're going to be mine, eventually."

"I'm yours." Brent didn't even have to think about it. They had a lot to talk about and discuss but he'd had more than enough time to figure things out. Calen might make him nuts sometimes, but he'd never had another Dom make him feel this way. He wasn't going to give it up without a fight, either. Calen might have some reservations because of what he liked but Brent was confident they would be good together.

Calen's serious expression changed to an almost wolfish grin. There was the Calen he'd been expecting when he'd come to the gym.

"I told you that you needed a reminder about who was in charge, didn't I?"

"Yes, Sir."

"Who do you belong to, subbie?"

"You, Calen."

"Very good. But to help you remember that, when you get in the shower you're going to jerk off. Not because you want to but because I want you to. Do you understand?"

He had to masturbate at the gym? Sure, the showers were private, but would he be able to be quiet enough? There might not be that many people there right now but what if someone came in while he was playing with himself?

Calen's cock rubbed against his, making it hard for Brent to think. There were probably a million good reasons why he shouldn't do it but the way Calen was scrutinizing him made them all fade away. If Calen wanted him to come in the shower he would.

"Yes, Sir."

"Such a dirty sub, aren't you? You always look so innocent and in charge but you're not. You're my dirty sub." The naughty words alone would have been enough to make his cock throb, but the thrusting of his dick against Brent's made him want to beg for more. The fact that they were in the gym and someone could walk in at any time was the only thing that kept him sane.

Calen must have seen how close Brent was, because he stepped back, smiling his wicked grin. "Go shower, subbie. The stall that's all the way down at the end. I'm going to be in the one right beside you."

Brent did his best to make his legs work right as he pushed off the wall and walked over to this locker. Getting his things out took longer than it should have but in his defense, his mind wasn't thinking about clothes and soap.

Doing his best to ignore Calen as he stripped down, Brent left his compression shorts on and made his way to the showers. He wasn't usually shy, but getting completely naked in front of Calen felt more intimate now. They didn't usually work out at the same time, and he couldn't remember if Calen had ever seen him changing before.

If he hadn't, now wasn't the time to start. Not that the shorts left a lot to the imagination. Still, it was better than walking around with his erection waving everywhere. Doing his best not to look at Calen, Brent still felt the hot gaze of his...Dom... lover...Master...his friend.

They needed to have a conversation before they did anything like this but it was too late to protest now. Not that he really wanted to. Calen was right. Brent was buttoned-up and very in charge at work, but he liked being able to give up control and let someone else run the show other times.

The fact that his new *someone* was Calen made it even better. He liked Calen's irreverence. He liked not knowing what the Dom would do. He liked the intensity Calen would get in his eyes when he watched Brent now. He liked everything about Calen.

Even though he enjoyed the unexpected, Brent had a feeling that Calen had something up his sleeve. Yes, Calen was proving his point that Brent belonged to him and that he would be the one to choose when Brent got to come, but there was something more. He just had to figure it out. Or maybe that was the point. He wasn't supposed to. He was simply supposed to follow his Dom's instructions.

He'd have to analyze it more later, but right now he had an order to obey.

Brent had never jerked off anywhere like this before. He'd played at the club occasionally but that was as close to public as he'd experienced. And he really saw that as more private than anything, no matter what other people might think. He was the most boring submissive ever.

Brent had a feeling Calen was going to change that.

Walking into the shower, closing the curtain behind him, Brent wished the gym had real doors on the stalls. He'd never felt exposed there before. In fact, he couldn't ever remember even thinking about the showers but this time it was different.

He was aware of every little gap and movement in the curtain. The way it swung when he hung his towel over the top of the bar. The way it wasn't quite wide enough to stretch all the way across without leaving a tiny space on one side or the other. As Calen pulled his curtain closed, the whole bar swayed, making the curtain flare out before settling back in place.

When he turned the water on, it only got worse. The fabric started pulling towards the spray just enough to make the gap even bigger. Could he actually do this? Hearing the water turn on next to him, Brent pictured Calen naked, water dripping down his body.

Had he ever seen Calen naked?

He didn't think so. Their schedules at the gym never seemed to have them in the locker room at the same time. And even if it had, Brent wouldn't have stared at another guy's junk. Friend or not, gay or not, it would have been a bad idea. But at that moment, Brent would have given almost anything to have been able to picture *exactly* how Calen looked.

"I can't hear you."

"Calen!" Brent couldn't believe that Calen would bring it up while he was in the shower. But the Dom laughed, sending shivers down Brent's spine. Brent's head was conflicted but his body knew what it wanted.

Even the worry over the curtain hadn't diminished his erection, and knowing Calen was listening only made him harder. Turning to face the water, Brent pushed his concerns out of his mind and did his best to obey. He took a deep breath and let Calen's image fill his mind.

Leaning into the water, letting it pound the stress away, Brent imagined himself pressed against the wall again, Calen leaning against him. The fear that someone could walk in any minute, that they would hear Calen's instructions, made him even more aroused.

Opening his legs wider, Brent tilted his body so that the water was running down his erection. Did Calen know how much Brent loved jerking off in the shower or was it a coincidence? With all his brothers in the lifestyle, he might have overshared at some point. But he was betting Garrett had been the one to say something, trying to tease him.

Growing up with so many brothers, no one was going to leave you alone if you had a habit of taking very long showers. It made Brent think. What else did Calen know about him? There were probably so many little things that he'd said or that his brothers had teased him about over the years. Did Calen know that much about him or was this a fluke?

Bringing one hand up to his chest, Brent braced the other against the wall. As the water pounded against him, he let his fingers trail over his skin towards his nipples. Going back and forth, he let them tease the sensitive skin.

Gradually, he stimulated them more until he was pinching them and tugging on them. He loved having his nipples played with. He'd orgasmed once just from having a Dom play with them during a demonstration of nipple clamps. Brent had been embarrassed at the time, but the Dom had loved it. They'd even dated a few times, but it hadn't worked out.

Doing his best to be quiet, Brent could hear Calen moving only feet from him. Knowing that the only thing that separated them was a flimsy wall gave him all kinds of naughty ideas. Spreading his legs even more, he pulled on his nipples as he pictured Calen sneaking in behind him.

Letting his hand snake down his chest, Brent imagined the feel of Calen pressed against him. The Dom would watch him playing with himself as he'd been ordered to. Calen would bring his arms up and wrap himself around Brent, teasing at his sensitive nubs until they were tender, each touch making Brent squirm and beg.

Calen would watch as Brent's hand wrapped around his cock. Running his hand up and down his shaft under his Dom's gaze, he could almost hear Calen's whispered orders telling him to speed up and then go slower. Calen would keep him on edge, not letting Brent come until he was ready.

Tightening his hand around his cock, Brent built the fantasy up in his mind and he fucked his fist. Calen was listening. And even though the sound of the shower muffled some of the noises, could he hear the rhythmic sounds of Brent thrusting?

It was like thunder to Brent. Skin rubbing against skin, the way the pulse of the water would change as his hand moved through it, the way his breath would hitch even though he tried not to moan...it seemed to echo in the quiet of the room.

Tilting his ass out, Brent wished he'd thought to ask if he could play with his hole. Did he need to ask? He had so many questions. Calen had told him to orgasm, but he hadn't been specific about what Brent was allowed to do. Would he be able to tell?

Shifting around so his shoulder was pressed against the wall, Brent braced himself then let his free hand slide around to his ass. If someone walked by and the curtain moved even the slightest bit, they would see. They'd see Brent teasing his fingers around his hole as he jerked off.

Easing one finger in just enough for him to feel the stretch, he gripped his cock even tighter. He wasn't in the right position to hit his prostate but the slight burn radiated out, pushing him right to the edge. Hips flexing back and forth, Brent felt the pleasure building.

His balls pulled up and he felt his orgasm swelling, like a wave that was about to crash over him. One last thrust of his finger and tug on his cock then it was there, pressing against him in an almost endless rush of pleasure. He tried so hard to be quiet, but he knew little sounds escaped before he stopped them.

Could anyone hear him?

Did they know what he was doing?

Calen knew what he was doing. The only sound from the next stall was the splash of water against the floor. He could almost picture Calen trying to be as still as possible so he could hear Brent's orgasm. Just the thought that Calen was listening kept the pleasure coursing through him.

When his orgasm had finally stopped, his cock was sensitive and his nipples were puffy and tender. He felt like he'd been hit by a train. Pushing away from the wall, he stood under the spray and let the water run over him. Pumping the button that released soap from a little dispenser on the wall, Brent worked on cleaning his body.

He'd been in the shower long enough that even if no one had heard him, they would still think it was strange. Quickly moving through his routine, Brent rinsed and turned off the water. Drying himself, he tried not to guess what Calen was going to say.

Would he tease Brent?

Would he ignore it just to make Brent crazy?

Had he found it erotic?

There were too many questions. As Brent wrapped his towel around his waist and pushed the shower curtain aside, he was surprised to see a dressed Calen leaning against the wall across from the stalls.

His body was resting casually, but his expression was intense and his eyes filled with desire. Brent felt his cock try to make a valiant effort to respond even though he'd already come. Something about the way Calen looked at him made him think that the man was barely hanging on to his control.

"You follow directions well, subbie. Very good."

Brent tried to fight the blush that he knew was starting to heat his face. He wasn't sure how to respond. Not hearing anything coming from the other parts of the locker room, he looked down at the floor then peeked up through his lashes giving Calen the same innocent slut expression he'd liked before.

"Thank you, Sir."

Calen shook his head like Brent wasn't fooling him, but he reached down to adjust his cock, so Brent knew he wasn't completely unaffected. "Get dressed. I'll meet you out front, but you've only got a few minutes. I'm starving."

The way Calen said it told Brent that his Dom was hungry for more than food. Was he next on the menu, or were they really only going to talk? He couldn't wait to find out.

7

CALEN

Sitting across from Brent at the diner was trying Calen's patience. He'd spent all night dreaming of the sexy sub, and all morning at the gym watching his body move and strain. He was quickly coming to his breaking point. What pushed him right to the edge was listening to Brent pleasure himself in the shower.

He didn't jerk off efficiently and get it over with. No, he drew it out. Calen had nearly climbed over the wall to get to him. And he didn't even seem to realize how sexy it had been. Brent had tried to be quiet, but the little moans and gasps had given him away. Calen had wanted to go peek around that curtain so bad, but he knew they weren't ready for that yet.

Conversation first, then he'd get to see Brent naked and hard.

Calen thought that doing it the other way around would probably be jumping the gun a little—even if Brent wouldn't have complained. Eventually, he'd have Brent recreate that scene so he could watch. They'd probably have to do it in a more private setting so they wouldn't get arrested, though.

"What are you grinning about?" Brent was giving him a quizzical smile as he looked over the menu.

"You." Calen didn't even try to hide his arousal.

Brent shook his head and went back to looking for breakfast, but Calen could see the smile in his eyes and the way his lips were trying to turn up. He might have been attempting to look calm, but Brent didn't seem to mind Calen's desire.

Setting his menu down, Calen leaned against the table, grinning. "I was thinking that I was going to have to make you do that again soon but somewhere I could watch next time."

Brent coughed and gave Calen an embarrassed grin before glancing around. "I'm not sure how to respond to that."

"All you need to say is 'yes, sir' because as long as our talk goes like I think it will, it wouldn't be up to you." Calen gave Brent a wicked grin that he knew hinted at all the naughty thoughts going through his head. "Would it?"

Brent went back to looking over the menu again, but shook his head. "No. It wouldn't. I would prefer that you decide those kinds of things."

So he wanted to go for the G-rated version of this conversation; Calen could work with that. At least, until they left the restaurant. "I would prefer that as well. And just to make myself clear, you would need permission for *any* of those types of activities. There will be no *private activities* without asking first."

Brent's eyes widened a little and Calen could see his pupils flare. He understood exactly what Calen meant, no masturbating without permission, and it looked like he didn't have a problem with that at all. "I assumed you would prefer something like that. I have no problems with that. I would like some rules spelled out in more detail, eventually. I like to know boundaries."

"I agree, that would be important as well. We can have specifics detailed later on today."

"That soon? Do you want to discuss a contract or something more informal?" Brent's question came out low and there was no obvious stress in his voice, but Calen could see that he'd been looking at the same picture of pancakes for too long. Especially considering Brent didn't like them. He preferred waffles if he was going to eat anything like that at a meal.

"It doesn't feel too soon to me. A contract illustrates my level of commitment correctly." Calen knew he was in it for the long haul. They had too many topics to talk about for him to insist on something more permanent yet, but he'd always had a very good long-term vision of situations and this was no different.

"I see." Brent was quiet for a moment but Calen wasn't worried. The sexy sub was a thinker and would always need time to process things outside of a scene. But Calen was curious to see how Brent reacted when his brain was turned off. "I think that a contract is an acceptable idea at this point."

Calen could almost hear the wheels in Brent's brain going when he paused again. "But you are already considering something of a more permanent nature?"

"Yes. I can very easily see a more long-term commitment." Calen wasn't going to hide his intentions from Brent...even if Brent wasn't sure yet.

"I see." Again, Brent seemed to be mulling over what Calen had said, and probably what Calen hadn't said. The fact that Brent was defaulting back to his business persona and trying to analyze their discussion didn't bother Calen. It was what Brent was most comfortable with.

And Brent might not have said much, but he hadn't said no.

"I think the idea has merit." Brent nodded like he agreed with Calen's conclusion. It made Calen fight to hold back his grin. Brent probably wouldn't find the situation as funny as he did.

"Are you ready to order?"

"Yes, are you?"

"Yes. I eat here a lot on the weekends. Cooking a big breakfast for one person isn't that much fun." Hopefully, he'd be able to cook for both of them soon.

Brent must have been thinking something along the same lines because he gave Calen a smile. "Maybe you can cook for me sometime."

"Sometime soon." Very soon if it was up to Calen.

The server walking up to the table pushed the conversation to the side for the moment. Asking questions and giving their order took a few minutes, but soon it was just the two of them again. Luckily, they'd gotten seated at the back of the restaurant and there weren't many people there. Too late for breakfast and too early for lunch gave them the perfect opportunity to talk without being overheard.

Picking up the folder he'd carried in from the car, Calen slid it across the table along with a pen. "I've printed out a list of limits. As you can see, I've already gone through and marked mine. You can take it home if you would like, or we can discuss them here. My preference would be to talk about it now so that I can make more informed decisions, but I won't pressure you."

He'd just flirt and tease and drive Brent crazy enough that he'd tell Calen what he wanted to know, anyway. Brent must have seen it written all over his face because he laughed and opened the folder.

"There's no way you'd calmly sit here with the list right in front of you and not want to talk about it. I'm not even sure I could be patient enough for that. There might be some things you've checked that I have to think about, but I can't picture you picking anything too out there."

Calen smirked. "You don't think I have a fetish for needle play or anything too interesting, huh?"

Brent laughed, shaking his head. "No. You got queasy that time we were all at the park and that kid fell and skinned her knee."

Attempting to control the urge to shudder, Calen fiddled with his silverware. "No. Blood is not my thing."

Trying not to smile, and failing miserably, Brent started going through the list. Carefully marking the different columns, he took several minutes to go through each item one by one. Calen appreciated the thought that he was putting into it, but he also appreciated the fact that he wouldn't have to wait hours to know what Brent would and wouldn't do.

As Brent finished up the list, the waiter brought over their food. After thanking him and getting everything settled, Calen opened up the folder and started reviewing it. Overall, nothing surprised him. They were both on the same page with most things. Brent had given a clear acceptance for restraints and most types of mild impact play.

"The items I marked as 'maybe' are ones we can talk about, but I would rather you not spring those on me." Brent was relaxed, eating his food as Calen read.

"I agree completely. You've checked yes for most types of restraints. Do you have any specific things that you would prefer not to happen while you are immobilized? Or, on the other hand, any particular things that you want to happen?" Calen was trying to behave himself and stay serious but it was hard. The only thing that kept him from getting too off track was the fact that they were in public.

Brent chewed slowly and squirmed in his seat. Calen didn't think he looked nervous, but he was definitely getting aroused. It took Brent a minute, but finally, he couldn't pretend to chew any longer. "That is a more preferred activity."

That seemed to be an understatement.

Imagining all the things he could do to Brent was getting him hard. He could see the scene perfectly in his head. It wouldn't even be that complicated to set up. Giving their surroundings another discreet check to make sure no one could hear him, Calen lowered his voice. "So if I decided to tie you up and say...spank you...because that's on the 'yes' list as well, it wouldn't be a problem?"

Brent choked on the bite he'd taken. When he caught his breath, he gave Calen a look like he was going to get even at some point. The feisty side of Brent had to be because of his brothers. He might be submissive in some situations but definitely not all.

"That would be fine." Brent was still trying to go for the businessman in public image. Calen decided his goal was going to be to shake things up a bit for the sub.

Calen pretended to glance down at the list again, but it wasn't necessary. The sexual activities that Brent found erotic were not something he would forget. Sliding his finger down the list, he glanced over at Brent. "So if I wanted to tie you up, for example, and use a prostate massager or dildo on you, that wouldn't be something you would find objectionable?"

After watching Brent cough when his water went down the wrong way, Calen thought that maybe he should stop asking questions when Brent had anything in his mouth. He didn't seem to be coordinated enough to swallow and listen at the same time.

"Do you have trouble swallowing? If you do, that should probably go on the list. It would be something that I need to know, as I plan on making great use of your mouth." Calen tried for dry and serious, but he could tell that he wasn't fooling Brent because after he stopped choking again, he glared at Calen.

Sliding Brent's water away from his plate, Calen shook his head. "I'm not sure it's a good idea for you to drink anything else. Explaining to your brothers that you choked to death is not high on my to-do list."

"Then stop asking me things like that when I have something in my mouth." Brent was shifting in his seat again but his eyes still seemed to be shooting daggers at Calen. He looked like he couldn't decide if he was angry or turned on.

Probably both.

Calen just seemed to have that effect on Brent.

"You still haven't answered my question. Should I repeat it?" He'd figure out a way to say it way naughtier if he had to.

"That will not be necessary." Then Brent's businesslike exterior cracked as he wiggled again. "That would be fine as well."

"Good to know. I'll note that you have no objections to being stimulated while restrained."

The shifting and fidgeting coming from Brent was getting worse. It gave Calen so many good ideas. "Do you enjoy being watched while you are being stimulated?"

Brent didn't even have anything in his mouth this time but he still swallowed funny and cleared his throat. "I...I have no objection to it, depending on the situation and scenario."

That was a yes. Calen wondered if Brent's enjoyment of being watched extended to the club. "Have you ever had that *situation* arise in a more public setting?"

Brent's eyes widened a bit and this time his body stilled while he processed the question. Calen thought the response was interesting. Did the change in behavior mean that Brent found the idea troubling or more arousing than he'd expected? Brent had marked exhibitionism as a 'maybe' on the list so it could have been either one.

Looking down at his breakfast and poking at his food, Brent took a moment before he responded, "I have always been more reluctant to consent to that type of scenario, but it is not completely off the table."

So he liked the idea, but he probably wasn't comfortable with it. The shower this morning might have made Brent think about being watched more than he had in the past. Calen wanted Brent to be his, but he found the idea of showing the sub off, even just a little, incredibly arousing.

Thoughts flashing back to the club, Calen could easily picture displaying Brent in one of the semi-private rooms while jerking him off or playing with him. Oh, they were definitely going to be coming back to this discussion.

"It will have to be a topic we go into in more detail. I find the idea quite...*interesting*." Calen didn't bother trying to hide his pleasure at the fantasies that were running through his head.

"Is it something you've done before? I can't remember you mentioning it." Brent set his fork down and looked at Calen curiously.

"Occasionally, when something arose at a particular estab-lishment we both belong to, but it was not an activity I set out to do. However, in this case, I find the idea of something more planned a distinct possibility—after our discussion, of course." Calen didn't want Brent to think he'd ever spring something like that on him. "And after we made sure of the surroundings and privacy from specific individuals."

Brent grinned and relaxed back in his seat. "I'd appreciate that. My family is pretty open but not *that* open."

"Agreed. And your family is entirely too bossy and opinion-ated. I'd never hear the end of the suggestions." Calen imagined Garrett fussing at him or Grant trying to run the scene.

Laughing, Brent shook his head. "That's just wrong."

"But I'm right. You know it."

"I'm not even going to respond to that—" Brent was inter-rupted by the buzzing of his phone. Looking down, he frowned and glanced back up at Calen. "I'm sorry, it's Garrett. If it's work—"

Calen cut in. "No, answer it. It might be important."

Brent slid his finger across the screen and picked up the phone. "Hello?"

Listening to the short, one-sided conversation, Calen didn't pick up much, but it seemed to be about some kind of meeting because Brent kept nodding and saying things like "I'll be there" and "Was there anything I need to bring?" At the end of the conversation, he looked up at Calen and smiled.

"No, he's right here. We're having breakfast at that diner over by the gym, if you must know. We met at the gym and worked out already this morning. I'll tell him. I'm sure he will. Now leave me alone and go back to work. I have the week off. Remember?" Smirking at whatever Garrett said, Brent hung up the phone.

"What was that about?"

"Garrett and Wyatt have invited us over to Garrett's house for dinner. Wyatt's handling everything and they want us to show up at six. Sound good to you?"

"Sure. But why just us?" They usually all hung out as a bigger group. Calen couldn't remember the last time he'd been invited to Garrett's without everyone else going too.

"My guess is he's trying to ease Wyatt into things. We're kind of overwhelming. He seemed a little unsure of how to act around us. He wants the lifestyle aspect but we're the most open family he's ever met. I'd think we were all a bit strange too."

"Small doses would probably be best. Hopefully, he'll be more comfortable in time." Calen thought back to the bouncy little creature that he'd first met, and he could already see the boy was much more comfortable now that he didn't have to hide what he needed.

Brent nodded. "He's already doing much better. He just needs to see that we don't mind. From what Garrett hinted at, Wyatt's family isn't the most supportive."

"Part of me understands, but I've been around you guys for so long it seems perfectly normal now. But when Garrett first told me about your entire family being in the lifestyle, it seemed crazy—like I'd walked into another world. It took some getting used to." To begin with, Calen had thought Garrett had been making the whole thing up. Meeting everyone for the first time had been a shock.

Brent laughed, but seemed to understand what Calen meant. "But dinner's okay with you tonight?"

"Yes, as long as we're not going to stay too late. I have plans for you that do not include leaving the bedroom." Calen had to suppress a smile as Brent started choking on his water again. "I worry about your ability to safely swallow. Are we going to need to practice that?"

Practicing watching Brent swallow could be fun...dildos...his cock...there were all kinds of interesting options.

Brent blushed, shaking his head. "Just stop saying stuff like that when I have something in my mouth."

"Am I going to have to worry about what I say when I have something else in your mouth?" There was no way he would be able to control the dirty talk coming out of his mouth when Brent was sucking him off. It wouldn't be possible.

His blush deepening, Brent tried to appear calm. "No. I'm not worried about that."

"Good. We might need to have you practice several times to be sure."

"Practice, huh?"

"Lots. Safety first, you know. And speaking of that, what safewords do you prefer?"

Brent shrugged, "I'm boring. I like red, yellow, and green. I think it's easier to remember."

"Easy to remember is good. Nothing kills the mood faster than randomly hollering out every fruit you can think of instead of saying green because you chose something too hard to remember."

Brent frowned at Calen. "That's not funny. I felt so bad for him. In the middle of that spanking demonstration and he was so close. It completely ruined everything. His Dom took it well but still..."

"Yeah, it was frustrating to watch at the time, but now it's just funny."

About a year ago, they'd gone up to observe some demonstrations that were being done by members of the club. One cute sub became so absorbed in the spanking he was receiving that when the Dom asked where he was, the sub couldn't remember the safeword he'd chosen to show that he was still good with the scene. He'd ended up hollering out random fruits and vegetables.

The Dom had later explained that because his boy got lost in subspace so easily, they didn't use verbal safewords at home except for brand-new activities. So when they were in a scene at the club, where verbal safewords were required, the sub hadn't been used to it. Needless to say, they decided playing there wasn't for them and just socialized there instead.

"I trust that we wouldn't have the same problem?"

Brent shook his head, obviously still thinking about the scene. "No, it's one of the reasons I stick with something simple."

"Good to know. Now, I am going to have one more cup of coffee and you are going to follow instructions." Calen had been waiting until Brent finished his meal for the next part of their day.

Brent gave him a suspicious look but didn't argue. He simply pushed his plate away and looked at Calen. He had a right to be worried, but Calen wasn't going to push him too much. "Yes, Sir."

The diner was still fairly empty so Calen lowered his voice a little and didn't worry about someone overhearing them. "Who does your pleasure belong to, subbie?"

The blush that had faded was starting to pink Brent's cheeks, but he didn't look away. "You, Sir."

Calen had a difficult time fighting the urge to adjust his hardening cock. "You are going to go into the restroom and jerk off again. You may fantasize about anything you would like, but no touching your ass. Are we clear?"

Staring at Calen, Brent's mouth opened and closed several times but nothing came out. Finally, he swallowed hard and managed to nod.

"You're my dirty little slut so I know it won't take long. But remember, if you're in there for a while, people will start to talk. I'm going to call the waiter over for more coffee, so off you go. If you dawdle, I might make you take a picture as proof next time."

"Next time? I mean, okay...um...yes, Sir." Clearly not able to talk coherently, Brent slid out of the seat and headed towards the restroom.

Calen hoped that no one would notice the hard-on starting to form in Brent's jeans—or the one in his. Adjusting his napkin to be on the safe side, Calen held his coffee cup up, trying to catch the waiter's attention. Giving the waiter a quick "Thanks" when he came over, Calen leaned back in the booth and tried to relax.

Well, as much as he could with all the wicked images running around in his head. One naughty fantasy was chasing after the other trying to make him crazy. What he wanted most of all was to be in there watching. Standing behind Brent, teasing him, touching him, while he masturbated. Not yet, though.

Not the time or the place.

Brent had been thinking about him as more than a friend for a while, but Calen wasn't sure that the sub saw him as a Dom. Seeing Brent as his sub wasn't hard for Calen. All he wanted to do was dominate and take Brent right to the edge. But going from seeing Calen as a friend to seeing Calen as his Dom had to be harder. Hopefully, little things like the jerking off when told would help with that.

And just to add something else for his mind to worry about, now they had to go to dinner at Garrett's.

Did Garrett even realize what was happening between Calen and Brent? Was that what the dinner was about? They did random dinners once in a while, but most of the time it was the barbecues on the weekends. Did this have something to do with Garrett's relationship with Wyatt?

Then there was the issue with his new relationship with Brent. Did he want to keep things quiet until they figured everything out or was he okay with talking about it already? How did Brent want his submission handled?

If it were solely up to Calen, he would have wanted everything out in the open, but it wasn't only up to him. Brent might be his submissive but that didn't mean that he wouldn't have strong opinions. And they still hadn't even written up their contract yet.

Calen hoped they would be able to get that ironed out before they had to see the rest of the group. He wanted to show Brent this was something he was taking seriously and committing to. Dinner was definitely messing up his plans.

He'd wanted to spend the afternoon talking about their contract and rules before having their first scene that night. Calen had envisioned a relaxing dinner after they'd had time to unwind and process everything.

Now with the invitation thrown in, he wasn't sure how much of that was possible. It would all come down to how much they agreed on right off the bat and how much they had to discuss and negotiate.

It only took a few more minutes and about a half a cup of coffee for Brent to come back to the table. He was flushed, with the same sleepy, just-fucked look that he'd had after he'd gotten out of the shower. Calen couldn't wait to see how he looked right after he'd come when he didn't have to put himself back together so quickly.

"That didn't take long. Did you follow directions?"

Brent didn't even seem to have the energy to blush. "Yes, Sir."

"Very good. How about we go back to your place and relax for a while? Then we'll discuss the contract." Calen watched as Brent yawned, nodding.

"And maybe a nap first." Brent's reply was almost unintelligible through the second yawn.

"Aren't you a forward sub? Asking your Dom to sleep with you before we've even gone through the contract."

"Calen! You know—"

Interrupting before Brent could get too worked up, Calen grinned. "I know. And a nap sounds good as long as it wouldn't be rushing you?"

"Not rushing at all." Brent tilted his head, giving Calen a sweet smile. "It sounds perfect."

"I agree. Nap, discussion, then dinner."

"Sounds good. You ready to go?"

"Absolutely."

When the two options were between sitting in the diner drinking coffee, and heading home to cuddle his sub, there was really no choice at all.

8

BRENT

Slowly waking, it took Brent a moment to figure out why he was so warm and comfortable. The sun streaming in through his bedroom window reminded him that he'd lain down to take a nap. But it wasn't until the warmth that was wrapped around him moved and tightened that he remembered Calen.

He'd slept with Calen.

Well, they'd taken a nap together was probably the best way to phrase it since they hadn't actually had sex. The rigid length that was pressed against his ass made him think that might change sooner rather than later. The idea didn't make him as nervous as he expected it would.

Wrapped in Calen's embrace and pressed tight against him, there wasn't anywhere he'd rather be. The only thing that would have made it perfect was if they were both naked. But he didn't think that was Calen's plan.

Calen seemed to be set on getting their contract and commitment ironed out first, before they got naked. It was sweet, but Brent was starting to wish Calen would be a little less cute and a lot naughtier. Maybe not lose the cute exactly, but spice it up with some of the wicked ideas Brent knew were floating around in his head.

His Dom had too much self-control.

The way he looked at Brent, it was easy to see not only his desire but his commitment. There was no need for Brent to second-guess what Calen wanted or was thinking. His Dom was making that perfectly clear. He wanted Brent, and he wanted to keep him too. Brent had dated and subbed, but most Doms seemed to want cute little twinks or guys who at least came across as more submissive.

Brent knew he was attractive enough that Doms noticed him, but they didn't want a submissive who was opinionated and not afraid to say what was on his mind. Yes, he wanted to surrender control in the bedroom and sometimes even out of it, but that didn't mean he was going to give it up lightly.

He wanted a Dom who would take the time for Brent to make that decision, and a lot of guys didn't have the patience. Calen might not realize it, but he'd been helping Brent to make the choice for a long time. Calen had never made him feel less for being submissive. He'd never questioned Brent's ability to lead at work. He never seemed to think it was odd that Brent could take control of the meetings but that he wanted to give up that control in his personal life.

The constant respect and understanding he'd always shown made it easier for Brent to picture submitting to him. All he had to do was make sure that Calen knew he was ready. It was hard to consider it rushing when they'd known each other for years and had both been obsessing about it for weeks. He was tired of thinking.

He wanted Calen to blow his mind and take away his ability to function, much less his desire to control anything. Snuggling closer into Calen's embrace, Brent couldn't help but imagine what Calen might do for their first time together. Would he keep it simple and sweet? Would he spank Brent? Would he relive one of the scenarios that he'd described at the diner?

Thinking of the diner made Brent's cock jerk. He'd already orgasmed twice today. His cock shouldn't have even been vaguely interested in anything, much less trying to get hard again. Maybe he'd been alone for too long, but he couldn't remember being this horny for anyone.

As the arms around him tightened, pulling him even closer to Calen, Brent couldn't help but imagine how good it would feel if Calen's hands were to wander lower. They would slide down his chest, teasing at the button of his jeans, before freeing Brent's trapped cock.

Easing the pants over his ass, Calen would run his hands over Brent's cock. How long would he make Brent wait before he got to come? Would he stop right before Brent's orgasm and deny him completely? Would he leave Brent naked and on display while Calen used his mouth, but not actually touch him at all?

His cock jerked even harder and Brent must have made some kind of noise because Calen shifted behind him. Giving Brent's neck a lingering kiss, Calen moaned and rubbed his cock against Brent's ass. "Are you thinking naughty thoughts, subbie? I can almost hear those dirty fantasies swirling around in there."

Glad Calen couldn't see his face, Brent smiled. "Possibly."

"Oh, it's more than that." Calen's warm voice came out deeper and filled with desire.

Then to Brent's shock and delight, the hand that had been resting against his stomach started moving further down his body. His hand was big enough that it didn't take long at all before it was resting on Brent's erection.

All he wanted to do was thrust into it and beg for more, but he knew that wouldn't get him what he needed. Calen's voice was thick with arousal but there was also a smile in his voice that made Brent want to blush when he spoke again. "This right here gives me a good hint at what you were imagining. The little moans you were making were a good clue as well."

Running his hand along Brent's cock, Calen didn't bother to hide how much he liked playing with Brent's body. Little moans and pleasure sounds escaped him as he cupped Brent's hard length. When Calen started rocking his hips, rubbing his erection along Brent's ass, he thought they were finally going to get naked.

He was wrong.

"As perfect as this is, subbie, we need to have our discussion before we go over to your brother's." Giving Brent's dick another firm stroke through the jeans, Calen kissed his neck again, sending shivers down Brent's spine. "I want you to go into the bathroom and jerk off again. But this time you'll stop hiding those sexy sounds. I want to be able to hear how good it feels."

He had to jerk off again?

Not that he had any issue with being told to masturbate, but Brent was confused—and too turned on to question Calen. As he pulled away, Calen must have seen something on Brent's face because he rolled Brent onto his back, leaning close. Pressing his lips to Brent's with the lightest, most tender touch, Calen kissed him.

It was sweet and loving, almost innocent, but when Calen pulled away, there was no mistaking the heat in his eyes. "Once I see you naked, you will be mine. But we're both going to be patient and talk about things first. Then tonight, I'm going to touch you, and kiss you, and lick you, and taste you. I'm going to do everything I've been fantasizing about for weeks."

He gave Brent another kiss, this time a quick peck. "Now, off you go. I want to hear your pleasure. Do you understand me?"

Brent's brain was in overload and all the blood in his body

was in his cock. All he could do was nod and give Calen a simple response. "Yes, Sir."

Calen's hot gaze followed him as he got off the bed and did his best to make his legs work. As he headed into the bathroom, propping the door almost closed, Brent knew coming again wasn't going to be a problem. His erotic thoughts on what might happen later and the knowledge that Calen wanted to hear him would have him orgasming in seconds.

The man made him crazy, but in the best possible way.

THE MAN WAS GOING to drive him nuts.

Certifiable, hide the body crazy.

Going over the limits again and discussing the contract was frustrating enough. But once they'd laid it all out and agreed on everything, Brent had thought he would at least get to touch Calen or maybe even go down on him.

No.

Calen had it in his head that they would wait until after dinner. So here he was, getting ready with another blasted erection, only this time he wasn't going to play with it. He was just supposed to ignore it and go to Garrett's house. He didn't want to. He wanted to get naked with Calen!

He wasn't feeling submissive at all.

Maybe that was the problem. He'd gotten little tastes of it all day long, but nothing completely satisfying. It was like getting a bite of dessert once in a while, but never enough to feel like he'd actually gotten a treat. It only made him want it more.

He was heading out to the living room to find his shoes when Calen came up behind him and wrapped his arms around Brent's chest, pinning his arms to his sides. "You are climbing the walls. What's bothering you?"

Brent sighed and leaned back into Calen's embrace. "I don't know exactly. I'm on edge. I'm not sure what it is."

It wasn't exactly the truth, but it wasn't a lie.

However, Calen didn't seem to need the full answer. He already seemed to have a pretty good guess what the problem was. "It's been a long time since you got to sink into your submission completely, hasn't it? When was the last time you got to surrender for more than a scene? Like all day or even over a weekend."

Brent loved the fact that Calen wasn't jealous and that he could ask questions about Brent's past, but he wasn't sure he felt like talking. The way Calen's arms tightened, though, Brent didn't think he'd have much of a choice. Sighing, he thought back. "A few years, probably."

"So you only had scenes, even though you had at least a couple of more serious relationships during that time?" Calen sounded surprised.

Brent shrugged. He wasn't sure why Calen was surprised. "A lot of Doms aren't interested in submission that goes beyond a scene or several hours at most."

Calen's arms tightened even more and Brent wanted to sink into him. It wasn't simply a hug, it went beyond that. The restraint and domination it implied were perfect. He must have made some kind of noise because Calen hummed and started rubbing his nose along Brent's ear, sending shivers through him.

"You like that, don't you?" Calen already knew the answer, but he waited for Brent to nod before he continued. "I know exactly what we're going to do. After we leave Garrett's later, we'll head over to my house. Once we get there, I'm going to take control. Not for a scene or even a couple of hours, but a day or two where you won't make any decisions. We'll go completely lifestyle during that time so you can relax. Once you've had a chance to escape your own head for a while and aren't so tense, we'll bring things back to normal. How does that sound? Neither of us is working right now so the timing couldn't have been more perfect."

"You wouldn't mind?" Brent thought the idea sounded perfect, but was it too soon? Was it too much to ask of Calen? "I know it wouldn't exactly be easing into the relationship if we did that."

"I don't mind at all. I love the idea of you being mine for days. Neither of us wants something like that permanently, but I think this is the perfect time to take a few days as a kind of break from real life."

Calen paused and seemed to be collecting his thoughts, but Brent wasn't going to rush him. Calen could take all the time in the world as long as he didn't let go of Brent. "Now, I'm giving you fair warning. I'm going to take complete control. Aside from necessary privacy, everything else would be up to my discretion."

"Everything?"

"Everything."

Brent was tired of thinking. Between work and trying to figure out what had been going on with him and Calen, he was done. "Please."

"When we get back, I'm in charge."

Calen sounded like he wanted one more confirmation from Brent. It wasn't really a question, but he answered again. "Yes, Sir."

"You won't need regular clothes, but let me see the stuff you have for the club. I've only seen you in the cuffs you usually wear. Do you have other things?" Arousal was clear in Calen's voice, even if Brent hadn't noticed the erection pressing up against him.

Pushing back the instinctive embarrassment, Brent nodded.

"I have a few pieces. Nothing complicated, but stuff to wear for the club or a scene."

"Okay. We'll see what you have and then we'll head over to Garrett's house." Giving Brent's cheek a quick kiss, Calen released him and stepped back.

Brent had to take a deep breath and shove the uncertainty away. He wasn't worried about submitting to Calen later, but the idea of showing him the drawer filled with clothes and toys made him...nervous. He knew it was silly, but it seemed more intimate, like he was inviting Calen to see the most private part of himself.

And considering he was talking about getting naked and submitting for days, that was ridiculous.

Taking Calen's hand, Brent led him back to the bedroom and over to the dresser. Kneeling down, he opened the bottom drawer and waited. He didn't have a ton of things because he hadn't gotten to play enough to justify buying that much. But what he did have, he knew he looked good in. It was just incredibly strange to have Calen looking at them.

Calen crouched down and started looking through the drawer. Pushing aside the cuffs and more obvious pieces, he seemed to gravitate towards the briefs and underwear. Well, almost underwear. Brent didn't think something that was a pouch with elastic holding it up should be called underwear.

Most of them he'd never even worn for someone else or to the club. They were fun and made him feel sexy. He couldn't help but wonder what Calen would think. Would he think they were hot or silly?

He shouldn't have worried. Calen zeroed in on them immediately, and one glance at his face had Brent relaxing. After picking out a few pieces, Calen looked over at Brent and smiled. "How often do you wear these to work? Every time I see you in a suit now, all I'm going to be able to focus on is what kind of sexy underwear is decorating your body. Because, subbie, stuff like this is just for decorating your cock."

Brent shook his head in disbelief. "I don't wear any of that to work."

Calen's heated gaze had a wicked look to it. "Oh, you will now. Maybe I won't have you do it all the time, but knowing that your cock is wrapped up in such a pretty package will make my day go by so much faster."

"*You wouldn't?*" Brent wasn't sure shocked was the right word, but wearing the underwear to work would have never occurred to him.

Maybe he *was* the most boring sub ever.

Calen leaned over and gave him a quick kiss. "Oh, you know I will. Come on, let's go. No more distracting me with sexy things."

Brent shook his head again. He seemed to be doing that a lot lately. "This was your idea. Stop molesting my clothes, then we'll go."

Waving the naughty scraps of fabric toward Brent, Calen grinned. "I'm going to do a lot more molesting before the night is over, subbie."

"You make me crazy," Brent sighed.

"You love it, though," Calen replied in a sing-song voice.

Brent rolled his eyes. "I plead the fifth."

Standing up, Calen reached out with his other hand to help Brent rise. When Calen started walking out of the room, Brent realized he was going to walk right out of the house carrying his stuff out in the open. Hell no.

"You're not carrying my underwear like that. Let me get something." Hurrying over to the closet, Brent quickly grabbed one of his old gym bags. Handing it to Calen, Brent made sure everything was hidden and zipped before they left the room. It seemed weird to be heading out for a couple of days with only the small bag. "So, no clothes?"

"No clothes. You can grab your toothbrush and razor if you have to, but that's it. I've got stuff you can use at my place, so that isn't even necessary." Calen's gaze scanned over Brent's body. It was easy to guess what his Dom was picturing. "Come on before I get sidetracked and we end up missing dinner completely. I don't want to have to explain that to Garrett."

"Me neither." Taking Calen's hand as they walked toward the front of the house, Brent did his best to push the thoughts about what would happen later to the back of his head. He'd never be able to focus on dinner with those images making him insane.

Calen promised a quick dinner. Hopefully, he could deliver on that because Brent had no desire to put things off any longer. He was ready to belong to his Dom.

9

CALEN

Dinner wasn't quite like he'd expected. Watching Bryce and Grant pull up as Calen parked the car was a surprise. Taking the key out of the ignition, Calen looked over at Brent. "I thought you said it was just going to be us?"

Brent looked at him and shrugged, "That's what Garrett said."

"Looks like he changed his mind or got ambushed at work."

He looked over at his brothers, responding automatically, "Ambushed. He probably said something, and those two didn't want to miss the action."

"Or free food." Calen knew no one in Brent's family could cook well enough to pass up free food.

Brent laughed, "Very true. Wyatt seems to be a good cook. He might even give you a run for your money."

Calen gave Brent a wicked smile. "You trying to be a naughty sub tonight? I might have to remind you how things work when we get home."

Giving Calen a grin, Brent's eyes were bright and teasing. "I don't know what you're talking about. You keep saying stuff like that, but so far I haven't seen anything."

Calen gave a little growl before reaching for the door handle, "Oh subbie, have I got plans for you tonight."

Climbing out of the car, they ignored the grins coming from Bryce and Grant and walked up to the front door. It wasn't like he and Brent were hiding anything, so he wasn't sure what they were so pleased about. Calen ignored it because he wasn't going to let them get to him.

"Fancy meeting you guys here." Grant's grin was filled with mischief as he and Bryce walked across the lawn.

Calen turned towards Brent, lowering his voice. "Is it just me, or has he been in a much better mood the last couple of days?"

Brent's mouth quirked up and Calen could see the laughter in his eyes, "Suspiciously so."

Calen looked over to Grant. "What has you in such a good mood? Does it have anything to do with a certain antique store owner?"

Bryce found that hilarious. By the time they got to the front door, Bryce was still trying to control himself, Grant was frowning at everyone, and Calen was simply enjoying the evening. Dinner was going to be interesting.

Before he could knock, Garrett and Wyatt were opening the door. Shaking his head at his brothers, Garrett stepped back. "Come on in. And remember, you're supposed to be on your best behavior."

They all mumbled polite agreements which no one believed and tried to give Garrett their best innocent smiles. He shook his head and gave them all his "I'm the big brother" expression that was supposed to keep them all in line. It never worked.

As they walked in, Wyatt glanced back and forth at them, giving them a peculiar look. Calen could almost see the wheels turning in his head. Wyatt might be bouncy and cute but he seemed to notice a lot more than Garrett did.

That wasn't hard, though.

Garrett had to be nearly hit over the head with something before it drew his attention. The way his relationship with Wyatt started proved that. At least they seemed to have moved past their initial reservations. He'd thought Wyatt's interest in Garrett had been obvious, but his friend hadn't been able to see it.

Grant and Bryce must have realized something clicked for Wyatt because they both had big grins, like cats that'd just eaten the canaries. Bryce chimed in, trying to look innocent. "We wanted more of Wyatt's food. And what better way to welcome him to the family than to invite ourselves to dinner?"

"In most families, I don't think that's how you welcome someone." Garrett stood there frowning and glaring, but Wyatt smiled.

"There's plenty for everyone. It's fine."

"See, he has manners." Grant smiled at Wyatt. "Thank you for letting us come over." Then he looked over at Garrett. "See, I have manners too."

Calen kept waiting for one of them to say something about him and Brent, but there was nothing. Well, nothing verbal. Bryce and Grant kept giving them winks and grins as they started towards the kitchen.

Garrett seemed oblivious, but Wyatt was clearly aware that something was going on. However, he didn't seem to know what. Calen had been prepared for questions about his relationship with Brent right off the bat, but so far no one had said anything.

Had the other guys not mentioned it to Garrett at all? Just the fact that he and Brent had arrived in the same car should have raised some eyebrows, considering they'd never carpooled anywhere before. But he had to remind himself that it was Garrett.

"So how's the vacation time going, you two?" Garrett's question seemed innocent, but it set off Bryce and Grant so much that they had to sit down at the table to catch their breath.

Grant got himself under control enough to respond before Calen could decide what to say. In his defense, he'd been a little distracted watching the hyenas in the kitchen. "They've been having *lots* of fun."

Bryce snickered and Garrett looked at the two of them like they'd lost their minds. Calen fought the urge to shake his head. He was going to end up looking like Garrett if he wasn't careful.

"It's been good." Brent did innocent better than anyone in the family. It was *almost* believable.

Wyatt was moving around the kitchen finishing things up, and it was clear to Calen that he wasn't sure what to say. They were all a little overwhelming when they were like this. Deciding it was time to distract everyone before it got worse, Calen called out to the nervous sub. "How's work going, Wyatt? Any new commissions?"

Wyatt looked up from doing something at the stove and smiled, clearly more at ease with the turn in the conversation. "It's been going great. I'm finishing up the pieces for the new club and I actually got an interesting phone call which might lead to a whole new line of furniture."

As he spoke, everyone started calming down and tried to listen. They were a curious bunch and Calen had known no one would want to miss what Wyatt had to say. Getting to know the newest member of the family was a priority for everyone.

The way Wyatt lit up and relaxed when he talked about his woodworking, it was obviously going to be the best way to learn more about him. So Calen tried to keep the conversation going. "What kind of stuff?"

Curious and kinky, all the brothers stopped goofing off

completely and focused on what Wyatt had to say. Luckily, he'd turned back to the stove and didn't seem to notice that he now had everyone's full attention. Calen thought that might have made him uncomfortable as well. "I've done some work for a woman who owns an adult store a couple of hours from here. She called and wanted to see if I'd ever done any items related to age play."

"She wanted to know if you'd made cribs for people in the age play lifestyle?" Bryce asked the question they were all trying to figure out the answer to.

Calen could see Wyatt smile as he stirred something. "That's what I thought to begin with, but no. She wanted to know if I'd ever made any hybrid pieces, like the spanking bench that looks like a regular bench. She said she'd spoken with several couples lately who were looking for more discreet furniture they could keep in their homes. Things that wouldn't automatically out them to neighbors and visitors. I thought it was a great idea."

"That's interesting." Brent had his head cocked and Calen could see the wheels turning. "For more traditional BDSM play, a lot of the equipment is easier to disguise or put away when it isn't in use. But even things like the spanking bench are hard. For a lifestyle like that, it's got to be even more difficult."

"Yeah, I hadn't even considered it, but she had some good thoughts on it already. I have to do some research and figure out if there's enough demand for it but it's got me thinking. I have some ideas already and I can't wait to see how they turn out." Wyatt was relaxed and smiling as he talked about his work.

"You'll have to show us what you come up with. There are probably even a few couples at the club that would be interested." Bryce had the same look as Brent and it was easy to see the business part of their brains going in circles.

"You might even be able to interview them to see what kinds

of things they'd like to have the most." Brent leaned back against the cabinets, a faraway look in his eyes. "They might even agree to do some product testing. See how easy the pieces would be to set up, usability, that kind of thing."

Wyatt beamed, "That would be a good idea. I hadn't thought of that. Then I could put them on the site, and maybe even see about doing some advertising on a few of the specialty websites to reach the right crowd."

"I'm sure the club does at least a small amount of advertising occasionally. They might be able to steer you in the right direction." Everyone had to agree with Bryce's suggestion. Ben and Conner would be a good place to start.

"You think they wouldn't mind me picking their brains a bit about it?" Wyatt looked hesitant but excited.

Garrett walked over and gave him a quick kiss. "They wouldn't mind at all. They love what you've made for the club and are always giving your name out to people interested in pieces for their homes. Why wouldn't they want to help?"

Wyatt blushed and shrugged, looking a little uncomfortable with the praise. "I guess so. I'll call them later this week, once I get some plans laid out."

Garrett touched Wyatt's face and leaned in close to whisper something in his ear. Wyatt's blush got deeper, but he nodded and smiled, then whispered, "Yes, Sir."

The little glances and touches the two exchanged made it clear how things were going. They were clearly very much in love. At one point, Calen might have been jealous, but not anymore. It was too early to use the word, but he wasn't going to deny how much Brent meant to him.

Looking over at his sub, Calen saw a smile on his face as he looked at his brother. They were all expecting invitations to Garrett and Wyatt's collaring ceremony sooner rather than later.

There was no way those two weren't meant to be. And as Brent glanced over at Calen, giving him a tender, loving expression, Calen thought his friends might not be the only ones talking about long-term commitments very soon.

10

BRENT

"I need to head outside and put some stuff on the grill..." Wyatt's voice trailed off as he reached into the fridge and pulled out two big dishes.

Garrett automatically grabbed one. "Here, let me take that." Then he turned to the rest of them. "I've got the chairs set up outside."

Taking the hint, they all started moving to the back of the house. Brent was the closest to the door, so he moved to open it. Wyatt smiled, "Thank you."

As they all piled out and found seats, Brent found that he enjoyed hanging out with everyone and not having to do a single thing. No planning, no making sure everyone brought something edible, it was perfect.

Dragging one of the chairs over to the shade, Brent was surprised to see Bryce follow him. Calen looked over, tilting his head in an obvious question, but Brent shook his head. It was sweet, but whatever Bryce wanted to talk about wouldn't drive him crazy, no matter what it was. But Brent had a feeling their conversation wasn't going to be about him, anyway.

Bryce sat down, leaning back and doing his best to look like everything was perfect. The only thing missing from making him the star in a summer commercial was the beer. Yeah, something was definitely up. If he wanted to pretend everything was fine, Brent would let him—at least, for a few minutes.

Finally, Bryce broke the silence. "Everything going okay with you guys? I'm assuming since you arrived together you had a chance to talk?"

"We did. We've discussed a lot and I think we're in a good place." Brent looked over to Calen and had to smile. He was trying to talk shop with Garrett but he was getting shot down. Garrett was going to make him take his full vacation no matter what.

"So, it's serious?" Bryce's hands kept moving, like he was wishing he had something to fidget with.

"Very. He had us write a contract earlier. No specific end date either."

"Wow. That is serious." Bryce didn't seem to be sure what to say.

"He's barely restraining the urge to collar me right away. He's trying to open up and show me that I'm important." His Dom was so cute, but Bryce didn't need to know that part.

"I'm glad. If anyone deserves to find 'Mr. Right,' it's you." Bryce seemed calm and relaxed, but there was something in his voice that made Brent think things weren't going so well.

"How's everything going for you?" Not sure where to take the conversation, Brent tried for something broad and hoped he'd be able to narrow it down. Bryce wasn't the most open person, but he'd always been able to share what was on his mind with Brent.

"Work's good. We've picked up several new customers lately. It's going to end up being quite a few new policies. Even a couple of business ones I need to talk to you about when you get back to work."

And there it was, the tiniest hitch in Bryce's voice when he talked about the new clients. "You had a new person come in the other day when I was there, didn't you?"

Bryce was quiet for a moment, then nodded. "Oliver Stanton."

Brent couldn't tell if Bryce was going to volunteer anything else, but his reaction was enough to make Brent keep pressing. "How did your meeting go? He was from the club, right?"

Again, there was silence for a long moment before Brent responded, "Yeah, it's going to be a good few policies. Auto, Life, the whole nine yards."

"Are they easy to work with? I don't think you said, have you met his partner yet?"

Bingo. There it was. The slightest flinch that he would have probably missed if he hadn't been watching Bryce closely. Something about that couple was bothering him. If it was just an issue with the policies or even that they were annoying, Bryce wouldn't have hesitated to say something. So this had to be personal.

"I did."

The short reply let Brent know he was on the right track. "What did you think of him?"

This time there was no hesitation. "Troy's nice. He's the strong silent type, but very in charge and aggressive when you get him going."

Were they still talking about insurance?

Somehow, Brent didn't think so. "What do you think of Oliver?"

"He's sweet. Chatty and open but a bit more laid-back than Wyatt. He's comfortable with himself."

There was absolutely no way they were talking about insurance. Brent had never heard any of his brothers describe insureds as "open" or "the strong silent type." "They sound like good people. How long have they been together?"

Bryce sighed, "About two years. They dated off and on for a year before that, though. They got serious once they found the club."

"Oliver's a little familiar but I can't picture Troy."

"He's taller than me by a few inches and built like a train." Bryce smiled and stretched his legs out. "He looks almost as rough as Grant but blonde, kind of like you'd picture a Viking."

Brent was starting to get a clearer picture in his head, of Troy the Viking and what was going on. "I think I can picture him. Didn't they do a demonstration with sounds a few months ago, maybe?"

Bryce nodded absently. "Yeah, Oliver loves being taken right to the edge. He's not a pain slut but loves that feeling of being totally owned and dominated."

The sounding demo had been hot. Looking back, Brent remembered how in-sync the couple had been. It had been very clear that they were together and not just for the occasional scene. Had Bryce gotten involved with them? "The scene was hot. I'm surprised I didn't remember it sooner."

"It was. They're perfect together."

Brent decided that it was time to prod the conversation, or they'd be slowly going nowhere all evening. "It sounds like you got to know them pretty well. Did you meet them after the demo?"

Bryce looked away, suddenly very interested in the fence that surrounded the yard. Eventually, he glanced back at Brent and nodded. "Yes." It was a short answer, but it was drawn out and filled with frustration.

"Want to talk about it?"

"I don't know." Bryce started playing with one of the buttons on his shirt, refusing to meet Brent's eyes.

It wasn't a no, so Brent kept going. "Was it just the once?"

"Yes."

"Did they want more than the one time?"

"Yes."

"Did *you* want more than the one time?"

"Yes."

Brent was fighting back a smile, but he wasn't that concerned since Bryce wouldn't look at him anyway. "Did they track you down? Is that why they're moving their policies over?"

Bryce sighed and tugged on the button, "Yes and yes."

"Do you know what you're going to do about it?" He figured he already knew the answer but he had to ask. Bryce just looked around the yard and sighed again. There was only so long Brent could watch him acting like Scarlett O'Hara with the dramatic sighs before he'd have to say *something*. It was his duty as a brother, after all.

"No clue."

They were moving on to more than one word, so Brent felt like they were making progress. "Have you talked to them about it, or are you ignoring it like Calen and I did?"

"Totally ignoring it." Bryce seemed to think it was a viable option, but Brent saw how well it worked out for him and Calen so he cleared his throat and tried to point that out.

"That has to be making them nuts."

"Yup." Bryce's short one-word answer made Brent want to sigh.

Trying to get things going again he pushed Bryce further. "But they're still interested?"

Brent nodded but ruined the calm façade by picking at the now loose string around the button. "Yes."

"Doesn't seem like your plan is working."

"Not at all." He seemed lost. Like he could see the crossroad ahead but didn't know which way to go.

"You know what you want?"

That seemed to have Bryce stumped, and he turned back to Brent again. "I don't know. It's not how I saw..." Bryce's voice trailed off.

"Things don't always work out like we'd planned." Bryce had dated Doms and subs but who said he had to choose. "Just because you hadn't considered it doesn't mean it's wrong."

Bryce was staring off again so Brent kept going. "Look at Calen and me. I never thought about him that way but now I wish I would have. Don't chase something away because it's different."

"Maybe." Bryce was quiet again. When he spoke, his words were filled with frustration. "We agreed to be discreet, though. There's no way I could keep something like that under the radar, even if I wanted to."

Brent hadn't even looked at it from that angle, so he wasn't sure what to say. Finally, he dove in. "We didn't mean to push away something special. The basic idea was not to do anything stupid here that would make the news or make the local gossips go crazy. If it's long-term and important, that's different."

"Would everyone else agree with that? Garrett's always bringing it up. It was one of the reasons he ignored what was going on with Wyatt for so long." Bryce's voice was quiet and Brent wanted to reach over and give him a hug, but knowing that would draw more attention than Bryce wanted, he held himself back.

"Garrett's an idiot, but even he eventually saw how stupid it was. We can talk to everyone but I know they'll want you to be happy. People are going to gossip no matter what, but most of our customers won't care." Brent wasn't one hundred percent sure about that, but he thought it was probably right. They had a variety of customers from traditional to unique, but he had to think that most of them wouldn't care what Bryce did in the bedroom.

Sensing that Bryce needed a break he reached over and poked him. "Come on. It looks like the chicken is done." Bryce was going to lose that button if they kept up the conversation any longer and none of them had the skills to sew it back on.

"Fuck, I'm starved. Let's go."

Dragging their chairs back to the patio, they walked over to the grill. The smells were amazing, and it looked even better. Looking around at everyone laughing and relaxed, Brent realized what a good idea dinner had been. Wyatt wasn't going to get comfortable with them just seeing everyone at the barbecues on the weekend.

Walking inside, the only awkwardness that cropped up was when they all walked over to the table. Wyatt had prepared a wonderful dinner of grilled chicken with all kinds of vegetables, and everyone was ready to fall on it like wolves. But Brent knew from his discussions with Garrett that Wyatt normally knelt for dinner.

It was clear that the other sub was hesitant to do it while they were there. The idea of family knowing would probably be odd to most people in the lifestyle, but it was what they were used to. He wanted Wyatt to feel comfortable enough to do what was right for him.

Brent debated for a moment whether he should kneel at the table as well, to make Wyatt feel less alone, but Brent knew that wasn't where he was emotionally. It wasn't the act of kneeling or even submitting in front of everyone. His head wasn't in it.

Luckily, Garrett stepped in.

Garrett was casual about it, leaning in to give Wyatt a kiss on the cheek and whisper in his ear. Brent could easily guess that he was telling his sub that the decision would be up to him. Brent thought it would have been easier for Wyatt if Garrett took the decision out of his hands. It might have just been where Brent's head was, though, not what was best for Wyatt. Brent couldn't tell anymore.

To Brent, if a submissive wanted a lifestyle relationship, it was a decision he shouldn't have to make. He probably didn't even want to be the one to decide. But Garrett would always want to make sure he wasn't rushing things, that he wasn't pushing Wyatt to be more open than he was comfortable with. Brent tried to remind himself that it wasn't his business and that Garrett knew his submissive best.

When he'd been going over the contract with Calen, their rules on kneeling had been a little more planned out, but not by much. They'd both agreed that kneeling in places like the club would be one of their rules. If they weren't in a long-term scene, it would be up to Brent as to his preference at the moment. So when they were at the barbecue it would be up to him, but when they were in more of a lifestyle mode like they were going to be for the next couple of days, kneeling would be required.

Brent thought that having clear-cut rules made it simpler for everyone. Maybe he'd see if Wyatt wanted to go out to lunch sometime with him and Bryce. It would give them all a chance to get to know each other better and for Wyatt to be able to talk things over with someone who knew Garrett. Deciding to text Wyatt tomorrow, Brent put it to the back of his mind. Wyatt had enough on his plate right now without Brent adding anything to it.

Whatever Wyatt decided to do, they would all be fine with, anyway. They were used to things being a bit different so it wouldn't be a problem. Wyatt evidently came to the same conclusion fairly quickly because after Garrett finished whispering to him, he'd walked over and grabbed his cushion before coming back over to the table.

Wyatt seemed much calmer kneeling and waiting for Garrett

to feed him. And Brent was glad to see him feeling more confident. Knowing what he needed and being able to do it in front of people who were just about strangers had to be difficult. Brent hoped that over time, Wyatt would become more at ease around them and that it would become second nature.

He wanted Garrett and Wyatt—well, he wanted them as happy and comfortable together as he was with Calen. Glancing over at his Dom, Brent couldn't help but think how lucky he was and how much he was looking forward to their lifestyle time together.

Part of him wished that Calen had insisted they start before dinner. Kneeling beside Calen, waiting to be fed, wearing only jeans and his cuffs sounded perfect. He should have said something earlier, but he hadn't even realized that he wanted it until he'd seen Wyatt's internal debate.

Reaching out to give Calen's leg a squeeze, Brent knew he was ready for whatever would happen. He was going to give himself to his Dom and let him take care of everything. It would be the perfect evening. As long as they could get dinner going a bit quicker.

11

CALEN

Dinner was going so well, Calen thought that he and Brent would be able to escape without having to explain the details of their new relationship. He wasn't trying to avoid it, but he liked the idea of having more time with Brent before they had to discuss it. But as Garrett and Wyatt came back in from the kitchen carrying dessert, that quickly changed.

"So how long have you two been seeing each other? I don't remember anyone mentioning it." Wyatt's curious expression seemed open and innocent. He obviously had no idea what he was stepping in.

"They're not seeing each other." Garrett paused and really looked at the two of them. "I mean, I didn't think they were. Are you?"

Brent coughed, trying to unsuccessfully cover a laugh, and Bryce wasn't having a much better time controlling his delight. But Calen shrugged and nodded, trying to keep it from getting out of hand. "Yes, we are. It's new."

Garrett looked back and forth between the two of them for a moment. "How new?"

"Very," Grant broke in, not willing to be left out of the conversation.

Calen looked at Garrett calmly, ignoring everyone else. "Since Monday, officially."

Sitting up in his chair, Garrett had one of those lightbulb moments because his eyes got wide. "That's the reason you've both been so nuts lately."

Brent nodded. "We were trying to figure things out and there was a bit of a misunderstanding. It's good now. I think we'll both be in a better place when we go back to work."

Wyatt watched everything play out as he sliced a chocolate cake. He looked upset that he'd started the conversation. "I'm sorry. I didn't realize that it was that new."

"No. It's fine. You had no way of knowing. And it wasn't like we were trying to hide anything. We're still getting our bearings and figuring things out." Brent tried to soothe Wyatt's worries because it was obvious he was afraid he'd made things awkward.

Kneeling back beside Garrett after the cake was passed out, Wyatt seemed to be mollified a bit, but it was clear he was still concerned. Calen noticed that he wasn't worried about the kneeling any longer, so maybe giving him something else to think about wasn't all bad.

"So what kind of lifestyle have you guys discussed, or is that something you're still figuring out?" In any other family, Garrett's question would probably have been weird, but Calen loved the fact that for their family it was a perfectly normal question.

He shared an amused look with Wyatt, glad he wasn't the only one to think it was at least a little humorous. Brent simply swallowed his bite of cake and answered as if Garrett had asked him about work. Calen found it all too funny, but he was careful not to let it show.

For the most part.

"Less lifestyle than you guys but not terribly vanilla either. We spent the afternoon going over limits and putting together a contract."

"Wow, a full contract already?" Garrett seemed surprised, but not in a bad way. His gaze went back and forth between them, like he was finally realizing how serious they were.

"Calen didn't want to give me the chance to realize how crazy he is and make a break for it." Brent's words were teasing and laughter filled his eyes, but to Calen, it wasn't that far off base.

"We're both kind of in the middle when it comes to where we fall lifestyle-wise, so getting everything spelled out and discussed made the most sense." Calen shrugged and tried not to worry about what Garrett would think.

He shouldn't have worried about his friend because Garrett smiled and leaned back in his chair. "That's wonderful. I'm glad you're both happy."

Reaching out, Garrett absently ran his fingers through Wyatt's hair, and it was clear to Calen that his friend was thinking about his own relationship. He might have had every intention of taking things slowly, but it was easy to see a more permanent relationship coming quickly for them. Calen couldn't blame him.

When you found someone who was perfect for you, why would you wait?

Glancing at Brent, Calen stretched out a hand and let it rest on his leg. Giving Brent a gentle squeeze, he tried to let him know how happy he was. The last couple of weeks had been incredibly stressful, bordering on painful, and Calen was glad they'd put it behind them.

Now if they could just get dinner behind them, so they could head back to his house, that would be wonderful.

Brent must have been thinking the same thing because as he

finished up his cake he looked over to Wyatt. "Thank you very much for dinner; it was wonderful."

"I'm glad you liked it. I love cooking."

Brent smiled. "Thank goodness, because Garrett's terrible. Now maybe we can put him in the rotation for something else at the barbecues. I might not be any better than he is, but at least I can put together a halfway decent salad."

Garrett snorted. "It wasn't that bad. Was that the reason I got banished to desserts permanently?"

"You didn't even realize the lettuce had gone funny and the dressing you brought was six months out of date. You almost gave us all food poisoning!" Brent was shaking his head and looking at Garrett like he didn't know what to do with him.

"If it weren't for Grant's obsession with the salad dressing, we wouldn't have even noticed." Bryce's words came out teasing but Grant frowned at him.

"It's not an obsession! You always bring the wrong kind."

"We're not doing this again." Brent's voice came out firm and decisive. Both brothers relaxed back in their seats, but it was easy to see they were still too worked up for it to actually be about the salad. They were both more stressed than normal, especially Bryce.

Wyatt was coughing, trying to cover up his laughter, but Garrett wasn't buying it because he frowned at the sub. "I'm shocked. You're taking their side."

"Of course not, Master. He's obviously teasing you." But the innocent act was ruined when he looked over and gave Brent a wink. That was one little sub who was deliberately egging his master on. Itching for a spanking, was he?

Garrett growled out something about punishments, making Wyatt blush and stare down at the floor, but his grin made it clear how pleased he was. Garrett looked like he was going to enjoy the evening too. Calen took that as their hint to leave.

"You two have fun. We're out of here." It might have been a bit abrupt, but everyone else seemed to have the same idea that he did because they were all grinning at Garrett and Wyatt. Those two weren't subtle at all. Not that anyone else in the family was any better.

"Oh, we will. You guys have fun on vacation. Barbecue is still going on this weekend, right?" Garrett glanced up and looked around at everyone.

Calen looked to Brent who nodded and replied, "Yeah, we'll let you know what to bring."

Deciding he wasn't going to be subtle either, he looked over to Grant and Bryce. "You two get cleanup for fighting at the table."

Grant snorted, "You're going home to—Shit, Bryce!"

Bryce evidently decided Grant didn't need to finish his sentence because he elbowed him in the stomach. "You have no manners. Or common sense. You have to wait awhile for that shit or he'll tell Mom you were trying to embarrass them."

"You two are a mess. Get your shit figured out or I'll be the one calling Mom about you." Garrett looked confused about their behavior, but he seemed to have reached the end of his patience.

Tired of the siblings bickering, Calen took Brent's hand, leading them to the front of the house. As they reached the car, Calen pulled Brent close. Wrapping his arms around Brent, loving the way he leaned into him, Calen whispered, "You ready to be mine?"

Cocking his head and giving Calen a curious look, Brent took a moment before he spoke. "I think I've been yours longer than I realized."

Leaning in to give Brent a quick kiss, Calen smiled. "Me too. Let's go home, subbie."

Stepping closer, Brent cuddled into Calen. "Sounds perfect."

Thankfully, the drive back to his place was short. Calen didn't think he had the patience to put off their night any longer. He'd been ready to make Brent his for days. He just hoped that everything would be okay with Brent.

Nothing that he had planned went anywhere near the sub's limits, but it might not be what he was expecting, so Calen wasn't sure what he would think. Pushing his insecurities to the back of his mind, Calen stopped as they walked in and shut the front door.

Giving Brent his full attention, Calen saw the stress in his friend's eyes and the weight of everything finally hitting him. "Who do you belong to?"

"You, Sir." Brent's voice was tired but Calen didn't think it was physical.

"Use your safewords if you need to, but other than that I simply expect to hear 'Yes, Sir' and to see you obey. Is that clear?"

Brent nodded and gave him a quiet, "Yes, Sir."

"Sometimes I'm going to tell you what will happen and sometimes I won't. You don't have to think about anything or make decisions. All you have to do is let me take care of you." It wasn't a question, but Brent nodded anyway. He looked so... fragile almost, that Calen wrapped his arms around him and pulled him close.

Brent rested his head on Calen's shoulder and sank into the touch. Standing there in the hall, Calen let his friend and submissive relax. When the tension seemed to fade from Brent's body and little sighs started escaping as Calen rubbed small, gentle circles on Brent's back, Calen knew it was time to continue.

Pulling back enough that he could see into Brent's face, he gave his friend a quick kiss. "We're going to go to my bedroom now and I'm going to get you ready."

There was nothing for Brent to say, so Calen took his hand and led the quiet sub back to the room. Next time he would have Brent strip for him but at that moment, he wanted to take care of his sub. Stopping Brent when he reached the center of the room, Calen began stripping off Brent's clothes. The T-shirt came off quickly, but Calen didn't rush to remove Brent's pants. He wanted it to last.

Running his hands up Brent's muscular chest, Calen felt little shivers racing through him. Calen had always admired Brent's body even when he didn't let himself think of the sub as anything but his friend. Now that he could touch Brent and there was nothing in their way, he let his gaze take in the beautiful man in front of him.

Letting his fingers tease around Brent's nipples and then dip down to trace the muscles of his chest and abs, Calen enjoyed watching Brent's body come alive again. He'd been a little worried that the sub was too worn out to play, but that wasn't going to be the case. Brent's mind might be exhausted but his body was still very much into what they were doing.

Seeing the way Brent's nipples tightened and his pants started to tent, Calen couldn't wait any longer to get him naked. Watching Brent strip down at the gym and not be able to touch him had been the hardest thing he'd ever done. He'd inwardly both cursed and thanked Brent for leaving his underwear on as he'd walked to the shower. A naked Brent would have been too much for Calen to handle.

Taking a little step back, Calen spoke. "Bend over and take off your shoes and socks."

There was no hesitation or question in Brent's expression, he simply leaned over and did what he was told. Calen took the opportunity to walk around and admire the sub. His ass was perfection. Calen might prefer to bottom but he loved a sexy ass, and he had all kinds of things he wanted to do to Brent's.

When Brent had his shoes and socks off, he straightened and waited for instructions. Calen couldn't decide if it was because his submission was starting to take over or if his brain had checked out completely. Thinking it could very well be either or both, Calen stepped closer and pressed his chest to Brent's back.

Brent leaned against Calen's body and sighed. To Calen, it looked like Brent was starved for the touch of a Dom. He wasn't questioning what Brent felt for him, but Brent had been on his own too long. He took charge so well that sometimes it was hard to remember he was more submissive than people realized.

Letting his hands caress Brent's chest, Calen brought his hands closer and closer to Brent's nipples. He'd wanted to explore them when Brent had stripped down the first time to see how sensitive they were, and now he would find out. When the pad of his fingers skimmed over the tight tips of Brent's nipples the sub inhaled sharply and let out a little moan.

Brent had indicated on his form and in their conversation that he enjoyed nipple play and mild pain. Imagining every-thing he could do had made Calen wild with need. He loved seeing a sub hover right at the point between pleasure and pain, where their nipples were puffy and sensitive and they were one tug away from orgasming. Brent was going to be beautiful to play with.

Teasing the hard little buds in small circles, Calen heard Brent's breath catch and felt the sub's muscles tighten as he tried not to move. Deciding to push Brent a little more, Calen took Brent's ear between his teeth and bit down gently as he pinched his nipples.

The moan of pleasure that tore through Brent filled the room. His chest heaved and little shivers raced through him. "Master!"

It was music to Calen's ears.

Giving his tender buds one last tug that had Brent arching

his chest and letting his head fall back, Calen reluctantly released the sexy toys. He'd be back to play with those again, but he needed to get his sub naked first. As Brent struggled to get his body under control, Calen reached down and released the button on Brent's pants.

Easing the zipper over the sub's growing erection, Calen pushed his pants down and watched them as they fell to the floor. Giving Brent's ass a quick pat, he stepped back. "Pick up your clothes and fold them neatly on the chair in the corner."

Brent's quiet reply was slightly breathy. "Yes, Sir."

Watching as Brent moved around the room picking up his clothes and putting them away as he'd been told, Calen had to admire the sub. He was beautiful. When Brent was finished, he came back over to Calen and waited.

He already seemed so much more relaxed, but Calen wanted to make sure he did his best to put the sub in the right frame of mind. Reaching up to cup Brent's face, Calen leaned in and gave him another quick kiss. "Go lie on the bed, face down."

"Yes, Sir." The low response held more curiosity than when they'd first started, but Brent didn't say anything else. He simply walked over to the bed and lay down close to the edge.

Taking a minute to walk around the room and grab everything he needed, Calen went to where Brent was patiently waiting for him. Head tilted to the side, Brent's gaze had followed Calen around the room. He hadn't said anything, but Calen could tell that Brent was wondering what the plan was.

Setting his supplies at the end of the bed near Brent's feet, so the sub couldn't see everything that he had, Calen grabbed the lotion first. Warming some up in his hands, Calen started at Brent's feet and worked his way silently up the sexy sub's body.

Brent's surprise was evident, but he still didn't say anything. The only sounds he made were low rumbles of pleasure. By the time Calen had reached Brent's butt, the sub was relaxed, his legs spread slightly open, and his whole body seemed to be sinking into the bed.

Letting his hands caress and touch, Calen took the time to not only help Brent calm down but to learn what he liked as well. Where he liked a firmer touch. Where it only took the lightest caress to make him sigh and arch into Calen's hand. Where it would make him moan with pleasure and need.

When Calen told Brent to roll over onto his back, it was no surprise to see the full length of Brent's erection straining up towards his stomach. He had plans for that, but not yet. Taking his time to learn the front of Brent's body as thoroughly as he'd done the back, Calen waited to touch the sub's cock until last.

By the time he'd worked his way back down Brent's torso to his cock, his sub was fighting the urge to move. No longer relaxed and pliant, Brent was straining to remain still. Running his hands up Brent's rigid length, Calen felt his own arousal surge. A large part of him wanted to keep going and see how far he could push his sub before he came but unfortunately, that wasn't the plan.

Letting his fingers caress the head of Brent's cock, Calen teased at the weeping slit which was dripping with pre-cum. Trailing his fingers down the sensitive underside, Calen smiled as Brent gripped the bed, doing his best to lay still. Calen knew that all his sub wanted was to thrust up and beg for more but even if he would've been that naughty, it wouldn't have done any good.

Brent had already gotten to come several times today, now it was time for him to focus on his Master's pleasure. Reaching down to the bottom of the bed, Calen grabbed the cock ring he'd picked out earlier. Because this model wrapped around an erect or relaxed penis, Calen didn't have to worry about easing it over his sub's impressive dick. Once he had it fitted, and he knew

Brent wasn't going to be coming anytime soon, he gave Brent one last touch to watch him squirm.

Picking up the remaining items off the end of the bed, he leaned over and gave Brent a slow kiss. He'd started out planning to give him a quick kiss but as soon as his lips touched Brent's, Calen knew that wouldn't cut it.

Tasting his soft, tender lips, Calen knew he'd never get enough of kissing Brent. Full smooth lips met his as he nibbled and claimed. By the time he pulled away, they were both breathing hard and desperate for more.

It was time for more, but not what his sub would expect.

"Go into the living room and wait in front of the couch. Show me how pretty you look kneeling for me again." The image in his head from the club was almost innocent, but this time, having Brent on his knees would be far from innocent.

Brent blinked up at him and it took a second for the words to connect. "Yes, Sir."

Watching his sexy sub climb off the bed, Calen followed Brent out to the living room, thoroughly enjoying the view. To Calen's way of thinking, anyone who thought a sub should follow their Master was an idiot.

As his beautiful submissive gracefully displayed himself in the center of the room, Calen found himself standing in the doorway admiring him. He knew Brent was sometimes frustrated because he didn't look like what people thought a submissive should be but to Calen, he couldn't be more perfect. He just had to get Brent to see it as well.

12

BRENT

The posture and movements were automatic for Brent, but the feeling of kneeling in Calen's living room while his Dom watched was very different. He was actually submitting for Calen. It was nothing like what he'd expected.

With slow, careful touches, Calen had his whole body singing. With a touch that was sometimes erotic and sometimes tender, Calen made him feel like the center of his entire world. And that was just the beginning.

Brent could see the plans and ideas dancing around in Calen's mind. He couldn't wait to see what else his Dom had in store for them. But he knew there would be no way to guess. Every time he thought he understood what would happen next, his Dom would surprise him. The massage was a perfect example.

Waiting while Calen stood in the doorway, all Brent could do was to try to be patient. Maybe it was the massage, or maybe it was knowing that his submission wasn't just for a few hours this time, but everything felt much easier than he'd expected.

He'd been so stressed and overwhelmed earlier but that had

all faded. As Calen pushed away from the doorframe, Brent took a deep breath and focused on the floor in front of the couch. He would have loved to have watched Calen, but he knew better, and he wanted Calen to see that.

Calen stayed right outside of his field of vision but Brent could sense him as his Dom came up behind him.

"You look incredible. So good, in fact, you're going to stay like this so I can admire my beautiful submissive." Calen's voice was sexy and rough.

Brent wasn't sure what Calen meant, but he was completely surprised when a blindfold was wrapped around his eyes. Calen must have noticed his start because his Dom made a soothing sound and started running his hands through Brent's hair.

"Shh. You're not going to move. Nothing is going to happen. You're going to stay right here for me to look at. The only thing that might be different is that I'm going to make sure you don't have anything else to focus on but kneeling right here." Calen's voice was warm and soothing, settling nerves Brent hadn't even realized he had.

There wasn't anything to say. It wasn't like the scene was anywhere near his limits and he didn't have any reason to be jumpy. But he wanted Calen to know everything was fine, so he responded anyway. "Yes, Sir."

"That's good. Now I'm going to put ear plugs in you, subbie. You're not going to be able to hear anything, but you don't need to." Calen's words came out slow and even, like he was trying to settle a skittish horse.

Why was he so nervous?

He trusted Calen. Hell, Brent wanted this. He'd wanted this for so long. It wasn't even a particularly edgy scene. He even liked sensory play. He knew how relaxing it was going to be once he got in the right headspace.

Maybe that was the problem.

It had been so long since he'd been able to turn over control to someone. Not only let them be in charge during a scene but really give himself to another person. Maybe he simply needed to remember how much he liked this. "Yes, Sir."

Again, there was nothing else to say. Eyes covered, head down, he waited until he felt the tickle of Calen's fingers near his ears. "That's it."

One hand trailed over his body as the other fit the plug in one ear. Calen's touch made him want to arch and beg but that wasn't possible, so he tried to let the warmth soak into him. Over his chest and down to caress his erection, Calen's words felt as good as his caress.

Little thoughts and phrases kept escaping his Dom, and Brent wasn't even sure he realized it. Telling Brent how incredible he was...how beautiful...how perfect...It was like basking in the sun and soaking up the wonderful warmth after a winter of cold, cloudy days.

Except this time, Calen was his sun.

As the other ear plug slid in and the sounds faded away, Brent could still feel the trail of Calen's fingers as they traced invisible paths along his cock and legs. When all he had to focus on was that gentle touch, everything seemed magnified.

The drag of Calen's fingers against his skin sent shivers through his body. And as ridiculous as it was, he could almost feel the heat of Calen's gaze. His Dom wanted to watch him— wanted to display his body just for his Dom's pleasure. As Calen moved away, Brent found that he could feel his Master's movements through the floor.

The shifts in the boards and the vibrations carried up through his legs. It was another little thing he never would have noticed, but now it made the sensation of being watched even stronger. Master was there and wanted to see what a pretty sub Brent was.

Master thought he was beautiful.

Thoughts tumbled around in Brent's brain. Imagining how Calen saw him. He tried to picture if he was sitting straight enough, and if he was kneeling correctly. Slowly, though, as he knelt in the quiet, some of the jumble in his head seemed to fade away.

Fleeting ideas floated into his head but just as quickly they were gone. His body seemed to settle into the floor and it was almost as if he could have stayed there forever. Knowing that by being silent and still he could please his master helped push the remaining thoughts from his mind.

He had no idea how long he knelt there waiting, but at some point, the time didn't matter. Everything was still and peaceful. It had been so long since there was that much tranquility, Brent let it draw him in.

When the touch came, the gentle caress sent lightning through his body. It was softer than the most delicate touch of a finger, but as the sensation moved up his legs and over to his cock, Brent thought he might lose his mind.

Uncontrollable shivers raced up his body, and he felt a moan vibrate in his chest. As the touch traveled up his torso and circled around his nipples, Brent knew he moved but he couldn't seem to help himself. Arching, he strained to get even closer but when his body begged for more, the caress moved away down his body again.

Circling his erect, trapped cock, it seemed to delight in pushing him to the edge. Shaking, Brent realized he was talking, but his brain couldn't keep track of the words. Every part of him was focused solely on the maddening pleasure that racked his body.

When the ear plugs finally came out, and the fabric was removed from his eyes, Brent was overwhelmed and desperate. It took a few long seconds before Calen's words made sense.

"You did such a good job. So beautiful. So perfect." The words were loving and filled with emotion. "Watching you present yourself for me. Having that incredible cock on display for me."

It wasn't until Calen's words brought Brent's attention back to his erection that the sub realized his Dom was still touching him. The feather dragged over his skin in the lightest, fleeting touch but it was overwhelming.

"Master." Brent could hear the plea in his voice but he wasn't even sure what he was begging for.

"Are you ready to please me? Are you ready for me to use your body for my pleasure?" The words were erotic enough that they sent passion through Brent, but the look on Calen's face made them even hotter. Seeing how badly he wanted his submissive sent need racing through Brent again.

"Yes, Master. Please."

Calen took his hands and started to rise. Following his master, Brent only wanted to obey. As Master helped him to stand, Brent felt the strain and prickles in his muscles. Giving him a moment to steady himself, Calen waited and watched.

When Brent was steadier, Calen started leading him back to the bedroom. His brain was still foggy and body oversensitive, but all he wanted to do was please Calen. The Dom's words were soft and low as he directed Brent to lie on the bed.

As Brent lay down, Calen went around and started adjusting something near the corners of the mattress. "Stretch out, love. That's good. Arms and legs open for me."

Then, to Brent's surprise, Master started attaching his arms and legs to cuffs fastened to the bed. Once he was firmly secured, Brent watched as Master started unbuttoning his shirt. It wasn't until Calen's grin turned wicked that Brent realized he was pulling at the cuffs. The desire to touch Calen and be the one to strip him was a desperate need that was uncontrollable.

Watching Brent squirm on the bed only seemed to make Calen more aroused. By the time his shirt was off, his Dom's impressive erection was straining against his pants. Brent cursed the bonds holding him down as Master reached down to flick the button on his pants.

The slacks and underwear slid to the floor with a thud that seemed to echo in the room. Master was naked and there was nothing Brent could do but lie there and wait. Calen had talked about using him for his pleasure, but what had he meant?

Brent thought back to their discussions and Calen's worried confessions, but he couldn't be sure what would happen. Watching as Calen started walking toward the bed, Brent found himself holding his breath in anticipation. When Master paused at the head of the bed and opened the bedside drawer, Brent's world narrowed to the condom and lube in Master's hand.

"You want to please me, don't you, love?" Crawling on the bed, Calen looked like a Greek god come to life. Muscles rippled over his impressive frame and his cock hung long and thick between his legs. Making no attempt to hide his desire, Calen was pure sex, but Brent could see the old fears lurking in his Dom's eyes.

"Yes, Master. Anything."

Calen's smile had a wicked feel as he knelt between Brent's spread legs. Brent could only watch as Calen opened the condom and covered his sub's aching erection.

"Maybe when you've shown me how good you can be, and when you've earned it, I'll let you come inside of me, but not yet. You have to be a very good boy to get to mark your master." Calen's words sent swells of emotion and need rolling through Brent.

The idea that he would be used bareback someday and that he would get to shoot his cum inside his master was overwhelming. They'd discussed the fact that they'd both been tested since they were last with someone, so it wasn't completely out of the blue, but the knowledge that Calen would let Brent orgasm inside him was incredible.

"I'll be good, Master. I...I'll be good..." Words tumbled out of Brent as Calen smoothed lube over the erection he was going to use to pleasure himself. That was when it finally hit Brent. He would be Master's life-size dildo—a flesh and blood sex toy for Master to use. And with the ring around his cock, Brent knew Master could use him as long as he wanted.

He knew that Calen could see the exact moment when Brent realized it. His smile took on a predatory gleam and his eyes flared with passion. There were no more worries lurking in Master's gaze, he was confident and thoroughly enjoying Brent's reactions.

To Brent, he couldn't have looked more amazing.

When Calen reached around behind him with two lubed fingers, Brent thought he would have a heart attack. "Please, Master. Please..."

"You want to watch? You want to see me stretch my hole so I can use your cock?"

Nodding his head vigorously in a desperate attempt to make sure there would be no misunderstanding, Brent pleaded. "Yes, Master. Yes. God, please. Master!"

Watching the hesitation creep back into Calen's gaze, Brent could only beg and try to let his master understand that he was more than okay with what his Dom wanted. Turning enough so that Brent could see, Calen slowly fucked his ass, stretching his hole with lubed fingers. The tight ring around Brent's cock was the only thing that kept him from coming.

It was the most erotic thing he'd ever seen.

Calen shivered, and Brent knew the pain and pleasure that had to be flooding his Dom. He couldn't decide what he was more jealous of, that Calen was readying his own hole or that he was getting to feel what Brent knew were incredible sensations.

"Can I...Master...sometime..." Brent didn't even know how to ask what he wanted. Would Calen let him?

Calen's voice was thick with desire. "You want to be the one to stretch me next time I use your cock? You have to be a very good submissive if you want that."

"I'll be good...yes...please..." Brent's brain wasn't working, but he needed Calen to know how much he wanted it.

Brent's reaction seemed to only inflame Calen because his Dom seemed to take great delight in putting on a show for him. Something about being tied down and only able to watch made it even hotter. By the time Calen was moving to straddle Brent's hips, they were both so turned on they were shaking.

Straining against the bonds that held him, Brent could only arch and moan as Calen sank down on his erection. The feel of his Dom's body as it gripped him was the best thing Brent had ever experienced. The whole thing was perfect. Brent loved getting to top, but this also fed his submission in a way that he'd never expected.

All he could do was lay there while his Dom used him for his pleasure. "Master!"

"Oh, love, you feel..." Moaning, Calen's head fell back as he sank all the way down on Brent's hard length. Squeezing his muscles and rolling his hips, Calen sent waves of pleasure through Brent, but there was nothing he could do.

And it wasn't like he could complain. Calen had already let him come several times today, but at that moment the memories were distant. It was the hottest scene he'd ever experienced. It pulled at every sense and at every kink he had. Even the pressure from the ring was perfect.

Watching as Calen fucked himself on his cock, Brent fought the urge to close his eyes. As much as he wanted to focus on the tight pleasure engulfing his cock, the need to see the desire racing across Calen's face was even stronger.

Time lost all meaning for Brent as Calen rode him.

Faster, then slower, Calen chased the pleasure, then seemed to want to draw it out. Brent had no idea how long he lay there and watched his Dom. When it was finally too much for Calen, he slammed himself down on Brent's cock and exploded. Squeezing his tight muscles, he milked every drop of pleasure from his body. Calen arched back and shook as cum shot out over Brent's body in long stripes.

The world narrowed down to that one point and soon Brent was flying. The aching fullness in his balls and the weariness in his muscles didn't matter. The bed seemed to swallow him up and everything else faded away. He could hear Calen's voice in the distance but it was warm and soothing, helping to lull him deeper into the haze.

The words were lost, but the love and emotion were clear. Master, lover, Dom, friend...Calen was everything to him.

"So you ready to head back to work on Monday?" Bryce's smile wasn't as forced as it had been before his time off, so Brent couldn't help but hope he'd started to figure out what he wanted—and maybe even how to go about getting it.

"Yes and no. This week has been perfect, but I'm ready to get back to the real world." But it was a hard call. Being able to completely submit and let Calen decide everything for those few days had been amazing. It felt more like he'd had a month off, not a week. But being so relaxed and centered made him ready to tackle real life again, so it was a double-edged sword.

Sitting around the outdoor patio of their favorite Mexican restaurant, Brent was glad he'd managed to drag everyone out to lunch. Wyatt and Carter had been a little hesitant, but Bryce had jumped at the chance to get out of the house.

Brent thought he'd probably been obsessing over his new *interests* too much lately. He hadn't had a chance to talk to Bryce much in the last couple of days. Calen had kept him *well-occupied*, but he planned on rectifying that once he got back to work.

Wyatt looked around, then leaned closer to the table. "You said you guys played a lot this week. Did you like being lifestyle for a while?" Wyatt's cheeks were getting a little pink, but the sub didn't let his nerves get the best of him.

Brent thought he was so cute. "Doing it all the time might drive me nuts, since Calen's bossy and completely takes over when you let him, but it was what we both needed. And it let us both get a taste for how things will work long-term."

Carter smiled and settled back in his chair. "I'm still new to the group and learning about everyone, but you guys seemed to be figuring things out pretty fast. I'm impressed."

"It might seem kind of quick, but it doesn't feel that way. We've known each other so long, it's like the logical next step. Calen is patient when he needs to be and has crazy amounts of self-control," he had to smile, his Dom had it in spades when he needed it, "but he's like a freight train when he wants something."

Bryce smirked, "And right now, what he wants is you."

"Not exactly," Brent shook his head, smiling. "It's more like he wants us together without anything in the way. And things like living in two separate houses and having busy schedules are in the way."

Wyatt's eyes got wide, "He wants you to live together already?"

"He'd have moved me in the day we signed our contract if I let him. We've settled on a schedule where we'll stay over at each other's places for right now. I think he'll end up selling his place and moving into mine pretty soon, though." And Brent wasn't going to fight the idea, either. There would be some bumps as they figured out how to live together, but he couldn't imagine putting it off too long.

Wyatt looked thoughtful, and he started to fidget, so Brent knew there was something on his mind. He liked the fact that he was starting to get to know Wyatt more. He wanted his new friend to feel like part of the family. "How are things going between you and Garrett? He still trying to take it slow?"

The cute sub leaned back in his seat, sighing dramatically. "God, yes. He's so sweet, but it's making me crazy."

Bryce laughed, "So you're ready for him to lock you up and throw away the key but he's giving you space, or some other nonsense like that."

Wyatt blushed an almost violet color at the mention of being locked up. Brent had a pretty good idea what the issue was about and so did everyone else, because Bryce and Carter started snickering. The sub shook his head, then stuck out his tongue at them, making Brent laugh. "Basically."

"Are you going to talk to him about it?" Carter managed to stop giggling long enough to question Wyatt.

A little grin escaped Wyatt as he answered. "Don't tease him or anything..." Then he gave them all a stern look before he continued. "But hearing that Calen wanted a contract right away made him rethink taking things as slow as he has been. He wants to start working on one tonight. I'm going to mention it when we talk about schedules."

"If it was up to you, what would you want?" Brent couldn't help asking. It probably wasn't his business, but it wasn't the weirdest thing that Wyatt would be asked now that he was part of the family.

Wyatt thought about it for a moment, then the blush started to creep back into his face. "I'd like for us to live together. Garrett might be right, but having him around all the time would be so much better than only seeing him occasionally. He calls a lot..." He paused and started shifting in his seat a little before he continued. "And he constantly shows me he's thinking of me, but it's not the same."

Carter shrugged, then reached out to squeeze Wyatt's shoulder. "You're a jump in feet first kind of sub. There's nothing wrong with that. You've found a great guy who loves you and gets what you want. Don't feel bad about that."

Bryce nodded and spoke up. "He's probably thinking the same thing you are. Talk to him about it. You don't need to go off of someone else's timetable for relationship steps. Do what comes naturally."

The thoughtful expression on his brother's face had Brent hoping that Bryce would listen to his own advice. Turning back to Wyatt, Brent had to agree with Bryce. "He's right. You'll know what feels right. Tell Garrett, and I think you'll be surprised at his reaction."

"But no collaring ceremony before Mom gets back. She'll kill you both if you make her miss something like that." Bryce laughed at the shocked expression on Wyatt's face.

"She'd want to come?" Wyatt looked dumbfounded.

Brent and Bryce spoke at the same time. "*Oh yeah.*"

Trying to calm Wyatt down, Brent reached out to pat his shoulder. "We'll make sure it's tasteful and Garrett will have you appropriately covered, if that's your fear."

Wyatt seemed to relax a little. "That's certainly part of it. But still..."

"It's weird and overwhelming, but that's our family for you." Bryce was thoroughly enjoying Wyatt's reaction.

"No offense or anything, but your family is strange." Wyatt shook his head, not bothering to hide his nerves.

"Oh yeah, but you'll learn to love us." Brent smiled at Wyatt's skeptical expression; the sub was going to fit right in with the rest of the family.

"We grow on you." Bryce was trying to be serious, and make Wyatt more comfortable, but Carter ruined it.

He chimed in, a wicked grin on his face. "Like a fungus?"

As everyone laughed and enjoyed themselves, Brent couldn't believe how fortunate he was. He had wonderful friends, a supportive—if crazy—family, and the best Dom he could have wished for. Now that everything felt perfect for him, he hoped that Bryce and Grant would find happiness as well.

However, Brent felt they might need a nudge in the right direction. Looking at Carter, he thought a trip up to the club might be in order. He'd have to see what Calen thought, but if he knew his Dom, he'd think it was perfect. Getting the chance to meddle in Grant's life, and maybe even Bryce's, as well as playing with Brent at the club; his Dom wouldn't be able to resist.

As much as he liked relaxing with everyone, Brent was suddenly ready to get home. Calen had promised him a surprise and Brent had a feeling it was a naughty one. But whatever it was, Brent knew Calen's love and domination would come through.

Brent had been on enough bad dates and met enough Doms that didn't understand him that he wasn't going to let Calen get away. Maybe it was time for Brent to surprise Calen tonight by telling his Dom exactly how he felt.

He'd never said the words to anyone else, and even thinking about saying them to Calen gave him a lump in his throat. Calen was his friend, his lover, and his Dom, and Brent couldn't have loved him more. Oh yeah, he thought with a smile. It was time to go home.

GRANT

FIRST EDITION AUGUST, 2017

1

CARTER

W yatt sailed through the door of Hidden Treasures, almost dancing while saying, "I heard from a little birdie you had a date tonight."

Carter fought to keep himself from rolling his eyes at Mrs. Jenkins as he handed her back her credit card. Hoping she would ignore Wyatt, he smiled and tried to keep things professional. "I'll let you know if I can find those chairs you wanted. I've got some good contacts, so it shouldn't be difficult."

Her eyes twinkled as she took back her card. "A date? You didn't mention anything like that." Then she turned to Wyatt. "Hello, dear."

He blushed a little. "Hello, Mrs. Jenkins." Then, glancing back to Carter, he mouthed, "Sorry."

She wasn't going to give up on good gossip, so she turned to look at Carter. "Who is your mysterious suitor? I can't remember hearing you mention anyone."

Carter wasn't sure what to say, because he still wasn't sure if it was a real date. Grant had asked him out for dinner and it sounded like a date, but Carter had been in this position before.

Pushing aside his worries, he shrugged. "He's a friend. We're just having dinner."

Not believing Carter for a minute, the little old lady looked at Wyatt and tilted her head questioningly. He gave Carter a shrug and then looked back to Mrs. Jenkins and shook his head, whispering conspiratorially, "He's lying. The way Grant looks at him, there's no way that man thinks they're friends."

She laughed like it was the best thing she'd heard all day. Ignoring Carter's rising embarrassment, she kept her focus on Wyatt. "Is he handsome?"

Wyatt leaned toward her and nodded. "He's one of my boyfriend's brothers. He's built like a tank but is very nice."

Her eyes lit up. "Like one of those body builders on TV?"

Wyatt shook his head. "He looks more like a bouncer at a motorcycle bar, but he's smart and works in insurance."

"Oh, the best of both worlds." Carter swore the older woman almost swooned.

Wyatt nodded energetically. "I'm completely gone over Garrett but—Oh, you're going to love him, Mrs. Jenkins."

She turned back to Carter. "Is your young man picking you up from work?"

Carter knew if he answered yes, she was going to find another dozen things she had to ask questions about. He smiled. "No. I'm meeting him at my house after work."

"They're going to dinner and I've heard Grant has a surprise." Wyatt was almost skipping around the store and Mrs. Jenkins was eating it up. She was the perfect audience for Wyatt's enthusiasm.

"You can't keep it a secret from me." She stepped closer. "We won't tell doubting Thomas over there."

Wyatt giggled and whispered low in her ear. She smiled and brought her hands together near her chest. "Oh, that's perfect. He's going to love it." Then she leaned close again and whispered something low to Wyatt. He nodded like she'd given him some sage advice, then they both looked over at Carter.

He was nervous enough about the date. He didn't need them adding anything else. He wasn't going to play the guess-the-secret game, so he ignored it. Wyatt was probably overreacting, anyway. *Please, God, let him be overreacting.*

Mrs. Jenkins smiled and gave Wyatt a conspiratorial look before turning back to Carter. "I'll come back and check on those chairs later in the week."

Carter knew he was going to get politely grilled about his date, but he wasn't sure if there would be anything to tell her. Most of his dates went terribly—and that was when he was sure it was a date. He and Grant had been talking and texting for almost two weeks, but when Grant mentioned dinner during one of their conversations, Carter had been too shocked to do anything but agree.

How much texting meant friendship, and how much meant something more?

His friendship with Wyatt might not be the best indicator, because they talked constantly. He didn't do that with many people, but maybe most friends didn't talk much. Had that been Grant's way of hinting he wanted more than just friendship?

Carter was starting to wish he'd asked a few more questions, like "Is this a date?" and possibly "Where are we going?" From the look on Wyatt's face, it might have been a good idea. Mrs. Jenkins hadn't been shocked, so it couldn't be too weird. Who was he kidding? That outrageous little old lady wouldn't have blinked no matter how strange the date might be.

As she made her goodbyes and left the antique shop, Carter turned to Wyatt. "What did we discuss last week?"

Wyatt sighed and flopped down on a chair. "Not to come in talking about personal things without making sure the store is empty first."

"And why did we have this discussion?"

Wyatt closed his eyes and tilted his head back, sighing even more dramatically. "Because Mrs. Jenkins doesn't need to know that Garrett likes to do fun things to me in bed."

"I thought you were going to give her a heart attack." Carter shook his head and leaned over to prop his elbows on the counter.

Wyatt opened his eyes. "I stopped before I said spanking."

"There was no way she couldn't guess how that sentence would end. Knowing that woman, she might have pictured something worse, though." She'd looked like a kid in a candy store, and Carter knew she'd run off to talk about what happened to the gaggle of little old ladies she played cards and drank with, calling it tea like it was something perfectly proper.

The good thing about it was that every time Wyatt did something like that, business went up for the next couple of days. They'd all find a reason to come visit to see if he'd say something outrageous again.

"I've been much better."

"Yes, you have." Carter knew he sounded slightly patronizing, but he wasn't that mad. Just a little frustrated. What happened to privacy? "Now, tell me what you know about my *date*?"

Wyatt must have heard the question in Carter's voice because his head popped up and he nodded excitedly. "Oh, it's a date. He's really excited and told Garrett about the plans. I'm not supposed to know, but I was—well, you don't need to know that part, but we'll just say I was close to the phone when they were talking, so I heard."

Whatever Wyatt had been doing was naughty, if the excitement in his eyes was any clue. "You're right; I don't need to know that part. Is it fancy? I was just going to wear something work-casual, but is that wrong?"

Clothes were the hardest part of a date. Trying to navigate the sea of options to figure out how "him" he could actually be was frustrating. He'd spent an hour picking out his clothes that morning, and if he had to change, he'd go insane.

Wyatt thought about it for a moment and sat up straighter to try to see over the counter. "What are you wearing?"

Carter came around the counter and stood there awkwardly. He'd picked out his most neutral black slacks that were technically from the women's section, but not so obvious most people would notice, and a button-down men's white shirt that was a little roomy on him. He'd look almost masculine, if it weren't for his subtle makeup, and his dirty blond hair that was a little longer than most men wore.

"Well, you look boring, but it will work." Wyatt frowned, disappointed. "Why didn't you wear your new skirt, or the dress you got a few weeks ago?"

Carter thought that was obvious. "Because I kind of want there to be a second date. I'm not going to do that to him." He liked Grant. The gruff exterior camouflaged a sweet guy who'd been nothing but nice and open-minded.

Wyatt cocked his head and looked at him like he was daft. "Why would that matter? The first time you guys met, you were wearing the sundress." Wyatt bounced up from the chair, making Carter wonder for a moment if something was wrong. "Oh, the sundress, wear that one again!"

"We were at a family get-together. That's different." Carter had learned that the hard way. No matter what you were wearing when you met or what you put on a profile, there was a very different standard when they were taking you out in public.

He looked down at his clothes. "And let's get real, it's not a total butch outfit. I'm probably pushing it as it is. Do you think the shoes are too much?"

They were women's flats. The pants went down far enough

he thought most people couldn't tell, but some men were into shoes and would notice right away. He had a feeling Grant wasn't one of those men. Grant was always dressed presentably, just in a casual, almost straight-guy way. The man couldn't even be called metrosexual, or any of those other trendy names straight guys got when they could show up well-manicured and fashionably dressed to an event.

As far as he could tell, the man only owned one suit, one T-shirt, and one pair of jeans, or else he wore the same thing over and over. Not that Carter had an issue with it; it was just cute. Wyatt snorted. "Like he's going to be looking at your feet. Your ass looks great in those pants. That's all he'll notice."

Carter laughed. "That might be in your imagination. He flirts a little, yes, but nothing that screams he's dying to get into my pants—or up my skirt."

"Then you haven't been paying enough attention because —oh, not supposed to talk about the phone call. Just ignore that." Wyatt looked sheepish. "I'm not supposed to talk about it."

"Will you get punished if you do?" Carter smirked.

"No, even worse, he'll be disappointed in me and that sucks. Also, disappointment does not lead to good sex." He slouched back in the chair. "And Master is great at—"

"TMI. We've had this discussion."

Wyatt smiled; it was innocent and wicked all at the same time. "But you don't mean it. You love my stories."

"Not when I have to see the man all the time and I'm possibly dating his brother. That makes it weird." Carter shook his head. Very weird.

"That's no fun. When did that become the rule?" Wyatt seemed honestly frustrated with the new no-TMI standard.

"When I had to sit down at dinner with the man who spanked you the night before, and I knew all the details. 'Pass the rolls and by the way, Wyatt said you're great in bed' is kind of strange."

"That's terrible. Does it mean I don't get to hear what happens on your date?" Wyatt looked eager for the date, but disappointed he might not get enough information.

"I'm not sure there will be much to tell. The last couple of dates I've been on ended early, and a couple of them ended before dinner was over." Carter even had a standby meal picked out; he'd looked over the Chinese takeout menu earlier and knew what he was going to order if it all went to pieces. Grant was polite enough Carter knew he probably wouldn't ditch him before dinner even started, but he wasn't going to plan on a night of wild, hot sex.

Wyatt shook his head and rolled his eyes like Carter was deliberately missing the point. "I'm going to say I told you so." Letting out a grin, he teased in a sing-song voice, "And then I'll get details as a reward."

"Who said anything about a reward?" Carter wasn't falling for that.

Wyatt's expression turned dreamy, like he was remembering something good. "Master says good subs get nice rewards."

Holding back a laugh, Carter leaned back against the counter. "First, I'm not required to follow any of your master's rules. Second, you're crazy."

"I'm not crazy. Grant is totally into you."

Carter knew his expression was skeptical, but he didn't believe his excitable friend. "How would you know?"

"Not going to tell because I'm trying to be a good boy for my master." Wyatt dug into his pocket to find his phone. "And speaking of my master, I have to go. I'm supposed to be at his office in just a few minutes."

In the weeks since Wyatt first started seeing Garrett, Carter had noticed a significant change in his friend. Being around so many people who understood the BDSM lifestyle and supported what he wanted had made a huge difference in Wyatt's confidence. No longer worried about Garrett's family and co-workers, Wyatt bounced out of the store, excited to see his master.

Carter might not have wanted a full-time master like Wyatt did, but he was a little jealous of the bond the two had. He wanted something like that. Not the kneeling and constant submission part, but the closeness and having someone who understood.

His phone calls with Grant had him thinking he might have found it. But there were still nagging voices in the back of his head that made him question things. Wyatt called him at random times just to chat, but most guys he knew didn't. Grant was another anomaly with the texting and phone calls, but maybe it did mean something more.

Grant had picked up the habit of calling him randomly throughout the week. At first, Carter hadn't been sure what to make of it. The initial conversations had been awkward and stilted, at least on his side. Grant never ran out of things to say and completely ignored how uncomfortable Carter's responses were. But now, he didn't even think about it when Grant called. They would simply chat and tell stories about their day. It was nice.

But was it flirting?

Did it mean something?

That was the part Carter wasn't sure about. He'd gotten so many mixed signals from guys and had been on so many terrible dates that he was more than gun-shy, he was paranoid. He thought recognizing it was a good step. It didn't make the crazy any less nuts, though.

Mindlessly walking through closing up the store, Carter couldn't help but imagine what might happen. The romantic evening...the romantic night...the hot, steamy, melt-your-panties kind of night. That thought was like a bucket of cold water on his fantasies.

He'd been wearing a dress the first time they met, and it hadn't stopped Grant from flirting and teasing most of the afternoon. So Carter wearing *other things* shouldn't be a deal breaker for the sexy Dom. Could it?

There hadn't been a good way to ask it, or at least, not one he'd found.

Great that you could call...what's your opinion on not-so-masculine undergarments?

Carter could almost hear the crickets on the other end of the phone, or worse, the horrified reaction where Grant would try to explain he thought they were just friends. Grant was sweet and wouldn't do anything to make Carter uncomfortable on purpose, but the not knowing was going to make him nuts.

Just because Grant's family was open-minded and accepting of their own preferences didn't mean that Grant would find Carter's intriguing. Sure, having a family where everyone was into BDSM in some form or fashion should make him more tolerant of others. However, tolerant didn't mean that the things Carter liked would turn him on, too.

Looking around, making sure everything was put away and locked up for the night, Carter headed for the front door. After double-checking to make sure it was locked, Carter went to his car. He probably should have had Grant meet him at work, but that felt too much like friends meeting—and no matter what he told Wyatt, he was hoping it was a date.

The ride home only took around twenty minutes, but it was about fifteen more than his nerves could take. By the time he'd parked and walked in the door, he thought he was going to need a drink to function. However, he was a giggly, flirty drunk, so that might not be the best idea.

Sober and queasy it was.

Heading back to his room, Carter looked over the house to make sure everything was perfect. He usually kept things fairly neat, but little things were always getting away from him; a pair of heels under the couch, sandals in the kitchen, flats in the hallway for some reason...okay, shoes got away from him. Everything else was much easier to keep control over.

Dragging the last-minute stragglers, who he swore escaped on their own, he went back to his closet. Carter looked at the full-length mirror that hung on the inside of the closet door. He didn't look bad. Sure, the shirt was looser than most men would wear it, but nothing too obvious. And he felt okay about the outfit. It wasn't so masculine that he was hiding. It was a good compromise kind of outfit.

He had several, but this was one of his favorites. The shoes were pushing it. He couldn't help himself with that. The only other option he'd considered was a pair of combat-style boots that could go either way, but didn't seem like a good choice in case they went to a nice restaurant.

He forced himself to smile in the mirror. "It's going to be fine. He's a nice guy."

Not sure if he was lying or not, he turned away from the mirror. Heading into the bathroom, he had to stop himself from reaching for his makeup. Running his fingers through his hair, his fingers itched to play and get creative. He liked cosmetics. They'd always made him feel beautiful, not just handsome. It was like the grown-up version of coloring and getting to play with paints. It was fun.

He had to admit he was attractive even when he was looking his most masculine, but that just wasn't how he saw himself. He liked the way his eyes flashed when they were outlined with a little mascara and some eyeshadow. He liked the way his lips looked highlighted with a little bit of gloss. He just wished other people did as well.

Would Grant?

Forcing himself out of the bathroom, Carter headed for the kitchen. He had a few more minutes to kill before Grant would be over; maybe the drink would be a good idea. Just a little one. Not enough to make him want to climb all over the sexy tank of a man, but enough to settle his nerves.

He didn't even get to the kitchen before the doorbell rang. Cursing Grant's punctuality, Carter turned and went to the front door. Opening it, he smiled, but before he could say anything, Grant beat him to it.

Grant was leaning against the door, filling the frame completely. Seeing how big Grant was always sent a shiver down Carter's back. Carter might not be that tall for a man, but Grant always seemed to tower over him. It wasn't just the few inches in height; his broad shoulders and whole demeanor made him seem even bigger.

Grant's short hair always seemed like it needed a brush to Carter, although he couldn't figure out why. Most men with short hair looked neat even if they didn't do anything with it, but Grant had a perpetually disheveled look that Carter thought was sexy. Maybe it was the attitude or the muscles, but nothing Grant did ever looked typical. His shirts always fit too well, T-shirts stretching across his broad, muscular chest. The tattoo peeking out of the short sleeve plastered to Grant's arm made you think bouncer or boxer, not insurance agent. Maybe if more people realized the tattoo was his family's names, they'd understand him more.

"I heard from a chatty little birdie that he thought your outfit was boring." Grant's deep voice would have seemed menacing if it weren't for the laughter and teasing glint in his eyes. Grant's eyes scanned down Carter's body, and for a moment he felt almost naked. It had his dick sitting up to take notice. "I'm not sure that's how I would describe it, but I'll admit I was hoping you were going to wear something pretty for me."

Carter knew he was standing there like an idiot, mouth hanging open in shock like it was some kind of sitcom moment. He just couldn't help it. Out of all the things he'd expected, the flirting and clear indication Grant didn't mind his usual outfits wasn't one of them.

Wyatt needed to keep his mouth shut.

Carter managed to find his voice. "Little tattletale."

Grant threw his head back and laughed, then leaned in, giving a startled Carter a peck on the cheek. "We still have a few minutes before we have to leave for dinner. How about you put on something you really wanted to wear for me?"

The spot where Grant kissed him tingled, and the simple act short-circuited Carter's brain. "Um...okay?"

"If you'd like, I can make it an order." Grant's words were deep, and Carter could almost feel the arousal pulsing off him. Most of the time, he could forget that Grant was a Dom, but sometimes he'd make a comment that would have Carter melting.

This was one of those times.

"Um..." Having no idea what to say or how to get his brain to work, he stepped back from the door so Grant could come in. The only thing his brain could come up with was a surprising realization that it probably was a date, after all.

2

GRANT

Watching his beautiful little obsession standing there in astonishment had Grant desperate to pull him into his arms. Knowing that would be pushing things, Grant kept his hands to himself, but it was harder than he thought it would be.

Stepping inside, he closed the door behind him. Even though Carter was still waiting there in shock, it looked like he'd been trying to invite Grant in. Fighting off a grin that might have been misconstrued, Grant looked down Carter's body again. "I like the shoes."

That made Carter blink. "Um, thanks."

He was talking; that was a start. Grant leaned back against the door, trying to appear casual. "I thought you might have put on that sundress for me, but the little birdie said you have something even sexier."

"The little birdie has a big mouth." Carter frowned, but he didn't seem upset with Grant. Wyatt, on the other hand, was probably toast the next time Carter saw him.

Grant grinned. "You can't kill him or Garrett would be upset."

Carter snorted. "How about I leave him alive but just make him suffer?"

"I've got a better idea; how about we let Garrett know that he told you I'd called and talked to Garrett about you?"

Carter's mouth fell open again. "He told you?"

Laughing, Grant's eyes sparkled. "No, but you just did."

A bark of laughter escaped before Carter frowned. "I think that's cheating."

"He tattled first. I'm just getting even. It's what you do with family."

Carter shook his head like the whole concept was foreign. "Your family always makes me feel like I've tumbled down the rabbit hole."

He shrugged. "You get used to it."

Cocking his hip and lifting one eyebrow, Carter let his skepticism show. "That does not make me feel better."

"I know what will make you feel better," Grant teased.

Carter looked suspicious. "What?"

Grant made his voice even lower just to watch Carter shiver. "Putting on something special for me."

Carter's mouth tensed up, and Grant could see thoughts racing through his head. Finally, Carter popped one hip out and folded his arms across his chest. "For you, huh?"

"For me—because you have to know how fabulous you looked in that sundress. And I have it on good authority you were just as hot in your new skirt. Don't you want to show me how incredible you looked?" Grant knew he was laying on the dress-sexy-for-me routine fairly thick. While he would have loved anything Carter wore, he knew Carter was worried about it. He would have realized it without Wyatt's help, but it was nice to know his suspicions were correct.

Carter couldn't decide how to answer. His mouth opened and closed several times until he finally shook his head and stalked off toward the back of the house. Hoping he wasn't pushing his luck, or Carter's patience, he called out teasingly, "I thought you knew you were supposed to look sexy for your boyfriend on a date. I dressed up for you."

Something crashed down the hall, and Grant was worried for a minute until he started hearing Carter's creative cursing coming from what he thought was his bedroom. Between his colorful uses of the word fuck, Grant caught that Carter had walked into his dresser and that he thought Grant should be creatively tortured. Wyatt, too.

Deciding that letting Carter cool down was probably a better option than the naughty comebacks that came to mind, Grant kept his mouth shut. Grant was pleased that even though Carter was frustrated with him, he never disagreed with the date comment, or the boyfriend one.

Wandering into the living room and being nosy, he'd been prepared to wait for a while, but Carter came back out within a few minutes. This time he looked more like himself, or at least, that's how it felt to Grant. The slim skirt went down to his ankles, hugging his frame beautifully, and there was something dark around his eyes that highlighted how stunning he already looked. Grant couldn't wait to see how the skirt looked from the back.

The little birdie might have dropped a hint about that, too.

Carter had kept the white shirt but changed out the shoes he'd been wearing for low-heeled boots. Grant knew they probably had a name, and he made a note to himself to look it up. He wasn't much for clothes, but Carter was, so that made it important to him.

Letting out a low whistle, Grant watched Carter blush as some of his residual anger faded. Carter's stance relaxed and his eyes lit up. His sweet man looked amazing. "You look sexy. You going to give me a turn, or do I have to wait until I follow you out?"

Shaking his head at Grant like he'd been a naughty kid, Carter gave him another sassy look and turned slowly. Once his back was to Grant, he looked over one shoulder and smirked. Carter knew exactly how incredible his ass looked.

Widening his stance, Grant slid his hands into his pockets to frame his cock and gave Carter an appreciative glance. Licking his lips, Grant looked back up to Carter's face. He made his desire obvious. It would have been too much for any other first date; he was smart enough to realize that. However, Grant wanted Carter to know how much he wanted him, so that there would be no misunderstandings and no second-guessing.

Carter finished turning around and did something with the way he stood. All of a sudden, he wasn't just long and lean, he was curvy and slinky—and somehow, knowing that there was a cock under all that sexy packaging made Grant hard and needy.

He'd always liked more feminine guys. However, they usually took one look at him and headed in the opposite direction. Carter must have seen Grant's arousal go from interested and fun to serious and desperate, because his blush came back and he straightened up.

Grant wasn't sure why Carter was always so surprised when he responded to the pretty man's flirting, but he was going to do his best to help Carter get used to it. Carter seemed to be pushing aside his embarrassment because he gave Grant a stern look. "I'm assuming this will do? Can we go to dinner now?"

"Oh, yes, beautiful. It will do." Grant hammed it up a little, wiggling his eyebrows like a lecherous cartoon character, and had Carter rolling his eyes again.

"Let's go. Before I decide I can't take you in public with all that teasing." Carter headed for the door, letting Grant hang back to admire his ass.

"Who said I was teasing?" Grant let his voice go deep and needy again. Carter's little shiver made his ass twitch, and Grant's mouth started watering. Maybe he could convince Carter to just stay in. No—he pushed the fantasy away immediately. Carter needed to see that Grant wasn't going to hide him.

Carter seemed at a loss for words, because he kept quiet and just shook his head as they walked out the door. Locking up the house, Carter turned to Grant. "Would you hold the keys? Skirts and dresses never have enough pockets."

"Sure." Holding out his hand, Grant took the keys. "What about a purse?" Grant was serious, but Carter narrowed his eyes like he was expecting more to the comment.

When Grant just kept looking at him questioningly, Carter shrugged and relaxed. "Never got into them. Keeping track of a little bag seems like a hassle."

Grant nodded, filing the information away. "Makes sense."

Carter kept watching Grant as they walked down off the porch and headed for the car. Grant felt a little like a bug under a microscope. Carter didn't seem to know what to make of him. Grant thought he'd been obvious in the house, but maybe not.

Opening the door for his date, Grant gave him a smile and a wink as he sat down. Before Carter could grab the seat belt, Grant had it and was leaning in the car, reaching across Carter's body. The beautiful man's eyes heated up, but Grant wasn't sure if he was turned on or frustrated.

He had that effect on lots of people.

"Is this a Dom thing, or did you think I couldn't figure it out?" Carter's voice volleyed between skepticism and sarcasm. Grant thought it was sexy.

He let his voice drop and his gaze wander down Carter's body as he straightened up. "Neither, although the Dom in me likes seeing you restrained. I just wanted an excuse to get close to you." Then, with a wink, he closed the door and walked around to the driver's side.

Thoroughly enjoying making Carter nuts, Grant climbed in the car with a smile. Trying to look innocent, he turned to Carter. "Steak sound good to you?"

Carter looked like he wanted to throw something at Grant. "Yes." Then, through clenched teeth, he managed to keep going. "Sounds delicious, thanks."

And because he just had to, Grant pushed it a little further. "Golden Corral has two-for-one tonight, so it'll be a good deal."

"He needs to keep his mouth shut!" Carter exploded in frustration, throwing his hands up in the air.

When Wyatt told Grant the story about how Carter's last date said he was going to take Carter to get steak for dinner but ended up taking him to the Golden Corral instead, he'd found it both humorous and sad at the same time.

Carter was such a sweet guy he should have had loads of men lining up to date him. Even though he felt bad that Carter had such a hard time, it didn't mean he wasn't going to tease him about it a little. It was too good a story for that, and Carter's reactions were so much fun.

Laughing, Grant leaned over and gave him another kiss on the cheek, dodging the hand that came up to smack him. "I'm teasing. I thought Italian sounded good."

Carter leaned back in the seat and sighed. "Sounds great. He's told you everything, hasn't he?"

Starting the car and backing out of the driveway, Grant headed for his favorite restaurant. "Yes. I'm sorry you've had such bad luck and shitty dates, but, and this might make me a bad guy, I'm glad you're still single."

Blushing lightly, Carter ignored this comment, which just made Grant want to push things further. Carter straightened up in the seat and looked forward out the windshield. "Did you have anything else planned after dinner? You didn't say on the phone."

He hadn't said because he hadn't been sure what they should do when he'd first asked. Grant had needed time to consult with the chatty bird first. "Yes."

Carter sighed again. "Yes, you have something else planned?"

"Yes." Grant grinned.

"You like making me insane." Carter said it like it was a statement and not a question, but Grant felt the need to answer him anyway.

"Yes." Then he gave Carter a wink. "I'm going to have fun making you crazy other ways, too."

The skeptical look was starting to fade, and Carter shifted in his seat. Grant wondered what was going through his head. Carter didn't give him any hints, though, he simply looked forward and ignored Grant's teasing.

If it weren't for the little blushes and stunned silences, Grant might have thought he'd upset his date. He was betting Carter wasn't sure how to handle someone flirting with him. Wyatt had made it clear Carter hadn't had the easiest time dating. Wanting someone more dominant and who could accept his desire for more feminine things was hard.

Grant wished Carter had been willing to go to the club years ago. Bound and Controlled, his favorite BDSM club in D.C., would have been the perfect place for Carter to have found more open-minded people. Wyatt said he'd been trying to get Carter to go for years, but his friend always resisted. Grant knew the idea of going to a club like that would have been intimidating if you didn't know how welcoming the owners were. Having friends and getting to know people with similar interests in a D/s lifestyle would have been good for Carter, though.

The fact that they would have also met sooner would have

been a bonus. There weren't too many subs who were like Carter, and he wouldn't have missed the sexy man if he'd shown up. Especially if he'd shown up wearing something flirty and feminine.

"I shouldn't ask, but I'm going to anyway." Carter sounded resigned to whatever answer he expected. "What were you thinking? The look on your face..."

Deciding to answer honestly, even if Carter might not really want to know, Grant grinned. "I was wishing you'd gone up to the club before, so we could have met sooner. Then I thought about what kind of outfit you might have worn..."

"You would have...you think I would have worn...but..." Carter kept stopping, never quite finishing his sentences, but Grant thought he could guess some of what he was thinking.

"I would have stalked you around the club and made a complete nuisance out of myself to get you to notice me. And I can picture you dressed up in so many naughty things for the club." He growled the words out, making sure Carter knew just how much he enjoyed the idea. "When we all go up, are you going to let me pick something out for you to wear? I bet you have some naughty things hidden in your bedroom, don't you?"

Grant wasn't kidding. Carter would look incredible in something tempting and feminine. If the man enjoyed skirts and dresses, Grant would bet almost anything he had some sexy lingerie hiding in a drawer somewhere. Would he let Grant dress him up for the club?

Glancing over, he saw Carter was giving him that shocked fish face again. Pulling up to a stoplight, he debated reaching over to close Carter's mouth, but he figured it might be pushing it. "I'm not sure why you're so shocked. Most Doms like dressing up their subs. You might not be mine yet, but the fantasy's hot."

Carter was quiet for a moment before he spoke. "You say things, and I have no idea how to respond."

"You wanted to know what I was thinking. I'm not hiding that I'm interested in you. If you're not into me the same way, that's a different conversation." Grant tried to appear calm, but it was hard. Even knowing Carter was interested in him didn't make it any less stressful. There was still a possibility that he wasn't ready to take the chance and admit it.

"Most guys aren't comfortable with who I am." Carter took a breath and kept going. "I've had time to figure things out for myself, but men usually want someone who's clearly masculine, even if they're a twink, or clearly feminine. I'm kind of in the middle, and that makes them unsure."

"I like men. I'm gay, that's no secret, but I've always been drawn to more feminine guys. I have no issue with the skirts or anything else that interests you." Grant would have had more questions, but he'd thoroughly drilled Wyatt about Carter's preferences.

That was something he wasn't going to tattle on the little birdie about.

Carter nodded and was quiet for the rest of the drive to the restaurant. Grant figured he was trying to sort things out, so he didn't push. He knew he was giving Carter a lot to process. Just the fact that he hadn't put up a fuss about the clothes was more than Grant had been expecting.

Little Italy was one of his favorite restaurants. His mouth started watering as soon as he parked near the building. Carter didn't seem to mind his choice. He glanced over and gave Grant a little smile. "At least it's not a buffet restaurant."

Grant laughed as he climbed out of the car. Carter didn't wait for him to come around and open the door, and that was all right with him. He didn't need to do that kind of stuff, and he didn't want a full-time submissive. But from the look on Carter's face, he'd been curious if Grant was going to say something.

Not yet. There were so many other things to drive Carter insane about.

Their reservations were ready when they walked in, so they were taken right to their table. "Your waiter will be with you in just a moment."

"Thank you." Grant gave the hostess a quick smile as she started to walk away after giving them their menus and the typical spiel.

Their service was one of the reasons he'd chosen this restaurant. Located right on the edge of the more conservative part of town and the trendier district, it had an upscale feel but none of the snobbery you would expect. It would take a lot to make one of their employees blink, much less be surprised at a skirt.

Carter seemed to know he looked fabulous, but that didn't mean he thought everyone else would appreciate his clothing choices. Grant was glad to see that when he realized the server wasn't surprised at all, his stress seemed to fade.

Hopefully, the rest of their date would go just as smoothly.

3

CARTER

I t was the strangest date he'd ever been on.

No drama that he wasn't dressed right to be taken out in public, well, not the typical drama. Grant's aren't-you-going-to-look-sexy-for-me pushiness wasn't the normal way his dates usually went. They'd gone to a real restaurant. And Grant really didn't seem to mind what Carter wanted to wear at all. He even liked the skirt.

He *more* than liked the skirt.

Grant thought he was desirable. He even wanted to take Carter to the club dressed up in something erotic. The look on his face let Carter know exactly what kinds of naughty things he was imagining, and it wasn't typical sub gear.

Carter wasn't sure what to make of it. He was tempted to look around for the hidden cameras that had to be following them. It couldn't be real—but it was. Grant was perfect. Well, perfect except the man had no subtlety when it came to flirting. Carter didn't mind, though.

It was nice to be wanted for who he really was. He just wasn't used to it. As they'd ordered and started eating, the conversation became more natural and it didn't feel so strange. Grant pulled back on the outrageous comments, talking about work and asking questions about Carter's shop.

Maybe it was all the time they'd spent talking on the phone and hanging out at the family events Carter had been invited to. Grant wasn't new; it was just the idea that he actually liked Carter that would take some getting used to.

By the time they finished dinner and were heading back to the car, Carter was feeling more confident. The usual sci-fi-sized moths that would try to beat their way out of his body were typical first date butterflies. It was nice.

Grant teased him through dinner that he wasn't going to tell what they were going to do next—unless sufficiently bribed by Carter. Carter just hadn't been exactly sure what Grant had meant, so he'd kept his mouth shut. The words had been teasing, but the desire coming from Grant had been anything but sweet.

What had he been picturing?

Carter knew he couldn't ask without Grant being very forthcoming about exactly what was on his mind. Carter was torn. He couldn't decide if that was a good thing or not. He liked not having to speculate about Grant's interest in him, but he didn't know enough about what the Dom liked to guess at how he would respond.

How much of a Dom was Grant?

No one in the family had said he was looking for a lifestyle relationship, and Carter was reasonably sure that information would have been freely offered. They didn't believe in hiding anything in their family. He hadn't been over that many times, but they'd all been very open and welcoming.

It would take some getting used to.

His own family hadn't bothered to hide what they thought of Carter's choices. Watching how differently another family handled things was...hard. Carter loved the way Garrett's family supported Wyatt. He just wasn't used to it. It gave him a peek at what his own family could have been like if they'd been more accepting.

Mostly, he was glad Wyatt had found someone who loved him and a place he fit in. No one thought he was odd for wanting to kneel or for needing more from Garrett than a typical boyfriend would. They'd all gone out of their way to show him he could be himself.

They'd also gone out of their way to show Carter he could be himself.

"Now are you going to tell me?" As they were pulling out of the parking lot and heading toward downtown, Carter was anxious to know what else Grant had planned.

"Possibly. I still haven't been bribed, though." Grant's tone was teasing, but the look on his face was pure desire.

He shouldn't play along. He was either going to encourage the crazy, or he was going to be embarrassed when he guessed wrong. Carter was completely out of his depth. He'd had some hookups and met a few guys, but nobody like Grant.

Deciding that looking at Grant's reaction would be too stressful, he looked out the side window, studying the signs and buildings as they drove by. "How about a kiss?"

Grant snorted. "Unless I really fuck up tonight, I thought that was already just about guaranteed on a first date. I think I'm going to need something a little more tempting."

Carter coughed to cover his laugh. The offense in Grant's voice was the funniest thing he'd ever heard. Glancing over at Grant, he tried not to smile. "Guaranteed, huh?"

"We've talked a lot. I haven't sent any dick pics or anything offensive. I took you to a nice restaurant, and I have something else fun planned, too. Oh, yeah, I get a kiss goodnight. It's in the bag and you know it." Grant grinned and looked incredibly pleased with himself. Coming from a man who looked like the leader of a motorcycle gang, it was an odd combination when talking about a kiss.

"I'm not sure about that. For argument's sake, I'll concede the issue." Ignoring the wicked grin coming from Grant, Carter glanced out the window again. He was already encouraging the crazy, but how much more was he going to play along? It'd been so long since someone was interested in him that even with Grant's sledgehammer approach to flirting, he still questioned it.

Grant was quiet while Carter's mind worked through the options. He didn't automatically give Carter an out, but they'd driven around the same section of downtown three times, and Carter knew he was running out of time. If he wanted to play, he would have to step up, or Grant was going to let him out of it just by parking the car.

"How about I let you pick out what I wear when we go up to the club?" Carter held his breath and waited to see what Grant would say. It was a ridiculously over-the-top bribe, but he wanted Grant to know he was interested but reserved, not blowing him off. And he'd already promised Wyatt he'd go, so he might as well let someone dress him who knew what would be appropriate and sexy.

Grant growled under his breath and actually reached down to adjust his cock. Then he looked over at Carter with a naughty, satisfied grin. "I like that. You know how to bribe a man."

Carter knew he was blushing again, so he looked out the window, trying to pretend he wasn't embarrassed. "So where are we going?"

"I thought we could do the night market. I haven't had a chance to go there in ages, and I heard that you haven't ever gone." Grant's voice was pleased, like his team had just made a touchdown.

"Oh." That sounded promising. Even though he'd been in Richmond quite a while, he hadn't gone to the farmer's market that was held in the summer evenings. Most of the time he was either busy with work or so tired he'd just wanted to go home and curl up. "That should be fun."

"And the website said they even have a craft market and some antique vendors there tonight, so I thought it could be interesting to see what else is out there." Now Grant sounded a little less sure of himself.

"That's a great idea. I like seeing the different things other businesses find. I've even made some good contacts at similar events. Thank you for thinking of it." Glancing over at Grant, Carter could see the smug expression back on Grant's face. The Dom loved being right.

Needing to get back at him just a little, Carter returned to looking out the windshield. "Are you ready to stop driving around in circles now and actually park?"

Grant laughed. "I had to make sure I got my bribe."

"Would you have kept driving around until I gave in?" Carter shouldn't have asked; he already knew the answer.

"Of course, or unless you said you didn't want to play." Carter saw Grant's casual shrug out of the corner of his eye.

Not sure what to say, Carter just shook his head again. Grant was going to make him batty. Thankfully, they parked before he could figure out how to respond. As they got out of the car, Grant surprised him by taking his hand. The skirt and everything, and Grant still didn't mind.

As they walked down the street and turned into the local park, Carter could see the stalls and booths that were set up. There were lots of traditional fruit and vegetable vendors, but there were also flowers and crafts and a variety of other things.

Meandering through the crowded walkways, Grant showed him some pictures he liked by a local artist, and Carter pointed out some antique vendors that were a few rows over. When

Grant dragged him over to a booth selling brownies and cookies, Carter had to laugh.

"These are my favorites. They look like regular chocolate chip cookies, but they have a brownie inside." Grant looked like a kid on Christmas morning. "I can either only get a couple to eat now, or enough that Brent can steal a couple when he comes over. He's a sneaky bastard and can smell cookies no matter how well you've hidden them."

He was so serious that Carter coughed to cover a laugh. Oh, the problems when you had a large family that didn't hate you. "I'll keep that in mind. How many are you going to get?"

Carter hadn't thought it was a difficult question, but Grant took it very seriously. After a quick internal debate, he looked back at Carter. "A couple for us now, but can I leave the rest at your house so they won't get stolen? The last time I bought some, Brent came over the next day and they were gone. I didn't even see him steal them. I went to get something out of the bedroom, and he and the cookies vanished."

It had to be the funniest thing Carter had ever heard, but he was trying to take it seriously because Grant was clearly concerned. "Yes. You can keep them at my house. I'll even keep them away from Wyatt if he comes over."

"Yeah, he can't keep a secret." Grant nodded seriously, and then turned to the vendor who was nearly dying while trying to be professional. "Two dozen, please."

After getting their treats and promising one more time that he could keep them safe, they set off toward the other side of the park where the furniture and used items were being sold. He recognized a few other shop owners from around the area and stopped to say hello.

The ones he'd met before were used to his more colorful personality, so they didn't even blink at the skirt, but Grant made them a little more cautious. Not because he was introducing himself as Carter's boyfriend, which Carter still wasn't how to take, but because even in his work clothes, he still looked out of place.

Bikers did not buy antiques or date men in more feminine clothing, evidently.

Carter finally started introducing Grant by bringing up Grant's business first, then letting Grant butt in to say they were together. Hearing the ties to a well-known local business seemed to smooth things over faster. Grant seemed used to the hesitation from the other owners, because as they left one very skittish older woman who was selling antique clothing, Grant leaned down to whisper in his ear, "That's why Garrett or someone else does most of the Chamber of Commerce stuff or the public face of the business. I make people nervous."

"I don't see why. I knew right away you were sweet." Carter wanted to add "and a terrible tease," but he thought that might get them off track.

Grant smiled down at him and squeezed his hand. "I liked that you weren't hesitant about spending time with me."

Carter held off on pointing out that they'd met at a family barbecue so he hadn't been worried about much going wrong, but Grant was so pleased Carter didn't want to burst his bubble. By the time they finished browsing around, Carter had some good ideas for the shop and a full stomach from all the cookies they'd eaten. As they wandered back to Grant's car, Carter smiled. "I had fun. This was a good idea."

Getting a chance to talk to Grant and get to know him in a casual environment had been a much better choice than a movie or anything like that. Even the few off looks they'd been given hadn't dampened his enthusiasm for the evening. The only thing that was pulling at him were the unanswered questions he still had but wasn't ready to ask—and wasn't sure how to bring up.

As they drove back toward Carter's house, Grant looked over and gave him a wicked grin. "You know I'm going to make everyone look at schedules tomorrow to figure out when we can go up to the club."

Carter barked out a laugh. "I had a feeling you were going to do that." He'd have been very surprised if that wasn't top on Grant's to-do list.

"You still going to let me dress you up?" Grant's gaze was heated, and Carter could feel the arousal radiating from him. How much did the idea of picking out his clothes appeal to the Dom?

"Yes. I won't back out." Even though he probably should. "I just want to make sure I won't look ridiculous or anything. I don't want to embarrass Wyatt or your family."

Imagining going up there with everyone made him queasy, but he wasn't going to change his mind. When Wyatt had initially brought up going a few years ago, he'd thought the hardest part would be all the strangers. Now it was going to be all the people that he knew.

"You are going to look incredible. Now, you know you're going to have to show me what you have before we go so I can pick it out. I don't want to wait until the last minute, in case I need to buy you something else." Grant's eyes lit up and Carter wasn't sure what turned his boyfriend on more, buying something new for him to wear or going through his lingerie drawer.

"I never said you could buy me something." That seemed too intimate, even though they *were* talking about going to a BDSM club.

"That's just understood as acceptable boyfriend behavior when he's a Dom." Grant nodded like the discussion was done and the issue settled.

"Hmm, we'll see about that." He had a feeling he would have

to learn to pick his battles with the train that was Grant, or he'd end up getting flattened.

Did he mind Grant buying him something?

The first thing that came to Carter's mind was yes, but he couldn't decide why. Grant was going to be looking through his lingerie. Why would buying something matter? Maybe it was because it felt more real...more nerve-racking.

If Grant bought him something, especially something that was sexy and feminine, it would mean that he really understood Carter. The idea was frightening—and that made him feel stupid. Just because he hadn't found a man who understood and supported what he liked didn't mean there was anything wrong with finding one who did.

He'd wanted a unicorn, but now that he had one, he was thinking about running in the opposite direction—that wasn't the most reasonable behavior. If it were something else besides lingerie, he wouldn't have thought about it. Flowers, fine. Dinner out, fine. He was going to have to do some thinking.

Carter hadn't even realized they'd pulled up into his driveway until Grant turned off the engine. He turned to Grant awkwardly and was relieved when the Dom didn't seem to care that his mind had wandered.

Grant smiled and gave him a knowing look before leaning back against the door. "I had fun tonight. Thank you for going out with me."

It was sweet and polite. Carter was immediately suspicious. "I had a good time. Dinner was wonderful, and the market was a great idea."

Grant's chest puffed up. "I know." His grin took on a serious note. "Don't forget to mention that when my mother asks."

What?

"Your mother?" Carter thought he had to have misunderstood something.

"With everyone finding 'Mr. Right' there's only so long she's going to stay traveling. We've got a bet going about how much longer it will be. I'm thinking about a week, but Brent thinks another three because she should be traveling for several more weeks. Bryce, on the other hand, is saying two weeks, and he was very confident. I think he's cheated somehow, but I can't prove it. Garrett refused to guess because he said she was like a ghost and talking about her could conjure her. He's been hanging around Calen too much." Grant frowned and shook his head. "Bryce is the sneaky one. You have to be careful, because he looked too innocent."

Carter was still reeling from the comment about Grant's mother, and was having a hard time catching up. "But your mother?"

Grant nodded seriously. "Will grill you to see if I behaved myself."

"Huh?"

The Dom looked slightly sheepish but waved his hand like it was nothing. "Don't worry about that part. You can just tell her I took you out to dinner and we walked around the night market, and that I was a perfect gentleman."

Oh, there was a story there. Carter wondered if Wyatt had heard it yet.

If he hadn't, it wouldn't be hard to figure out. The brothers were always trying to tattle on each other, and someone would be glad to fill Wyatt in on the family gossip. Carter nodded reluctantly. "Sure. I'm just not supposed to mention the lingerie stuff or the fact that you thought you'd earned a good night kiss?"

Seriously considering the question, Grant nodded. "Probably not, just to be on the safe side."

What had the Dom done?

"Okay. I won't, but you're going to owe me." He wasn't sure if he was teasing or not, but from what Carter had learned of Grant's family, if he wanted to fit in he was going to have to learn to fight dirty.

Grant smiled wickedly, leaning closer. "What am I going to owe you?"

"You'll find out." To keep from having to decide what to say, Carter gave him a haughty look and opened the door.

Laughing, Grant climbed out of the car and went around to walk Carter to the door. Carter needed to get his head wrapped around everything before he invited Grant in, but he was hoping that wouldn't be an issue.

Grant seemed to be one step ahead of him because the Dom stopped at the bottom of the steps and didn't make any attempt to go in. "Do you want to go out on Friday or maybe stay in and relax?"

"Staying in sounds perfect." Carter took a deep breath and looked at Grant. "How about you come over around seven?"

"Great." Grant smiled and took a step closer to Carter. "Do you need me to bring anything?"

"No, we've got the cookies for dessert, and I have everything else." If he was going to hang out with Wyatt, he might have suggested some beer or a bottle of wine, but he had a feeling he'd need a clear head with Grant. Too much alcohol, and he'd be up for anything the Dom suggested.

"I'm looking forward to it." Grant stepped even closer, until Carter could feel the hem of his skirt brushing against Grant's legs. "Do you know what else I'm looking forward to?"

He shouldn't ask, but he had to. "What?"

"Seeing what kinds of *stimulating* things you have hidden away. I'm thinking that I might need you to model a few things for me. Just so I can make a good choice, of course." Grant's voice was low and made Carter's stomach whirl.

While he tried to get the butterflies under control, his mind was too mixed up to respond. Grant gave him a wicked grin and pressed his body against Carter's. Looking up at Grant, he gripped the post behind him for support. Suddenly his knees didn't feel strong enough to support the rest of him.

Tilting his head, Grant slowly brought his lips down to Carter's. The maddeningly slow descent left plenty of time for Carter to move or to say something, but he had to taste the full lips in front of him. He wanted to know if their chemistry was going to be as explosive as he'd thought.

It was.

Grant's mouth touched his, brushing their lips lightly together. It was like fireworks went off. Grant nibbled with his lips and teased at Carter's mouth until he opened for the Dom. A deep moan escaped when he felt Grant's tongue slide across his.

He felt cherished, but there was no doubt who was in charge.

It made him want to melt into Grant and beg for more. For the Dom to drag him inside and strip off his clothes—and that thought chased some of the desire-filled haze from his mind. He wanted to believe Grant would take one look at his lingerie and say he was the sexiest thing the Dom had ever seen. The little doubts eating away at the back of his head had him hesitating.

Grant must have realized something was wrong because he gentled the kiss, pulling back slowly. Giving Carter one last peck, he straightened up. "I had a good time tonight. I can't wait for this weekend."

"Me too. It's just..." Carter wasn't sure he could explain it without sounding like a wimp.

"It's all right. We'll go at our own pace. We both had fun tonight, and that's what mattered." Then his expression grew teasing. "Well, that, and I got my kiss goodnight."

Carter couldn't resist. "Behave, or I'll tell your mother."

Grant laughed. "You cheat like the rest of the family. You're going to fit right in."

He made it sound like he could see Carter in his life. Not just as a new boyfriend, but something more. Like Carter had a place in their family and it was just waiting for him to step into it. Grant said boyfriend, but the word seemed to mean more than that.

Carter couldn't decide how he felt about that...elated or terrified.

4

GRANT

"Is that everything for now? Anything else about the radio campaign on the agenda tonight?" Brent looked around at everyone in the meeting, then glanced down to make a few more notes. "I think that's everything, then."

As some of the staff from the different insurance offices started to head out the door, Bryce tried to slip out with them. He had to have known the interrogation was coming, but he hadn't ducked out fast enough. Garrett cleared his throat and spoke up over the chatter. "Bryce, not so fast."

There were a few giggles and a couple of teasing remarks as everyone else filtered out. With Grant, Bryce, and Garrett each running a different branch of the family insurance company and Brent running the claims department, the employees all felt like family, so the comments had to be expected. When it was just the five of them, Bryce tried to play dumb. He went back over to the table and sat down, looking at Brent. "I thought we covered everything. Did we miss something?"

"Don't play stupid," Grant barked out. "What's been going on with you? We heard you skipped out early almost every day this week."

It was more like Bryce had simply been leaving on time, but since that was such a huge change, Grant didn't feel bad for exaggerating a little.

"Bullshit." Bryce snorted. "I just haven't been putting in lots of extra hours."

Garrett leaned back in his chair and cocked his head. "Care to tell us what has you working such reasonable hours lately?"

Bryce glared at Brent like he'd snitched, but Brent just gave his head a little shake like he was denying whatever he was being accused of. Interesting. Even Garrett noticed the interchange, because he frowned. "You told Brent?"

"Lord, this family is nosy." Bryce slumped back in his chair. "It's nothing."

"It's something if you were mad at Brent for telling. So what's the secret?" Grant knew they all had a good guess, but it was time for Bryce to fess up.

Bryce sighed and looked up at the ceiling, his head falling back to rest on the back of the chair. He waved his hand at Brent. "Brent, you do it."

Clearing his throat, trying not to laugh at the drama coming from Bryce, Brent looked over at Garrett, Calen, and Grant. "Bryce met someone...two someones, actually, and he's afraid—"

Bryce growled out, "Not afraid, just concerned."

"Excuse me." Brent rolled his eyes. "Bryce is *concerned* that his entering into a relationship with two people—"

Bryce interrupted again. "Dating. We're not entering into anything."

Calen laughed at the unintended sexual innuendo. "Do you want to tell the story?"

"No." Bryce sighed again.

"Then sit there and don't talk, drama queen."

Trying not to laugh, Brent started again. "Bryce is *concerned* that *dating* two men who are already in an established relationship may not be as discreet as we agreed to be."

It was quiet for a moment, then Garrett looked at Brent. "Is it serious?"

Grant thought it was hilarious that Garrett was asking Brent about Bryce's love life, but he managed not to make an ass out of himself. Brent nodded and looked over at Bryce before speaking. "Yes. I'd say *very*."

Bryce didn't disagree with him.

Grant had a few more questions. "Are they in the lifestyle? Where'd they meet?"

"Yes, and at the club a few months ago. The last time we were all up there, evidently." Brent answered without even looking at Bryce. "They've been testing the water, but Bryce is nervous about getting serious with a Dom and a sub and how it will look."

Bryce had dated a variety of people. As a switch, he was drawn to Dominants and submissives, but he'd never dated both at the same time. Grant could see that being difficult already without adding in the worries about what clients and friends would say.

Bryce was still staring at the ceiling, ignoring them all.

Looking around at his family, Grant wasn't sure what all the fuss was about. "We said we weren't going to do anything stupid to draw attention to ourselves. We never said we wouldn't fall in love and date who we wanted to. You morons are taking that conversation too far."

Calen's snickering turned into gasps of laughter. Brent frowned at him, but when that didn't get the desired response, he balled up a piece of paper and threw it at him. That got Calen to stop laughing, but it was easy to see he was planning his retribution. Brent blushed, but ignored him.

Brent cleared his throat. "That's basically what I said, just nicer. There is no reason for him to chase away people he really cares about."

Even Garrett was nodding. "We just want you to be happy. We'll deal with anything that comes up, but I think most clients won't care. We might lose a few, but not enough for me to be worried. Other areas, like the number of new customers we've picked up from the club, are growing, and I think that will more than make up for anyone who might have a problem with it. But let's face it. Most people see their insurance person once a year, tops, and don't care who he's married to."

"Agreed." Grant was glad that was settled. Maybe if Bryce got serious quick enough, it would distract his mother from his relationship with Carter. "So who is it?"

Bryce managed to find his voice with that question. "Troy and Oliver."

The names were familiar, but Grant couldn't place them. Everyone else seemed to be in the same boat until Brent spoke up. "The guys with the sounds."

"Oh." Now Grant could picture them. The demonstration had been—

"They were hot," Calen piped up.

"Calen! Not helping." Brent frowned at him, but Grant could see things heating up between the two of them, and he couldn't help but wonder if they'd make it home before they got into it. Now that they were both back from vacation and not trying to hide how they felt, the heat always went up a few degrees whenever they were in the same room together.

Grant had to agree with Calen. "They were hot. The little one's a firecracker."

Bryce laughed, and some of the stress seemed to be easing. "That's Oliver. He's sweet."

"So when are we going to meet them?" Garrett tried to get things back under control, but Calen interrupted.

"Meet them with their clothes on, he means."

Bryce blushed but smirked, clearly not upset by Calen's teasing. "Don't make them feel weird." He laughed. "I thought about inviting them to the barbecue next weekend?" It came out more as a question than Bryce probably intended.

"That sounds good," Garrett said, and everyone nodded.

The sound of the conference room door easing open had them glancing over. Wyatt's head peeked around the door hesitantly. "Master? You said not to let you stay late."

Garrett glanced over at the clock on the wall. "You're right. Thank you."

Everyone started heading toward the door with greetings for Wyatt and one last teasing remark thrown at Bryce. Grant still had a while before he needed to head over to Carter's place, so he hung back, waiting for the room to clear.

When everyone but Wyatt and Garrett had cleared out, Grant turned to the men. "So what did Carter say about our date?"

Wyatt had made a science out of avoiding Grant for the past couple of days. Even when Grant thought he had timed it perfectly to catch Wyatt at Garrett's office, he'd missed the sub by minutes. Wyatt started fidgeting and looking around the room, probably for a way to escape. "Nothing."

Garrett and Grant both laughed. Garrett moved over to hug Wyatt and Grant leaned back in his chair, propping his feet up on the table. Garrett growled at him to move them and Wyatt laughed, breaking the tension.

He shifted around and stood up, walking over to Wyatt. "If Carter asked you not to say anything, that's fine. I won't bug you." He probably should have said that he wouldn't bug him much, but that was probably understood.

Wyatt leaned back in Garrett's arms and smiled. "He didn't say that. Not specifically."

Grant loved loopholes. "See, then, it's fine."

Trying not to giggle and failing miserably, Wyatt's smile widened. "He had fun. Thank you for making him change."

"I didn't make him. I just encouraged him to dress up for me." Grant's grin was naughty and infectious. They both shook their heads at him.

"And the farmer's market thing was a hit. He loved that." Wyatt gave Grant an approving look.

Garrett perked up. "You have cookies?" He looked down at Wyatt. "You didn't mention the market. Did they get cookies?"

Frowning at Garrett, Grant shook his head. "No. I was on a date, not shopping for you."

Wyatt winked at Grant, then looked up at Garrett. "Is it okay to mention that Carter is a bit anxious about tonight?"

"I'm sure Grant's guessed that part already." Then Garrett gave Grant a firm look when Grant started to laugh.

"He was nervous the other night. I know it will take a while for him to get completely comfortable with me." Then he decided to push his luck. "Is he uneasy about something specific?"

Wyatt blushed a vivid red and pretended to zip his lips and lock them. Shaking his head, he threw away the key like he was a kid again. Garrett laughed. Stepping back, he looked up at the clock again, then took Wyatt's hand. "Come on, before you answer that and make Carter lose it."

Nodding, Wyatt refused to open his mouth, and just waved to Grant as they left the room. Grant followed behind them, not wanting to make them late for whatever plans they had. Grant hadn't missed the fact that neither of them mentioned what the reason was that Garrett couldn't work late.

Whatever it was, it wasn't going to stay a secret for long. Nothing did in their family. Grant knew Carter must have already figured that out, otherwise Wyatt wouldn't have blushed so red and refused to talk. There was only one thing Grant could think of that would get that kind of reaction. Carter must be very nervous about showing off his sexy collection.

Considering they hadn't talked about safewords or even BDSM in general terms yet, Grant knew he probably should back off a little. The Dom part of him balked at that idea. Grant thought the best way to tackle it would be to jump in headfirst, so Carter could see right away how beautiful Grant saw him as. Carter wasn't going to believe it until the proof was right there in front of him, or pressed up against him.

Grant shoved the dirty thoughts out of his head. He couldn't show up for dinner with a hard-on. That would give the wrong impression. He wanted it clear he was looking for something long-term, not a hookup. He'd known that by the time the first barbecue Carter had come to was over.

Carter was his; the sexy sub just wasn't ready to admit it yet.

5

CARTER

"Dinner's ready to be put together...cookies are still safe...movies picked out..." Carter wandered around the house, aimlessly trying to make sure everything was in order. Distracting himself was a bonus. It wasn't that he didn't want Grant to come over; he did. He just wasn't sure what was going to happen.

Did Grant really want to see his lingerie?

Carter knew Grant wasn't like most men—he was starting to understand that. But going from being okay with a dress to accepting lacy underwear was another thing. Some of his stuff was made for guys, but other things were clearly designed for women.

Would Grant really be okay with that?

Everything the Dom had said made Carter feel like he would, but it was still a big leap. Carter wasn't sure if he was ready for it. He wasn't ready for everything to be over if Grant changed his mind. He liked Grant, but it wasn't just that. It was starting to feel like he was part of the family, and Carter didn't want to lose that.

He'd tried to sort through his clothes and see what kinds of things he'd be okay with showing Grant, but that had been a little too stressful. So he'd gone back to cleaning the house and getting dinner ready. He should have picked something harder to cook. Not letting Wyatt shoo him out of work early would have been a good idea, too.

Having too much time on his hands was not a good thing.

On his third trip around the living room and kitchen, the doorbell finally rang. "You can do this. It's just a movie date. Nothing stressful."

Opening the door, he saw Grant leaning on the frame trying to appear casual, but Carter could see the excitement in his eyes. Was it for the date, or was he thinking about the clothing? Stepping back, he tried to smile. It felt forced and weird. "Come on in."

Grant gave him a smile and a quick, surprising kiss as he walked in. "Thanks for keeping my cookies safe."

Carter laughed and shook his head. "So you're not excited to see me. You're just glad I kept your cookies safe?"

With a heated look, Grant had him squirming even before he spoke. "I'm *very* excited to see you. The cookies are just a bonus. It's hard to keep secrets in this family, so it shows me we were meant to be."

Carter couldn't decide how much of that was Grant's teasing, and how much was serious. Deciding to ignore the part that made him nervous, Carter started leading Grant back to the kitchen. "You just have to have the right blackmail to keep people quiet."

"You must have something good on Wyatt because I couldn't get much out of him at all. He avoided me all week. He had some kind of sixth sense because I missed him repeatedly." Leaning against the counter, Grant laughed, clearly still enjoying the game of avoidance he'd played with Wyatt.

"Wyatt's very smart, and yes, I've got good dirt." Going over to the fridge, Carter started getting everything out to assemble dinner. "I hope you like pizza. I made the dough earlier, but I wasn't sure what you liked on it."

He might have gone a little overboard with prepping the toppings. He wasn't sure if Grant would be a complete pizza carnivore or if vegetables would be okay, so he'd gotten several different things ready. It wasn't until he had the dough ready that he'd realized he didn't know if Grant liked homemade pizza. That had just given him something else to worry about.

"Oh, homemade? That sounds incredible." Grant sounded entirely too enthusiastic for pizza.

"It's not hard." He didn't want Grant to think he'd gone all out and done something outlandish.

"You're talking to someone whose family can't even boil water without ruining it. Trust me, I'm impressed." Grant was looking over the dough and toppings like it was some kind of all-you-can-eat buffet.

"How can none of you cook? Couldn't your parents?" The guys could grill, and Carter had seen a few homemade dishes that looked good, but Grant wasn't exaggerating by much.

"Yes, but teaching us was almost impossible. My dad said we didn't pay enough attention, and my mom got tired of butting heads with us. It was one of those always thinking we were right kinds of things. They finally gave up and said we'd better marry someone smarter than we were, or learn how to order enough veggies off the takeout menu so we wouldn't end up with scurvy." Grant sounded serious enough that Carter didn't think he was teasing, but he just couldn't imagine his parents saying anything like that.

"Well, it looks like you haven't died of malnourishment yet, so you've got takeout down."

"And I plan on marrying someone smarter than me." Grant winked, making Carter forget what he was doing for a moment.

Deciding that was another comment he was just going to ignore, Carter finished putting the toppings on the table. "I wasn't sure what kinds of things you liked on pizza, so I figured we could do that part when you got here. It's not going to take long to cook."

Grant gave him a look that said he knew Carter was avoiding some of his comments. Carter walked over and turned on the oven to preheat before going back to the table. Yup, avoidance to the rescue. "So meat, veggie, or both?"

Grant's eyes twinkled. "I like meat." His eyebrows went up and down, giving him a comically naughty expression. "Vegetables are good, too. I'm not into just one thing. I like variety."

They were talking about pizza, right?

"Um, okay, um... both, then." Carter had a hard time getting the words to come out. Focusing on spreading the sauce on the pizza, Carter almost jumped out of his skin when Grant came up behind him. Wrapping his arms around Carter, Grant took the spoon from him and started spreading the sauce.

"Let me help. I don't want you to think I'm just going to lay back and let you do all the work." Grant's husky voice made Carter tingle all over.

Pizza. He was talking about pizza.

"Um...yes...Um, thanks." The heat from Grant's body as it wrapped around his made Carter want to moan in pleasure. Grant's chest was pressed against his back, but the Dom was being careful not to press his cock against Carter.

One little shift of his hips, and then Grant's cock would be right there. It was tempting, but as confused as he was feeling, he knew it would be sending mixed signals to the Dom.

"How does that look?" Grant's voice was husky, and Carter could imagine him saying all kinds of dirty things.

"Looks great. Now for the cheese." Bracing his hands on the

table, trying to get his knees to stop shaking, Carter watched as Grant reached for the cheese.

He expected the Dom to dump it on, but Grant was slow and methodical. Watching Grant carefully sprinkling the cheese all over the pizza, Carter couldn't help but think of what kinds of other things the Dom might do with such a gentle touch. It made a shiver run down his spine, and he heard a low groan radiating from Grant.

When the cheese was finally finished, along with most of Carter's nerves, Grant set the bag down and growled into Carter's ear, "Now, what else sounds good?"

Pizza. What toppings for the pizza.

"Um..." Carter felt the heat rising on his face but he couldn't help it. "Sausage?"

Grant chuckled low, his breath sending more shivers down Carter's back. "How about you do that part? Show me how the sausage should be handled."

With his face still hot and his nerves frayed, Carter reached over and started spreading the sausage over the pizza. Food wasn't what was running through his mind, and trying to push back the naughty images wasn't helping.

He was stupidly disappointed when he was done spreading out the meat. "Um, any more meat?"

"I think you handled the sausage perfectly. Let's put some vegetables on it. How about the peppers? Some of the sweet ones and some of the hot ones. I like how juicy the sweet ones are, but sometimes you want a little spice. What do you think?" Grant nearly growled the words out, making it hard for Carter to think.

"Um...yes...both's good..." Sweet and spicy would be perfect.

Toppings—they were talking about toppings.

"Good." Grant reached out and started methodically putting the vegetables on the pizza. When the peppers were on, he reached for the tomatoes. "Since these are already cut, let's put some on too."

When the last of the diced tomatoes went on, Grant brought his fingers up to his mouth and licked the juice off. It made Carter's toes curl. The man was trying to make him crazy.

"That looks perfect." Grant's low voice made Carter's insides turn circles.

Carter was saved from having to think of a response when the oven bell dinged. Not sure his knees would work, he was glad when Grant stepped back and reached out to grab the pizza. Taking the pan over to the oven, he carefully put it in.

"How long until it's hot and ready?" Grant's words didn't help clear the fog from Carter's brain. If anything, they just made it worse.

"Um...fifteen minutes, then we'll check and see if it needs a few more." Pizza, they were talking about pizza.

"Perfect. I think we have time for a little talk." From most people, those words would never be good, but Grant had a hungry expression that had Carter's pulse rising.

"Um...sure." He was starting to sound like a moron, but his brain wasn't firing on all cylinders.

Humor flickered through Grant's eyes before the hunger settled back in again. He reached out and took Carter's hand, then led him out of the kitchen. Not wanting to argue—not enough brains for that—Carter followed quietly.

Grant brought him over to the couch and sat down, pulling Carter onto his lap. "Oh!"

Wrapping his arms loosely around Carter, Grant smiled. "Would you prefer to sit somewhere else?"

Hell no.

"Um, this is fine." It was more than fine. It was sexy and hot as hell. Not that he was going to say that.

Grant seemed to understand, because he grinned and pulled

Carter in to snuggle against his chest. Carter sighed and curled up against the big man. God, he loved the way Grant could wrap himself around him. It was like curling into a big, naughty teddy bear.

One with very wicked intentions.

Hands wandering up and down Carter's back in a slow, soothing motion, Grant cleared his throat. Carter wasn't sure if the Dom needed time to think or just to figure out how to say what was on his mind, but Carter wasn't in any hurry.

When Grant spoke, his voice was low and even. Carter could feel the vibrations of the Dom's voice through his chest. It was soothing, like listening to a cat purr. "We haven't spoken much about the fact that I'm a Dom. I know you're aware of that because you've spent time around everyone else, but I thought you might have some questions."

Carter nodded but didn't say anything. He wasn't sure where to start.

Grant paused for a moment, but kept going when Carter didn't speak. "I don't need something lifestyle or even submission all the time in the bedroom, but I come across a bit stronger in sexual situations, so I couldn't say that I'm ever vanilla."

"I get that," Carter managed to comment, and pushed forward more. "You said you like playing in the club."

"Yes."

"How much playing at the club? I've never been, but Wyatt's told me stuff and I'm not sure..." His nerve started to fail, but Grant seemed to understand where he was going.

"We'd never do anything you weren't comfortable with. The first couple of times we went, I wouldn't even think of participating in a scene. I'd want you to watch and see how it felt. Give you a chance to get comfortable. Just going will feel weird, and there's no reason to rush."

"But if I never want to do anything there?" Carter couldn't

even begin to guess how it would feel. He didn't want to make any promises that he couldn't keep, but he also didn't want to ignore the possibility that he'd actually enjoy it.

Rock, meet hard place.

Grant didn't even pause to think. "That would be fine with me—as long as I get to show you off in something sexy to make everyone jealous."

Carter would have laughed, but he could hear the seriousness in Grant's voice. The fact that the Dom thought other people would be jealous and not shocked was sweet. "I think I can deal with that."

Maybe.

He'd try for Grant, but even thinking about having other people see him while he was dressed up had his stomach turning in knots. "Just not show off *too* much."

Grant laughed but didn't make any promises. "From the little you've said about the lifestyle, I know you're curious but haven't seriously dated anyone who was into it."

Carter nodded, not sure if Grant wanted a real response. That seemed to please the Dom, because he gave a satisfied grunt and tightened his arms around Carter. "How much first-hand knowledge of BDSM do you have? Have you ever been spanked or tied up?"

There was no way to hide the shiver that raced through him when Grant started listing off the options. Grant chuckled but didn't say anything. Carter wasn't going to wuss out, even though killing spiders in the house sounded like more fun than admitting it out loud.

"I don't have personal experience with either, but I'm not opposed to trying. I'm also not sure about my pain tolerance. But I've read scenes in books, and Wyatt overshares about *everything,* so I've gotten more exposure than most people who aren't involved in the lifestyle." Pleased that he'd managed a real sentence that made sense, Carter felt some of his nerves settle. Talking to Grant wasn't as hard as he'd thought it would be.

"Have you ever seen a contract?"

Not sure where the conversation was going, Carter kept his answer short. "No."

"Well, one of the parts is usually a list of activities and limits. How about next time I come over, I bring over my list so you can go through it and see what catches your eye? I can answer questions, or you can look stuff up online before we talk about it, whichever you prefer." Grant made it sound like they were talking about a grocery list, not a list of BDSM activities.

It was logical, though, and Carter thought it was nice that Grant had obviously put some thought into it. "Okay."

"I can deal with the short answers, beautiful, but do you not know what to say or are you overwhelmed?" Grant was clearly trying not to laugh—he was losing the battle.

"Both?" Carter hadn't meant to give him another short answer, and he chuckled. "Sorry. A little of both, probably. It's a lot to take in."

"I can see your brain going a hundred miles an hour, but you're only letting a little out."

Grant didn't say it like it was a bad thing, but Carter felt the need to apologize. "Sorry."

"Don't be." Grant shifted to give Carter a kiss on his forehead. "We're still figuring things out."

"Okay." Carter took a deep breath. "How about I try to open up more?"

He knew Grant was doing his best to be transparent and share what he was feeling. It was only fair for Carter to do the same.

"I'd appreciate that." Grant gave him another tender, quick kiss.

In an effort to be more honest, Carter spoke up again.

"Thinking about showing you my...stuff tonight is giving me ulcers."

Grant hugged him tight. "I know, but I'm not letting you out of it. You need to see it's not going to chase me away, and I want to see how tempting you look. It's my reward for behaving so well."

Laughing, Carter shook his head and looked at Grant. The goof had started out so sweet. "I think your mother would be very interested to know how often you expect to be rewarded for good manners."

"Meanie." Grant frowned and started to say something else, but at that moment the oven timer went off.

He leaned close and gave Grant a quick peck. "Let's go check the pizza."

Grant grumbled about cheaters, and Carter laughed as he climbed off the Dom's lap and went back into the kitchen. He was going to have fun making Grant nuts.

6

GRANT

The sexy little thing was going to make him crazy.

After their talk, Carter had gotten more comfortable with Grant, but that only meant he would tease and flirt more. The shy, hesitant man who'd been nervously pacing the kitchen was gone, but the racy looks and grins were making Grant's pants too tight—and they hadn't even gotten to the best part of the night yet.

The pizza had been delicious and the action movie Carter had picked out had been fun, but Grant was starting to think Carter was just finding ways to keep putting off showing Grant his lingerie when he started talking about cookies and another movie.

"Yes, cookies. No movie." Grant stood up and wrapped his arms around Carter. "As much as I loved cuddling with you, I'm ready to see your sexies."

Carter visibly swallowed nervously. "My sexies?"

"Oh yes, all those erotic things I know you're hiding under your clothes. I'm supposed to be picking out something for you to wear, or have you forgotten?"

Carter blushed and looked down to stare at Grant's shirt. "I didn't forget."

Kissing the top of Carter's head, Grant tried not to smile. His nervous sub was getting worked up over nothing, and it was time he realized that. "Then let's go see them. Unless you want to bring it all out here?"

Carter looked around the room and must have felt it was too open, because he shook his head. "Let's do it in my room." He stepped back and took Grant's hand, holding on tightly. When he was facing away, he spoke again. "I don't have to put it on? Just show you what I've got?"

The images that flashed through Grant's mind were erotic and beautiful, but the nerves in Carter's voice made him want to pull him close and promise him everything would be okay. "You don't have to, pretty, but I'd like it if you would."

Maybe if he kept saying it, Carter would eventually believe him. Grant thought seeing was going to make the biggest impression, though. He saw Carter's head go up and down, but he didn't think the worried man was actually agreeing with him.

As they walked back toward Carter's bedroom, Grant felt his excitement rise, along with his cock. Sexy men in feminine lingerie just did it for him, but knowing it was Carter made it even better. He wished that Carter trusted him enough not to worry about his reaction, but Grant knew that would come in time. His sweet sub had experienced enough bad reactions to be gun-shy.

Carter's room was an interesting contrast to the rest of the house. The kitchen and living room were contemporary and warm, but his bedroom was completely different. It had antique furniture and was done in simple colors, but it had a more feminine feel. Nothing that Grant could point out specifically, but it felt like he was seeing more of who Carter really was and less of what he actually showed people.

"Your room is beautiful. I love your dresser."

Carter seemed to relax more and smiled at Grant. "It's stuff I found when I was buying things for the shop. These are my favorite pieces that I just couldn't sell."

"You've done a great job putting it together." Everything wasn't matching, but it felt like it went together. Grant wasn't much for decorating, but he was impressed with Carter's skill. It made his own bedroom seem sad and blank.

"Thanks." With a more confident stride, Carter let go of Grant's hand and walked over to the dresser. Bending over, he opened the two top drawers, then moved back.

Refusing to let Carter hide awkwardly, Grant reached out and pulled him close. Wrapping his arms around Carter, he tucked him close to his chest. "Do you want to show me your favorite things or should I just look?"

"You look." Carter had to clear his voice twice before the words came out, but he seemed to be trying to sound confident because they were strong and sure.

"Okay." Taking Carter at his word, Grant held him close with one hand and reached out for the silky clothing with the other. One drawer looked like it contained panties and different kinds of stockings. The other seemed to have different kinds of night-gowns and sexy things that Grant didn't have the right words to name.

He needed to do more research so he wouldn't look stupid.

The first piece that caught his eye had thin little straps and seemed like a silky tank top. It was a deep red color, and Grant knew it would skim and hug Carter's body perfectly. Grant had seen sets like it before and he knew there had to be another piece to go with it.

He set the top on the dresser and started looking for the matching part. "I bet this has sexy panties or something like that."

Carter nodded and reached out. Sorting through the drawer, he pulled out a pair of tiny panties. Grant could easily see his sweet man in the outfit, but there was no way it would have hidden anything. Erotic didn't even begin to describe it, but he didn't want to share that much of Carter at the club—at least, not the first time they went.

And not when his family was around.

Tightening his grip on Carter, his voice came out rough and filled with arousal. "You would look incredible in this, pretty one. But I want you a little more covered for our first time to the club. You'll wear this for me sometime when it's just the two of us, won't you? God, you'd look..."

Carter gave a jerky nod and a little whine escaped before he clamped his lips together. Grant grinned and pulled Carter close enough that he would be able to feel Grant's arousal. He wanted it clear that he was turned on by the thought.

"Let's pick something out that I can show you off in." Grant let his hands slide down Carter's chest enough that he'd under-stand what Grant was trying to say. "Just not *too* much."

A needy shiver raced through Carter. He reached down to the drawer filled with nighties and dug down until he found what he was looking for. No second-guessing or thinking; he knew what he wanted to show Grant. Carter might be nervous, but he'd been thinking about their trip.

It had to be a good sign.

Black lace and a soft, shiny material Grant thought might be silk came out of the drawer, and Carter laid it on the dresser. Grant helped spread it out; Carter's hands were shaking too much. The top was very similar to the first one Grant had seen, but the new one had lace and looked a little longer. It would flirt right at Carter's groin, giving teasing glimpses of his cock.

The bottoms were even better.

Grant didn't think they were panties, but he wasn't sure

what to call them. They were almost like shorts but sexy and tight. They would show every curve, every hint of arousal. The same lace edged the legs and waist, and Grant thought that the lace waistband would peek out every time Carter moved. It might even cover his cock, as long as he didn't get too turned on.

If he did, well, Grant might have to help him with that just so no one else would see Carter's hard length poking out. It was the perfect outfit to wear to the club, but would it push Carter too much?

"Oh, God, that's...it's perfect. You would look incredible."

"It's...it's not made for men. Some stuff is, but this one..."

"Was made for you, pretty one. It was made for you." Grant knew without a doubt how perfect it would look. "It's going to tease at your cock and hint to everyone that if they look close enough they might see your beautiful body."

Carter couldn't seem to decide what to say.

He opened his mouth and closed it, but nothing came out. Grant knew Carter had been expecting him to be shocked at the women's underwear and frilly things, but he still wasn't sure why. He'd done his best to make it obvious what he thought.

Maybe he'd been too subtle?

That was easily fixed.

"How about you go in the bathroom and try it on for me— you know, so we can make sure it fits." The words came out thick with arousal, and Grant couldn't resist rubbing his cock against Carter's full ass.

There was only so much temptation a man could fight.

"You...you want...now?" Carter managed words that time, but it was a long way from a sentence. Luckily, Grant was learning to read his sub.

"Oh, yes. I want to see how perfect you look. We need to make sure it's right for the club." He wasn't going to pass up the perfect opportunity to see his man dressed up in something sexy.

"We do?" Carter didn't seem convinced, but he hadn't said no, so Grant was taking that as permission.

"Most definitely." Grant took a step back and gave Carter's ass a pat. "Hurry, pretty one. You don't want to make me wait, do you?"

Carter snorted and shook his head, but grabbed the lingerie and straightened. Heading toward the bathroom, he seemed to give his hips a little extra sway and did something that made his ass look even more incredible. As he crossed the threshold into the bathroom, he turned and gave Grant a little wink.

"I wonder how pleased your mother would be to learn you were making very suggestive statements to me on our second date." Then with a grin, he closed the door.

He was a sassy little thing, but Grant loved it.

"Then I'd have to tell her you were tempting me and showing off those sexy legs."

"You wouldn't!" Carter's voice came out high-pitched and squeaky.

Grant laughed. "You know I would."

"You're terrible!" Carter didn't seem upset by that fact.

"You love it."

He heard laughter coming from the bathroom but no more comebacks. Grant hoped Carter was putting on the erotic outfit, but he had a feeling Carter was talking himself out of it. "There are still a lot of your things I haven't had a chance to look at yet. You don't want to leave me unsupervised too long."

There was rustling and more laughter. Carter might have thought he was kidding, but the drawer was calling his name. It was begging him to come touch and find more lingerie for Carter to try on. Just as he was about to give in, he heard the bathroom door.

Opening it just a crack, Carter's toes with their deep purple polish were visible, but that was about it. Grant stood up from where he'd been leaning against the dresser and tried to be patient. "As sexy as I'm sure your feet are, they aren't the part that I was interested in—unless that's something else we need to talk about. I might be up for kissing them, but I'm not sure about anything else. I dated a foot guy—"

"I don't think you're supposed to tell me about other guys you dated when I'm dressing up for you. One of those dating rules, I think." Carter had pushed open the door. Leaning against the frame, it gave him the illusion of curves, but there was no hiding the outline of his cock as it pushed against the short-like bottoms.

He was still soft, so Grant knew he had to be nervous, but he looked beautiful. Grant gave a low whistle. "Damn, pretty, look at you."

Carter blushed, but Grant could see he was doing his best to pretend he wasn't nervous. "Thank you."

He glanced down, then back up at Grant. "It would be okay? It feels..." Carter couldn't seem to find the word, because his voice trailed off and he started to move restlessly.

"Probably very exposed and nerve-racking, but God, you look...mouthwatering."

Carter grinned. "Better than the cookies?"

"Better than a dozen cookies." Grant let his eyes eat up every glimpse of Carter he could see, but the stubborn man hadn't moved from the doorway yet.

"Just a dozen?" Carter let one foot trail up the other leg, and it made his cock move deliciously under the silky fabric.

"Two dozen. All the dozens." Carter was worth everything. "Don't just stand there teasing me, pretty. I think I've earned a little show."

"You earned a show, huh? What makes you think that?"

Carter smirked, but straightened like he was contemplating leaving the bathroom.

"I left your drawer alone, and I picked out an outfit that leaves you mostly covered. Yup, I earned a show." Grant watched as the top teased right at the beginning of Carter's cock just like he knew it would. With each little step, he was watching Carter's shirt kiss the head of his dick.

It was mesmerizing.

"You've got a very interesting definition of good behavior." Carter didn't seem to mind because he had a wicked look on his face. Putting one foot in front of the other, he walked closer to Grant, who finally had to lean against the dresser to keep himself from pushing Carter too far.

Had to keep his hands to himself, it was Carter's show.

It was getting harder and harder to remember.

Carter's hips swayed, making his cock swing, and it looked like he was getting harder. Not so nervous now that he'd seen Grant's reaction? Grant hoped so. He wanted Carter to feel confident and beautiful, no matter how he was dressed.

"Damn. Every Dom there is going to be looking at you, pretty."

Carter shook his head like he didn't quite believe it, but the little smile on his lips let Grant know how much he liked the compliment. When he finally got within arm's length of Grant, he stopped and did a slow turn.

The outfit looked just as good from the back as it did from the front. The top dipped down in the back showing creamy skin that Grant wanted to lick. The bottoms cupped his ass but left the lower part of his full cheeks peeking out temptingly.

Grant thought it probably wasn't the time to tell Carter how erotic he'd look with a pink spanked ass spilling out of the shorts. Maybe another time. Carter hadn't seemed opposed to the idea, so Grant might be able to fulfill his fantasy one day.

One step at a time.

Giving up on being good, Grant pushed off the dresser and closed the gap between them. Pressing his body tight against Carter's, Grant knew his erection would be obvious. "You look amazing. You have no idea what you're doing to me."

Carter leaned back in Grant's arms, rubbing his ass up and down Grant's erection. His voice was teasing but thick with his own arousal. "I think I have an idea."

"Oh, the things I want to do to you." Grant leaned down and nuzzled Carter's neck, loving the breathy moan that escaped and the way Carter's soft hair curled around his ears, teasing Grant's cheek. "I can't wait to see what other sexy things you have hidden away. Are you wearing things like this all the time under your clothes? Panties under your sundress, maybe, or lacy little things under the skirt you wore to dinner?"

Carter's face flushed red, but he didn't back down. He just nodded and cleared his throat. "Yes. I like...sexy things under my clothes. Even when I'm dressed more traditionally masculine."

"You know I'll think about that every time I see you. Every date, every family barbecue, all I'm going to be able to think about is what's under your clothes. You might need to be punished for making me distracted." The words came out low and Grant knew Carter could hear the need in his voice. He wasn't teasing, though. It would be all he'd be able to focus on.

"Punished?" The words were soft and hesitant, giving the impression Carter knew he shouldn't ask but was going to, anyway.

"Oh yes, my pretty one. I might have to spank you for getting me hard and teasing me with your sexy lingerie."

"Spank?" It was more of a squeak than a word, but Grant understood.

"Naughty subs would get bent over and their panties pulled down. Then I'd bring my hand down on your ass until you'd learned your lesson about teasing me. When I would finally pull your panties back up, you'd be able to see how red it was, and every time you sat down you'd think of me." So maybe he'd gone further into the fantasy than he'd meant to. But the way Carter was rubbing his ass along Grant's cock, he didn't seem to mind.

Grant thrust his cock harder against Carter and his sexy sub moaned in pleasure. Looking down at his perfect man, he could see Carter's straining erection pushing the front of the little shorts out obscenely, the head of his cock just escaping the lacy waist of the shorts.

Letting his hands slowly move closer to Carter's beautiful cock, Grant lowered his voice and let his breath tickle Carter's ear. "If we were at the club, we'd have to take care of this. I don't want anyone else to see your sexy cock—at least, not yet."

7

CARTER

"Take care?" His voice came out high-pitched and sounded needy to him, but he couldn't help it. Grant was making Carter's brain melt. "Yet?"

Grant's breath sent shivers down Carter's spine, and the naughty words only made it worse. "We'd have to find a private spot where I could help you. Do you want me to show you what I'd do? Are you curious, pretty?"

He had a good idea what Grant would do, and he knew what Grant was trying to ask. He should say no. He should slow things down and put his clothes back on, but it'd been so long...He broke. "Please. Show me."

A low groan vibrated through Grant's chest, making Carter's nipples tighten and ache. Grant's hands slowly kept working their way down, and the measured pace was making Carter want to scream. With the silk rubbing along his cock and the feel of Grant's erection pushing against his ass, Carter could hardly hold on as it was.

Ridiculous little sounds kept escaping, but he couldn't hold them in. In the quiet moments when he let himself believe the insane fantasy that Grant might want him like this, he'd dreamed about how the sexy Dom would touch him. The reality was even better than his fantasies.

His touch was sure and strong. Grant knew what he wanted, and he wasn't shy about telling Carter exactly what it was. Carter hadn't let himself believe Grant could want him, but there was no denying it now. When Grant's hands reached Carter's cock, he let one finger gently trail along the rigid length that was pressing against the fabric.

Carter's knees buckled and he would have gone down if not for Grant's firm grip. "You like that, don't you?" His finger went up and down the sensitive underside of Carter's cock, and the light touch made him moan and shiver.

"Please."

"Whatever you want, pretty." Grant growled low, tightening his grip around Carter's waist. The next trip down Carter's length wasn't just one finger. His whole hand tightened around the shaft and jerked off Carter in a slow, earth-shattering rhythm.

"Grant, please." He needed more, or he was going to combust.

Somewhere between leaving the bathroom and being held by his Dom, he'd lost his fear—and gained a need that frightened him. He'd never wanted anyone like he did Grant. The force of the desire took his breath away.

Grant seemed to thoroughly enjoy how insane he was making Carter. He could feel the pleasure and cocky confidence radiating from Grant and it made him want to throttle his Dom —right after he got off.

The pressure building inside him was the most important thing at that point.

When Grant finally pushed down the front of the boy shorts and freed Carter's erection, he thought he'd feel better, but it just made the need worse. Watching Grant's strong hand wrapped around him while he was dressed in his favorite lingerie was a fantasy come true. But the Dom needed to hurry up or Carter was going to finish things himself.

"Damn it, Grant." Fantasies were great, but Carter needed to come before he went insane.

Grant's low chuckle made Carter's nipples tighten even more. He must have moved or done something, because it drew Grant's attention to his chest. Carter was afraid for a minute that Grant would stop playing with his cock, but instead, the Dom braced one leg between Carter's thighs and let the hand that had been holding his waist slide up to his nipples.

The feel of Grant's fingers trailing up the silk made him shiver, a moan escaping. When Grant finally let one finger circle the tightly puckered nipple poking at the fabric, Carter thought he would come right then.

"I bet that feels good, doesn't it? Your nipple's all sensitive and needy, rubbing against the soft material. I think you need more, though. Do you want more?"

He had to talk? What kind of sadist was his Dom?

Finding the words, Carter shoved them out desperately. "Yes, please."

Grant moaned again, his cock jerking against Carter's ass. "Should I play with them gently or do you like it rough?" The words were growled out, making Carter's need almost frantic. He loved how aroused Grant was getting simply by touching him.

"Anything, please!"

Grant took him at his word because the next circle took Grant's hand right over the hard tip, and he pinched down. It didn't hurt, exactly, but it made his knees weak. He pushed up for more. The pleasure was tinged with pain and it was perfect.

Working Carter's nipple and cock, Grant made wicked sounds of pleasure that had Carter squirming in his arms.

Grant's arousal had Carter even more desperate. He was so close. "Grant! I need...please..."

He wasn't sure how to ask for more. His brain was fractured into a thousand pieces, but Grant knew what he needed. The grip on his cock tightened, speeding up, and the next pinch to his nipple sent waves of fire shooting through him.

With no warning, his orgasm crashed over him. Grant held him and kept teasing his body, making the pleasure go on and on. When it was finally over, Grant scooped him up and walked the short distance to the bed. Laying Carter down on the mattress, Grant curled around him and held him while the aftershocks of pleasure faded.

"Just in case you couldn't tell, I liked the outfit." Grant's words were almost serious, but Carter could hear the dry humor running through them.

"I never would have guessed. Thanks for clarifying it." Snuggling into Grant's warmth, Carter yawned and rubbed his face against Grant's firm, broad chest.

Silent laughter had his head bobbing up and down. Giving Grant's side a pinch, he got comfortable again. "Pillows don't get to move."

"Got it, boss." Grant's laughter made Carter have to get settled again.

Smiling, Carter tucked himself close to Grant and closed his eyes. He told himself he was going to relax for just a minute, then he had plans to explore the sexy Dom.

In just a minute...

As another yawn forced its way out, Grant's arms wrapped around him and he felt a kiss to the top of his head.

"You know this means I'm keeping you, right?"

He yawned and shook his head. Not denying the sentiment, just the presentation. "So romantic."

"Yup. That's me." It wouldn't have been funny, but Grant

seemed completely serious. Carter told himself he would set the Dom straight on a few things, right after he closed his eyes for just a minute. The warmth of Grant's body was soothing, and as the lull of sleep pulled at him he felt another kiss.

Carter had to smile. Grant might be a bulldozer, but evidently, he was Carter's bulldozer.

"How did your date go? Are you proud of me? I didn't tell… Well, I didn't tell much, and I kept my mouth shut when it counted. Garrett was very proud of me! Do you want to know my reward?" Wyatt bounced into the shop like a hurricane on steroids, nearly knocking over Mrs. Jenkins who'd stopped in for gossip, or, as she'd said, "To browse around, dear." He hadn't found her chairs yet, but she was innocently browsing around the store again.

Her eyes lit up as Wyatt bounded in. He was the real reason she'd been stalking the shop lately. Carter knew how to keep things to himself, but Wyatt—not so much. "Hello, dear."

"Sorry, Mrs. Jenkins." He looked suitably contrite, although Carter knew he was desperately holding back his curiosity.

"That's all right. You were very excited about something. It's understandable." Her voice was soothing and warm, lulling people in so they'd spill their guts. Wyatt fell for it every time.

He leaned in close and whispered conspiratorially, "Carter had another date with the insurance guy. He didn't call last night complaining that things ended badly, so I'm thinking it went very well."

"Oh." She turned to smile at Carter. "And here you said nothing exciting happened lately."

Wyatt was starting to look like he'd realized he'd overshared, but before he could decide what to do, she charged ahead. "It's so nice things are going well. They're such a nice family." She gave Wyatt a wink. "I've heard most are very take-charge and... strong-willed."

The little pause let Carter know she'd been tempted to say something else. Knowing her, something naughty. He'd thought the guys had been fairly discreet, but evidently not enough to fly below Mrs. Jenkins' naughty band of ladies. The smile on her face, deceptively sweet, let Carter know she didn't mind.

Wyatt was looking at Carter, frantically trying to ask for help. He clearly wasn't sure what to do. He'd overshared before, but now he looked like he was backed into a corner, not sure what to say without getting into more trouble. Deciding to save his friend, Carter spoke up. "They're a very interesting family. I'm enjoying getting to know him."

"So things are going well?" She smiled and reached out to pat his hand. "You didn't seem to have that good of luck with dating, and we were starting to get worried." She perked up and her smile seemed slightly wicked. "We'd even thought of introducing you to Maggie's baker's boy. He's an interesting thing, and we thought you'd do well together."

Carter knew he shouldn't, but he had to. It was just too tempting.

"Interesting?"

She nodded and tried to look very innocent, but he knew that was when she was at her most devious. "He's another... strong-willed young man, you might say." Then her voice dropped, coming out at a low whisper. "He has tattoos and some very *interesting* items that he carries in a backpack when he goes out on a date."

What the hell?

"Um." Carter wasn't sure what to say, and he really didn't think he wanted to know what "interesting" things the Dom carried around. "I'm very happy with Grant, but thank you."

"We'll keep him in mind for someone else. He might not be ready to settle down just yet, and his parents might need time to adjust." She shook her head and shrugged. "They think he's seeing the woman who owns the used bookstore, but that's not believable. Maggie saw him talking to a very cute young man a few weeks ago. It was evidently a very passionate discussion because the young man kept blushing. She wasn't close enough to hear the exact details."

Carter was stumped again.

Wyatt knew exactly what to say. Losing his fear of over-sharing quickly, he straightened. "Does he have a tattoo of Chinese symbols going down his left arm?" He pointed to his forearm.

"Yes, he does." Mrs. Jenkins perked up again, ready for the good gossip.

Wyatt gave her a knowing nod, but didn't exactly say the man was gay. Then he leaned in and whispered, "He's an interesting one. I'm not surprised the guy blushed. I know someone who...dated him for a while."

Her eyes lit up like it was Christmas, and Carter just watched as the flighty gossip and the busybody went at it.

"We had to do some research to figure out what some of the items Maggie saw were. It was *enlightening*." Mrs. Jenkins nodded. "A man like that needs to be settled down and have someone to devote his...attention to."

Wyatt shrugged his shoulders but seemed to be agreeing with her. "It's hard. He's supposed to be very nice, but some...*qualities* are harder to find in a partner."

What the hell was the man into?

Mrs. Jenkins nodded again and clucked her tongue. "We're going to find someone to fix him up with. Once we find the right young man for him, then we'll start working on the parents." She shrugged her shoulders and shook her head. "With his backpack, they have to know. If Maggie could get a peek that easily, they're just playing dumb. Not very enlightened of them, but we'll work on it."

Wyatt smiled, but he seemed at a loss what to say. "I'm glad he has you on his side, ma'am."

She beamed at him. Then, giving his arm a pat, she headed for the door. "I'm late for coffee with the girls. I'll see you gentlemen later."

"Yes, ma'am." Wyatt seemed a little relieved to see her go.

"Thank you for stopping by, Mrs. Jenkins." When she was safely out the door, he turned to Wyatt. "What was that all about?"

Wyatt blushed and looked around. "Um, I probably should have pretended I didn't know him. Right?"

Carter barked out a laugh. "Too late now. What is he into that she and those outrageous old ladies found so interesting?"

"He's a Dom, but he likes puppy play. He probably had a leash and plugs in there. Maybe some knee pads. I'm not sure what they had to look up; it could have been anything." Wyatt shrugged. "He's a nice guy."

"Well, the ladies have evidently adopted him. I just hope he's ready." Carter shook his head. Those crazy women were going to find a pup for a Dom. It made him incredibly grateful he'd found Grant before they'd turned their focus on him.

Wondering what kind of guy they would have picked out for him would give him ulcers.

"That's just…"

Wyatt nodded. "Weird. Those ladies are strange."

Carter had to agree. Before he could say anything, Wyatt seemed to remember why he'd come to the shop to begin with. "Your date! How did it go?"

Moving around the room, straightening little things, Carter

tried to keep his response simple. "It went very well. We had a nice time."

"Carter!" Wyatt wailed out his name like he was exasperated.

Laughing, Carter gave in. "It was wonderful. We picked out something, and he seemed to like...my things."

Wyatt giggled. "Of course he did. Garrett said Grant loves lacy things on sexy guys. You're his dream come true."

Carter blushed and looked away. "I'm not sure about that, but I'm not quite so worried."

"Does that mean you did more than give him a kiss goodnight?" Wyatt walked over and leaned on the counter, elbows braced on the wood and his head in his hands, a hopeful expression on his face.

"Possibly." Carter wasn't the natural oversharer Wyatt was, but he couldn't hold everything back. "I tried something on for him, and let's just say he liked it a lot."

"Which one!"

Wyatt's enthusiasm was contagious. Carter smiled, and he knew it looked slightly wicked. "The black outfit with the lace, it has the boy shorts that go with it."

"Oh, I love that one. It will be perfect." Wyatt's delighted expression dimmed. Tilting his head, he leaned closer. "So you're really coming to the club?" Wyatt sounded skeptical. Not that Carter could blame him.

"Yes. It seems like it. I'm still not sure how I feel about it but...I'm going to try." Nervous did not even begin to describe how he felt about going there.

Having everyone see him dressed up. Having everyone seeing him as a submissive with a Dom. Having to see everyone else. It was all too much when he started to think about it. So he'd been doing his best not to.

"Everyone's nice and open-minded. It's not going to be as weird as you think. Well, it might be weird, but not the bad kind." Wyatt was very earnest and Carter didn't want to burst his bubble, so he nodded and tried to give Wyatt a smile.

"It will be fine."

"Grant will take good care of you. It's easy to see how much he likes you."

Carter wasn't sure how he felt about the idea that Grant would take care of him. There was a lot rolling around in his head. Knowing he was submissive in bed and experiencing it with a real Dom and not just a bossy wannabe was difficult.

When Grant had taken charge the previous night, it'd felt right. Carter had felt cared for. Maybe that's what Wyatt was trying to say. There would be time to figure everything out. Grant might charge in like a bull, but he wouldn't push Carter too far. It was clear he was going to shove Carter outside his comfort zone, but he wasn't going to make him go alone. As he'd firmly announced the previous night, his Dom was there to stay.

8

GRANT

"Why are we here?" Grant cocked his head to give Garrett a curious look.

"What?" Garrett glanced around the living room. "I thought since Brent and Bryce took the guys out it'd be fun. We already talked about it. You know why you're here."

Grant laughed. When Garrett had first brought up hanging out since the other guys were going to dinner, he'd thought it would be fun. What he hadn't expected was to be eating pizza at Wyatt's while he was out. "Wyatt knows we're here, right?"

Calen was laughing so hard he was having a hard time holding his pizza. The plate kept tipping, and Grant expected it to go sliding to the floor any minute.

"Why would he mind?" Garrett was honestly confused.

"Because he's not here." Grant thought that was obvious, but he was starting to think Garrett was hiding something. He'd known Garrett was spending a lot of time with Wyatt lately, and that Garrett had stopped enforcing the whole "taking things slow" routine. However, making himself at home while Wyatt was out for the night seemed a bit much to Grant. He couldn't imagine being that presumptuous with Carter. It made him think the two men were a lot deeper into their relationship than they'd admitted.

Garrett looked around again and shook his head. "It's fine. It's not like I asked Wyatt to cook or something."

Calen snorted. "Five bucks says he offered."

Grant had to fight back the urge to laugh. "Of course he did. And I bet the idea of Garrett ordering pizza made him nuts."

Garrett frowned at them both, but the truth was too easy to see. Shaking his head, he took a bite of his pizza and mumbled, "I'm not letting him cook for us on his night out."

Calen laughed. "I'm telling your mother about your table manners. She'd have a cow."

"You do and I'll tell her how miserable you made her sweet baby Brent. She won't care about my talking with my mouth full then." Garrett grinned at Calen's wince.

Ignoring them both, Grant turned the conversation back to what he was curious about. "How often are you over here?" Grant had a nagging suspicion it was more than he'd expected.

Garrett shrugged. "It's more comfortable and Wyatt cooks better."

"You mean he cooks, period." Calen managed to catch his breath long enough to respond before laughing again.

Fixing his shit with Brent had improved Calen's mood, but it hadn't improved his sense of humor. Grant frowned at him. "We're not that bad."

"Yes, you are." Calen snickered.

Ignoring the hyena, Grant turned to Garrett. "How often?"

Garrett looked like he'd rather not answer, but he knew when he was cornered. "Most of the time. We're actually talking about moving in together and getting rid of my place. I'm never over there anymore, and he's already started bringing over my pictures and stuff. He wants it to be my home, too."

"Before he even meets Mom?" Grant knew the look on his face was wicked, but he couldn't help it. "And before some kind of collaring ceremony?"

"Don't tell her. She keeps talking about coming home early. If you start telling her shit like that, she'll be here tomorrow. You really want her butting in on your relationship with Carter?" Garrett frowned, clearly conflicted about the idea of having their mother home. "Besides, they've talked on the phone, so it's not like she doesn't know him at all."

Calen snorted. "That won't count at all with her."

Garrett frowned at him. "It counts."

"Not if you move in together—and if you do that without something more permanent she's going to kill you." Grant could almost see the explosion. She'd go crazy. "You'd get the lecture big-time."

Garrett shuddered. "I'm not going to piss her off."

They'd all gotten different versions of the same lecture growing up, once they'd come out and admitted their sexuality and D/s preferences. Basically, it was a lecture on being a responsible Dom or making sure they picked a trustworthy Dom. Between that and the sex talk, it was like baptism by fire. They'd all gotten over any natural shyness quickly, because she wasn't one to back down on something she felt was important.

Grant loved his mother, but something about her innate need to dominate and her mothering instincts made her...overwhelming. Helicopter mothers had nothing on his mom. She had a hovercraft complete with spy glasses and guns. Having her home would be great, but there was no way she would keep her distance from their private lives.

Calen stopped laughing long enough to nod and turn the conversation around to Grant and Carter. It was hard to tell if he was honestly curious or if he wanted to give Garrett a reprieve. "Speaking of you and Carter, how is that going?"

Garrett leaned back against the couch. If Grant had to guess, he was glad to be out of the spotlight. "Wyatt's excited, but he's worried for Carter."

Grant wasn't sure what to say, but telling them to mind their own business didn't even occur to him. "I think it's going good. I'm not going to try moving in with him tomorrow or anything." He gave Garrett a teasing grin. "He just needs to accept that I don't mind who he is. He attracted more douches than Brent did."

He'd been doing his best to make sure Carter knew he was serious about them and that he liked what Carter wore, but he knew it would be an uphill battle. Carter knew who he was and what he wanted, but he'd had so many guys shoot him down that Grant thought his confidence was battered all to hell. Grant knew he just had to keep showing Carter honestly how sexy he was and letting him be himself when they went out.

Some people would always have a problem with them, but other than a few looks when they'd gone out, it hadn't been as bad as it could have been. Overall, the communities closer to the city were more welcoming than they had been when they were younger, and he hoped it would keep moving in that direction.

Thinking of the local area brought something else to mind he'd been meaning to ask the other men. "You guys have a strange lady come in to get insurance quotes last week?" His clients were all over the map and he did a lot of business policies which attracted a different sort, but she was more interesting than usual.

Garrett and Calen looked at each other and nodded. "Little Southern lady? Bossy and asked a ton of questions?"

Grant nodded. "None of which had anything to do with the business."

They both nodded again, and Calen spoke up. "Lots of crazy ones about your family. It was more like an interview than an insurance quote. She even insisted Garrett and I both sit in on it. She wasn't going to budge on that, either. It was like trying to move a very polite brick wall."

Grant smiled. "Definitely an interrogation. You guys get the feeling she knew more about us than she should have if it were just about insurance?"

Garrett nodded. "I'm not sure I've ever been asked about who I was seeing. I wasn't sure how she was going to take hearing I was seriously involved with a man, but she was surprisingly…"

He trailed off, clearly not sure how to explain it. Calen spoke up, not conflicted at all. "Gleeful. She got a kick out of it. It was weird."

Garrett looked like he wanted to argue, but he didn't. Grant had to chuckle. "Yup, sounds about right. She asked who I was dating and had all kinds of questions. She never even asked about the policies or costs."

Calen glanced between the other men, then settled on Grant. "Did she buy anything from you?"

He shook his head. "Nope. Just said she enjoyed meeting me and she thought I was a good fit."

Calen grinned. "We got something like that, too."

"Some people are weird." Grant was serious, but Calen found the comment hilarious. As he was laughing so hard he couldn't catch his breath, Grant and Garrett both just watched him, wearing matching confused expressions.

When Calen could finally speak, he gasped out, "Some people," before laughing again. Grant reached over to take the plate away before the pizza went everywhere. That just set the nut off even more.

"How much have you had to drink?" Garrett was leaning toward Calen, a stern expression falling over his face.

Calen snorted. "Completely sober. You guys are just hilarious."

Garrett looked over to Grant, and they both shrugged. Sometimes it was just easier to ignore Calen than to try to understand him. "I worry about your sanity sometimes."

That didn't help.

By the time Calen stopped laughing, the pizza was cold and Grant's beer was hot. Taking his trash to the kitchen, Grant went back into living room only to see Garrett and Calen whispering, heads close together. Straightening quickly as Grant walked in, they tried to make it seem like they'd been debating what movie to watch.

That didn't look guilty at all.

Ignoring the elephant in the room, because he was starting to get a good guess of what all the crazy was about, Grant flopped back in his chair. "If I'm coming over for dinner, at least let Wyatt make dessert."

Calen nodded. "That wouldn't have been much work."

Garrett ignored both of them. "I don't want to see the Bond movie again. We watched that already."

Snorting, Calen threw a crust at Garrett. "You shit. He volunteered, didn't he?"

"That's just mean. I bet he was going to make that cake he was talking about last week. The fudge one." Grant had to agree with Calen; turning down dessert was just wrong.

Garrett gave them a shifty look that was too familiar. Grant didn't even get the words out before another crust had Garrett ducking and growling out a threat. "Hey, you make a mess and he'll never make another dessert for you."

"Where is it?" Calen wasn't going to fall for the guilt trip. "I know you guys. You're worse than kids hiding cookies in their rooms. Where is the cake?"

Garrett let an evil grin escape. "I have no idea what you're talking about."

It was a challenge Grant and Calen couldn't resist. Movie forgotten, they headed to the kitchen. They'd find it somewhere. Family was fun sometimes, but Grant was glad he had Carter. His sub would never hide a cake from him. He was too perfect for that.

9

CARTER

"So, I take it things are going well between you and Grant?" They hadn't been seated for more than thirty seconds before Bryce started in on the questions. It was clearly a way of preemptively diverting the conversation from his own love life.

Carter wasn't going to hide his relationship with Grant, but the rest of the guys weren't going to let Bryce get away with it. Brent grinned, and even Wyatt shook his head before speaking up. "That's not going to work."

Brent laughed. "We've been waiting for days to see what else you've been up to with your new guys. Spill it."

Slouching back in his chair, Bryce looked around before speaking in a low tone. "We went out on a date the other night. They were okay with me wanting to keep it low-key in public, but it was good."

Wyatt looked like he was trying not to laugh, but Brent wasn't holding back. He grinned and shook his head, chuckling. "Only good? Next you're going to be telling us they're nice and you had a lovely time."

Bryce blushed and shifted in his seat. Rearranging the silverware on the table, Bryce tried to relax as he responded to their teasing. "Okay, so it was more than good."

"How much more than good?" Wyatt smiled gleefully, looking around to make sure they couldn't be overheard. "You have to give us more details than that."

Carter was glad Wyatt was feeling comfortable with the other guys, but Carter wasn't sure if he wanted to know more about what Bryce had been up to. If Bryce shared too much, he had a nagging feeling it would make keeping his own growing relationship low-key almost impossible.

"Nothing crazy. Mostly getting to know them kind of stuff." Rolling the knife over and over on the table, Bryce seemed to be lost in his head. "It's weird. I've always either been in charge or been the..." He paused and looked around again before continuing. "Not in charge. It's hard trying to balance both at the same time. I have to think about reactions more. Even little things at dinner or when we're talking."

They all nodded, understanding what he was trying to say, but Brent was the one who spoke up. "Have you told them that? I would hope they'd want you to be yourself and not overthink it."

Bryce nodded. "Yeah, they knew already, though. It's easier when we're talking one-on-one."

"Does being with both of them feel wrong?" Brent leaned forward, elbows on the table. "If it doesn't feel right, you can't force it."

"No. It's not like that. I'm just not used to it." He took a breath and it looked like he was trying to sort it out in his head. "It's always been separate. Working out how to balance both sides of me at the same time is weird. I feel like a scale that's not quite balanced—almost, but like it's not right yet."

"That might come in time." Brent gave him a serious look. "You seemed to be running from the relationship for a while, and maybe that's made you overthink it. Do you guys spend all your time together, or is it mostly separate?"

Bryce shrugged. "A bit of both. The date was together, and they came into the office together a few times to sign paperwork. When we talk on the phone, it's usually just two of us at a time."

"Do you talk to them a lot?" Wyatt's curiosity was showing again, but Bryce didn't seem to mind.

"Yes. At least one of them, almost every day. Most of the time we talk after work." Bryce blushed again, and he stared off into the distance. Relaxing back in his chair, Bryce shifted, and for a minute reminded Carter of Wyatt.

He couldn't help wondering what Bryce was thinking about. Something he was remembering clearly flipped the switch to sub for Bryce. Carter had a feeling it was one of those occasional work conversations Bryce had hinted at.

Most of the time wasn't all the time.

Giving Wyatt a look before the curious sub could even open his mouth, Carter shook his head. Wyatt frowned but didn't push it. Brent didn't seem to feel the need to restrain himself, since he leaned back in his chair and gave Bryce a grin.

Brothers.

Carter did his best to hide his frustration, but the way Brent grinned, he didn't do a good job of it. Brent's wicked smile turned to Bryce. "Your Dom keeping you on your toes? I can't imagine any Dom behaving that well with someone they're interested in."

"He's not my Dom." The *not yet* clearly implied, Bryce gave Brent a stern look. "And we agreed to behave at work."

Laughing, Brent shook his head. "Knowing all of us, I'm not sure that rule will work."

Carter decided Brent was easier to deal with when he was sad and moody.

The way Wyatt was nodding enthusiastically, a dreamy

expression in his eyes, Carter knew the rule had already been tossed out the window. Bryce just hadn't gotten the memo yet. Had Grant? Not that he wanted Grant to invite him to work and do something outrageous. Not yet, anyway.

Wyatt giggled. "Just don't get caught."

Bryce gave them a curious look, sitting a little straighter. "I'll have to remember that next time Oliver comes in to pay a bill."

Wyatt couldn't restrain himself. Carter didn't blame him; the whole conversation was too tempting. "I'm sure Troy could help you remember."

Laughing, they all took turns heckling Bryce until the waiter arrived with their food. After starting to eat, the conversation turned back around to Wyatt and Garrett. Oversharing and tattling on each other seemed to be part of the family dynamics, so Carter felt it was his duty to make Wyatt feel more at home. "Did I hear you say that Garrett had invited Grant and Calen over to your house for dinner?"

Wyatt looked suspicious, but he couldn't see the issue. Nodding slowly, his brain was rolling things around, trying to see what Carter was up to. "Yes. He thought it would be fun, since we were hanging out."

Carter glanced at Brent and Bryce, then with an innocent look shoved Wyatt under the bus. Picking up an oversized steak fry, Carter gestured with it to Wyatt. "I think the exact words I heard were more like *our* house?"

That got everyone's attention.

Wyatt squirmed and tried to play it off, but no one was having it. They latched on like the gossip bloodhounds Carter had suspected they were. Bryce seemed to be glad it wasn't him getting the third degree and jumped right in. "*Our* house, huh? You two have something you want to share with everyone?"

"If Garrett thinks he can hide moving in with someone from

Mom, he's lost it." Brent grinned and reached for his glass to take a sip of his soda. "I think a phone call might be in order."

Bryce had an odd look on his face, but seemed to push it away because it was gone before Carter could decipher what it meant. Bryce nodded, a grin that matched Brent's on his lips. "I think she'd want to know that he's moving in with Wyatt before collaring him or something more traditional."

They both nodded like it was a serious topic that was a terrible breach of etiquette, but Carter could see the gleam in their eyes. They were going to have fun tormenting Garrett. Wyatt was bouncing back and forth between nervous and eager. "Don't get Master in trouble."

The other guys missed what Wyatt hadn't said, but Carter didn't. Wyatt was doing his best not to deny or confirm anything, but he was so excited he was ready to pop. What had he and Garrett been up to lately? Carter knew Garrett had been spending more and more time over at Wyatt's house, but he hadn't realized it was getting that serious.

Wyatt couldn't keep a secret like that for long; his natural inclination was to share. It could embarrass Carter, but it was who Wyatt was. In the beginning of their friendship, it was what had drawn him to Wyatt. Finally meeting someone who was just as unique in their own way as Carter was had made him feel so much more normal. He'd needed Wyatt's outgoing, sweet oversharing. Without it, he probably wouldn't have found the courage to be himself.

He wouldn't out Wyatt now, but the next time they were in the shop the nut was a goner, because Carter was going to corner him and find out what was going on. Wyatt looked excited but too nervous for Carter's comfort. Wyatt had always been the more outgoing person between the two of them, but to Carter, it felt like he was the one corralling Wyatt.

It might technically be Garrett's job now, but Carter knew it would always be a big part of their friendship. He had a feeling he knew what they were up to, though. Wyatt's reaction...yeah, Carter knew they needed to talk.

"We won't get him in too much trouble." Bryce had a wicked look on his face that Carter didn't believe for a minute.

"Don't get *me* in trouble!" Wyatt was starting to understand that getting Garrett in trouble was the goal.

Brent laughed so loud that it drew attention from several other tables. "Now you're learning. That's a better argument."

Huffing, Wyatt gave them dirty looks before going back to picking at his pasta. "You guys are nuts. It's like learning a foreign language."

"Family's fun." Bryce grinned, then started to cut into his steak.

That earned a skeptical look from Wyatt. "Funny ha-ha or funny nuts?"

Carter was nearly rolling on the floor, his burger long forgotten. He couldn't help it. Wyatt fit right in with the rest of the brothers, but it was going to take Carter a while to get used to the dynamics. Carter wasn't sure if he'd ever fit in as easily as Wyatt did, or if he even wanted to, but Wyatt was meant to join their crazy family.

"Both." Brent and Bryce spoke at the same time, then laughed.

Wyatt shook his head. To Carter, he looked like a parent who was getting to the point of being fed up with his kids. Time to change the subject by throwing himself under the bus. "Grant keeps talking about going up to the club. Is he actually serious, or is it one of those things he talks about but it never actually happens?"

They all perked up and looked at Carter like a bunch of puppies hearing the treat bag rattle. He tried to keep a straight face, but he wasn't sure it worked. Wyatt spoke up first. "Yes. Club trip."

Bryce and Brent both nodded. Bryce spoke up. "He's serious. We used to go a lot more often. The stuff with Wyatt and Garrett, and with Brent and Calen, got things sidetracked."

Brent gave Carter an understanding look. "It's not as bad as you're probably imagining. You won't be going by yourself, and if it's too much, just tell Grant. He'll understand."

"We'll be there for you. Unless you want us to back off so you can have some fun." Bryce gave Carter a big shit-eating grin. "We've gotten good at backing off so things don't get weird."

Carter couldn't imagine things not being weird. Not only was he going to a BDSM club with his...boyfriend...lover... maybe Dom...he was going with his—significant other's family. It was the strangest thing he'd ever considered doing. Even with all of Wyatt's pushing, he could only see himself doing it for Grant.

That, more than anything, let Carter see how much Grant was coming to mean to him.

As much as he fought to keep the steamrolling Dom at arm's length, he was starting to get under Carter's skin. He wanted to make Grant happy, but he was also getting tired of feeling like he was holding himself back.

He was comfortable with who he was, but it had been a hard-won comfort. He'd all but lost his family and didn't have that many close friends. Everyone wanted you to fit into a neat category and when you didn't, they gradually found reasons to drift away. Sure, some of it had been his fault for not trying harder to keep friends in his life, but when they hadn't understood, why should he?

Wyatt had understood.

Even when he hadn't, he'd refused to be ignored. Even if it was something as simple as having found another strange soul to make him feel more normal, Carter was grateful for him. Maybe he should have gone with Wyatt earlier.

Knowing Grant was going to be at the club made it feel different. Having someone to lean on and who would take control made it easier. He wouldn't have to be in charge or make any decisions. He could leave everything up to Grant.

He just needed to make sure Grant knew he was in control.

Maybe it was time for a talk.

"I'm sure it will be fine. Wyatt survived, so I'm sure I will, too." Ducking when Wyatt threw a balled up napkin at him, Carter laughed.

"I'm not that bad. I had fun, which is more than I can say of some people who act like they're closer to eighty than twenty." Wyatt laughed when Carter threatened to send the napkin sailing back at him. "At least I don't have little old ladies trying to fix me up."

Carter groaned. Brent and Bryce smelled blood and pounced on the gossip. Bryce spoke first. "What lady, and who was she fixing you up with?"

"She's an older lady who comes into the shop. She's funny and looks so proper, but she's a dirty bird." Wyatt grinned and shook his head. "She pretends to shop, but she just wants to gossip and hint at the outlandish things she gets up to with her friends."

Carter jumped in when Wyatt took a breath. "She thought I needed to be fixed up, so she was going to fix me up with the son of a friend of a friend. They found out he's into *interesting things* and thought I'd like to meet him."

"What did they think was so interesting?" It was clear Bryce was expecting something fairly innocent, so Carter loved the expression on his face when Wyatt started to explain. By the time Wyatt quietly whispered "Puppy play," Bryce's jaw was nearly on the floor.

"How did they even know about that?"

Wyatt lifted his hands palm up and shrugged. "They looked it up online, evidently."

"And they thought Carter would be a good fit?" Brent was looking at Carter like he was trying to visualize it.

"No. It would not have been a good fit." Carter couldn't see himself in that kind of a situation.

"They're going to find someone for him. I've seen the Dom at the club a few times, but not that many. I wonder if he's started going back. If he has his stuff out, then he has to be meeting someone." Wyatt leaned against the table, and Carter could tell his friend's mind had started to wander.

"Not our business." There were a thousand things running through his own head and Carter didn't need Wyatt adding to them.

That earned him a frown from all three men. Wyatt shook his head sadly. "You're no fun."

Biting back the slightly inappropriate comeback that sprang to mind, Carter cocked an eyebrow and gave him a look like he should know better. "Eat your dinner."

"See, he's not bouncy enough to be a pup. I'm not sure what they were thinking." Bryce was looking at Carter like he was inventorying his parts.

"They were thinking he was sexy in a skirt, so he might be into other things." Brent's dry answer had them all choking on their food.

When they could finally breathe, the waiter came over and set the bills down pointedly. They might have been too loud, but the stern schoolmaster look was out of place on a guy who looked like he was barely out of high school.

Evidently, grown-ups weren't allowed to be a nuisance, only teenagers.

They managed to behave while they paid their bills and

headed out of the restaurant. Brent stopped outside the door. "We might have to pick a different restaurant next time. They didn't seem to think we were that funny."

His dry delivery had Carter fighting not to smile. He really was such a different person now that everything with Calen was worked out. He hadn't met Brent that many times, but he was so much more relaxed that Carter almost wanted to check and make sure he hadn't been taken over by the pod people.

Wyatt only focused on the idea of going out again. "Yes. We should do this again soon. Every couple of weeks, at least."

Carter had to agree that it sounded like fun. "Once a month. Maybe we'll even talk Wyatt into cooking sometimes."

After making tentative plans to have dinner again, they separated and started heading for their cars. Even before he got into his car, Carter knew what he wanted to do. Taking his phone out of his pocket as he climbed in and locked the door, Carter pulled up his text messages.

Dinner over or you guys still hanging out?

It didn't take long for Grant to reply.

I'm heading home. Why? Booty call?

Carter's head fell back against the seat and he grinned. Maybe—but he wasn't going to tell Grant that.

Just thought you might come over for a drink. Unless you have to work early.

Grant's reply was so cheeky Carter could picture the look on his face.

I might have an in with the boss. I think I can swing it. Your place?

Before Carter could stop himself he typed out the answer.

Yes

His response was so typically Grant he made Carter laugh.

Gonna wear something sexy for me while we have that drink?

In for a penny…

Yes

Grant's reply came back so fast it had Carter worrying he would get into an accident.

Oh pretty I can't wait

Telling himself that it wasn't a booty call to text someone he was actually dating, Carter pulled out of the parking lot and started heading home. He knew exactly what he was going to put on for Grant. He just had to get home before his Dom so he could get it on. Picturing greeting Grant at the door in nothing but the white nightie had his pants getting tighter.

It was time to stop running from what he wanted.

What they both wanted.

10

GRANT

He'd teased Carter about it being a booty call, but it didn't have that kind of feel to it. Carter wasn't the type. He wouldn't have done it without deliberately trying to send Grant a message—but what? A late call for a drink wasn't something he would have expected from Carter.

Carter had a lot of walls and uncertainty that came from people who hadn't understood or supported him, but Grant had a feeling when he was ready to let those walls come down, it would be amazing. He'd thought they'd made progress when Carter tried on the sexy outfit for him, but he didn't want to assume anything, so he hadn't pushed.

They were going to explore their relationship at Carter's pace. Grant was just hoping Carter wouldn't make him guess how fast or slow it was supposed to go. He was better than Garrett at interpreting subtlety, but he didn't want there to be any miscommunications with Carter. Some people might like teasing and hinting, but he could see that backfiring with Carter.

The drive to Carter's house wasn't that many miles, but it felt like forever before he was pulling in the driveway. Turning the car off, he climbed out and headed toward the door.

Longest thirty seconds ever.

His brain was going back and forth, trying to figure out what Carter meant by the texts. Asking would probably ruin the mood, but unless it was obvious, he might have to.

It was obvious.

Carter opened the door before he could knock. Grant was left standing on the porch, arm raised and jaw falling to the steps. His sexy sub was stunning—and thankfully not hinting at all.

"You requested something sexy, I think?" Carter had a teasing glint in his eyes but his nerves were also showing. Little nibbles to his shiny lips and shifting hands with polished nails that didn't quite know where they belonged let Grant see how hard it was for his pretty sub.

"You are incredible." Grant let his hand fall to his side as he stepped closer, invading Carter's personal space. Not touching, but so close he might as well have been. "I've never seen anything hotter. I don't remember seeing this in your drawer."

Carter's cheeks heated, drawing attention to the subtle powder sparkling around his eyes, and his hands came up to brush down his chest. "It's new. When I saw it, I thought you'd like it."

"You were right." Grant's heated words left no doubt how much he loved the outfit, even if Carter had missed his raging erection.

The outfit was white lace that seemed to mold to Carter's skin. Little straps went over his shoulders, leading to the stretchy looking lace tank top Grant knew probably had a name, but he could hardly remember his own in that moment. It clung to Carter's lean body, accentuating every dip and hint of curve.

The bottoms were even more incredible. They were tight little shorts that reminded Grant of the other ones, but these left nothing to the imagination. Carter's thickening erection was beautifully outlined, and by the way they went up on the sides, Grant had a good image in his head about how much of Carter's tempting ass would be showing.

Carter gave a low chuckle that had Grant's gaze trailing back up his body to look at Carter's pleased expression. No more fear, no more nerves. Just pleasure and a wicked humor that was enjoying Grant's reaction. "Glad you like it."

Grant licked his lips and gave Carter one last, thorough glance. "I think I'm ready for that drink now."

Sexy clothes didn't mean Carter was going to get out of them, so Grant needed something in his hands before he closed that last step. Carter was entirely too tempting.

Carter grinned and a low chuckle vibrated through Grant. "Wine okay?" Then Carter's grin turned positively evil as he turned and walked back toward the living room.

The view was perfect.

The little shorts rode high on his ass baring most of his cheeks, giving teasing glances at the seam that hinted at other tempting places Grant wanted to explore. There was only one thing missing to make the picture perfect.

"Oh pretty, the only thing missing is a pink bottom peeking out of those panties." Grant's words came out low and husky. If he hadn't been watching Carter's body so closely, he might have missed the little hitch in his step and the way his ass clenched tight. His sub liked that idea.

It was enough to make any Dom crazy. Keeping his hands to himself had never been as hard before as it was in that moment. Carter was trying to kill him. His heart was pounding, and with all the blood rushing toward his cock, it was entirely possible. Reaching down, he didn't try to hide his movements as he adjusted his dick into a more comfortable position.

Carter peeked back in time to see Grant's hands. The pink in his cheeks flared to life again, and he quickly glanced forward.

He might have been a little embarrassed, but there was an extra swing to his step that let Grant know he wasn't too flustered.

By the time they reached the living room, Grant was even harder and Carter's sexy walk was making it hard to think. It took Grant a minute to hear the words that Carter was saying. "Sorry, what?"

"Wine? Is that okay?" Carter's eyes were dancing. He liked knowing he'd melted Grant's brain.

"That's fine." Grant didn't care what it was at that point. His body and brain were occupied with more important tasks: keeping his hands to himself and not doing anything stupid.

Carter chuckled and walked toward the kitchen, calling out behind him, "Have a seat. I'll be right back."

Grant threw himself down on the couch and took several deep breaths. There was a message tonight, all right. No matter what happened, Grant knew Carter was at the very least showing he was comfortable with Grant. That Carter would let Grant in like this meant everything to him. He could almost see the walls crumbling, and he felt proud of Carter for opening up to him.

It wasn't exactly submission, but it felt the same to Grant. Carter was sharing who he was and what he liked on the deepest level. It took an amazing amount of trust. He pushed back the emotions welling in his chest as he waited for Carter.

He was worth the wait.

Walking out slowly, hips swinging back and forth making his arousal evident, Carter carried two glasses of red wine. Watching intently, Grant almost missed the obvious as Carter kept walking toward the couch. His pretty sub had no intention of sitting beside him.

Making himself at home on Grant's lap, Carter gave Grant a deceptively sweet smile as he handed one of the glasses over.

Taking a long sip, Grant fought to keep his control. Carter was going to kill him.

Carter took a drink that looked more like he was playing with the glass than actually consuming it. "What do you think?"

It was a loaded question and Grant's mind wasn't stocked with any answers. "What?"

"The wine? What do you think?" Carter's innocent expression wasn't fooling anyone. He knew exactly what he was doing.

"Delicious." Grant felt Carter's body rub over his cock and the one word was all he could manage. Taking another sip, he tried to clear his head. It didn't work. "Did I tell you how much I liked your outfit?"

"Yes." Carter reached out and took Grant's glass before turning to set them both on the end table. The twisting motion highlighted his lean muscles. "I hoped you'd like it."

"I do." He more than liked it.

"You know you shouldn't drink and drive." Carter tried to look confident, but Grant could see the cracks showing.

"You're right. It's dangerous." Starting to see where things were going, Grant continued, "I should probably stay here tonight."

"That might be best." Carter's gaze broke away, and he started looking around the room. "I should have thought of that before I offered you a drink. It was...naughty of me."

Finally feeling like he had a true green light to loosen his control, Grant wrapped his arms around Carter's body. Letting his hands caress the lace-covered skin, Grant pulled Carter closer. Bodies touching, Grant's hands came to rest on Carter's hip, teasingly close to his ass. "You're right. That was very naughty. I'm going to have to punish you. Do you understand why?"

Carter's body practically vibrated with nervous excitement,

but his words came out soft and even. "Yes, Sir. I understand you have to spank me when I'm bad."

It was where Grant's mind had automatically gone, especially with Carter's reaction to his comment earlier, but it was nice to hear the words from his nervous sub. Grant let one hand ease back so he was caressing the top of Carter's full bottom with his fingers, gingerly stroking the sensitive skin where the two pieces separated.

A shiver raced through Carter. His cock visibly jerked under the panties that kept giving teasing glances at the naked skin underneath. Grant couldn't control the growl that escaped, and he knew Carter would be able to feel how hard he was. "I think we should head back to your bedroom. I'm going to stretch you out across my lap so I can give you the spanking you need."

The little gasp that escaped Carter's wet, parted lips made Grant fight the urge to kiss him. As tempting as it was, it would have to wait. He knew that one taste would distract them both, and he wanted to give Carter the taste of submission he was craving.

Carter hadn't really been able to discover that part of himself, and Grant wanted to give him the space to explore those needs as well. Short and breathy, Carter's answer was to the point. "Yes, Sir."

Beyond a few brief conversations, they hadn't talked much about the D/s portion of their relationship. He was supposed to have brought over a sample contract and list of preferences so they could discuss it in more detail. It just hadn't felt right yet. To Grant, they'd had other things that they'd needed to get comfortable with first. He wanted Carter to believe he was going to stay, and that he loved the way Carter expressed himself. Those things were more important.

But it looked like Carter was ready for a taste of submission.

Reluctantly helping Carter off his lap, Grant took his hand

and led him back to the bedroom. Turning on a lamp near the bed, Grant left the rest of the lights off. The dark felt more intimate to him and he was hoping it would help Carter relax easier.

Giving Carter's ass a quick pat, Grant ordered him up on the mattress. Watching a shy Carter slowly climb up, Grant thought he'd come right there. The sweet nervousness combined with the sexy clothes that showed every line of Carter's body had his arousal surging.

Before Carter could sit, Grant climbed up beside him and gestured to his lap. "Over my legs, pretty."

Carter's endearing blush was back, but he didn't let any worries stop him. As erotic as Carter looked, Grant was proud of him as well. He might be nervous, but he was going after what he wanted. As Carter hesitantly draped himself across Grant's legs, Grant brought his hands down to soothe his beautiful sub. "That's right. God, you look...perfect."

Ducking his head, Carter still looked nervous, but it was edging toward an aroused excitement and less like he was ready to bolt. Grant let his fingers trail up and down Carter's body, letting him get used to being touched.

Warm skin and soft lace teased at his fingers, making him want to rub his body against Carter's. Torn between wanting to feel Carter's naked skin and loving the way the lingerie made him look, Grant compromised and took the lace panties in his hand. Carefully easing them over Carter's ass, Grant left them just under his cheeks so they framed his bottom perfectly.

Carter's breath hitched again, but he didn't say anything, so Grant pressed forward. "You were a naughty boy. We're going to make sure you remember to be better next time. Do you understand that?"

A needy whine escaped Carter as he nodded, pressing his head into the covers. "Yes, Sir. I'm sorry."

Tightening one hand around Carter's waist to hold his trembling sub securely, Grant rubbed circles over the smooth, pale skin. Deciding that teasing too long would be more torture than pleasure, Grant brought his hand up and down quickly before Carter had a chance to brace himself.

Making sure to keep his strokes light and ease Carter into the spanking as gently as possible, Grant was pleased to see Carter arch up, silently begging for more. Within seconds Carter's quiet need was traded for moans of pleasure and gasps as the sensations started to flood his body.

Grant knew the heat was building and with every smack the feelings would radiate through Carter's body, making him need even more. It would be confusing as the pleasure and pain started mingling, but Carter's reactions were beautiful. Writhing against Grant's lap, Carter's full erection let him know more than anything that his pretty sub loved his first spanking.

Making sure not to hit the same spot too many times, Grant watched as Carter's bottom grew pink. The tender seat of his ass was a rosy color that would look incredible against the white of the panties. With each pop, Carter's gasps and needy moans grew louder and more desperate.

Knowing it wouldn't be long, Grant started spacing out the spanks, caressing Carter's heated bottom, drawing out the pleasure. Carter was shaking, grinding his cock against Grant when Grant decided his sweet sub was at his limit.

Letting his hands run small circles over the beautiful pink skin, Grant made sure to have his fingers graze Carter's tight pink opening that kept peeking out as he writhed. Pleading noises broke out as Carter fought the urge to beg for more.

He was trying to be so good that Grant had to reward him. Grazing his fingers lightly around the sensitive pucker, Grant watched as Carter's resolve broke.

"Please, Grant. Please, Sir. I—I..."

Pushing his thumb against the tender opening as he let his fingers caress the beautiful pink skin, Grant didn't make him fight the need any longer. "Come for me, pretty. Show me how good it feels."

Grant wasn't sure if it was the permission, the touch to his heated ass, or the feeling of Grant's thumb on his tight opening, but Carter exploded, pleasure ripping through him. Holding his sub gently as his orgasm sent waves of arousal through him, Grant caressed him tenderly, urging it higher and higher.

When Carter finally collapsed, body spent and relaxed, Grant carefully gathered him up in his arms. Turning to lay them both on the bed, Grant held him close. Carter's gaze was foggy like he wasn't really there, and while Grant didn't think he was in subspace, it was clear he was close.

Giving his sub a gentle kiss on his head, Grant ran his hands up and down Carter's back while he snuggled close. When he'd gone out that night, he'd never imagined that his evening would end curled up in Carter's bed, holding him while he came.

He didn't think it could get more perfect.

He was wrong.

F ighting his way back up through the pleasure, Carter fought the temptation to sink into the sleepy oblivion that called to him. As perfect as falling asleep cuddling in Grant's arms would be, he wasn't ready yet. He wasn't going to leave Grant hard and needy.

That he'd get to touch and enjoy the big, broad man was a bonus.

Rubbing his face against the soft cotton of Grant's T-shirt, Carter felt the well-defined muscles of his chest. Forcing his eyes open, he wished it was skin instead of cloth. "If I'm almost naked, I think you should be, too."

He felt a chuckle rumble through Grant's chest. "I'm not sure you learned your lesson. You might need another reminder about how to talk to your Dom."

Grant's hands wandered down Carter's back and squeezed his ass. The rough touch sent arousal flaring through his body, even though there was no way his cock could recover that quickly. Rolling his hips, Carter let his cock brush Grant's thigh. Dropping his voice low, filling it with all the desire still running through him, Carter let Grant know how much he still wanted him. "Yes, Sir. I'm sure I'll need lots of reminders. Being good is hard."

Letting his hands slide down to caress the edges of Grant's shirt, Carter spoke again, low and husky. "Will you get naked for me, Sir? I want to touch you."

Calling Grant Sir felt right, but didn't feel as serious as it sounded when Wyatt said it. There was an edge of teasing and a lightness he hadn't expected. Was he doing it wrong? BDSM always sounded so serious when Wyatt talked about it, but with Grant it was fun. Maybe it was because Grant didn't seem to need the domination to extend outside the bedroom.

When he'd been laid out over Grant's lap, his panties pulled down and his ass bared, it had felt overwhelming and so much more erotic than he'd ever imagined. The few times a lover had come close to introducing pain, even by accident, Carter had loved it, but the spanking was incredible. He had a good guess that he'd feel it tomorrow, but he didn't mind that at all.

Pain and pleasure had mixed until he really couldn't tell one from the other. They were rolled together somehow until he craved them both equally. He couldn't wait to do it again. Carter knew that Grant hadn't been rough with the spanking, but part of him wanted to see how it would feel to go even further.

Eventually.

Just not right then.

Grant groaned as Carter's fingers worked their way under his shirt. Carter gave him a cheeky grin. "I think you're not moving fast enough...Sir."

"Naughty boy..." Grant didn't look upset, though. He rolled away long enough to sit up and tug his shirt off. Then, leaning back, he gave Carter a wicked look and ran his hands down his chest to flick the button on his pants. Dragging the zipper down, he had Carter's mouth watering as he slowly opened it.

By the time everything was off, Carter was tired of waiting.

He wanted Grant naked right then. Even Carter's cock, which should have still been spent, was trying to come to attention again. Grant's boxer briefs hid more of his body than Carter would have preferred, but they outlined his cock beautifully.

It was long and thick, well-proportioned for his body but not overly large. Carter was all for a nice-sized dick, but there could be too much of a good thing. Finally coming to his limit, Carter reached out and helped Grant along.

Grant laughed and shook his head as Carter pulled down his last remaining clothing. Carter couldn't resist touching Grant once his body was finally bared. He figured he'd been patient long enough. Grant didn't argue, he just stretched out and let Carter explore.

Running his hands down Grant's chest, Carter felt the muscles ripple under the smooth skin. The only hair he had was a small treasure trail leading down to a trimmed bush around his cock. Letting his fingers wander down through the hair, he circled Grant's straining erection, not letting his hands touch it yet. Grant had teased him before and Carter wanted to return the favor.

At least until his patience gave out.

Grant's cock jerked and bobbed as Carter's hands caressed the sensitive skin around his groin. Making low sounds of plea-sure, Grant was still as Carter's hands stroked closer and closer before moving away to run down his legs. Grant's moans took on a frustrated, demanding tone as Carter went farther from where he wanted to be touched.

But Grant never demanded Carter touch him and never made a move to direct what Carter should do. He was patient and seemed to have endless control as Carter eased Grant's legs apart so he could climb in between them.

Seeing his sexy lover spread out on display had Carter's hands sliding back up Grant's legs. Teasing was fun, but he was ready for more. Even his own cock was half-hard with desire again. Kneeling up, Carter moved his hands off Grant just long enough to push his panties all the way down before reaching up and stripping off the rest of his clothes.

Grant's hungry eyes watched him, and Carter knew it wouldn't be long before his Dom took control again. Settling back down on the bed, Carter brought his hands back to Grant's firm thighs. Grant's cock was damp with precum by the time Carter's fingers wrapped around the aroused length.

Grant growled and Carter could see his entire body tense. Even his Dom's cock pulsed in Carter's hand, demanding more. Slowly jerking him off, Carter stared intently as his hand moved up and down. Before he could even bring his other hand up to play with Grant's balls, his Dom spoke.

"I need to know how much more you want, pretty." Low and filled with desire, Grant's words sent a flood of naughty images through Carter's imagination.

Tightening his grip, Carter's remaining fears had scattered, and he knew what he wanted. "Everything."

In that moment, he wanted it all with Grant. He wanted to feel his lover stretched out over him, covering him with his body. Carter wanted to feel Grant inside him, taking him higher and filling him. He wanted to feel Grant pressed against him, kissing him and tasting him.

He needed everything his Dom had to give.

Taking him at his word, Grant seized control. One moment, he was still letting Carter set the pace and the next, he had Carter on his back looking up at the sexy man pinning him down with his desire and strength. Carter's breath caught in his throat, his cock jumping that final leap from half-hard to fully aroused.

Grant couldn't miss the excitement that surged through Carter at the sudden role reversal. Grant might be sweet and tender, but Carter could see the erotic need and desire flooding him. It made Carter ache, and he wanted more. He wasn't sure he was supposed to ask, though.

Was he supposed to wait and take what Grant would give him, or was the game something else? There were so many questions he should have asked, but jumping in with both feet seemed like a better idea. Grant had to have seen the questions running through Carter's mind because he gave him a soft smile and leaned in.

Pressing the softest kiss to Carter's lips, Grant tasted him and soothed ragged nerves Carter hadn't even been aware of. Melting into Grant's arms, Carter let his hands wrap around his lover to feel the straining muscles of his back. Grant's body was strong and broad. Carter loved every inch of it.

Trying to thrust his hips up, Carter could barely move, Grant was pressed so fully against him. As much as he wanted to be able to move and rub his cock against Grant, Carter loved the feeling of being pinned down. He'd never trusted a lover enough to let them restrain him, but suddenly all he could picture was being tied to the bed.

Grant pulled back and looked down at him with a more commanding expression than Carter had seen on his lover before. "What were you thinking, pretty? What naughty things went through your mind?"

Knowing he could trust Grant, Carter fought the instinctive need to hide what he was thinking and pushed out the truth. It felt like trying to work his way through quicksand, but he eventually got it out. "I like feeling you this way. Having you pinning me down like this. I was picturing you tying me to the bed."

"I would love to tie you up, pretty." Grant pressed a quicker, hotter kiss to Carter's mouth before pulling back. "There are so many things I could do to you. I'd stretch you out to the corners of the bed and then lick you all over."

Grant shifted, moving to bring Carter's arms over his head. "I could restrain you like this. Then I could flip you over and make you scream with pleasure. I could spank you again, then take you while you writhed for me."

Carter could hardly breathe.

Fire licked through him as he listened to Grant's fantasies. It was like his lover could read his mind. Chewing on his lips and trying not to pull against Grant, it was all he could do not to beg for it right then. Nodding, Carter felt his hips thrust up, and he knew needy sounds were spilling from his lips but he couldn't stop them.

"God, you're beautiful." Grant looked at him like Carter was the most incredible thing he'd ever seen.

Carter wasn't sure how to respond. His brain wasn't working. But even without desire frying his brain, he wouldn't have known what to say. Grant made him feel beautiful. Carter felt comfortable in his own skin. He wore what made him happy, but Grant looked at him like he was perfect.

It was scary and wonderful and everything in between.

No one had ever looked at him like that. It made Carter fight to hold back irrational things that shouldn't be said yet. Things that he couldn't be feeling so early in their relationship. Not having the words to respond, Carter lifted his head and poured out his emotions in a long, deep kiss.

Grant turned the passion and emotion around and took his mouth. Commanding and thorough, it felt like he was dragging the feelings out of Carter. Like he wanted everything Carter had to give him. Too soon—too much—it didn't matter to Grant.

When he finally released Carter's mouth, Grant had them both desperate and needy. Carter could feel Grant's arousal pressed hard against his legs, and all he wanted was for Grant to slip inside him. For Grant to take him and send them both into orbit with pleasure.

There was no doubt in Carter's mind that it would be incredible between them. When Grant leaned close and started kissing his way down Carter's chest, he thought he would lose his mind. The warm heat from his soft lips, the flick of his tongue as he traced unseen patterns in Carter's skin, the heavy press of Grant's cock against his leg all combined to have him begging for more.

Grant's low chuckle rippled across Carter's skin as his mouth inched closer to Carter's straining cock. Trailing his tongue along the edge of Carter's leg where it met his groin, Grant made him writhe and plead.

When Grant bypassed his cock completely to kiss lower and lick his balls, Carter wasn't sure if he was in heaven or hell. As Grant pushed his legs open and settled in to lick the seam that ran down Carter's sac, he knew it was both. The first touch of Grant's tongue on Carter's tight hole had him nearly coming off the bed. The only thing that kept him down was Grant's tight grip pinning his hips to the mattress.

Whining and begging, Carter pleaded for more, but he couldn't have said exactly what he wanted. All he knew was that it wasn't enough. The light flick of Grant's tongue as it circled his hole just made the need to be filled worse.

When Grant's tongue finally breached him, Carter's tone took on a demanding, desperate edge Grant seemed to love. Looking down at his Dom stretched out between his legs, Carter could see the wicked pleasure that radiated from Grant's eyes as Carter's need grew. The more frantic Carter got, the more Grant loved it.

He was like an old-fashioned rogue ravishing the maiden in the love stories that Carter would never have admitted he'd read. Wicked and devilish but sweet and careful, it was a combination Carter loved and knew he'd never get enough of.

When Carter's begging turned into a mess of jumbled words

and sounds, Grant finally took pity on him. Rising up, his eyes showed just how much he wanted Carter, even if the heavy arousal standing out from his body could have been missed.

It took Carter a minute to understand what Grant was saying, but finally the words made sense. "Supplies? Pretty, do you have any?"

Nodding clumsily, Carter looked toward the nightstand. Grant had been on the forefront of his mind when he'd been running errands the other day. Carter had come home with some items he hadn't intended to purchase. They were going to come in handy sooner than he'd expected.

Grant made quick work of reaching over and getting out the condom and lube. Carter was glad Grant didn't ask him to help, because he wasn't sure if he would have been able to make his hands work enough to get the condom on Grant. Luckily, Grant didn't seem to have the same problem. He was confident and sure as he rolled it down his cock, then lubed up two fingers.

Carter was already well-prepared from Grant's teasing and thorough tasting, so Grant's first finger slid in with only the slightest resistance, sinking deep. Gently sweeping his finger back and forth, Grant grinned as he found what he was searching for.

Starting to shake as Grant lightly caressed the sensitive bundle of nerves, Carter pressed down, demanding more. Grant's wicked chuckle sent shivers down Carter's back. He pulled out, and when he pushed back in Carter felt the delicious burn of two fingers filling him.

Gently stretching the tight ring of muscles, Grant enjoyed making Carter squirm and beg. The sweet burn was just enough to make him need more, but not enough to fill him. Perfection was just out of his reach, no matter how he pleaded.

Fire and pleasure danced in Grant's eyes as he watched. Carter loved the way it made him feel, like he was being chased by some fierce predator. But in this case, he couldn't wait to be caught. He was begging to be taken, but the beast wasn't done playing with him yet.

Carter was stretched and ready long before Grant moved to take him. Laying out over Carter, Grant finally slid his fingers from Carter's body. Even through the empty feeling, all Carter knew was relief.

The wait was finally over.

Slowly entering him, Grant was so careful it made Carter crazy. Every demand for more was met with that iron control that made Carter want to completely unravel. It was sexy and perfect. No matter how he cried out for more, Grant would make him wait until he was ready. It was even better than the spanking.

Not having to worry about what he said or how he had to behave was an incredible release.

It was freeing and unlike any sexual experience he'd ever had. No decisions. No fear of what Grant would think. No overthinking about being masculine enough. No worries that Grant would rush through. Just slow perfection and an honest desire that he'd never experienced with anyone before.

At some point, Grant must have realized Carter was hovering on the edge of insanity because his pace increased and every deep thrust was suddenly more intense. When Carter couldn't hold his legs up any longer, Grant's arms were there, looped under his knees.

The new position not only allowed Carter to let go even deeper, but it made Grant's cock rub over his prostate with every thrust. The constant caress against the sensitive bundle of nerves made the shaking even worse, and gray started hazing the edge of Carter's vision.

Almost trapped beneath Grant, with the pleasure radiating through him, Carter lost control. One minute he was riding the waves of sensation and the next he exploded. His orgasm burst through him like a tsunami of desire. Clenching around Grant's thick cock as he continued to thrust, Carter watched as Grant finally lost his iron control.

A low growl radiated out from deep in Grant's chest and his smooth rhythm faltered as his body tightened and bowed. Maybe it was the intimacy, maybe it was the feeling of Grant's body jerking in his, but it kept the pleasure rushing through Carter until he was almost floating.

It was almost like he wasn't actually in his body. It would have frightened him if it weren't for Grant. No matter what, Carter knew Grant would keep him safe. His Dom wouldn't let anything happen to him.

When the world returned to normal, Grant was wrapped around him on the bed, condom gone. His eyes were warm and filled with emotion. "There you are."

Carter just rolled closer and tucked his face against Grant's chest. "Stay."

"You'd have to shove me out the door, pretty. I'm not going anywhere." Low and soft, Grant's words were probably responding to Carter's demand, but Carter thought he heard something else. Somewhere between the words, the emotions made it sound like Grant was talking about so much more.

Closing his eyes, Carter felt the pull of sleep winning. It didn't matter what Grant really meant, there was only one response. "Yes. Mine."

The sound of soft laughter might have chased him into his dreams, but the world was gone before he knew for sure.

12

GRANT

Waking up to the warmth of Carter's body pressed against him, Grant couldn't imagine a better way to start the day. It made it easier to see why Garrett wanted to live with Wyatt so soon. Tightening his arms around Carter, Grant pulled him closer, loving the way his sexy man pressed his face into Grant's chest. Waking up like this every morning would be something he could get used to.

Rubbing his face against the muscled skin, Carter settled in, ready to sink back into sleep. He had to agree that it sounded like a better idea than getting up, but unfortunately, as much as Grant wanted to, he couldn't sleep all day. Going in late was one thing, but he hadn't planned on taking the day off, and he had meetings that couldn't be rescheduled.

Pressing a kiss to the top of Carter's head, Grant ran his finger down his pretty's back, loving the way he squirmed and scrunched up his face. Mumbling something about morning people that sounded ruder than what would usually come out of his mouth, Carter wrapped one arm around Grant. Grant heard his breathing even out again, and he knew Carter was almost asleep. He hated having to leave, but Carter would understand.

With feather-light caresses, Grant teased the top of Carter's ass, letting his fingers trail down slowly. "I have to go, pretty."

"No work. More that." Pushing his ass back into Grant's hand, Carter rubbed his cheek against Grant's chest again. Grant thought he felt a little tongue caressing the skin around his nipple, making the bud tighten and his whole body tense in anticipation.

His sub was a firecracker when he was awake, but evidently, he wasn't much of a morning person—unless it involved sex. Then Grant expected his man to be a little more forgiving. He thought it was cute, although he was smart enough to realize Carter might not appreciate being told that.

Sliding his hand over a little, Grant gave one cheek a squeeze. "Don't you want to have breakfast with me before I have to go?"

Carter moaned and twitched. He couldn't seem to decide if he wanted to press harder into Grant's hand or if it was too much. "Are you sore, pretty?"

He'd tried to be careful, but Carter was so new it would take time to learn his limits. His bottom didn't look red, but Grant couldn't be sure from that angle. He'd have to get a good look once they got up.

Carter shook his head, though, and peeked up at Grant through almost-closed lids. "Not like you mean. I can feel it, though, and it's...not bad but not good, it's..." He shrugged, not sure what to say.

"You're going to remember it today. Do you know how erotic that is? How much I like knowing you'll continually think about what we did last night? Remember that you're mine every time you sit down?" Grant knew he could be a little possessive, but he loved that Carter would think about being bent over his lap all day.

Every time Carter sat or leaned over, the scene would come

to his mind. He'd recall how it felt to lay over Grant's lap, exposed and needy. He'd think about being touched and spanked, the memories making him hard and ready.

Carter didn't even blush. He just shook his head at Grant's words, but the grin let Grant know that he didn't mind. The little reminders of what they'd done, and hopefully of how Grant felt about him, would follow Carter. It wasn't as permanent as a collar or other symbol of their relationship, but it was a step in that direction.

They weren't at that point. Grant understood it would take time before Carter would be comfortable with a symbol of their commitment, but he also knew he'd be finding subtle and more obvious ways to show it. There were a thousand ways to make sure Carter knew how much he was wanted. Grant was looking forward to trying each of them out.

"You like that." Carter was enjoying the sensation, but seemed to find Grant's reaction funny.

"I *love* that. I love knowing you'll remember being mine all day." Grant growled out the words, tightening his hand enough to make Carter moan again. "I'm also going to love keeping you turned on."

Carter rubbed his cock against Grant's leg. It was impossible to miss the aroused length. "Horny, yes—"

"But not now." Grant grinned at Carter's exaggerated frown. Carter didn't seem to know what Grant was trying to say—but it was clear he didn't think he'd like it. His boy was aroused and ready to do something about it right then.

Carter looked over at the clock, then back at Grant. "It's still early..." His voice trailed off and he gave Grant a meaningful look.

Grant smiled, lifting his head to give Carter a quick kiss. "But I like the idea of you going to work with your cock hard and your bottom reminding you about what we've done."

"But..." Carter couldn't seem to decide how he felt about that idea. "Going to work..."

Grant sensed the unasked question. "Yes. Not even playing with your sexy body by yourself. You can do that for me, can't you?" Grant dropped his voice low but gave Carter a playful look. He was going to do his best to get his way because Carter would love it. "I know we don't have a contract or a lot of rules, but what do you think about trying this for me?"

Carter's brain seemed to be racing around in circles. Grant could see his mind warring over the different choices. He might not like the idea of waiting, but Carter seemed to thrive when he got to stretch the limits of what he'd done before. There were probably moments in the past where he'd submitted unconsciously to someone or in a particular situation, but it was different when you were making a deliberate decision to submit.

Choosing to gift that to someone wasn't easy. It probably felt strange. No matter how much Carter had enjoyed the spanking the night before, letting Grant make other decisions in the bedroom wouldn't come easy.

The best things never did.

Finally coming to a conclusion, Carter nodded hesitantly. His words came out skeptically, like he wasn't sure he wanted to know the answer. "Okay, but for how long? I mean, how long am I waiting? Wyatt overshares and I'm not sure..."

Grinning, Grant could only imagine what kinds of things Wyatt had told Carter. The cute little sub loved to chatter and his first instinct seemed to be to tell Carter everything. "We're not lifestyle and you're not ready for something as intense as they might do. I'll probably take control in the bedroom without thinking about it. That's automatic for me at this point unless you say something. Extending things outside of a scene isn't something I'll ask of you very often. And never if it turns out to bother you, pretty."

Leaning down again, Grant gave Carter a quick kiss to his lips. "I think you'll like it, though."

Carter settled into Grant's chest again and sighed. "But how long this time?"

"How about I come over tonight and take you out to dinner? Then we'll see if you've been good and need a reward." Grant couldn't help his smile at the hitch in Carter's breathing. He was curious to know what had caught his man's attention.

Carter shifted his head and licked Grant's nipple again. Was it something he thought Grant would like, or was he unconsciously showing Grant what *he* liked?

Pulling back, Carter's words came out husky and low. "I like it when you talk about me being good and getting a reward. It feels...wicked somehow."

"I'll like rewarding you when you've been a good boy. I'll like it even more when I get to pull down your panties and spank you for being *naughty*." Grant felt a shiver race through Carter's body. "No spanking or orgasm tonight, though, if you play with yourself."

"That sounds sexy, too, when you say it." Carter shook his head like he couldn't quite believe it.

"I'm glad. It's important to me that you want what we do in a scene. I want it to feel right to both of us. And if there are things you want to try that I don't bring up, I want you to talk to me about it. Just because I don't mention it doesn't mean I'm not willing to do it with you." There was such a variety in BDSM that Grant would never be able to guess. "Eventually, we can sit down and go over the list that can be in a contract so we can talk about specific things, activities you're curious about or things that don't sound good at all. We'll also talk about safewords."

"I'm good with what we've done so far." Carter traced around one nipple with his tongue, making Grant fight to keep his body under control. "I'm curious to know what you want to do tonight when I get my reward."

"So you're confident you can be good?" Grant couldn't help but think of it as a challenge now.

Carter nodded, then took one of Grant's nipples in his mouth, teasing at the tight nub with his teeth. Grant moaned and his hips thrust out, his cock brushing against Carter's bare skin. Carter moved away long enough to answer, flirting, with sex dripping from his voice. "I know I can. I'll be a good boy for you, Sir."

"You're trying to cheat, pretty." His words came out breathless. Carter was making it hard to think. If he thought he'd be able to con his way into an orgasm, he'd be sadly mistaken.

Carter's words came out mumbled. "I'm being good."

"Even if I fuck you right now, you won't get to come. Is that what you want?" His sub was devious. Grant loved it.

It took Carter longer than Grant thought it would to pull away and shake his head no. He'd expected an immediate denial. Grant was left curious again, wondering what had been going through his mind. Did Carter like the idea? It hadn't been meant as a reward or even a scene, he just hadn't been willing to let Carter win, but something about the reaction pulled at Grant.

"Sometimes if you've been naughty, teasing me like that, I might have to lock up your cock and you wouldn't get to come before I made love to you. Of course, I'd have to be sure you were *very* ready before I slid into you. I wouldn't want to hurt you, pretty. I'd stretch you and taste you and make sure your body could take me without any pain before I took you." It was a scene Grant would thoroughly love, but it wasn't something he would have mentioned for a while. Not everyone was into denial to that degree.

But his man just might be.

Another little shiver raced through Carter and his teeth tightened, pulling at Grant's nipples. His pretty didn't mind that idea at all. Now *his* mind was racing. Would Carter misbehave today just to try out the punishment? Grant mentally added stopping by the adult store on the way home to his to-do list.

He needed a cock cage.

Carter didn't seem ready to voice his thoughts about the *punishment* option just yet, so Grant let it drop for the time being. If it came up that night he'd be ready, but if not, it was something that they could come back to later. If Carter liked denial, there were so many ways they could incorporate it into their scenes. Grant's cock throbbed just thinking about it.

"You never did say if you wanted to have breakfast with me?" Grant laughed at Carter's frustrated sigh.

"This conversation was just an evil plot to get me out of bed. Wasn't it?" Carter frowned, sure he'd been had. "There's no rule or punishment, you just wanted food."

Laughing, Grant shook his head. "Sorry to disappoint, but the rule stands. How about we take a shower together? Then coffee and I'll scramble some eggs for you if you have some." That was about all he could make in the kitchen, but they weren't bad. Usually, they turned out reasonably edible, and he was a master at toast. That made a reasonable breakfast.

Carter's frown turned into a grimace as he wrinkled his nose like he smelled something off. "I'm not letting you anywhere near my eggs. I'll cook."

"Mine are fine." Grant thought he should probably be offended. He would have been—except Carter had a right to be skeptical.

"Nobody in your family cooks worth a damn." Carter shuddered. "We'll end up with food poisoning, or they'll be burnt."

"It takes talent to burn eggs. Scrambled ones go rubbery first. They don't burn for a while."

"That you even know that makes my stomach hurt." Laughing, Carter shook his head. "Nope. Not letting you near my food."

"I think I might be offended." Grant knew his grin made the words less than believable.

"Should I help soothe you in the shower? Help you feel better?" Carter's grin held wicked anticipation.

Grant pinched his butt. "You're not going to get to come yet, pretty. But jerking one out sounds like a good idea. I should make you watch."

Carter cocked his head and gave Grant a look like he wasn't sure if that sounded good or not. His sub was going to analyze everything. Hopefully, he'd come to realize that sometimes it didn't matter why something turned you on, it just did. Still giving Grant a questioning look, Carter shifted away slightly. "Let's go get a shower. I'll let you make the coffee if you promise you can actually make it right."

Not sure what was going to happen in the shower, Grant tried for a neutral look. Figuring he'd play it by ear, he gave Carter a quick kiss as he sat up before starting to get off the bed. Visions of taking his time washing Carter thoroughly had his cock jerking and starting to leak precum. "Let's go, pretty."

"Just to let you know, that innocent act is failing miserably." Carter looked like he couldn't decide if he was excited to see what would happen in the shower or not.

"I'm just thinking about how helpful I can be." Pulling Carter close as he rose from the bed, Grant let their bodies rub together, loving the way Carter's cock pulsed against him. "I like being helpful."

Carter snorted. "That sounds more like a threat than a promise."

Grant laughed. "That's because you're more than just a sexy man in lacy panties. Your brains are just as hot."

Laughing, Carter stepped away and headed for the shower, giving his hips a little more swing than usual. "You like my lingerie."

"I love it." It was an understatement, but saying he was a bit obsessed sounded wrong.

"You'll have to wait and see what goes under my clothes today. I think I'm going to keep it a surprise." He looked back, grinning. "Just to make sure you think about me today."

Grant couldn't help but smile. His man was wicked.

13

CARTER

"Hello, dear." The cheerful voice of Mrs. Jenkins wasn't what sent shivers of dread racing down Carter's spine.

Where was Wyatt when he needed backup?

No, it was the sight of Mrs. Jenkins followed by a gaggle of innocent-looking older ladies that had his heart racing. She'd brought reinforcements. What could she want? He wasn't even going to pretend it would be about his actual job. No, those ladies had a mission and it had nothing to do with antiques.

He could see it in their eyes.

When he'd casually spoken about wanting a distraction to keep himself from thinking about what Grant might do when he got home, Mrs. Jenkins wasn't what he'd had in mind. He'd been picturing something less dangerous. Like an invasion of snakes.

It took him a moment to realize he hadn't answered. With a shaking voice, he managed to force out a weak response. "Hello, Mrs. Jenkins, ladies."

It sounded good to him. Evidently it hadn't fooled her, because she gave him a grin and clucked her tongue. "No, you're safe today. Although don't think I'm forgetting your recent dates. I'm going to wait for another day when Wyatt is working to ask about your new beau."

Relief flooded through him, but it didn't last long. If she wasn't there for Carter, what could she want? The options weren't good. Wyatt had the best radar for the woman Carter had ever seen; he always walked in just as she was starting to interrogate Carter. However, there was no reprieve in sight. He counted to five in his head to try and calm down. It didn't help. "What can I help you ladies with today?"

It was a loaded question. One that he didn't want the answer to.

Whoever said the customer was always right had never met someone like Mrs. Jenkins.

"We," She gestured with fluttery hand movements to her flock, "found the perfect young man for the baker's son."

A short woman with red hair that Carter was sure was found nowhere in nature perked up like a little poodle. "My baker. The boy's so sweet. A bit rough around the edges. The best ones always are. You know that, though. Your young man." She fanned herself. "Benji's so sweet but—"

"Benji?"

"Benjamin." She frowned, head shaking like she shouldn't have to repeat herself. "My baker's son."

The big Dom who was into puppy play was named Benji? Carter had a memory of that being a dog in an old children's movie. Who named their kid after a dog?

"You know he likes to be called Ben or Xavier, that's his middle name." Mrs. Jenkins clucked her tongue again. "Not that his parents listen."

All the women nodded in unison. Carter stared, not sure what to say. Luckily Mrs. Jenkins charged ahead, not waiting for Carter to comment. "They seem to be ostrich parents."

"*Ostrich?*"

Her hand waved around again. "You know how they name things these days. Those parents who hide from everything they don't want to see, even if it's right under their nose."

Ostrich. It worked and, as much as Carter hated to admit it, made sense. "I bet he's frustrated."

It seemed to be the right answer because she smiled at Carter like he'd said something brilliant. "And it's making it very difficult to find Mr. Right. All that stress isn't good. Not that he's admitting there's a problem. You'd think that someone who takes charge in other areas of his life would stand up to his parents, but evidently not."

Listening to Grant's brothers talk about their mother, Carter understood where Ben might be coming from—or was it Xavier? Carter wasn't sure. Not that it mattered, but he had a sneaking suspicion it probably would.

"Sometimes that's hard." Again, she gave him that smile. Was it weird he was enjoying her approval? Yes.

"Yes. We've found the perfect young man for him, though, and we had a few questions about his...lifestyle preferences." She looked over to a woman with white hair in a short bob who could have been anywhere between fifty and seventy.

She was striking and well-manicured but nothing like what Carter expected as she started to speak. "Yes, according to the fetish definitions on Wikipedia. Although some of those pages really should be updated. We need to make a note about that."

What the hell?

"You're right. We forgot to make a note of that at the last meeting. Charlotte, will you write that down for us?" Mrs. Jenkins shook her head and gave Carter a smile. "Memories, you know. As you get older you have to write everything down."

Carter was back to not knowing what to say again. Commiserate? Agree with her? Just nod like an idiot? Yup, that one.

She smiled and gave him an understanding smile before bringing the conversation back to the original awkward topic. "The other young man is a model in Charlotte's art class. He's a very sweet young man."

Charlotte broke in. "Bouncy and happy like you'd expect in a submissive who's drawn to that lifestyle. He focuses well, though, when he's modeling for the class, and thrives when given clear instructions. He also seems to respond well to praise."

He shouldn't, he knew he shouldn't. He did. "How did you find out he's into puppy play? I'm surprised that came up at an art class."

What kind of art was she studying?

They all looked at him like he was now failing the class and they were very disappointed in him. Mrs. Jenkins tilted her head and frowned at him. "His current lifestyle preference is not the most important thing. What matters is that we need to know the best way to introduce them."

To Carter, it sounded suspiciously like they had no idea what the guy was into. He took a few mental steps back. "He's gay, right?"

A few of the women looked guilty but Charlotte, Mrs. Jenkins, and the redhead all shrugged. Charlotte spoke up. "That seems to be the case."

He was an idiot but he couldn't stop himself. "But you don't know?

"He stood naked in a room full of mostly women, several well-endowed younger women in their early thirties, I'd say, and didn't...*react,* if you will. I'd say gay. We also debated that he might be confused about his sexuality, because there are some indications of that, but it's unclear." She spoke like they were analyzing flowers or what to bake for the church bazaar, not what turned on some guy who got naked for little old ladies.

Lord. Where the hell was Wyatt?

Carter wanted to know when they'd dubbed him the kink expert, but he had a feeling he was only a stand-in since Wyatt wasn't there. He knew he should have sent them on their way with a lecture about minding their own business. He couldn't make himself do it.

"Invite Ben to art class? Maybe get the naked guy to pick up something at the bakery?" It sounded like a bad romance novel plot. They seemed to think so, too, because he got the you're-not-so-bright-are-you look again.

"We've considered those. We're just not sure how much of a discussion we should have with the young man first. Would you recommend that? We're torn and decided to get a tiebreaker, if you will." She smiled at him like he should be pleased they'd included him.

He wasn't.

He'd never gotten peer pressured into doing something stupid as a kid. He'd always been a little too different to get included in things like that. It looked like he was going to get his chance to experience it. "Um, a little? Not cold turkey. That could go bad."

Very bad if the guy turned out to be straight with a temper. Looking cute and sweet for little old ladies wasn't hard. He could be some kind of an ax murderer and they probably wouldn't notice. He'd seen a few guys in bars and clubs lose it when they were assumed to be gay. You just never knew about people.

They looked at one another and seemed to be having a silent discussion before Mrs. Jenkins leaned close. "How much is a little?"

"At least make sure the guy is gay first." Carter shrugged helplessly. He tried to think back to his first awkward conversations with Wyatt. "Maybe hint that bakery guy is a little interesting, not say kinky exactly, but talk around it."

He received an innocent smile from all the ladies and got a sinking feeling. The redhead smiled the biggest. "How would you describe puppy play to someone new to the fetish community?"

He was going to die surrounded by crazy women.

14

GRANT

Leaning over in his seat, Grant gave Carter a quick peck on the lips. "Chinese sound good to you? I've been thinking about it all afternoon."

Carter smiled, leaning back against the seat. "Sure. Sounds good."

"Perfect." Grant put the car into reverse and backed out of Carter's driveway. He'd been very well-behaved as he picked up Carter. Wanting to get a feel for his sub's mood before he jumped into the reward or punishment part of the evening, he thought they'd talk about dinner and their day first.

Carter had a different plan.

"I was very good today." His voice was light and teasing. Grant glanced over to see Carter's eyes sparkling with laughter and desire.

"You didn't touch yourself at all?" Grant had been busy enough that he'd only managed a few teasing texts and one short phone call over lunch as he'd prepared for his meetings. The next time they played the same game he was going to make it much harder on his boy.

Much harder.

Long, dirty texts and phone sex kind of difficult. He could already see it in his head. Carter's voice stopped Grant's mind from wandering too far. Still teasing, it was laced with heat, and Grant knew Carter had been looking forward to their evening as much as he had. "Not at all. I just wanted to make sure you knew I deserve a fabulous reward."

"I've got that planned out." Grant let his voice go deep, passion heating his words. "I thought about it all afternoon. I even stopped somewhere after work to make sure I had everything I'd need to punish you or reward you. I have to admit, I'm not sure which would have been more fun."

Carter shivered, and a quick look let Grant see that his words had the desired effect. Carter's hardening cock was starting to tent his skirt. The long material was light and full enough that Grant thought the movement of the fabric would hide Carter's arousal. It was also going to make the evening more fun.

Taking one hand off the wheel, Grant reached over and draped it on Carter's legs. Slow caresses he hoped seemed fairly innocent had more shivers running through Carter. Grant had to push back a wicked smile. He wasn't going to make it easy for his sub to behave. He hadn't pushed his sub too hard that day, but Grant couldn't let that continue.

Carter would be disappointed if it wasn't a little bit torturous.

At least, that's what he was going to tell himself until Carter said otherwise. The way the sub had taken to spankings and the little playing they'd done made Grant think he was on the right track. Letting his fingers slowly caress Carter's leg as he carefully worked his way closer to Carter's groin, Grant started asking questions about his day.

Carter squeaked, then tried to cover it up with a cough. "My day?"

"Yes. I didn't get to talk to you as much as I wanted today.

One meeting after another." He wasn't exaggerating, either. Several meetings with restaurant owners about new policies had left him hungry and ready to skip out early. The smells that always came in with them, plus all the talk about food, made it hard to ignore his rumbling stomach.

"Mine was fairly busy." Carter shifted in his seat but made no move to adjust Grant's wandering hand. "I had several good sales. Some of the larger pieces that I was afraid wouldn't find a home. People make impulse purchases of the smaller items all the time, but not so much when it comes to a couch or full dining room set."

"That's great."

Carter smiled, for the moment distracted from Grant's touch. "I was surprised. It means I'm going to have to rearrange things in the store and look for some new pieces to add. I know someone who does estate sales down in North Carolina. I'm going to give her a call and see what kinds of things she's been seeing. I got several good tables from her last year and the couch that just sold."

"Were they just random sales, or have you done something different?" Grant loved that he and Carter could talk about more than just BDSM. They'd spent countless hours over the past couple of weeks talking about marketing and business plans. They were getting to know each other on what he felt was a deeper level than just finding out Carter's favorite color.

Which was an odd color of blue that wasn't called blue but had something to do with the ocean.

Carter laughed. "I have this group of women who come in on a regular basis for gossip. They love Wyatt with his oversharing and lack of filter. Well, they came in today wanting to get some advice about fixing up two guys. That's a crazy story that I'll have to tell you about later. I guess they've been in so often lately that they finally broke down and bought the pieces they'd been eyeing. Who knows, it might have been guilt about making me nuts, but I'll take it because I've earned the sales. Those crazy old ladies make me insane."

Grant smiled and couldn't wait to hear the rest of the story. "I'm having a hard time picturing older women stalking your store for gossip."

"They're terrible." Carter shook his head. "And Wyatt always plays right into their hands, telling them everything they want to know. It started with just one of the women, but then they all started trickling in for good gossip and antiques. Some days it feels like I should charge admission."

Their casual conversation continued until they got to the restaurant. Carter had done his best to ignore Grant's touch but it was becoming increasingly more difficult. By the time they parked, Grant had his fingers caressing the length of Carter's hard cock while Carter's fingers dug into the sides of the seat. He was doing his best to be good, but with Grant pushing his resolve at every turn, he was starting to lose the battle.

Turning off the car, Grant looked over at Carter and gave him an innocent look. "You ready for dinner?"

Carter let out a low huff of frustration but took a deep breath and nodded. It would have been more believable, but Grant could feel the way Carter's cock jerked and strained against his panties. Letting his hand slide over Carter's erection, Grant shook his head. "I'm not sure you are. I don't think I can take you in like this."

Slouching back in the seat, Carter gave him a skeptical look. Smart man, Grant thought with a grin. "I think we have to do something about this. I wouldn't want you to get tempted to disobey and lose out on your reward. You don't want that, do you?"

Carter shook his head, narrowing his eyes. "No, I want my reward. I was good."

"Then you agree that something has to be done." Grant gave him a smile that was far from sweet. "Pull up your skirt for me. I have something that will help."

"What? Pull up..." Carter was shocked, but Grant could see interest flaring in his eyes. Looking around outside the car, Carter relaxed as he realized they were at the back of the lot, well away from prying eyes. "What are you going to do?"

Grant cocked an eyebrow and gave him a questioning look before reaching behind his seat to the bag. He'd gotten everything ready before leaving the store, so it was easy to pull out the cock ring. Carter's eyes widened. Grant would have worried, but the sexy way Carter licked his lips and started nibbling on the bottom one let him know Carter wasn't upset—just surprised.

When Carter's hands went down to start drawing up his skirt, Grant's cock started to throb. He'd be the one to need a ring if he couldn't keep his arousal under control. Knowing what was going to happen had pleasure coursing through him.

Carter's hands were shaking by the time he'd pulled the skirt up far enough to bare his panties. They were very similar to the white pair that Grant loved. This time they were blue and looked like they would offer more support, which would be a good thing since Grant was going to make him even more turned on.

When Grant reached over and pulled the silky front down, Carter looked like he wasn't breathing. His teeth were working his bottom lip so hard, Grant was afraid he'd make it bleed. Leaning over, Grant gave Carter a deep kiss. Using the distraction to free Carter's cock, he slid his hand up and down the rigid length, swallowing Carter's moan of pleasure.

Pulling back, Grant gave him one last quick peck as he teased Carter's erection. "We can't have this getting out of control in the restaurant."

Carter's brain hadn't caught up to what was going to happen, because he just nodded with a stunned look on his face. Not wanting to push his luck, Grant kept the playing to a minimum as he wrapped the restraint around Carter's dick.

When Carter was secure, Grant tucked him back in his panties and arranged him as comfortably as he could. They wouldn't be eating for long, but he didn't want Carter to be too frustrated. Smoothing down the front of the floaty skirt, Grant gave him one more kiss and one last long caress.

"Ready?" Grant smiled at Carter's slow nod. "Safewords are red to stop and yellow to slow down. Do you need a minute?"

He wasn't going to ask if Carter wanted him to take it off. He knew Carter wouldn't hesitate to let him know if something didn't turn him on. Carter was just a little bit uncertain about what did arouse him. Grant didn't mind pushing a little so he could figure it out.

"Red and yellow." Speaking slowly and carefully, Grant thought his sub's brain was still coming back online. Carter finally shook his head like a dog clearing his coat of water and found his voice. "No. I'm ready." Clearing his throat, he continued, "I've been hungry for most of the day. The crazy ladies came in just as I was going to grab something in the back. By the time they left, I was too distracted to eat."

Smiling, Grant took the key out of the ignition and opened his door. "Let's go, then. I'm starving." Then, with one last teasing pat to Carter's arousal because he really couldn't help himself, Grant hopped out of the car listening to Carter growl about getting his big lug back.

Grant couldn't wait to see what kind of revenge Carter would get on him. He knew he'd deserve it by the end of dinner— because they were going to have fun.

By the time they'd finished eating, Carter couldn't seem to decide if he was going to jump Grant and take what he wanted, or if he was just going to kill him. Grant knew he probably had a screw loose, but he was thoroughly enjoying himself—and as frustrated as Carter was, he never called a halt to the teasing. His sub just liked to complain, but that didn't seem to mean he was ready for the game to be over.

The drive home was incredibly distracting. Carter's little moans and wiggles had Grant ready to pull over and jump him. That seemed to be what Carter was aiming for, but it wasn't the plan. One day he'd play that game, if it was something Carter was interested in.

Grant had planned their night in great detail and he wasn't going to be rushed. As they got closer to Carter's house, Grant reached over and started rubbing slow circles around the head of Carter's cock. It had leaked so much precum that the front of his skirt was damp. His panties had to be soaked.

"Someone's being a naughty boy. Distracting me and not letting me drive. I'm not sure if you're being good enough to get your reward." Grant hoped the darkness hid his smile as Carter let out a low, frustrated moan.

"Please. I was good." His words were low and breathy, need in every sound. "I didn't touch myself all day. That was the rule." Then he shot Grant a sharp look like he wasn't going to let him change the rules now.

"I guess." Grant pressed a little harder and loved the gasp of pleasure that echoed in the car. "And you were very good in the restaurant. They didn't even know that you had this under your clothes."

By the time they pulled in the yard, little mewling sounds were starting to escape Carter. Grant thought the ring might not hold him back much longer if they didn't change things up. Helping Carter out of the car, the walk to the house and into Carter's bedroom was the longest ever—for both of them. All they both wanted was for Carter to be naked and Grant to be touching him.

They just had different expectations about how quickly they'd get to the part where Grant was naked too.

Stripping Carter of his shirt and skirt, his beautiful sub stood in the bedroom in just his panties and tight, silky tank top. His cock strained against the fabric, the head poking out of the panties that were soaked with precum. As much as he'd teased Carter during their meal at the restaurant, they should probably be glad it hadn't shown sooner.

"God, you look..." Grant couldn't find the words to explain how incredible Carter was. The feminine clothing caressing his hard cock—the contrast was beautiful. Grant didn't know how everyone else couldn't see it that way as well—masculine and feminine mixing together in the most incredible way.

Carter's smile was tender and frustrated, muscles shaking and hands clenched by his sides. Not in anger, but Grant knew that if he didn't take more control of the situation, Carter wouldn't be able to resist touching himself.

Tossing the bag on the bed, Grant stepped close to him and cradled Carter's face in his hands. Giving him the lightest, most tender kiss he could, Grant rubbed his thumbs on Carter's cheeks, loving the way Carter flushed and blinked up at him, need and love showing in his eyes.

"Up on the bed, pretty." Giving him another quick kiss, Grant stepped back. "On your hands and knees facing the wall."

Carter's gaze was foggy and unclear, but eventually the instructions broke through the need. Arms and legs not quite working right, it took him a minute to climb up and get himself settled. No embarrassment or awkwardness, desire and trust were the only things radiating from Carter.

It made Grant's heart tighten and he had to push back the emotions that were starting to rise. It wasn't the time for that yet.

Forcing his body to move, Grant walked over to the bed and got the next surprise out of the bag. Carter was straining to see what Grant was doing. When he saw what must have looked like stiff pink ribbon, he frowned.

Grant grinned and stretched out the straps until it was clear. Carter gasped, which only made Grant's smile more wicked. "I knew your bed was made for restraints the first time I saw it."

Moving slowly around the room, Grant attached the pink cuffs to the iron posts of the old-fashioned bed. Keeping one eye on Carter as he watched spellbound, Grant finished hooking them to the bed. They weren't true BDSM restraints in the strictest sense, but he thought they'd feel less overwhelming for Carter since they wouldn't be impossible to get out of on his own.

With careful, deliberate movements, Grant reached out and wrapped the first one around Carter's left arm. Leaving enough slack for Carter to be able to bend his arms and be comfortable, Grant wanted to give him the experience without making it too difficult. There would be time to play with other setups if Carter liked the feeling.

Carter was still staring as Grant went around to attach the cuff to his other arm. Carter didn't use his safeword and Grant could see little shivers racing through his needy sub, so he didn't worry about Carter's lack of reaction. He knew he'd get a good one when he moved to the next part of their night.

Climbing on the bed behind Carter, Grant let his hands slide up Carter's soft legs. Grant wasn't sure if he shaved or if he had less hair naturally, but he didn't care. He just loved the way the smooth skin felt over the tight muscles and lean body beneath him.

Carter was moaning and thrusting his hips back by the time Grant worked his way up to Carter's ass. Teasing the edge of the panties with one finger, he watched as Carter started to shake and his demanding sexy sub found his voice again.

"Damn it, Grant." Carter growled out the words, making Grant laugh.

Giving Carter's bottom a quick smack, he loved the gasp and deep moan that followed. Carter's ass arched up and the words came out pleading, less demanding as he tried to figure out what would get him what he wanted. "Please, Grant."

Easing the panties over Carter's ass, Grant palmed the full, beautiful muscles. "You've been very good. Don't make me have to punish you now. You want that ring off your cock, don't you?"

Grant could have sworn he heard low cursing under Carter's breath, but the only thing that came out loud enough to be sure was a frantic agreement. "YES!"

Chuckling, which set off the grumbling again, Grant slid them down even lower until he could get them all the way off. He probably should have stripped Carter first, but he loved the way his sub's ass looked in the silk and lace. They had to come off, though, because he needed more room than the panties would allow.

He could easily picture keeping Carter clothed in the lace underwear and shoving them aside, taking him while he was still wearing the sexy things. That wasn't the plan, though, but next time...Grant pushed the fantasy to the back of his head and moved to lay down behind Carter.

Carter froze as he realized what was going to happen. Grant could feel his muscles twitching and shaking as his fingers gripped Carter's hips to hold him still. At the first touch of his tongue to the smooth skin of his taint, Carter gasped and demanding words came flooding out.

They didn't quite make sense, but the overall theme was that Grant needed to hurry or Carter was going to hurt him. Grant decided that his sub needed a lesson in patience. Taking his time, Grant ignored Carter's demands and slowly began to explore his lover's body.

Lapping at Carter's balls, teasing circles around his tight hole, Grant kept him on the edge of insanity for longer than he thought Carter would hold out. Carter never used his safeword, though. His demands gradually faded away until all that came out were random words and sounds that didn't make real sentences.

Pliant and trembling, Carter sank into the pleasure as Grant slowly pushed him higher and higher. By the time Grant was fucking Carter's tight opening with his tongue, Carter seemed to be riding the pleasure, lost to everything else. Reaching down for the bag, Grant carefully kept up his teasing as he found the lube. Needy whimpers escaped when Grant eased the first finger in.

Carefully avoiding Carter's prostate for the time being, Grant gradually stretched the muscles until Carter was pushing back, whining for more. When Grant eased the second finger in, he stopped avoiding Carter's small bundle of nerves.

The first time he caressed Carter's prostate it was like lightning shooting through his boy. His head came up and frantic sounds flooded out of his mouth. Grant thought it was the most beautiful thing he'd ever heard.

When a gasping Carter forced out one quiet, pleading word, Grant knew he couldn't take any more. "Sir?"

Sliding his fingers out of Carter's stretched hole, Grant quickly grabbed a condom out of the bag. Tossing it on the bed between Carter's splayed legs, Grant stripped his clothes in record time, grateful that Carter couldn't see his frantic, awkward movements. He just needed to be naked. It wasn't a Chippendale's routine.

Not this time.

Racing to put the condom on and coat it in more lube, Grant was back kneeling behind Carter before his boy could lose the beautiful subspace he'd sunk into. Gently easing into Carter's body, Grant fought the urge to thrust and made himself go slowly.

Sexy noises flooded out of Carter as Grant kept up the tortuously unhurried pace. He wanted this to be something that Carter would remember, not a hurried fuck just to orgasm. He wanted to blow his sexy man's mind and show him how incredible they would be together.

By the time he bottomed out in Carter, they were both desperate for more. Pulling out, he pushed back in with measured, even strokes. Fighting back the need to come, Grant started mentally reaching for anything to take his focus from his own impending orgasm. Crazy things came to mind, but nothing that distracted him from how incredible his boy was.

Finally giving up, Grant reached under a squirming, shaking Carter and opened the ring so it fell to the bed. That was all Carter needed. One more thrust and as Grant's cock caressed Carter's prostate he exploded. Carter's orgasm flooded through him in waves of pleasure, making it impossible for Grant to hold back.

His own orgasm broke through as Carter's muscles rippled and tightened around his cock. Frantic thrusts that made them both shout was the only thing that could be heard above the slapping of skin as Grant fought to keep Carter's orgasm going.

When they were both spent, Grant collapsed over Carter. Carefully removing the cuffs, Grant rolled them to their sides. Wrapping his arms around Carter, he knew he'd have to move in just a moment, but he wasn't ready to let go yet.

Carter snuggled into his arms, long slow breaths making Grant think he'd fallen asleep, but a quiet voice spoke up. "I think next time I'm going to disobey. I think that would be fun, too."

Laughing, Grant gave Carter's ass a half-hearted smack, which made Carter giggle. "That was incredible, Grant."

Giving the top of Carter's head a kiss, Grant smiled. "You are just...unbelievable, pretty." He didn't have the words to tell Carter how he felt, but the smile he could see on Carter's face let him know his feisty sub knew even if he didn't say it.

Carter's eyes closed and he pushed back closer to Grant. Feeling his muscles relax, Grant knew sleep was claiming his exhausted sub. Easing away from Carter so he could clean them both up, Grant was almost off the bed when Carter spoke one last time, sleep and confusion clouding his voice. "Why were you quoting the Preamble to the Constitution?"

Damn it.

15

CARTER

"Hurry up—but don't drop that. I don't want them to think I'm incompetent in the kitchen. If we have to show up with something from the store, I'll die. They'll never let me forget it." Carter might have been panicking over nothing, but as the plate of fudge tipped precariously sideways in Grant's hands, his heart rate jumped. "I should be holding that. You drive."

Carefully taking the plate from Grant, Carter shoved his keys in his pocket. "Yes. You drive this time." He'd drive on salad day, or maybe when they were in charge of bringing paper plates and plastic silverware. Grant just grunted and shook his head but was smart enough not to argue.

Carter had wanted to bring something different from what the guys might have been able to do for themselves, and competing against one of Wyatt's cakes seemed like he was setting himself up for failure. So he'd picked one of his favorite desserts, making several flavors of fudge for the barbecue.

When Grant had seen what they were bringing, he'd immediately made Carter box up some to hide in the house, knowing that none would be left by the end of the day. Since no one in the family but Wyatt had come to his house, he hadn't seen the need to actually hide the candy. Grant had refused to budge until it was *protected*.

Carter thought it was cute—but paranoid.

He'd humored his nut, though, and tucked the plastic container full of fudge behind a bag of seaweed chips in the pantry. He had a feeling none of the brothers would pick that as their first choice of snacks if they ever did come over.

They didn't strike Carter as the adventurous type when it came to junk food.

Grant thought it was perfect. However, he'd also seemed to question Carter's sanity, because he had a hard time moving past the idea that Carter had green chips in his cabinet. After reassuring him the chips hadn't gone bad, because then they might spoil the fudge, Carter couldn't manage to keep a straight face at Grant's disbelief. Shock didn't even begin to describe Grant's reaction.

Revulsion.

Horror.

Fear.

They'd then spent several more minutes with Carter reassuring Grant that he didn't have to taste them, and yes, he would brush his teeth before kissing Grant if he ate them. The ridiculous conversation had not only been frustrating and ridiculous, it had made them late.

"It's a family get-together. We're not late—and I wasn't going to drop it. They're going to love it. I don't know why you're panicking over this." Grant frowned and gave him a kiss before opening the door to his car. After helping Carter in, he walked around the car to get in the passenger seat.

In Carter's mind, there was so much to worry about it was staggering. Would they like him as much as they did Wyatt? Would they like dessert? Should he have made a pie instead?

What kind of pie would have been best? Would Wyatt's announcement—one that Carter wasn't supposed to know about—go according to plan? The list could go on and on.

The drive to Brent's house was over before he had a chance to get his nerves under control. Why couldn't he have lived farther away? Coming as Grant's boyfriend was a lot more stressful than coming as Wyatt's friend had been. He hadn't thought that would be possible—he was wrong.

After they parked, Grant came around and opened the door before Carter could situate the plate right. Shaking his head, Grant crouched down, putting his hand on Carter's leg. "It will be fine. They're going to love the fudge. They like you, and something tells me that we're not going to be the center of attention for long."

"Wyatt?" Did Grant know? He hadn't been supposed to tell. Had Garrett said something?

"What about Wyatt? I was talking about Bryce and his men." Now Grant looked confused. "Do you know what's up with those two?"

Carter tried for innocent—and failed miserably. He finally gave up. "I'm not supposed to talk about it. Wyatt was...worked up and talked about something he wasn't supposed to."

Grant's eyes widened. Carter saw a knowing look flash through his eyes before Grant's focus turned back to him. "I'm going to enjoy punishing you tonight."

"What?"

"Call it lying. The sin of omission. Hiding things from your lover. Concealing vital family gossip from your boyfriend. Call it anything you want, but pretty, I'm getting even tonight." Grant's words should have made him worried, but the wicked expression on his face made Carter shiver.

How long were they supposed to stay at the barbecue?

Not sure what to say, Carter kept it simple. "I'm sorry?"

The fact that it came out more as a question than statement worked against him. Grant shook his head and frowned. It made Carter want to squirm, and his cock started to stir. That was the last thing he needed, and the fear that he'd have to walk up to everyone with a hard-on sticking out of his panties cleared his head. "I'm sorry, Sir. I won't hide something important again."

It came out more believably. Not that he had any intention of actually keeping the promise. Grant didn't seem to think so, either, because he coughed to cover a laugh. "I hope you remember that promise when I'm punishing you tonight."

He shook his head at Carter, giving him a pitying look. "You're going to regret being naughty when I get out my special toy."

Toy?

Was he talking about the cage again?

Mind-blowing didn't even begin to describe that night. Would Grant get it out again, or did he have something else in mind? The carnally wicked look in Grant's eyes said it would be good, but Carter couldn't even begin to guess what he was thinking.

"Thank you for punishing me, Sir. I want to be good for you." Damn fantasies were making his cock thicken. If he didn't get it under control, when he stood up his skirt was going to be awkwardly tented. This wasn't the club, and he wasn't quite ready for that yet.

Mischievous light danced in Grant's eyes, but the rest of his face didn't give anything away. "I'm glad you're being a good boy. But if you don't get that cock under control I'm going to have to take care of it right here, and I'm not sure you'd like what I had in mind."

Carter's emotions ping-ponged around and he couldn't decide what he wanted. The longing to find out exactly what was giving Grant that look was so strong, but part of him was nervous and thought he wasn't ready yet. Taking the more prudent path, because yeah, they were in Brent's front yard, Carter took some deep breaths and thought of every gross thing he'd ever seen on a CSI episode.

Having a bit of an obsession for that and gory hospital dramas, he had a wealth of images to pull from. Before long his body was under control, even if that wasn't what he really wanted. He leaned over, careful of the plate, and gave Grant a quick kiss. "Let's go. Before I get myself in more trouble."

Grant's laughter wrapped around him like a warm hug as he climbed out of the car, and they headed around the side of the house. The barbecue was in full swing, but they weren't the last to arrive. Bryce and his men were conspicuously absent.

Carter tried to be subtle as he looked around the yard and back at the house. Grant didn't seem to feel any need to hide his curiosity. He just glanced at the yard, then called over to Garrett, his booming voice echoing, "Bryce chicken out on bringing his guys?"

The crowd of people laughed, and Garrett and Brent both started berating Grant for having no tact. Calen, on the other hand, completely agreed with Grant and immediately stood up for him. Carter just hung back and watched as chaos ensued. They were such a strange family, it was like watching aliens sometimes.

"Does it always feel like we're watching a circus or some kind of reality show to you?" Wyatt stepped up beside Carter and grinned. "It's not a bad thing. I love Garrett and his family is wonderful, but it's like a zoo over here sometimes."

They both watched as the arguing—if that's what it could be called because no one seemed angry—started to wind down. The general consensus seemed to be that Grant and Calen were going to leave Bryce and his guys alone when they finally showed up, but yes, he was probably being a shit and ditching them because he was nervous.

When they all finally calmed down enough to see what Carter had brought, nerves started fraying again. Grant was hovering over Carter, and while he would have loved to have thought it was because he was concerned about Carter, he knew it was more because Grant wasn't ready to share.

It was like watching toddlers war over the last cookie.

He finally pulled Grant aside. "You have more at home. Let me put this down. If they want some, that's fine. We brought it to share—" Carter barely got the words out before Grant clamped a hand over his mouth.

"You're never supposed to say that." Grant looked horrified, like Carter was giving away the intimate details of their sex life in the middle of Brent's back yard. Aliens, they were aliens. Before he could decide if he was going to lick him or bite him, Grant wisely removed his hand. Looking around like a bad James Bond, he dropped his voice. "I don't know if they heard or not. We have to find a better hiding spot when we get home."

"They're not going to come steal your fudge." It was like trying to reason with a three-year-old. Grant wouldn't be swayed.

"You have no idea. One time we went over to Garrett's house and raided his house of all the good stuff. He'd gone to the French bakery on the other side of town and thought he could hide it. He was at a late meeting, so we snuck over. When he came home, there wasn't a cookie or pastry in the place." Grant said it so reasonably, Carter had to run the conversation back a few times in his head.

"You broke into his house?" Carter's words tumbled out in shock, but he managed to keep his voice down enough that no one noticed.

"No." Grant looked at him like he was a few crayons short of a full box. "We had a key."

He was surrounded by lunatics.

"They'd better not break into my house for chocolate." Carter gave Grant a stern look. "If I come home to ransacked cupboards, I'll hang them all."

"They don't have a key." Grant shook his head like Carter wasn't thinking things through. "They'll invite themselves over, or come by to borrow something. It will be subtle, but by the time you turn around, they'll have left in a hurry and the fudge will be gone."

Grant sounded a bit like one of the alien conspiracy theorists on TV. Firmly convinced he was right—but paranoid and a little freaky to listen to. Carter shook his head and tried to talk some sense into his nut. "I won't let them take the fudge. I'm not even sure they know where I live."

Grant seemed to take some consolation in that, but not for long, because he started rambling about Wyatt not being able to keep a secret. Carter wasn't sure how long the insanity would have continued, but Bryce's arrival stopped the crazy train mid-station.

He was alone.

Hands in his pockets, Bryce tried to maintain a neutral expression as he walked around the side of the house, but he failed miserably. His eyes were shifting around the yard nervously. It was clear he was expecting an interrogation.

Everyone was stumped. Even the normally levelheaded Brent was standing there shocked. They'd all been so happy for Bryce and so excited to meet Troy and Oliver that him showing up without them stunned everyone. Luckily, Wyatt was the first to recover.

He walked over to Bryce, hands on his hips, and shook his head. "You forgot the salad, didn't you?"

Bryce gave him a half-shrug and nodded, grateful for the reprieve. "I'm sorry. It got burned."

Brent spoke up, frustration clear in his voice. "The damned salad wasn't burned, it was charred!"

Laughter rippled through the group, and the tension eased as conversations resumed. Carter wasn't sure what was wrong, but he hoped the other man would talk about what happened when he was ready. Grant shifted, drawing Carter's attention back to his lover. Grant looked ready to charge in and fix whatever was wrong.

Taking his bulldozer's hand, Carter leaned close. "I don't think he wants to talk about it right now, babe."

Grant tightened his grip on Carter's hand and started absently caressing the back of Carter's hand with his fingers. "But..."

"I know you guys are a close family, but some things are private. Do you think he wants to talk, or do you think he needs some time?"

Grant sighed but nodded. "Time." He said it begrudgingly, like he would have rather admitted anything else.

"Maybe it's not as bad as everyone is imagining. It could be something small." Carter tried to come up with something, but it felt wrong. Bryce's expression didn't make him think the other men would be coming later. Bryce seemed...resigned.

Bryce was so excited when they'd had dinner last week. He hadn't talked to him since, but what could have changed in a matter of days? They watched as Wyatt led Bryce around the yard, keeping him distracted.

Carter squeaked as Grant shifted and pulled him into his arms, Carter's back pressed against the bigger man's chest. When Grant's arms wrapped around him, pulling him close, Carter's heartbeat started to go back to normal.

Leaning back against Grant, Carter sighed. "He was so

excited the other day." He felt Grant's body shift and looked up
to see him nodding.

"Whatever happened, it sucks to see him like this." Grant
didn't seem to know what to say.

Carter let his fingers wander along Grant's arms, caressing
the muscles that enveloped him. He hadn't been involved with
the family for long, but they were all worming their way into his
life and emotions. As eccentric as they were, they were
becoming more of a family to Carter than his own had
ever been.

Wyatt and Garrett had a big part in welcoming him, but
Carter knew if it weren't for the big Dom with the even bigger
heart, he'd still be standing on the sidelines watching. Maybe he
needed to make sure Grant knew how much he was coming to
mean to him. "I'm sorry for what Bryce is going through, but I'm
glad I have you."

It wasn't a huge declaration, and it wasn't the three little
words that were dancing around in his head, but the way Grant's
arms tightened, Carter knew he understood. Grant's whispered
words were just for him, deep and filled with emotions that
echoed Carter's, and they were pure Grant. "Of course you have
me. You're crazy if you think I'm letting you go."

It wasn't a declaration of love, but the slightly stalkerish
sentiment filled the last empty places deep inside of him. Grant
might come across as the overbearing one, but Carter knew he'd
fight just as hard to keep their relationship alive. New as it was, it
felt stronger and better than anything he'd ever dreamed of.

EPILOGUE

As the barbecue started to wind down, Carter walked over to the long table to grab his plate. Hearing a car door slam, he glanced up. Brent had neighbors, but that'd sounded too close to be one of them. Brent must have thought so, too, because he looked around like a mother hen counting her chicks.

Carter hadn't met everyone that many times, but aside from Bryce's guys who were MIA, everyone else seemed to have made it to the party. Bryce was still being cagey about why they weren't at the barbecue. The fact that he wasn't saying anything gave Carter some hope for his new friend.

If it'd been a real breakup or something equally as dramatic, Bryce wouldn't have had any reason to hide it. Since he was keeping it close, only giving vague comments about them being busy, then their relationship might not be a total loss. It was new, but the way Bryce had looked when he'd talked about them told Carter it was something special—and relationships like that didn't end easily.

The only other real damper on the evening was that Bryce's turmoil seemed to have put a dent in Wyatt and Garrett's secret plans. They'd shared some pointed looks and had disappeared into the house for a while. There hadn't been a private moment to corner Wyatt, but he knew he'd get the full story later. Grabbing the empty plate that looked like it had been licked clean, Carter looked around for Grant.

He was hard to miss.

He was frozen in place, along with just about everyone else. Only a few people, like Wyatt, were confused and looking around. Everyone else was focused on the side of the house as a short, dark-haired woman came around the corner dragging a suitcase that looked nearly as big as she was.

Booming voices all called out at once, startling everyone into reacting. "Mom!"

Wyatt slowly walked up beside Carter as they watched the guys fight for her attention. "Is it bad I hoped she'd stay gone for a while longer? I'm not ready to meet her yet."

Carter glanced over at his nervous friend. "Wasn't she supposed to be gone for a couple more weeks?" He could have sworn Grant had said something like that.

Wyatt nodded. "Yes."

There was no doubt from the glances she was giving Wyatt, Carter, and Calen why she'd come home early. She wanted to see what her boys had been up to. The idea of meeting Grant's mother made his stomach turn in circles, but the knowledge that Wyatt was a lot more serious with Garrett gave him hope.

He and Grant might be getting serious, but Wyatt and Garrett were way ahead of them. He had a feeling she was going to love that. There was no way those two could keep their plans a secret for long. Wyatt was probably going to have a heart attack, but at least Carter knew he wouldn't be the center of her attention. He might not be willing to throw Wyatt under the bus, but he wasn't going to get in its way either.

Friendship only went so far.

He hadn't even met her yet, but that one short look had spoken volumes. She was curious, and if the stories he'd heard were true, she wanted to see her boys happy and settled down. The dramatic way they spoke about her and how excited she was that they were starting to get in serious relationships was freaky.

Carter knew that his connection with Grant was the best thing that had ever happened to him, but he wasn't mom-level ready yet. He might have had a closer relationship with his banker than he did with his own mother, but that didn't mean he was clueless when it came to what real mothers wanted for their children.

Love.

Happiness.

Commitment.

Wedding bells.

Collars.

Well, she'd want collars and ceremonies for her boys, but Carter thought that it was just a more intense version of what other mothers wanted. He knew he wasn't ready for all that yet. Some of it. Most of it, if he was honest with himself, but would she be able to accept that? Would Grant?

His gentle giant always seemed to know what Carter needed. He couldn't imagine Grant pushing them into anything they weren't ready for—but family was hard. Even a loving one that was slightly off their rockers.

Obsession and ridiculous worries aside, he knew how he felt about Grant, and he had a good idea about how Grant felt about him. His Dom wasn't exactly subtle and that was one of the things Carter loved best about him. He just needed to keep that, and how much he trusted Grant, in the front of his mind and not let the fear take over.

Grant had never given him any reason to question him.

Looking over at his bulldozer vying for his mother's attention, Carter had to fight back a grin. If someone had said he'd be head over heels in love even a month ago, he would have had their head examined. Now he couldn't imagine being anywhere else. Standing there with Wyatt and their new extended family, he knew he was where he belonged.

Surrounded by acceptance and love.

BRYCE

FIRST EDITION SEPTEMBER, 2017

1

BRYCE

He knew he should stay away, but he couldn't. Something about the couple had called to him from the first moment he'd seen them. He'd tried to leave them alone and find someone else that attracted him, but it wasn't possible.

Watching as Troy carefully wrapped a still-shaking Oliver in a soft blanket, he told his feet they needed to walk away from the intimate moment in front of him, but the traitors kept taking him closer. Inch by inch he worked his way toward the darkness.

The sounding scene had been for the audience at Bound & Controlled as well as the men, but now that it was over, the after-care was only for the two of them. It was intimate, private. Every rule and piece of etiquette he'd ever learned screamed at him that he needed to leave them alone and give them their space, but something kept him orbiting their private world.

Bound & Controlled was a gay BDSM club that was open and accepting, but there were rules and boundaries. Bryce knew he should find someplace else to be, but it was impossible. It didn't matter that he was supposed to let them have their space after a scene. Bryce couldn't leave them. He'd managed to walk away in the past, but it was quickly becoming impossible.

He had to seem like an idiot, or worse, some kind of weird stalker. They were just so perfect together. The passion and the emotion, it was incredible. He loved watching them, but standing outside looking in wasn't satisfying him any longer.

Troy's firm voice echoed from the dark corner where the two men sat at the L-shaped sofa, startling Bryce. Even in the low light, he could picture the tall, blond Dom, built more like a Norse god than a mere mortal. "Come sit next to him. He's still flying, but he'll want to see you when he comes down."

His heart stopped.

He felt like he was standing right on the edge of an entirely different universe, and he didn't know if he could do it. The two warring sides inside of him were finally both on the same page. They didn't care if they got to dominate Oliver or submit to Troy, they simply wanted to curl up on the couch and hold them both. His brain, on the other hand, kept shouting to walk away.

It was confusing.

A relationship where he was the Dom *and* sub couldn't work.

They wouldn't want him for more than a scene or two, anyway.

His brain was adamant; luckily, his feet listened to lower parts of his body. He took the first step closer and didn't even realize he was going to say something until the words were already out. "He will?"

It wasn't much, but Troy didn't seem to mind. His stern voice warmed a few degrees, sending pleasure through Bryce. "You know he will. Come sit down." His voice dropped low and heat threaded through it. "Don't make me tell you again."

His inner sub rolled over and squirmed for attention. Bryce felt his skin flush and his heart rate increase. It'd been so long since someone really understood what he needed. Would they be able to see who he was and grasp that he was both a Dom and a sub at heart?

Was he willing to take the chance?

Yes.

One last step and he was standing by the couch. The lighted stages around the room gave off a low glow, but the way the room had been designed left the quiet corner in near-darkness. Even sitting, Troy's massive frame made Bryce feel small. It made the sub inside him whine and plead for more.

Troy held Oliver in his arms, the sub's lean, muscular body cradled in his lap. Bryce wasn't sure where to sit. Troy, thankfully, took the decision out of his hands. "Sit by his feet. That way he'll see you when he wakes up."

Bryce curled up next to Troy, close but not touching, and observed Oliver. He'd been so beautiful up on the stage. Needy and desperate but wanting to be perfect for his Dom, giving everything over to the pleasure. At some points while he watched, he'd wanted to be Oliver, strapped down and helpless. Other times, he'd imagined he was Troy, standing over Oliver, teasing and pleasuring him.

His family didn't really understand, but it felt like there were two different people inside of him struggling for dominance. What he really wanted most was someone who could under-stand that and help him find a balance.

"You're thinking too hard. Scoot closer, I won't bite—unless we go over limits first." Subtle hints of laughter flowed through his words, making Bryce want to squirm. He inched closer until he was pressed tight against the Dom. "That's better. Hold his legs and let your hands rest on him. He likes to be held lightly right now, but tighter once he wakes up."

Something squeezed inside of him as Troy shifted to let Oliver's legs rest in his lap. Softly wrapping his hands around the slim, strong limbs, Bryce let his head fall to Troy's shoulder. "Thank you."

He wasn't sure for what, but the words were important.

Troy hummed a low tone that sounded pleased, but Bryce wasn't sure what it meant. "He knew you were there. He wanted to be perfect for you."

"I...I..." His mind was blank.

Oliver's eyes started to flutter, and he shifted in their arms, turning to get closer to the radiating warmth of Troy's body. A little frown created creases between his eyes, and he shifted, trying to get comfortable.

"Is he okay?" He'd seemed fine on stage, but Bryce wasn't sure.

"He's going to be a little sore from straining against the straps, but he's fine." There was a warmth in Troy's voice as he talked about his boy. "He's just whiny when he's sleepy. He won't even notice it once he's awake."

"Good." Bryce let his hands glide slowly up and down Oliver's legs as the man slowly come back to them.

"We'd hoped you'd be here to watch. It was the only thing on his mind this week."

"It was?" Bryce wasn't sure how he felt about it. He liked knowing that Oliver had been thinking about him, but it also meant they'd realized how drawn to them he was. He also didn't want to cause any problems between the two men. "Was that okay with you?"

Bryce felt Troy shift, and a hand came up to wrap around his neck, fingers caressing the short hairs at the back of his head. "Yes, we talk about everything, and we've both noticed you around the club."

He wanted to make sure they were all on the same page before it went any further, but the wonderful sensations Troy was sending through him made it hard to process what he wanted to say. "I...I'm...I can't think."

Troy laughed and stilled his hand, but didn't move away from Bryce. It was just enough to let his brain work again. "I'm a switch. I can't sub all the time."

"We know. We asked around when we first realized we were both drawn to you." Troy's fingers started moving in slow, soothing circles. "Are you okay with letting me take charge for now?"

Bryce nodded. He realized how hard Troy was fighting to stay calm and not push too fast. But his inner Dom was quiet, unsure of what to do and what was happening. He didn't need to be in control. He wanted Troy to handle everything. It would take time before he could give his complete submission to the man, but he was already well on his way to kneeling and needy, and they hadn't even done anything together.

"I need to hear the words. I want to make sure we both understand."

Bryce fought a frustrated moan that tried to escape as his cock jerked and thickened. He loved the firm, soothing sound of Troy's voice as he gave the order. He didn't bark it out. He wasn't trying too hard or forcing it out because he was unsure. His command was simple and firm. It made Bryce's toes curl.

"Yes. I'm okay with you taking charge." He didn't add Sir, but the word was right on the tip of his tongue. They weren't there yet, he still had too many questions, but it was so close he could almost taste it.

"Good." The low word vibrated through Bryce, and that time he didn't try to hide his reaction. He let his head fall back against the Dom's hand and a little moan escaped. If he was even thinking about submitting to the Dom, there was no reason to fight his needs or suppress his reactions.

Troy made that low hum and Bryce understood he'd pleased

the Dom. It sent a shiver racing through him that only got worse as the hand at his neck tightened and fingers threaded their way through his hair. He loved having his head caressed and his hair played with. It was one of those odd things that could flip his switch and bring his submissive side right to the surface with almost no thought on his part.

The legs on his lap shifted again, and he fought the sensation that was making his brain foggy. Looking down, he saw beautiful green eyes peering up at him in surprised pleasure. "Hello."

Again, it wasn't much in the way of a greeting, but it seemed to please Oliver. He smiled a beaming grin and curled into Troy, letting his legs brush against Bryce's cock. "Hi."

Oliver looked up at Troy and whispered. "Sir, he's here."

A low chuckle had both submissives shivering. "I know. He came over to check on you."

Oliver preened and glanced back at Bryce, but still talked to Troy. "He did?"

"He did."

"You were beautiful." Bryce thought his words were inadequate, but Oliver looked like he couldn't have been happier. He blushed and wiggled again, then blushed even deeper when he realized exactly what his legs were rubbing against.

Oliver looked up at Troy and whispered, "He thought I was beautiful."

Bryce smiled, and he felt a deep rumble of laughter go through Troy. The Dom's short response was full of delight. "I heard."

Sighing, Oliver snuggled deeper into their embrace, not making any effort to avoid Bryce's hard cock. His innocent smile looked like it hid wicked intentions, and Bryce couldn't wait to learn more about the sweet sub.

"There's water on the table beside you, can you grab it,

Bryce?" Troy's words startled him and it took a second for his brain to make sense of them.

"Oh, yes." Looking to his right, Bryce saw the table he'd missed earlier and grabbed the bottle of water. Opening it, he handed it to Troy. Watching as the Dom carefully brought it to Oliver's lips, Bryce wasn't exactly jealous, but it had been so long since he'd given his submission to someone, he longed to feel that care.

Oliver drank it greedily, and Troy handed Bryce the empty bottle. Setting it on the table, he turned back to see Oliver smiling at Troy. "May I have kisses, Sir?"

Troy didn't respond with words, he simply lifted Oliver higher in his arms and brought their mouths together. It was tender and caring, almost innocent compared to everything going on around them, but Bryce watched intently. He wasn't sure if he should have looked away or not, but he didn't want to miss a single moment.

When Troy pulled away and let Oliver relax back into his lap, Bryce thought the moment was over. He startled as he felt the hand on the back of his neck tighten and push him down toward Oliver. "I think you want another kiss, don't you, kitten?"

Troy's words sent shivers of need through Bryce. His hand was firm and Bryce knew it wasn't so much a request as a silent order. The tender stroking of his fingers as he guided Bryce was a combination that made his cock throb. It was tender yet firm, and Bryce couldn't help but wonder if he would be the same in bed.

"Oh, yes." Sated, but somehow still needy eyes watched as Bryce drew closer. "Thank you."

Bryce wasn't sure who the sweet sub was thanking, but either way, it was hot. To be thanked so prettily for a kiss was just as erotic as the fantasy that Troy was giving him to Oliver as a present. His mind went wild with the fantasies, but as their lips touched, every other thought faded away.

Full and soft, Oliver's lips caressed Bryce's, sending waves of need through him. It was so much more than just a kiss...it was almost frightening. Troy must have sensed something because he slid his hand down from Bryce's neck to caress his back. Slow circles had his heart rate easing and his brain turning off.

The kiss was slow and filled with unexplored desire. He'd watched Oliver for so long, but he'd never dreamed of being beside him, kissing him. Tasting him. Bryce didn't deepen the kiss. He didn't know what he had permission to do, but the temptation was there. So he kept it light, using his lips to nibble at Oliver's, breathing in every gasp and exhale.

When he pulled away, Oliver settled into Troy's embrace, a satisfied smile on his face. Troy's hand worked its way back up to Bryce's neck. The possessive position tightened things low in Bryce's stomach. Troy let him ease away from Oliver, but not as far as he'd previously been. Troy kept him close, tucking him tightly against the side of his body.

"That was..." Oliver's words drifted off, but his Cheshire cat grin spoke volumes.

"Sexy." Troy growled out the word, the heat and passion sending precum streaming out of Bryce's cock.

Bryce wasn't sure what to say. Anything that came out would give away how long he'd watched them. How long he'd needed their touch. He shouldn't—

"He's wanted that for a long time." Troy's words stopped the roller coaster of worry and nerves that were crashing through Bryce. "I have, too."

It wasn't an order to kiss the Dom, but Bryce knew the request was hidden in the words. Bryce looked up into Troy's eyes and was drawn in like a moth to a flame. He twisted, holding tight to Oliver's legs, and let his gaze fall to Troy's lips.

They should have looked hard, since Troy's strong features couldn't be described as soft, but when his tongue flicked out and licked them, they suddenly looked tempting and delicious. Inching up, drawing closer to the Dom, Bryce made sure his intentions were clear, but Troy never told him to stop.

The Dom studied him, what Bryce thought was anticipation and arousal flashing in his eyes. When his lips finally touched Troy's, Bryce didn't know what to expect. Was he supposed to take charge of the kiss? Would Troy? Was it supposed to be light and quick, or deep and needy?

He melted in relief as Troy took control. The hand on his neck tightening, firm strong lips pulling him close, Bryce felt deliciously trapped and wanted. The passionate, demanding kiss made Troy's feelings clear. He'd wanted Bryce and he was going to have him.

Oliver's needy moan echoed the feelings swirling around in Bryce. "God, you guys are so hot."

Troy pulled back, the first hint of laughter dancing in his eyes. "You like watching us together, kitten?"

Bryce saw the shiver that raced through Oliver, but he also didn't miss the shifting that said he was still sore. "You two are so perfect together, Sir."

"Don't get any ideas. You are too sore to play." Troy's words came out stern, but Oliver didn't seem to mind.

He pouted prettily, blinking up at Troy. "But, Sir...He's finally here with us."

"He'll understand you can't play tonight. I'm sure he'll play with us again. I think he wants to give you more kisses. And I'm sure when you tell him how you've dreamed of laying yourself over his lap while he spanks your bottom, he won't want to deny you."

The deep words were tempting and magical. Bryce would have agreed to almost anything they said. When he talked about kisses and spankings, Bryce found himself nodding absently. He didn't want this to be the only time he got to touch them both. He wasn't sure what he was doing or what they wanted, but he knew he had to have more.

Oliver turned his charming, clearly-designed-to manipulate gaze to Bryce. "You'll play with us again? You'll spend time with us?"

"Yes." Bryce nodded, letting his head fall against Troy's shoulder. "I will."

Joy and pure excitement radiated from Oliver. "You have to." His voice dropped low, arousal and anticipation clear. "But what about tonight? I'm the only one who got to come."

2

TROY

Troy watched as Oliver shifted his legs, dragging them over Bryce's straining arousal. There was more than one reason he called his boy "kitten." He was sweet and cute, but had determination and claws you never saw coming. Bryce didn't stand a chance.

At least, not until he knew Oliver better.

"We talked about having you with us."

Bryce blinked and stared. He couldn't seem to believe they'd wanted him as well. Troy noticed him swallowing hard, not sure what to say. "You did?"

Oliver nodded, his deceptively adorable expression pulling Bryce in. Troy had seen Bryce when the Dom in him was in charge, and he knew how erotic and decisive the man could be. But Troy loved seeing him befuddled and aroused just as much. He could picture how incredible it was going to be when Bryce unleashed his inner Dom on Oliver.

"We did." Troy flexed his fingers on the slender column of Bryce's neck, loving the little gasp and shiver that escaped.

If he loved that little bit of dominance and the feeling of being almost trapped, Troy couldn't help but imagine how he would react if he was tied up and helpless. He would bet almost anything the man would be incredible.

Bryce looked up at him, confused and too aroused to think. He nodded, agreeing to some kind of internal debate, or maybe just to Oliver's comments about having him play with them again. Oliver's continued torment of the man didn't help his thought process, either. Bryce had already been hard from watching the sounding demonstration when he'd come over to them.

Having a nearly naked sub wiggling on his lap and begging for kisses hadn't helped his condition.

Oliver tightened his legs, and Troy knew his naughty kitten was teasing Bryce again. Oliver gave Troy a pretty, wide-eyed expression and nibbled on his bottom lip. "He's so hard, Sir. I don't want him to suffer just because I'm too sore."

Naughty kitten.

But oh-so-perfect. Bryce's mouth opened and closed several times, but eventually, he forced it closed and watched Oliver. Troy threaded his fingers through Bryce's hair, which was long enough at his neck to be able to caress and play with. Bryce dropped his head back and tried to hide the moan threatening to escape.

"Are you still hard? I saw that long, hard cock in your pants as you saw me fuck Oliver with the sound."

He waited while an unsure Bryce decided what to do. Did he want to play or was it all too much? It could go either way. They'd watched him for longer than he should admit, and in the past, every time Bryce got close he'd find a reason to walk away. Was he ready?

A stuttered breath and a hesitant nod were all he got, but Troy understood how hard the admission could be. He wasn't only acknowledging what they all knew already. In that moment, he was giving his submission to Troy. Troy knew he wouldn't have it for long; Bryce wasn't ready, no matter how much they wanted him to be. He was going to cherish the gift while he had it, though.

"I think we need to take care of that. Don't you, kitten?" Troy let the teasing, heated words work their way through his reluctant, albeit temporary, submissive.

"Oh, yes. I want him to feel good like I do, Sir." Oliver pulled his legs up slowly, letting Troy help him scoot around until he was cuddled on the other side of Troy. Flanked by two sexy men, Troy couldn't help but feel incredibly lucky.

One man he loved beyond all reason, and the other was someone who drew him in and made him want to discover everything about him. When Oliver was tucked into the corner of the couch, comfortable and warm, Troy took his now-free hand and brought it over to rest on Bryce's chest right below his throat.

Bryce's eyelids drooped, closing halfway, and he bit his lip trying to contain the little noises that wanted to escape. Troy growled, "Don't hide from me. I want to know I'm pleasing you."

The words were gravelly even for him, but Troy loved how they affected Bryce. Shivers raced through him and his head dropped back again, baring his throat in the most beautiful, naturally submissive way.

Troy traced the soft skin at the base of his neck and wondered if the smooth skin kept going or if the man had more hair under his tight T-shirt and supple leather pants. When they'd seen Bryce play at the club in the past, it had always been as a Dom, even though he was known as a switch. Troy had never been sure if it was because he'd never found the right Dom, or if there was something more to it.

He'd tortured Oliver with endless fantasies about what the sexy man might look like.

"So sexy." Troy trailed his fingers down Bryce's chest, seeing his labored breathing and feeling the way his muscles shook as he fought to stay still. "You're going to let me take care of you now."

It wasn't a question, more a statement of fact. Bryce seemed to understand that because his only agreement was a whimper that sent pure satisfaction through Troy. Flicking Bryce's puckered nipples through the thin, dark fabric, Troy loved the needy sounds that escaped the man who he hoped would become his boy.

Plucking the stiff peaks, he watched as Bryce finally broke his stillness. Arching up into the painful pleasure, he moaned as Troy worked the sensitive skin. Little shifts led to needy squirms as he tried to hold back. That wasn't what Troy wanted, and he didn't think Bryce really did, either.

Something in him said that if he couldn't break the man's walls down in that initial encounter, he'd never have another chance. If it was going to be his only time with Bryce, Troy wasn't going to waste even a second hinting at what he wanted.

He would take it.

To Troy, the best thing about Bryce being a switch was that he'd understand the emotions and needs from both sides of a scene. He'd know how incredible it felt to push a sub higher and higher, and how a good Dom really wanted his sub to fly. He'd also understand how powerful it was to give yourself over to someone else, for them to be in control.

"Oh, he's so sensitive, Sir." Oliver's quiet words pushed Bryce even higher.

"Please." As far as begging went it was mild, but Troy cherished it.

"I think he needs clamps on these pretty nipples. Would you like to see him decorated like that, kitten?" Troy let the words flow out filled with desire. Bryce liked something about it, if the desperate look in his eyes was any clue.

Was it the clamps themselves? Was it knowing Oliver wanted him to wear them? There were so many things that could have spoken to the sexy man. Troy wanted to have the time to get to know him well enough to figure out every tell and hidden need.

"He's beautiful now, Sir, but you would make him incredible." Oliver's whispered words made Bryce whimper. It was filled with pleasure and a desire for more, but Troy could only guess at what.

Bryce's hips finally started to move, frantic thrusts he couldn't seem to control. Moving away from the tempting nipples, Troy trailed his fingers down the sculpted chest. "You need more, don't you?"

Another broken plea tore from Bryce. "More, please."

It gave him the same feeling he got when he heard Oliver beg and scream out his pleasure. It was filled with so much emotion, even though it was so simple and quiet compared to his kitten. "You're so good for me. Letting me hear your pleasure. Giving me what I wanted. You want to please me, don't you?"

Bryce gave a jerky nod, and his hips humped the air again. Having to acknowledge his submission and his desires seemed to amplify the need. Troy couldn't wait to see how high he could push the beautiful man.

Beautiful and conflicted.

"Do you want to know what would please me?" Desire surged through Troy as Bryce struggled with the answer.

The man's submission was instinctual but not easy. He needed it, but it would be on his terms. Troy wanted to crawl inside him and understand what made him tick. To learn what took him from Dom to sub. To discover how he felt about his submission and giving that gift to someone.

It felt important to Troy. Significant. Special. But he wasn't sure if he was only seeing what he wanted to. He wanted it to be different for Bryce. Just the fact that he was submitting to Troy in the club gave Troy hope, but he didn't want this to be a random encounter for the complex man. He needed Bryce to want them as much as they desired him.

Bryce nodded again, this time looking up at Troy with need-filled eyes. "Yes, Sir."

That one little word was perfect.

Troy hoped Bryce could see it in his eyes. He knew he wasn't the most romantic man or the most eloquent, but it was important to him that Bryce understood how much Troy cherished his gift. Sliding his hand down, he palmed Bryce's impressive erection in one long movement.

Bryce threw his head back and arched into the touch, silently pleading for more. Troy let him get away with it, but if Bryce wanted to come, he was going to have to stop hiding his need and remember his manners.

He gave Bryce's cock a firm squeeze. "Do you get to fuck yourself against me?"

Bryce stilled and fought to control his body. Lifting his head to look at Troy, Bryce blushed and shook his head. "I'm sorry, Sir."

Troy loved the fact that he could make Bryce forget even the most basic of rules, forcing him to just react. But the sweet embarrassment flooding Bryce's face as he realized he'd been naughty was gorgeous. "Who does your pleasure belong to now?"

Bryce shivered again, something wild crossing his eyes for just a moment. "You, Sir."

"Very good." Troy gave his cock a long, gentle caress as a reward.

Straining to stay still, Bryce bit his lower lip and shook with the force of his desire. It was such a desperate need that Troy didn't want to hold him back. He needed to give the exquisite man everything he wanted. Working open the buttons on

Bryce's leathers, he never broke eye contact. He wanted Bryce to see how much he meant to him.

When the pants were open and Troy could feel the smooth, hard skin of Bryce's erection, he finally looked down. Bryce's shaft was long and thick with a broad head that would stretch and caress the person taking it. He wasn't going to convince himself they were there yet, but it was so easy to picture how incredibly Oliver would react as it slid deep inside him. It would stretch his kitten and rub his prostate with every thrust.

Bryce was still, but his shaking let Troy know how hard it was. Having to focus on his body freed something in him because he no longer seemed to think about how he was reacting, his moans and pleas flowing out of him without the need to censor himself.

Gripping him tightly, Troy slowly jerked him off. The pace was too slow to actually make him climax, but Troy loved watching the pleasure build. He loved teasing and pushing a sub to their limits, and he wasn't going to hide that from Bryce.

"You're being so good for me. And you have such a pretty cock. Oliver's going to love sucking on it and licking it when I give him permission. Next time we play, do you want that? Do you want Oliver down on his knees for you? Tasting your dick?" Frantic nods and incoherent words fell from Bryce.

It was a jumble of pleas, and yes, and more, and broken bits of fantasies that had run through Bryce's head. Fierce emotion surged through Troy as he realized that Bryce had been lusting after them just as long as they'd been obsessed with him.

Troy tightened his grip on the long shaft but still went tortuously slow. Bryce jerked and squirmed, trying to be good while Troy teased him with all the sexy things they could do together. When he started telling Bryce about how he wanted to bend him and Oliver over the couch together so he could spank them both at the same time, something snapped in Bryce.

One hand let go of the couch where it had a death grip on the leather and flailed out until it found Troy's leg. Sliding his hand over the Dom's body, he reached out until he found what he was looking for, which was Oliver. Watching the two men cling to each other while Bryce flew higher and higher, Troy couldn't wait any longer.

Using Bryce's precum as lube, he moved his hand faster, finally giving Bryce what he needed to reach his pleasure. Bryce held Oliver's hand in a vise-like grip, and all he could do was beg.

"Please, please, Sir. Oh god, please." Eyes closed and face full of concentration, Troy knew it was all Bryce could do to stop himself from exploding.

"Come. Show us how much you need...give me your pleasure..."

Bryce's orgasm burst out of him, cum covering Troy's hand as he kept going, pushing the pleasure higher and higher even though Bryce's cock would be sensitive. He stroked and teased until Bryce sagged back on the couch, head rested on Troy's shoulder as he just trembled under the onslaught of sensations.

With one last slow caress, he moved his hand away from Bryce's cock, but he left the tight grip on the man's neck, not wanting Bryce to feel deserted. Placing a kiss on the top of Bryce's head, Troy felt Oliver's hand wrap around his arm.

"Please, Sir. Can I taste him?" Oliver's soft pleading words went right to Troy's heart.

That meant so much more than Bryce would understand.

Troy knew his relationship with Oliver wasn't conventional, but it worked for them. After a bit of a rocky start, they'd made rules and had spent countless hours talking about what they needed and wanted. Oliver submitted to other Doms occasionally, and they had threesomes when it felt right to both of them, but one of their big rules was that no one else came inside

Oliver, in any way, unless it was someone they wanted a long-term relationship with. For Oliver to even ask to taste Bryce was his way of letting Troy know how invested he was becoming.

"Yes, kitten." Troy brought his hand up, watching as his sweet sub licked cum off his hand.

Bryce watched them both, sated and quiet while curled up against Troy, completely unaware of how much was being said with the one sexy act. Troy just hoped that they'd be able to talk things out and see where it could take them because he couldn't see walking away from Bryce.

It would already be too hard.

3

OLIVER

"But I still don't understand. Why would he play with us at the club and even talk on the phone, but not want to see us again?" Oliver knew he sounded frustrated. However, he just didn't understand the logic.

"I think he's conflicted about liking us both." Troy pulled Oliver into his arms, bringing one hand up to play with the hair framing Oliver's face. It still amazed Oliver what a tactile person his Dom was. Troy always came off as cool and probably emotionally distant to most people, but Oliver always felt loved and cared for. "He's dated Doms and subs, but never in a relationship like ours."

That was one of the pieces Oliver couldn't quite work his head around. When it came to most people, he understood why they would push back against a relationship like what they wanted. He didn't understand Bryce's hesitance, though.

"This is the best type of relationship for him." Oliver pushed his head close to Troy's lips, encouraging a kiss. He loved forehead kisses; they made him feel warm and cuddly inside. "This way, he gets the best of both worlds. Both of us when he wants to be cuddled and loved. You when he's feeling submissive." Oliver gave Troy a flirty look when he got his kiss. "And me, when he's all take-charge and controlling."

"You're looking forward to that part, aren't you?" Troy's smile was wicked, and Oliver could tell he was thinking about all kinds of fun things.

"Oh, yes." Oliver's toes almost curled. "He was so hot with you. I loved being able to sit back and watch you like that, especially since I was worn out and feeling fabulous."

Oliver smiled as Troy gave him another kiss at his hairline. He almost moaned as Troy started to run his fingers absently through Oliver's hair. It was so good—but they'd miss their appointment if they kept it up. "You're going to make us late."

"But those little moans sound so good." Troy's voice sent shivers down Oliver's spine. Damn him. He was doing it on purpose.

"I want to go. You don't have to protect me." He pulled back enough to lean up and give Troy a quick peck on the lips. "If it goes bad, I won't fall apart. Promise."

Oliver thought it was the perfect way to see Bryce in person and figure out what the hell was going on, but Troy had found one excuse after another to put off the appointment. Once he hadn't been able to talk his way out of it anymore, Oliver thought Troy would be fine. It turned out he was just going to try another tactic. He also thought Troy wasn't just worried about Oliver's emotions, but his own as well.

His blond giant had a mushy heart that he hid well most of the time.

"All right. Let's go." Troy pulled away, taking Oliver's hand in his. Heading out to the truck, Troy looked at the clock as they climbed in. "You said it only takes ten minutes to get to the office?"

Oliver nodded. "Yes, so we still have time."

He ignored the soft *damn it* he heard coming from the passenger seat.

They drove to Bryce's office in silence—too much silence. It gave Oliver too much time to think. He'd been on cloud nine when they'd called Bryce the day after their evening at the club. They'd thought they would have to bribe Ben or Conner for his number, but they'd found it online fairly easily. Bryce had been surprised to hear from them, but it hadn't felt weird or like they were intruding.

The next couple of calls had gone just as well. To Oliver's surprise, Bryce had even called them a few times. It was only when they'd started talking about dinner and going out somewhere that things had gotten awkward. They could talk for hours, the three of them together or just Bryce with one of them, but the minute dinner or even a movie was mentioned, suddenly something came up.

The first time it had happened, Oliver had been convinced they would never hear from Bryce again. He'd been floored when Bryce had called the next day, wanting to talk to Troy about a football game that was on.

He'd acted like nothing out of the ordinary had happened.

He knew Troy was worried that Bryce was ashamed of seeing the two of them together or that Bryce didn't want to admit it was more than a casual fling, but Oliver knew it was more than that. The way Bryce talked about his family and his little comments about BDSM in general let Oliver know he wasn't ashamed of anything. He just seemed hesitant...and confused.

Oliver didn't understand what was making it so difficult, though.

What they wanted should have been perfect for Bryce.

He'd have someone who would take charge when he needed that and someone to dominate when he went all alpha. There would always be someone to do something with, sexually or just fun, and with three people the sex was off the charts hot as long as it was done right. And he and Troy had enough practice to make sure it went right, even if Bryce had never had a threesome.

He was slightly frustrated...that little piece of information hadn't come up in conversation yet.

Not that he hadn't tried to bring it up—Bryce was just playing it very close to the vest.

Bryce was turning out to be the king of mixed signals, and Oliver wanted some answers. He'd managed to make an appointment to get new insurance quotes with Bryce's office last week when the regular assistant at the front desk was gone. Whoever had answered the phones only asked a few questions about the nature of the meeting. His name wasn't one of them.

Oliver thought he'd done pretty well managing that one.

He'd managed to get the last appointment of the day on Friday, when he knew from phone conversations that most of the office was ready to start sneaking out the door by mid-afternoon. By the end of their meeting, even if they only talked about new insurance—which they really needed—everyone else would be gone.

It was *perfect*.

Once they could get past whatever was holding Bryce back, they would all be perfect for each other. He just needed Bryce to honestly admit it. He wouldn't have been calling and talking to them so often if they didn't mean anything to him. Not after the night at the club.

He'd felt completely worn out from the sounds and so thoroughly sated that he couldn't have gotten it up if his life depended on it. So as he'd watched Bryce and Troy, he'd gotten to see the beauty in their reactions and the need, not just the desire.

They'd been beautiful together.

Troy didn't let that many people see his tender side first-hand. The way he'd stroked Bryce and let his façade crack enough for Bryce to catch glimpses of what was underneath let Oliver know he wasn't pushing anything his Dom didn't want. Troy just wasn't going to butt in where he suspected he wasn't wanted.

Oliver didn't have those reservations.

Especially when he knew deep down they *were* wanted. Desperately. Then he didn't mind pushing and making a nuisance of himself. Sometimes he thought that was why the universe made subs, to push the Doms into taking what they really wanted but wouldn't always go get. Too many over-developed morals about not wanting to talk people into something they didn't want.

Some people needed a little shove. And he thought Bryce was one of them.

So that's what they were going to do. Give him a little nudge and hopefully get the dominant side of him revved up. Oliver had a suspicion it wouldn't take much to get that part of Bryce ready to jump into whatever would have Oliver submitting to him.

Then they could finally figure out what all the hesitation was about.

By the time they'd gotten to the office, Oliver was even more confident about the meeting. No matter what Bryce said or tried to avoid saying, his actions spoke louder than his words. And his actions screamed out that he wanted them both.

So that's what Oliver would give him.

Walking through the door, they were greeted by a smiling woman who clearly had no idea why they were there.

Her brows pulled together, and she shrugged. "I don't see anything on the schedule, but if you give me a minute, I'll figure it out. I'm a temp; the regular receptionist is out of the office. I'll go get Mr. Ryder for you."

They heard a whispered conversation coming from a back office. Something about calendars and updating schedules, but he couldn't catch it all. Troy was giving him an are-you-sure-about-this expression that Oliver just ignored. He had a plan. And he wanted to experience what Bryce was like when he was in charge. Oliver had a feeling he would be a fiery Dom. Troy was always so in control with a cool passion that made Oliver crazy, but he thought the two Doms would complement each other perfectly.

When Bryce came out of his office with the temp, there was a moment of awkward silence before Bryce seemed to push away his concerns. "I'm sorry about the confusion. Please come back to my office."

He started in on a fairly rehearsed speech about quotes and coverages as he ushered them into his office. When he closed the door and they could no longer be overheard, he gave them both a skeptical look.

"This is a surprise."

Oliver was just pleased that he wasn't angry, so Bryce's cool welcome didn't dampen his excitement. He smiled sweetly at his uncertain expression. "We've known we've needed new insurance for a while, but I kept putting it off. Finally, we decided just to get it done."

Bryce nodded, trying to hide a grin. He didn't believe Oliver's innocent act for a minute, but there was nothing he would be able to call them on because they really did need a new company. Troy sat down in one of the sumptuous leather chairs and Oliver sat down on his lap.

Curling into Troy, Oliver watched Bryce closely as he talked about their current insurance. They'd had a small independent company that they'd used for years, but when they'd been purchased by a larger one, Oliver hadn't been impressed with the service.

He always felt like he was annoying the people at the call center when he had a question, and he'd run into more than a few of the customer service people who seemed homophobic. He was tired of dealing with it. When Bryce realized that they really did need new insurance, he relaxed.

He asked good questions and understood what they were looking for without making it seem like a canned sales pitch. Even if Oliver hadn't been desperate to taste the man again, he would have bought the coverage from him.

They were quoted auto insurance and a new homeowner's policy right away, and Bryce asked some questions about other policies he was going to quote for them. He never mentioned Oliver being cuddled up on Troy's lap, but Oliver could see the little glances and questions that would run through his eyes as they talked.

When Bryce tilted his computer screen so they could see how he'd changed the coverages on the house quote, Oliver took it as a sign. "I can't quite see that. Can I come around there?"

It was innocent and not that crazy of a question, so Bryce couldn't think of anything to say before Oliver started to move around the room. A pat on his ass from Troy as he walked away was the only thing that could possibly be thought of as unusual, until Oliver walked over and made himself at home on Bryce's lap.

Bryce made a startled sound, one that Oliver would *never* identify as a squeak, but wrapped an arm around Oliver's hips to keep him in place. Bryce gave him another skeptical look, but Oliver gave him a crooked little grin and wiggled his bottom over the Dom's growing erection. "This is much better. Thank you."

Then he pointed to the screen and started asking coverage

questions, which really threw Bryce off. Oliver might want to drive Bryce a little crazy, but he had questions, so it worked out well for both purposes. It took Bryce a few minutes to get his head back in the conversation, but soon they were ironing out the quote and Oliver was pleased with the price.

He gave Bryce an excited little peck on the cheek, not even thinking about it. "Thank you. I love it. It's much better than what we've got now."

Bryce cleared his throat, then smiled at Oliver. "I'm glad. I'll have everything finalized when you come back to get the other quotes."

Troy laughed. "He's been bugging me about this for six months. I'm just glad we're getting it done. I'm tired of talking about it." Troy gave Oliver an indulgent smile. "He's always right about this stuff. I don't even know why I ever put it off."

Oliver tried not to smile. "I'm going to remember this conversation the next time you question me." Bryce grinned as Troy gave him a stern look.

"Someone's itching for a spanking." Troy growled out the words, sending a shiver down Oliver's spine.

He sighed and relaxed against a now-stiff Bryce. Deciding to push his luck a little, Oliver turned and whispered in Bryce's ear. "He looks all stern and growly, but he knows how much I love being pulled down over his lap. Do you like spanking cheeky subs, Sir?"

Bryce groaned and tried to fight whatever was going through his head, but he finally gave in. Letting the hand that had been on the mouse come down to rest on Oliver's legs, he caressed them with long, slow strokes. "I do. I think a sub looks wonderful with a pretty pink bottom."

"So does Troy. He loves making my bottom red. He says it helps me to remember to behave, but I think it's just because he likes it so much. I'm a good boy. I don't need the reminder. You know I'm a good boy, don't you, Sir?" Oliver turned back to Bryce, letting his voice drop low, and almost whispered the words into the Dom's ear.

He could feel Bryce's cock jerk, and the Dom laughed. "I think you're a handful."

Then to Oliver's delight, Bryce gave his ass a pat before he continued. "I bet you have to be constantly watched."

Oliver gave him an adorable expression and pouted, shaking his head. "I'm such a sweet sub."

Troy cleared his throat to cover up a laugh. "Kitten, you're adorable and sexy, but you're a handful."

Oliver gave Bryce a wide-eyed look and gave the Dom a confused expression that he knew looked sexy. "Sometimes Troy says he needs an extra set of hands just to keep me in line."

"And you have no idea what he means, do you?" Bryce grinned and shook his head.

"No." Oliver leaned close again and let his lips get close enough to touch Bryce's ear. "I'm such a good boy. I'm obedient and I always try to do my best. When Troy tells me to bend over for my spanking, I do it right away. When he tells me to kneel down so he can use my mouth, I take his cock in and relax my throat so he can sink in deep where it gets tight. When he wants me to fuck myself on his cock, I climb right up and ride him until he lets me come. See, I'm a good boy." Oliver clenched his legs together and shifted just enough to make Bryce moan. He could almost see the restraint slipping away from the tightly controlled Dom.

Oliver knew the passion would explode out of him when he was ready to let it all go.

"It sounds like you're a *very* good boy." Bryce growled out the words, staring at Oliver like he wanted to devour him. Bryce's eyes flitted over to look at Troy for a second, and whatever he saw pleased him because he relaxed even more and his hand moved back to caress the top of Oliver's ass. "Good boys get rewarded."

And he had him.

Oliver let the need he was feeling flow right out through his voice, making it husky and breathy. "Do you know I want for my reward, Sir?"

Bryce tightened his hold on Oliver and seemed to stop moving. "What?"

"For you to come out to dinner with us."

Bingo.

4

BRYCE

And he was very neatly trapped.

Sweet, sexy, and devious.

He should have guessed it was coming. Seeing them at his office had thrown his brain for a loop, though. When the temp, Maddie, maybe, or Mandy, he couldn't remember, came in to tell him about the surprise clients who said they had an appointment, they were the last people he'd expected to see. Lack of blood in critical thinking organs may have played a part in it as well.

Bryce had known that they couldn't be put off forever, but he never suspected they'd show up at the office. He should have. Bryce thought that Troy wasn't the type to push, but one look at Oliver and he knew there was no way the sub would back down. Under all that innocence was pure fire. Bryce could see why Troy called him kitten.

It was dinner. Just dinner.

It wasn't like they were asking for a collaring ceremony.

Pushing that stray thought to the back of his head, Bryce nodded. "All right, trouble."

Oliver sat up, shock clear in his eyes. Bryce glanced over to

Troy, not sure what to expect. The pleased expression on the Dom's face was a surprise, but a good one. Then he jerked his head, gesturing to Oliver and giving Bryce a knowing look.

The permission was unexpected.

Looking at a slightly confused Oliver, Bryce wrapped his arms tighter around the sub. "I would love to go out to dinner with you. We don't have to use that as your reward, though. I can think of other, more fun things for that."

He placed a tender, slow kiss on Oliver's lips, loving the gasp and low, breathy moan that escaped. It was just as tender as it had been the first time. But in the light of day, it felt...odd, maybe, to have Troy watching. The man who'd dominated him so thoroughly was seeing him dominate his lover. It was a little...odd.

So maybe it wasn't the right word...but it made him feel vulnerable.

Oliver must have felt something change in the kiss because it deepened and his hand came up to gently cup Bryce's face. It not only got him even more aroused than he already was, it helped to turn his brain off so he could simply focus on the man on his lap.

When Oliver finally pulled back to breathe, he had an amused, affectionate expression on his face. "Thank you for coming out to dinner with us."

Bryce glanced at Troy to make sure he knew he was still included in the conversation. "Where do you want to go?"

Oliver, still on Bryce's lap, turned to look at Troy. "What sounds good? Italian? Steak?"

Bryce laughed. "That's what I would have said."

Oliver gave him a grin. "Great minds think alike."

Troy shook his head as they flirted like awkward teenagers. "Italian. We can go for steaks next time."

Next time?

Oliver nodded and bounced off Bryce's lap, glancing down with heated laughter in his eyes at Bryce's obvious erection. Bryce's hand came out and popped Oliver on the bottom, completely without thinking. "Naughty boy."

"I told you. We'll have to keep him in line." Then Troy gave him a look like he was daring Bryce to say something.

His stomach did circles at the fantasies that were running through his head. The scariest part was that most of them weren't even dirty. If his brain put them in the play and leave category, it would have been easier to sort through.

He was selective with who he played with, especially who he subbed for, but he'd still met a good few subs that he'd liked and had fun with. He'd even submitted for a few Doms who'd made him think, but never both at the same time, and never where it felt so real...so permanent.

They'd made it clear that they weren't looking for something casual.

He wished it was as easy as they made it seem.

"Sounds good." He wasn't going to pretend he didn't want to see them. Holding off on the phone had been hard enough, but with both of them watching him, it was impossible to say it. "Let me get a few last-minute things done and we can go—or I can meet you there?"

Oliver immediately shook his head, still smiling but stubborn. "No, we'll wait for you."

"I'm not going to disappear on you." Bryce would have been frustrated, but Oliver was just so cute.

"I have no idea what you're talking about." Oliver smiled sweetly. "I'm just excited—and hungry."

Troy snorted, wrapping his arms around Oliver. "You're always excited."

Oliver waggled his eyebrows, grinning as Troy pulled him so

he was pressed close to the Dom's chest. "Oh, yes, and with the two of you in the room, it's only getting worse."

"I think I can keep you occupied while Bryce finishes up his work." Troy's deep voice had conflicting signals bouncing through Bryce. Submitting to Troy was still so recent in his mind, he could almost feel himself back on the couch in the dark club, but having just held Oliver, the Dom inside him wanted to tease and pleasure the naughty sub.

It felt like he had multiple personalities and they all wanted different things.

Oliver moaned, sinking against Troy. As Bryce tried to log off his computer and do the things he had to get done, he watched as Troy's hands slid down Oliver's chest. Bryce's fingers wouldn't work the keyboard as Troy slowly worked his hands under Oliver's tight, preppy-looking polo shirt.

Something about those big, strong hands inching up under Oliver's clothes had Bryce nearly drooling. It was so easy to picture himself standing in front of Oliver, helping to make him crazy. Kissing him while Troy took his clothes off or while Troy teased at his nipples.

Distracting.

What was he supposed to be doing?

Reports, logging out, quotes organized...he could do it. It didn't help when Troy's wandering hands finally reached Oliver's nipples. It really didn't help when the litany of dirty words started. Hearing Oliver's little moans and gasps went right to his cock.

Torture.

Pure torture.

By the time Oliver was crying out and grinding his ass against Troy as he straddled the Dom's leg, Bryce was ready to explode. Was Troy trying to drive him crazy or Oliver? Bryce was starting to get the feeling it was both of them.

When he stood, everything completed, Troy looked over at him and cocked an eyebrow. When Bryce nodded and mouthed *ready*, Troy released the nipples he'd been working so thoroughly. He was still more closed off than Bryce was used to seeing, but his eyes held wicked laughter as he smoothed Oliver's shirt down.

"I think you owe Bryce an apology, kitten. You were trying to make him crazy, and that wasn't nice." The words made Oliver shiver and his unfocused eyes fought to look at Bryce.

"I'm sorry. I shouldn't have teased you, Sir." Oliver was pure sex. The husky words went right through Bryce.

"Are you going to be good tonight?" Bryce wasn't sure if he was asking about Oliver's behavior at the restaurant or whatever might happen later, but Oliver nodded, probably understanding what Bryce was trying to say better than he did.

"Yes, Sir."

Bryce still didn't know if it was the best idea. Even if he put aside dating a Dom and a sub at the same time, there was still the issue of him dating two people at once. How was he supposed to explain that?

He'd agreed with Garrett, Brent, and Grant that they wouldn't do anything in their personal life that would bring attention to the business. Just dating two people in a more vanilla relationship wouldn't be within the boundaries of their agreement.

How would he explain that to prospective customers?

His family would understand if the business wasn't involved —but it was. Mentally shaking his head, Bryce tried to remind himself that he was jumping the gun. Dinner didn't mean serious. Dinner didn't mean a ménage or polyamorous relationship. Just because that's where his mind was going didn't mean anyone else would see it that way.

Dinner could mean business meetings or hanging out with

friends. Dinner could be casual and innocent. It didn't have to mean spankings and domination. That's what came to mind when he thought of dinner with the two of them, but it didn't mean it had to be that way.

He was so screwed.

"I'm all finished. Are you two ready for dinner?" Dinner, it was just dinner.

"Yes." They both spoke at the same time, one voice aroused and needy, the other confident but slightly hesitant, if Bryce read Troy right. He couldn't blame him. It was hard to put himself in the other Dom's shoes, but he couldn't imagine how hard it would be to bring someone else into his relationship. They were obviously in love, and they wouldn't want anything to come into their lives that might fuck it up.

As he led them out of the office and locked up, he tried to focus on enjoying their company and nothing else. They deserved his undivided attention. He was also looking forward to spending time with them. They'd talked multiple times since the club, and no matter what the topic, he got a kick out of both of them.

Troy was so serious but had a dry sense of humor and could get crazy wrapped up in anything sports related. Oliver was cute and loveable and could charm his way into just about anything he set his heart on. Evidently, he'd set his heart on Bryce.

Bryce wasn't sure how he felt about that.

Flattered?

Yes.

Worried?

Possibly.

He just couldn't picture it working out in reality like his fantasies had everything playing out. Obsessing over it wouldn't help. He locked up and walked out the front with them to their car. Luckily, they'd been talking so long everyone else in the office had gone home, so he didn't have to explain why he was walking out with their new insureds.

The temp would have been confused, but the rest of them would have been able to guess.

He knew he couldn't hide his interest in either of them.

They were just...hot...perfect...sexy...funny...naughty...in other words, the picture of every fantasy he'd ever had. He was completely screwed.

Oliver walked around to the driver's side after giving Bryce a tempting, teasing look. Troy gave his boy a tight grin. "In the truck, kitten. I'll be right there."

Oliver had a knowing grin, but nodded and climbed in the driver's seat. Waiting not-so-patiently, he fiddled with things on the dashboard and watched the two men intently. Bryce wasn't sure what Troy was going to say, but he was relieved he didn't have long to wait because he didn't think his stomach could handle it.

Troy turned away from the truck. "You want to do this, right?"

Was he asking about the food or something else? "Dinner or—"

"Everything." Troy leaned back against the truck looking cool and collected, but Bryce could see the stress around his eyes and in the set of his lips. "If you only want to be friends, we need to know that up front. I'm going to be honest, we're already more invested in this than you are, I think, and—"

"No, you're not." Bryce wasn't sure what would happen, but he didn't want Troy feeling unwanted or like Bryce wasn't emotionally invested in the two men. Because he was. As crazy as it sounded, even to him, that one night changed everything. "I want to be here, and if we're being honest, I'm not sure how I feel about everything, but you're not the only one who feels something."

It wasn't much, and it definitely wasn't romantic, but it satis-fied Troy. His no-nonsense attitude and guarded exterior made Bryce sense that he'd rather have the truth laid out than anything flowery and dramatic. Oliver, on the other hand, would probably love something romantic. He glanced over at the man in the car, head cocked, looking like he was trying to read their lips.

Bryce got a big grin from Oliver, but he seemed more worried than he had when they were in the office. "If you make him wait any longer he's going to pop."

Troy grinned, nodding. "My kitten is very curious."

"So, Little Italy, or did you guys have another restaurant in mind?" Standing in the parking lot was awkward. He wanted to get back to the more relaxed atmosphere that they'd had before. Sitting down eating seemed like the best way to get there.

"That's fine." Troy's expression turned guarded again. "We need to talk about things before this gets too far."

His insides felt like they were at war with each other. The firm way Troy was looking at him was making it hard to think. His internal sub wanted one thing and the Dom another. Bryce slid his hands in his pocket to keep from fidgeting and nodded. "I agree. What topics did you have in mind?"

Something flashed through Troy's eyes, but Bryce couldn't catch it. "You need to understand what Oliver and I want, and we all need to talk about expectations in a scene and in general. I want to make sure we're all on the same page."

"Understandable. And after dinner?"

"We'll see what comes up at dinner, then we'll go from there. If you'd like, you can come over to our house for a drink after-ward." Troy seemed to be waiting for Bryce to pull away and make an excuse not to go, but while he knew he probably should, he didn't want to.

"Sounds good." He glanced over and gave Oliver a wink to

help keep him from worrying. "I'll follow you over to the restaurant."

"All right."

Bryce watched as Troy turned and headed for the passenger side. Walking over to his vehicle, a sedan that looked small when compared to the truck, he got in and turned on the car. He knew Troy was concerned for Oliver, and he couldn't blame him. Bryce wasn't sure how long they'd been together or what their story was, but he knew he'd be worried if the situation were reversed.

He just didn't know what he would say.

He wasn't even sure what he wanted. Maybe that wasn't quite true. He could see some of it, but he wasn't sure it was realistic or the best idea. He knew long-term BDSM relationships could work. His own parents were proof of that. It was when you added in a Dom and a sub to the mix that made it more confusing.

Would they accept that as an answer?

I like the idea of this, but I'm not sure it can work wasn't the most eloquent response. It was honest, though. That had to count for something.

He hoped for the drive over to magically take longer, but it seemed even shorter than usual. He still hadn't worked out what to say by the time he'd pulled in and parked beside their truck. Excitement poured from Oliver, making Bryce smile. Even knowing the little brat would try to manipulate him into getting what he wanted didn't dampen his grin.

Kitten was right.

Opening the car door, he got out and walked over to his dates. Not that he would call it that. Not yet, at least. "I'm starving."

"Me too." Troy didn't look like he was talking about food.

Oliver laughed and smirked. "I'm *always* hungry."

Oliver didn't seem to be talking about food, either.

Bryce shook his head. "Come on, you two. Behave."

They both gave him little smirks. Oliver's a bit naughtier and Troy's a bit more reserved, but still very similar. If they could get through dinner without drawing undue attention to themselves, he was going to count it a win. He wouldn't bet on it, though.

5

TROY

It was going better than he thought it would, but he wasn't ready to relax yet. Bryce was a little too hesitant for Troy to understand what he wanted. One minute he would look confused and skeptical, the next he would watch them like he didn't want to let them go.

Oliver had been over the moon with the way the meeting had gone, and Troy had to agree with him. Once Bryce had found his footing, he'd moved past the awkward phase quickly. They'd gotten a lot of good information, and Oliver's little stunt had proven Bryce wasn't just seeing them as potential customers.

They'd had a long talk about flirting and how far things could go without them needing to discuss it more. Troy had wanted Bryce to understand that he didn't just want his submission, they wanted him to be a true Dom with Oliver as well. It would be a balancing act, but he wanted to make sure Bryce understood that.

He didn't want Bryce to feel pigeonholed into one role and expected to stay there.

It could work. Bryce just needed to see it.

As they relaxed with their drinks, waiting for the food and eating the breadsticks Oliver loved, Bryce brought the conversation back around to more personal topics. "So how long have you two been together?"

Oliver gave Troy a sweet smile. "Two years as a couple, and before that we dated off and on."

"Dating as in vanilla dating?" Bryce took a drink of his soda and relaxed back in his seat.

"Sort of." Oliver shrugged. "We met at a bar and hit it off. It was mostly vanilla for the first couple of months until we both started opening up."

"It was easy to see that Oliver wasn't the dominant kind of guy and I liked that, but I wasn't sure if he'd realized what it could mean." Troy mentally shook his head at the time they'd wasted not talking about what they really wanted.

"I'd met a few people online that were into BDSM and played around a little, but never anything serious. Troy looked like a total Dom, which was one of the things that had me flirting with him to begin with, but when he didn't mention the scene, I just pushed it to the back of my mind." Oliver frowned and started playing with the wrapper to his straw. "We were both trying for a traditional relationship, but wanting something else."

Troy broke in because he knew Oliver didn't like this part of their story. "We actually broke up several times over the course of a year, but would always get back together. I was still trying to force myself to ease up on the dominance I really wanted, and Oliver was trying to fight his needs as well."

He reached under the booth and took Oliver's hand. "It was never big fights or cheating. We just weren't happy but weren't talking."

A smile broke over Oliver's face, this time reaching his eyes. "Until that night."

"What night?" Bryce was leaning forward, elbows on the table, looking curious.

"We hadn't seen each other in a few weeks at that point. Not long for most people, but at the time it felt like an eternity. I'd met a guy, another sub, who told me about the club. We went one Friday night when they were allowing new people who were curious to come check things out. Well, I'm hanging out with my friend and we're flirting with some of the Doms. Nothing serious, but it was nice not to fight what I wanted."

Oliver looked over at Troy and grinned. "My friend started talking about a sexy Dom he saw across the room. I looked over and there was Troy." Oliver gave Troy a mock frown. "Surrounded by little twinks who were going crazy."

Troy shrugged. "I didn't do anything with the twinks. They all looked like I could break them with one thrust."

Bryce choked on his drink and shook his head. "Then what?"

Oliver laughed. "I very sweetly went over there and told him how surprised I was to see him."

Troy snorted, almost sending water out his nose. It had to be the biggest reaction Bryce had seen from him. "Sweet? How about we tell him the truth?" He looked over at Bryce. "This *sweet* sub here made a hell of a scene. Marched right over and demanded to know what the hell I was doing there. He then proceeded to tell me off, saying that if I needed to practice on little twinks to figure out how to be a Dom then fine, but I could come begging him back when I knew what I was doing."

Bryce laughed so hard he couldn't breathe. Finally he managed to speak. "Why haven't I heard this before?"

"There were mostly just new people there. Many of the regular club members don't go on those nights for privacy reasons. I think Ben and Conner were the only regulars there in the bar area to see it." Troy let his hand come up to rest on Oliver's shoulder.

Oliver leaned into his touch and picked up the story again. "I started to storm off dramatically. Pissed doesn't even begin to describe how angry I was. He'd never mentioned anything about wanting BDSM, but there he was with a dominant band around his arm. It was like waving a red flag in front of a bull."

"Pot, meet kettle." Bryce gave Oliver a teasing look.

"Sure, that part is obvious now, but at the time, I didn't see it that way."

"I did." Troy broke in. "I knew right away why he was there, and I was ticked he'd thought to ask strangers to do things to him and not me. So I grabbed his arm and told him that it sounded like he needed a Dom to teach him some manners."

"What was Ben doing with all this going on?"

"He was dying. Jealous lovers screaming at each other with all those newbies standing around watching? It wasn't the first impression of BDSM that he wanted to give them." Troy's lips twitched at the memory.

"So Troy pulled me against him and somewhere in there called me a brat and said he should teach me a lesson, or something like that. I might have egged him on a bit. Ben was watching all our drama and just stood there while we hollered at each other. I think he understood what was happening faster than we did, really. I was nearly panting, I was so turned on. Troy looked like every bratty sub's fantasy." Oliver leaned back against the seat, fanning himself dramatically.

"Between how turned on he made me and how frustrated I was, I couldn't think." Troy leaned over and gave Oliver a kiss. "Ben stepped in at that point and asked us if we wanted to talk things out or if we needed to separate."

"I yelled something about how I wasn't going anywhere because I wasn't going to leave my Dom with anyone else." Oliver's smile turned wicked. "Ben said that if Troy was my Dom, then I was going to have to behave or Troy would have to punish me. Well, I egged both of them on because by that point, all I could think of was going over his lap. God, that was so hot."

"I sat down and pulled him over my lap. Gave him a good lecture about screaming at me in public and explained we were both going to talk. Then Ben talked us through Oliver's first spanking, making sure we were both safe, but also using it as a teaching experience for the newbies. I think some of them thought it was a planned demo, but it turned out all right in the end."

"All right is an understatement. It was so hot, I came all over his lap." Oliver shivered at the memory. "Then he had to punish me again later for that."

Bryce shook his head. "Ben never said anything about it."

"I think he was trying to keep us from losing it again at the club. Once we started talking and explaining what we wanted and needed out of a relationship, things improved. We learned to be honest with what we were thinking." Oliver looked over at Bryce with a loving expression on his face. "We both realized how much I liked the exhibitionist part of what had happened and started talking about adding a third to our relationship pretty quickly after that."

"Having the club helps, but we both enjoy having another with us, and it satisfies the part of Oliver that likes to be watched and to see me with someone else. That was one of the things he hadn't wanted to tell me about. He was afraid of how it would sound, but it wasn't something that bothered me." Troy was watching Bryce as they explained, but he couldn't tell what the other man was thinking. Did he get it? "It fits us. We like playing, but what we really want is a permanent person in our life. Another lover or boyfriend, whatever you want to call it."

Bryce took a sip of his drink. He seemed to be rolling things around in his head before speaking. The silence wasn't long, but it was heavy. "Did you talk about a switch, or were you thinking of another sub or Dom?"

"It's not like ordering a hamburger." Oliver snorted, breaking the tension. "We just talked about meeting someone. Finding a guy that would fit with us, someone we could love."

Some of Bryce's tension seemed to fade. Had he thought they were just looking for a switch and he fit the bill? They'd been watching him for a while, and maybe he needed to understand that. "We noticed you a few months ago. You were doing a flogging demo and—"

"And it was so hot we had the best sex ever." Oliver sighed, giving Bryce a heated look. "Best. Night. Ever."

The waiter came back over with their food before Bryce could find his voice. Troy was just glad the guy hadn't come a few seconds earlier. They'd eaten there enough in the past that the restaurant knew to automatically seat them in the back where the tables were more spaced out. Their booth was round and fairly private, set back in the corner, which was a good thing for them.

By the time the food was passed out and the waiter left, Bryce had managed to sort through everything they'd told him. "I saw you that night. You made it hard to concentrate on the guy I was flogging. We weren't together, it was just for the demo, but even after we were done and I was making sure he was alright, you were still on my mind."

"I told Troy that we were going to have to thank you. He thought that would be kind of tacky, but now it seems fine. So, thank you." Oliver beamed, pleased to be able to tease both of them at the same time.

"You're welcome. It seems like you owe me, though." Bryce's words dripped with sex, sending a shiver through Oliver.

"Oh, yes." Oliver nodded, his mind obviously whirling with naughty thoughts.

"Eat your dinner." Troy looked over at Bryce, cocking one eyebrow and giving him a stern look. "Don't encourage him."

"Is that how this would work?"

Troy wasn't following the change in topic, but Oliver got it right away. He nodded, swallowing a bite he'd taken. "Yes. He gets all bossy with both of us, but you both get to be all sexy and take charge with me." Oliver gave him wide Bambi eyes and shrugged like he was confused. "He says I'm a handful, but I just don't see it."

Bryce laughed. "I can see it." Then he looked over to Troy and started playing with his pasta. "I'm just not sure how it would all work."

Troy glanced around and, seeing they were fairly isolated in the back of the restaurant, turned back to Bryce, wanting to answer honestly. "I think it's going to have to be something you experience and not simply something we talk about. It's one thing for me to say that I want to dominate you in the bedroom while you're spanking Oliver, but I'm not sure you'll believe it or really understand it until we're actually doing it."

Pushing the ravioli around on his plate, Troy tried to think of what else he needed to say. "In everyday life, I don't need multiple submissives. Oliver isn't exactly a full-time sub, but we probably lean more toward that end of the scale."

"He wants someone to share the burden that is Oliver-the-sub, not someone else to boss around all the time." Oliver leaned back in the seat, hand dramatically draped over his forehead like a bad stage actor, then grinned, taking the sting out of the teasing statement.

"Basically," Troy said dryly.

Bryce snorted his laughter and choked on the bite of alfredo he'd just put into his mouth. After swallowing and taking a few sips of his drink, he seemed more relaxed. "I'm getting the picture. I still think that nothing beats firsthand knowledge, so that's still important."

Troy let another smile escape. Between Bryce's not-so-subtle flirting and Oliver's dramatic "Yes," it looked like their evening was about to get more interesting. He glanced over and gave Oliver a tight look. "Behave."

Oliver gave him a pretty pout, then bit his lower lip enticingly. "I'm sorry, Sir." He tilted his head, giving Bryce a shy look. "Sirs."

"Oh, you're a handful." Bryce didn't seem to mind, though.

"He looks so adorable and obedient, but that's when he's at his most devious." Troy reached out and let his fingers slide over Oliver's ear, playing with his hair. "That's when he usually desperately needs a spanking. He needs help remembering to be good. Don't you?"

Oliver gave a jerky nod, leaning into Troy's touch. "Oh, yes. I need lots of help."

Bryce's hand tightened on his fork, and he knew the other man was desperately trying to behave in the restaurant. He was making it too easy on him, though. That would have to change. He leaned in close to Oliver's ear, all the while watching Bryce, letting him see the heat that was building, and whispered, "I think you need to tell Bryce more about that spanking."

Oliver gave a breathy whimper. "Sometimes it's hard to remember to be good, Sir. I need to be bent over your lap and have my bottom spanked until it's red."

"How do we spank a naughty sub's bottom?"

"When it's naked, Sir. You have to pull down my pants and see what you're spanking." Oliver squirmed in the seat and a quick glance downward, which let Troy see how hard his boy was. "No playing with yourself in the restaurant, kitten. I see that hard cock."

"Yes, Sir." Oliver's breathy response was to Troy, but he was looking at Bryce. "I have to ask permission to touch my cock. But he's so good to me that he almost never tells me no."

"Because you ask so nicely, kitten." Troy growled the words out, loving the way both men reacted to his words. "What are you thinking, Bryce?"

There was a long pause when he thought Bryce might not answer. He looked at Troy like he was having some kind of discussion in his head. But then Bryce seemed to make the decision to share his thoughts because he leaned back in his chair and reached out to play with his glass. The small nervous fidgeting spoke louder than his silence. "I was envisioning both of us having to ask you to play. Thinking about how it would feel to be caught in that moment of wanting to...say, spank Oliver... and knowing that I not only have to talk to you about doing anything to myself but have to ask to control Oliver. It's hard to think through—"

"But it's so hot." Oliver broke in, seemingly unable to control himself. "You having to call Troy while he's out at work or running errands. Then he could give you instructions for both of us and you would get to carry them out." Oliver shivered, loving the fantasy he was building up in his head. "He would give you permission to touch me or to spank me. God, it would be so..."

"I'm with him on it." Troy knew the words came out dry as he cocked his head toward his dramatic sub. "I think it's hot, but we'd talk about what parts you liked and what parts didn't fit within your limits. It's going to be about compromise. Not just what I, or the drama queen over there likes."

Bryce gave them both a slow nod, fighting a little grin. "It all comes down to communication, firsthand knowledge, and seeing what works." He picked up his fork, giving them a heated look. "I think we've started the communication process. Working on the physical side should probably be next."

6

OLIVER

"Thank god!" He hadn't meant for that part to come out so excitedly, but he couldn't help it. He'd been dreaming of being topped by both of them for weeks. If they were dominating him at the same time, and he thought that was what Bryce was suggesting, it would be even better. "Sorry. I'll behave."

Being naughty enough to get a spanking was one thing, but he didn't want to drive both of them bad-crazy. That wasn't the goal. He just liked making them both a little nuts. Doms, in general, seemed to be so serious, and Troy fit that mold to a T. Bryce wasn't as bad, but Oliver still thought he needed to relax a little, or he was going to give himself a heart attack worrying about everything.

Bryce coughed, trying poorly to cover a laugh, but Troy just rolled his eyes and shook his head in a you're-going-to-regret-that way. Oliver couldn't decide if he was looking forward to that or not. With Troy, it was hard to decide sometimes.

As their relationship had transitioned from traditional to something closer to full-time Master and submissive roles, pushing Troy's buttons had gotten more fun, but sometimes,

Troy had the most incredibly devious mind when it came to punishments. Thinking about it made a tingly sensation shoot down his spine again, right to his cock.

He squeezed his legs together, trying to relieve the pressure somehow. He didn't even realize he'd closed his eyes until he heard Bryce's voice coming from right next to him. They'd put Oliver in the corner of the round booth. At the beginning of the meal, there had been plenty of room between him and the Doms, but somehow they'd both worked their way closer, first Troy, then Bryce.

"Are you supposed to be doing that?"

He tried for innocent. "Doing what? I'm just smelling the food and talking to you guys."

"Naughty boys don't get orgasms. You want to be touched and get to come, don't you?"

The sinfully rich voice had wicked thoughts running through Oliver's head. "Yes, please."

"Then stop playing with your cock, kitten." Troy growled out the words on the other side of Oliver. He was sandwiched between the two sexy men and it was making it hard to think.

"Yes...but...yes...I...no, I won't..." He took a deep, stuttered breath and tried to get things to make sense in his head. He finally went with something easier. "I'll be good."

He could say that in his sleep; it didn't mean he actually meant it, though.

Bryce's low chuckle told Oliver he might have guessed that. "We'll see. Right now, you need to open your legs a little. I don't want you trying to rub that pretty cock of yours."

Oliver nearly purred. Bryce thought his cock was pretty? He opened his eyes, watching Bryce out of the corner of them. "You think it's pretty?"

"Beautiful. When I saw you strapped down to that table with your cock straining and begging for attention, it was the most incredible thing I'd ever seen. You have no idea how hard it was to stop myself from going up to the stage." Bryce's sincere words were hot and erotic but, in a way, sweet as well.

"I'll be good."

"Now it sounds like you really mean it." Bryce watched him intently. There was always so much behind his eyes, it drew Oliver in.

Oliver nodded, then tried not to melt in his seat as Troy traced around his ear with a delicate touch. "You've got to be very good if you want a reward when we get home."

He held his breath, then forced it out. "A spanking?"

Please let Troy say Bryce was going to spank him!

"Only if you behave." Bryce teased the words against Oliver's skin, making the nerves dance, sending shivers down his spine.

"I will. Whatever you want." Oliver would have given them anything and promised even more, as long as it meant he'd get to go over Bryce's lap.

"Good boy." The men spoke at the same time, both rich, deep voices leaving Oliver panting with need.

All he could do was nod. The fantasies in his head were making it hard to function, much less talk. When Bryce prodded his hand and told him to finish eating, Oliver tried to follow the instruction, but the food was a lot less interesting than it had been a few minutes earlier.

He forced himself to take a few bites, but he lost the struggle when Bryce's hand moved over to Oliver's leg. He wasn't sure what he'd missed when he was zoned out on the spanking fantasy, but it had to have been some kind of discussion because Bryce went from reserved to making Oliver crazy.

The hand that was resting on Oliver's thigh leisurely started moving up and down his leg. Bryce's hand would caress one long, slow stroke from his knee to just below his cock. It was incredible. And maddening. And erotic. And mean, because if he didn't behave then he wouldn't get the spanking he desperately wanted—needed, even.

He finally gave up eating and just tried to sit there quietly, moving food around the plate so it looked like he was behaving. When Troy added a hand to Oliver's other leg, he gave up even playing with the food.

The two men teased in tandem. One's hand would slide up as the other was inching downward, neither ever touching his aching dick. When the waiter came back to check on them, he thought he would get a reprieve. Bryce wasn't ready to let anyone know he was even casually dating two men, much less fooling around with them in a public restaurant.

He was wrong.

Very wrong.

"Is everything still all right with your dinner, gentlemen? Do you need a refill on your drink, sir?" They were simple, innocent questions that Oliver's brain couldn't generate a response to. Because in that moment, Bryce let his hand inch close enough to caress the head of Oliver's dick.

If that had been it, he might have been able to force his brain to at least manufacture a short sentence. But no, Troy brought his hand up to cup Oliver's tight, full balls. It was beautiful torture.

"I'm sorry. Can you say that again?" Ha, he managed a sentence. He still didn't know what the waiter had asked him, although the man was patiently waiting for an answer.

"Did you like the penne? It's a new recipe the chef is trying." The young waiter was so earnest and polite it made Oliver's head hurt. Why couldn't he have been rude, so he didn't have to answer?

"It's delicious. Thank you." The guy didn't seem to believe him, so Oliver picked up his fork and tried to make his body behave by eating another bite. It was beyond difficult. Making him use machinery while being sexually aroused should be against the law.

"I'm glad you're enjoying it. I'll let him know." Then the smiling, too-sweet waiter was gone.

Oliver carefully set the fork down, then sagged down in the seat, trying to keep his ass on the bench. If he gave in to the need to thrust up, he might *never* get his spanking.

"Are you done with your dinner, kitten? I thought you were hungry." Troy's words sounded like he was serious, but Oliver knew him better than that.

"I am. Please." It just wasn't food that he needed.

"Do you want dessert? They have a delicious chocolate cake." Bryce's words were more teasing, but just as designed to make him crazy.

The hands rubbed gentle circles on his cock and balls, making it harder and harder to think. "Please."

It was whiny and filled with desperate desire, but he didn't care. If begging got him what he wanted, then that's what he would do. He just needed the teasing to stop and the real pleasure to begin. "Please, Sirs."

"Do you think he's ready to go home? I can't tell." Bryce's tone was almost mocking, but it made Oliver's frustration even greater, which turned him on even more.

He moved his focus up to glance between Bryce and Troy. He couldn't decide who he'd have a better chance with to get what he wanted. The mental coin toss had him focusing on Troy. "You've talked about it for so long, please."

If they didn't get him naked soon he was going to come in his pants. And that wouldn't get him his spanking.

"You've been a good boy, kitten." Troy's fingers inched down to slide across Oliver's jean-covered opening. "Let's get you home."

"Thank you." Oliver wanted to sag down against the seat and

let the sensations roll through him, but they were still in the restaurant and he had to behave. It would only be a few more minutes. He had to keep telling himself that as Troy called the waiter back over and asked for their check.

There was a quiet discussion on who would pay the bill. Troy thought they should because they'd asked Bryce out, and Bryce wasn't ready to back down from the idea of him paying. Oliver finally leaned over and whispered in the insane Dom's ear. "I'm so hard I hurt, and I need to be spanked. Does it really matter who pays?"

Bryce barked out a laugh, letting Troy pay.

As they got up from the table, Oliver had to discreetly adjust himself so that he didn't scandalize the other customers. Once they'd moved their hands from his groin, it had become easier to think, but his body wasn't relaxing as fast. He was still hard and ready to be taken.

Troy took his hand as they walked out of the restaurant and back toward the vehicles. A look flashed across Bryce's face and Oliver knew he was thinking about taking his other hand. As much as the Dom wanted to, it was too big a step for that moment. Oliver was a little disappointed, but he understood. He wanted both men with a need that still surprised him, but he was starting to understand where Bryce's nervousness was coming from.

He could be patient.

Oliver gave Bryce an understanding smile and reached out to run his free hand down one of Bryce's just for a moment before pulling back. The Dom smiled but gripped his keys tighter and shifted slightly closer to Oliver.

It wasn't a grand public gesture, but it meant a lot, coming from Bryce.

After making sure Bryce knew where they lived, Troy asked for the keys, and Oliver gratefully handed them over. Driving required too much concentration and coordination, and his body wasn't thinking of anything beyond getting home and getting naked.

Bryce leaned against the truck and gave Oliver a wicked grin before looking over at Troy. "I think you'll have to make sure he doesn't relax too much in the car."

Troy nodded, a fiery glint in his eyes. "I agree. It would be a shame if he wasn't still hard and needy when we got home."

He loved the look that passed between them, but he knew it spelled trouble for him. Sexy, naughty trouble.

Climbing in the truck while the two Doms spoke quietly for a moment, Oliver tried not to worry. He knew Bryce wouldn't lie about coming back to their house, but there was so much depending on one night. Bryce was clearly worried about the balance of the BDSM part of the relationship, and Oliver knew that if it was awkward and even the slightest bit off, it would chase him away.

There was a huge part of him that was relieved that nothing about the evening was up to him. All he had to do was obey the Doms' instructions and let them lead, but it still made his stomach start to turn. As Troy climbed in the truck, he took one look at Oliver before reaching over and grabbing his hand.

"It will be fine. You'll see."

"I know. I just want it to be..." Perfect wasn't the right word. It implied too much order and neatness to his mind. "I want it to be right. I want it to be so right between us that he doesn't think about backing out."

"We're not going to do anything crazy tonight. It will just be the three of us, no toys or props. He's going to see how incredible it will be between us. He will have a lot of things to work through, just like we did. We have to be patient."

"I can be patient, it's just—"

Troy snorted. Oliver wrinkled his nose. "I can be patient when I have to. I just don't see the need most of the time."

Troy gave a grudging acceptance of the revised statement, then continued. "It took us months of talking before we knew what we wanted in a relationship, and that was after a rocky start. This isn't going to be an overnight relationship. If it works, it's going to take a lot of communication, honesty, and time."

Oliver sighed, leaning back against the seat. "I know."

"Now come over here and give me a kiss. I was supposed to keep you horny and desperate and I'm failing." Troy sounded a bit frustrated with himself. Was it a competition with Bryce, maybe? Oliver could see that spurring on some incredible scenes.

Oliver unbuckled and leaned across the cab. What he wouldn't have given for a bench seat in that moment. The kiss was hot and demanding, making his toes curl with anticipation. Demanding entrance to Oliver's mouth, Troy's tongue danced against his, sending shock waves of pleasure through him. By the time Troy pulled back, Oliver was lightheaded and his cock was pressing against the zipper of his jeans.

"That's better." Troy's mouth tilted up on one side, giving him a rakish look. "Buckle up for me, or he's going to beat us home."

Oliver fumbled with the belt, finally managing to get it across his body and in the slot. It seemed to take incredible amounts of coordination to make it work. When he completed the monumental task, he leaned back in the seat and tried to calm his racing heart. He was just so damned excited.

"You don't need to calm down, kitten. I want you all needy and desperate. Reach down and take out your cock." Troy said the words like they were perfectly reasonable, and for him, they were.

Oliver fumbled with the button on his jeans, grateful that

the truck was high enough few people would be able to see in. A quick shift of his shirt would have him covered if a big rig drove by, but that was pretty much all he had to worry about.

Shoving his jeans down just enough to free his cock, he breathed a sigh of relief as it was released from the snug confines of his briefs. Troy only wanted him to wear tight little briefs, and as sexy as Oliver thought he looked in them, more room for his growing erection would have been wonderful.

"I want you to play with your cock. Not for long, though." Troy's voice rumbled through the truck, making Oliver shiver. He reached over and obediently started fisting his cock. He wasn't going to waste time teasing unless Troy specified that it had to be a specific kind of touch. Until then, he was going to get as much pleasure out of it as he could.

Troy let him play with his cock as they drove out of the parking lot and turned on the main road heading toward the house. Before they got to the first stoplight, the instructions changed. "All right, hands on your legs."

His cock arched out from his pants obscenely and he ached to touch it. He gripped his legs tightly, trying to think of how good it was going to feel when he got his reward. It didn't help his painful arousal. He couldn't wait to get home.

"Now, what do you want us to do when we get home?"

"Huh?" His brain wasn't working right.

"I want you to tell me what you would have us do if you got to pick. You're not going to, but I want to hear it, anyway." Troy growled out the words and they vibrated deep in Oliver, making his dick jerk.

He moaned helplessly. It was going to be a long ride home.

I t was a long ride to their home. Bryce kept going back and forth about the right thing to do. For once, his heart and his cock were on the same side, but his head kept trying to intrude. He finally gave up, pushing his worries to the back of his mind. He wasn't going to think about how it could affect the business or how complicated it would be. Bryce told himself that he was going to see where it went, and that was the only thing he would focus on.

Keeping up with the truck had been easy, but he'd never managed to see what they were doing inside it. He'd gotten a glimpse of movement from Oliver as they'd reached a stoplight, but that was about it. His brain kept all the possible options running around in his head. Troy's expression had been wicked when he'd said he would keep Oliver good and wound up on the ride back.

By the time they pulled into the driveway, the only thing Bryce could think about was seeing them both naked and all that might happen. He had a good imagination, but not enough practical skills when it came to a threesome. That wasn't to say he hadn't been approached by people for a ménage in the past. There just hadn't been many couples that felt right.

Finding a single Dom or sub to play with wasn't that hard at the club, but finding a couple where both people pulled to him was a lot harder. When he added in personalities and preferences to the mix, it hadn't seemed worth the potential hassle. Two additional people in his bed didn't just double the potential drama, it looked like it would quadruple it, and that wasn't what he was looking for.

He was hoping that he was right about Troy and Oliver. No matter how dramatic their start into BDSM together was, they were a strong couple who seemed to know what they wanted and agreed about how to handle it. He'd never even heard anything negative about them from other people at the club. The only thing that came close to a criticism was that Troy was too reserved, but Bryce didn't mind it.

With his family being so insane and dramatic, he liked Troy's calm manner and dry sense of humor. It was a nice contrast to the craziness he dealt with from everyone else. Oliver provided enough character for the two of them, anyway.

Bryce watched as the two men climbed out of the truck. Troy had a gleam in his eyes that screamed how pleased he was of himself, and Oliver looked like he'd been put through the wringer. His clothes were all a little out of place, and even from a distance, the bulge in his jeans was noticeable. Very noticeable.

Taking one last deep breath and pushing the remaining worries to the back of his mind, he got out of his car. He was going to focus on the two beautiful, tempting men in front of him, and that was it. The area around their house was quiet and dark. It looked a lot more private than his home, even though they hadn't driven very far.

The two men watched him walk up. Troy wrapped his arms around a shaky Oliver and pulled him back to rest against his chest. Oliver looked grateful for the support but desperate for more. His ride from the restaurant had to have been interesting.

"I had this naughty boy here telling me all the things he's been fantasizing about doing in bed with you. I have to say he has a beautifully dirty mind." Troy's fingers started fanning out and caressing Oliver's chest. Oliver and Bryce both seemed to think they were heading for his cock because he started to shake and Bryce couldn't stop watching the wandering fingers. "He had a hard time tucking his hard cock away when we pulled up. I probably should have made him leave it out, but I didn't want to surprise you."

Bryce blinked; the image in his head was too perfect. It took a long few seconds before he could make anything come out of his mouth. "What about neighbors?"

No, he didn't mind Oliver's exhibitionist tendencies, but he also wasn't looking to end up on the front page of the paper. Troy's lips quirked upward slightly. "We don't have any, do we, kitten? The house down the street is empty right now and our house backs up to some state land. There's no one around to see anything that we do. Isn't that right?"

Oliver shivered and nodded slowly. It was clear his thoughts were still focused on Troy's hands and not the words coming out of the Dom's mouth. Bryce swallowed hard. "No neighbors?"

"None." Troy watched Bryce like he could see right through him. "No one can see, no matter what I do to him. You'd like neighbors, wouldn't you, kitten? You like being watched."

A whimper broke free and Oliver nodded desperately. His legs looked unsteady, and it seemed like Troy was making sure he stayed upright. Troy's hands kept working their way lower, and Bryce could only watch as Oliver tried not to beg for more. He was trying so hard to behave, but even in the low light of the dark yard, Bryce could see he was fighting a losing battle. Bryce could tell that Troy didn't want him to be able to be good.

"These pants are hurting you, aren't they, kitten?" Troy didn't wait for a reply. He closed the gap between his hand and the button and opened Oliver's jeans. In an instant, his cock was pushing against the fabric of his underwear, no longer restrained by his pants. Oliver sighed at the relief, but then whimpered again as Troy's huge hands caressed his covered length.

Oliver's erection strained against the fabric, pushing it away from his body just enough so that Bryce could see the thick base of his arousal. Watching as Troy caressed the pale band of Oliver's stomach just above his pants had Bryce frozen in place. He wasn't sure what he was supposed to do, but the need to move closer to them was overwhelming.

"I think he still looks uncomfortable. What do you think, Bryce?" Troy's deep voice sent warring signals through Bryce. His inner Dom and sub both perked up.

Watching the needy, hard Oliver squirm, something clicked in Bryce and he stepped forward. Just one step closer, but it changed the dynamics. He didn't want to submit with Oliver, he wanted to dominate the sexy sub. "I think he's being good, so we don't want him too uncomfortable."

Troy slid his hands up Oliver's chest, baring the lean body. "You should help him, then. Kitten, you want Bryce to free your cock, don't you? Won't it feel so good to let it out and not have anything pressing against it?"

A low moan tore through Oliver and his head fell back against Troy. Bryce took it as a yes, even though Oliver hadn't managed any words. His body language made it easy to see what he wanted. Bryce took a few more steps, putting him right in front of Oliver. Not close enough to touch, but one more small step and he'd be able to press himself tight to the writhing sub.

Bryce slowly telegraphed every movement, wanting to give Oliver a chance to change his mind. When his fingers gripped the straining fabric of the tight briefs, Oliver whined and his hips thrust toward Bryce. Bryce stopped his movements and shook his head as Troy made a sound like Oliver had been a naughty boy. "Is that how a good boy behaves?"

Oliver pleaded with his eyes, but Bryce was starting to know him well enough not to fall for that every time. "I'm sorry. I'll be good. You're just so...and it's...please..."

He was beautiful when he begged.

"You have to stay still and follow directions or you won't get to come." Bryce loved that idea, but the image of a desperate Oliver getting to orgasm was incredible, too. It would be hard to pick which sounded better.

"Yes, Sir. I will." Oliver shook with need and the force it took to remain still in Troy's arms. Bryce knew how hard his body was working to move with the need to grind his cock against anything.

Mentally giving himself a shake, Bryce started easing the briefs over Oliver's erection. It was long and hard and shone like a beacon in the darkness. He took Oliver's cock in his hand and slowly jerked him off. It was too soft a grip for Oliver to come, but the pleading noises that escaped from Oliver had Bryce's own cock aching.

Bryce continued his painfully slow touch and looked up at Troy. The other Dom's eyes were heated, and even though his expression didn't give much away, Bryce knew how turned on he was. "I think he feels much better now."

The painfully aroused noises coming from Oliver told another story entirely. Troy's grin broke free for just a moment and it was thoroughly wicked and beautiful. "He has to be." Troy moved his hands farther up Oliver's shirt and had to have started teasing his nipples because the most delicious wail broke out of Oliver. He was either incredibly sensitive or Troy was teasing him mercilessly.

Maybe both.

Oliver's cock jerked, and Bryce could see the precum leaking down the long length. Oliver squirmed and fought to keep his begging quiet, but it wasn't working. Bryce wasn't sure what the plan was, but he knew if they didn't pull things back, no matter how gently he was playing with Oliver's cock, he was going to come.

Easing off of whatever he was doing under Oliver's shirt, Troy let him calm down enough for Oliver to catch his breath. "I think you've been good enough to get your spanking, kitten. What do you think? Have you behaved?"

His head bobbed up and down in a haphazard way that made him seem even more unsteady. "Yes, Sir. Please."

The words were choppy and forced out, like Oliver's brain wasn't quite working. They stirred images up in Bryce's mind that had a growl trying to escape. Picturing the desperate, needy sub draped over his lap, or even Troy's, had him adjusting his cock in his pants.

Troy didn't miss Bryce's arousal. His wicked grin flashed before his calm mask settled over him again. "I think Bryce wants to spank your bottom, kitten. What do you think? Do you want to be bent over for him?"

"Yes! Please." There was no questioning Oliver's agreement or desire.

Bryce's brain had given up questioning what would happen or debating what was best. His only thoughts were about what was happening right then. He wanted Oliver's full bottom, naked and on display. Preferably over Bryce's lap.

"Let's take him inside." Troy's voice promised there would be more to come.

Bryce moved to step back and release Oliver's cock, but Troy shook his head. "Why don't you lead him in? We wouldn't want him to forget who was in charge."

Oliver whimpered and his cock jerked in Bryce's tightening grip. Bryce had to agree. It was hot as fuck. Using Oliver's hard dick as a handle, Bryce led him away from Troy. They followed the other Dom up a large porch and into their home.

Bryce couldn't focus on the details of the house. The feel of Oliver in his hand and the way the sexy Dom moved through the house took all his concentration. Flashes of wood and leather registered as a living room and a tall staircase meant they were heading for the bedroom.

That was all he needed to know.

Carefully teasing and tugging at Oliver's cock as they walked through the hallway, Bryce's heart rate jumped as they entered the bedroom. An impossibly wide bed took up most of the space and Bryce noticed a long dresser and a large chair in a corner, but that was about it. The rest of his attention was aimed at Troy and Oliver.

Oliver had been good going through the house, but the promise of his spanking was making it hard for him to stay focused. Troy had to say his name twice to get his attention. "Are you going to listen and be good?"

Oliver nodded but whimpered as Bryce let go of his cock. "Yes. Oh, yes."

Bryce didn't hide his pleasure. He loved Troy's control, but he wanted Oliver to know exactly how much Bryce was loving the sub's reactions. Troy watched them both through passion-filled eyes. "Bryce, why don't you go sit on the bed. Then we'll have Oliver lay down over your lap."

Oliver nodded as Bryce walked around the room and climbed up on the tall, wide bed. He pushed the pillows up behind his back and settled in, comfortable on the soft mattress. He glanced at Troy, trying not to think about how it would feel to be draped over the Dom's lap, and nodded.

Troy walked over to the dark chair in the corner and sat

down before looking at Oliver. "Push your pants down a little. We're going to offer your ass up to Bryce. You need a spanking so bad, don't you, kitten?"

Oliver's hands shook as he whined and eased his jeans over his ass. His shirt and pants framed his cock and bottom beautifully, putting him on display. Bryce knew how naked it would make him feel, and probably how naughty.

"Now up on the bed. You know where I want you to be." Troy's voice dropped low, making both men shiver as Oliver walked over to the bed, slightly hobbled by his pants. Oliver blushed, and Bryce thought it was probably because he wasn't as smooth or graceful as he wanted to be, but to Bryce he looked perfect.

He gave his lap a pat and let his gaze wander over the sub. Oliver's cock jerked and Bryce's made a matching move. Trapped behind his pants, he couldn't wait to be naked. It wasn't time for that yet, though. Oliver awkwardly climbed up on the bed and it made his naked ass stand out even more.

Cock bouncing, he crawled over to Bryce and laid himself over Bryce's lap. His hard length pressed against Bryce's legs, and every muscle was tight as he tried not to move. When he spoke, his voice was thick with need. "May I have a spanking, please?"

Bryce instinctively glanced over to Troy, whose eyes crinkled in pleasure as he nodded. Did he like that Bryce looked to him for permission, or was it just everything in general? He wasn't sure, but he didn't think it mattered. "Yes."

There was so much more he wanted to say, but it was all rolling around inside him. Instead of fighting for the words, Bryce brought one hand to rest on Oliver's back and the other to his bottom. It was full and round, completely at odds with his lean frame, but still perfect for spanking. It would look wonderful when it was red and heated from Bryce's touch.

Oliver stiffened, but sank down onto the bed when all Bryce did was rub gentle circles on his skin. Bryce didn't want to rush. He wanted to remember the moment and savor it. It wasn't a quick one-night stand, and it wasn't doing a scene at the club. He wasn't one hundred percent sure where everything was going, but he knew it was the start of something important.

He caressed the soft skin, loving the way it felt under his hand. Warm and firm, it filled his grip. When his thumb grazed the crack of Oliver's ass and inched closer to Oliver's tight pucker, Oliver arched and moaned with pleasure.

"When he lets go and relaxes into a scene, my kitten is very sensitive. Once he's given himself over to it, it's like he's given his body complete permission to simply react and feel."

"He's beautiful."

"You're both like that." Troy's voice was husky and sent shivers through both Oliver and Bryce.

Lifting his hand, Bryce brought it down forcefully on one cheek. Oliver moaned and shook, desperately trying not to move. Bryce ran his fingers over the handprint, loving the way his mark looked on Oliver's body. He loved it more than he should have.

They hadn't even known each other for that long. Surreptitiously watching each other at the club didn't count as actually meeting. He shouldn't feel this much this soon. There was just something about seeing the pink color blooming on Oliver's skin, knowing that it was because of him, that squeezed his heart. It was ridiculous but completely overwhelming.

Oliver held his breath and Bryce could see the anticipation building. He brought his hand down again, alternating where he placed it and spreading out the impacts until Oliver's bottom was a stunning shade and he squirmed in Bryce's lap. Needy little pleas and rambling sentences that showed how desperate he was tumbled out of his mouth.

Pleasure flowed through Troy's quiet words. "He marks so easily, but they also fade away quickly."

"It just means we have to do it more. So he'll remember." Bryce watched as Oliver's bottom quivered and arched up to beg for more.

He kept half an eye on Troy as he spanked Oliver, gradually slowing and lengthening the time between each smack. He'd tease and caress the sensitive skin before bringing his hand down again. Troy's gaze was almost feral, but his body was deceptively calm. Bryce knew he was giving them time together, and it was sweet, even though he knew most people wouldn't understand.

When Oliver was shaking and so hard it had to ache as his cock pressed against Bryce's leg, he knew it was time to give his boy some relief. He'd been so good. Bryce looked over at Troy, cocking his head questioningly. Did he have an opinion, or was he going to leave it up to Bryce?

Oliver was right on the edge. He seemed to still be fighting the urge to grind himself against Bryce because he was gripping the covers so tight they were coming off the bed. Troy gave him a little shrug that didn't seem to mean anything, then lifted his chin toward Bryce. He was leaving it up to Bryce?

What Bryce really wanted was all of them together.

He picked up the hand that had been rubbing up and down Oliver's back and crooked his finger in a *come here* motion. They were going to top Oliver together. Troy gave him a look, probably trying to guess what Bryce wanted, but stood up.

Bryce dipped one finger in the crease of Oliver's ass and teased circles around his hole. Oliver clenched down, wanting more, and his head arched off the bed. His long, lean body was like a living sculpture. "I think Oliver wants to come. What do you think?"

Troy gave a low hum of pleasure. "I'll need to check and see, but you might be right."

The broad, tall Dom climbed on the bed and relaxed next to them. Bryce moved both hands to knead at Oliver's flushed bottom, and he watched as his sub moaned and writhed. Troy brought one hand between Oliver's legs and grabbed his cock.

Whatever he'd done had Oliver mewling, nearly coming off the bed. Bryce wanted to see what Troy had done to get such a reaction out of their sub, but it wasn't time for twenty questions. Troy turned his gaze to Bryce, almost ignoring the pleasure rolling off Oliver. "I think he's ready for you."

For him?

8

TROY

Troy had seen the questions on Bryce's face, but he didn't pay any attention to them. He simply jerked his head toward the side table and continued to torment Oliver, twisting his fingers and rubbing the little spot that made Oliver dance in pleasure. "Grab the stuff out of the top drawer."

Releasing Oliver's cock, Troy lifted his shaking sub onto his lap. When Bryce turned back around with the lube and condoms, he still hadn't seemed to recover from his surprise. Troy wasn't sure what Bryce thought would happen, but he wanted Bryce to know that he saw him as just as much a Dom as a sub. When they'd first noticed him, he'd spent a lot of time considering what Bryce being a switch would mean.

Oliver was watching them both with hungry eyes. His little kitten was needy. Knowing not to trust Oliver's legs or balance at this point, Troy moved him around again so he was on his hands and knees between Troy's legs. Bringing their faces together, he gave Oliver a kiss. "You need, don't you, kitten?"

Oliver nodded and sighed, arching up his ass and giving Bryce a come-hither look that was worthy of any of the Hollywood legends. Bryce didn't stand a chance until he'd built up some immunity. But considering how long it had taken Troy, he wasn't going to hold his breath for it to happen anytime soon.

Bryce watched them, hesitant and aroused, as he moved to kneel behind Oliver. Troy wanted him naked, he desperately wanted to order him to strip down completely first, but he was determined to restrain himself. This time.

"I bet Bryce would strip down if you begged him nicely, kitten."

Oliver smiled wickedly, then turned his head to glance at Bryce. Troy couldn't see his face, but something sent Bryce into overdrive. He looked like he wanted to devour Oliver as he started slowly removing his shirt. He either had lots of practice stripping or he'd been watching Conner at the club, because even kneeling on the bed it was hot.

Oliver was nearly panting by the time Bryce was naked, cock arching up toward his muscular abs. If Troy was being honest, they were both panting, he just hid it better than his kitten. Bryce was eating up their expressions because there was a distinct swagger to his movements as he closed in on Oliver again.

Bryce brought his hand down on Oliver's ass again, and both Doms thoroughly enjoyed the moan that echoed through the room. Oliver loved having his bottom spanked, and he wasn't the type to hide his desire.

When Bryce reached for the lube, Oliver and Troy held their breath. To distract them both, Troy brought Oliver's lips back to his, but he let his eyes follow Bryce. He let the cautious, confused man see how much he wanted him and hopefully a little of how much he was coming to mean to Troy.

Bryce only faltered for a moment, but he caught himself quickly and pushed aside whatever was running through his head.

Turning his focus back to Oliver, Bryce teased the lube around Oliver's sensitive opening and slid one finger in. Oliver squirmed and arched into the breach, earning another smack from Bryce.

Bryce took his time, slowly stretching Oliver. Troy could see he was being careful, but he was also enjoying how crazy it was making Oliver. By the time Bryce had the condom sheathed and lubed, Oliver was back to desperate and unsteady. Troy had only wanted to watch, but he found himself keeping Oliver from sinking down to the bed.

It was beautiful.

He loved being able to see Oliver come completely undone. Most of the time Troy was so focused on Oliver's reactions and pleasure, he lost some of the beauty. Being able to hold Oliver and love on his kitten was wonderful. Especially when he was being pounded and taken apart.

Oliver gasped into Troy's mouth, making delicious noises as Bryce inched his cock into Oliver's tight hole. Troy pulled back enough to catch Bryce's eye. "He's ready. Kitten loves being taken hard. Bent over the couch, shoved up against the wall, he wants a lover to really own him."

Did Bryce understand?

Maybe. His easy, slow rhythm faltered before Bryce leaned over Oliver and started riding him hard. Bryce's hips flexed and Troy watched as his cock fucked Oliver, making his kitten howl out his pleasure. More kisses or focus on the stunning show in front of him? With his two beautiful men, it was an impossible choice.

He finally decided to share in both pleasures. He'd kiss and distract Oliver enough to keep him from coming, then he'd sit back and tell them both how incredible they looked, how sexy and erotic, how much he wanted them both. By the time they were ready to come, their lust had a desperate edge to it. Troy wanted to feed the desperation and see how high he could take them, but it wasn't the right time.

Conscious of Bryce's needs, he gave Bryce a long, thorough look, then slowly reached down to Oliver's cock. "Has he been good enough? Does our kitten get to come?"

They both exploded.

Bryce growled out something low and fierce and Oliver called out a desperate plea, but it was too late. Troy wrapped his fingers around Oliver's pulsing length and caressed him, keeping the pleasure going. Bryce gaped at them both and shook as his orgasm crashed through him.

When they'd wrung out every bit of pleasure from their orgasms, Bryce pulled out and wrapped his arms around Oliver to give him a quick, tender kiss. He got rid of the condom in the trash can by the bed, then cuddled into them.

Oliver was sandwiched in the middle, making soft, satisfied sounds. As Bryce settled back in close to them, his kitten smiled sweetly and reached around to hold them both tight. "You're staying, right?"

Troy didn't like the hesitation in Oliver's voice, and, evidently, neither did Bryce. He pushed himself even tighter against Oliver and rained kisses down his neck. "I'm staying."

Watching his two men, Troy gave them both a predatory glare. "Until I let you go tomorrow."

It wasn't a question, but Bryce nodded slowly. "Until you let me." Then Bryce sat up a little. "I have a family thing on Sunday."

Troy nodded. "I'll release you by then."

"Release?"

Oliver yawned, pulling Bryce down close to him again. "You think too much. I'm tired."

Bryce let Oliver bring him back down to the bed, a matching yawn making Troy smile. "But..."

"You'll love it." Another yawn cracked his jaw. "Troy, don't make him crazy."

"Go to sleep." Troy leaned over and gave both men quick, tender kisses. Oliver took his with a sleepy passion that made Troy smile, but Bryce opened his lips to let Troy thoroughly claim him. Giving him permission, maybe?

Pulling back when the temptation to restart things was too high, Troy gave him one last kiss to his forehead. "Sleep."

Bryce nodded, closing his eyes and sighing as Troy pulled a blanket from the bottom of the bed over his men. Troy didn't understand how he'd gotten so lucky, but he could only hope that they weren't moving too fast for Bryce. It was a lot to take in, but it was so easy to see they had so much between them all. Wrapping his arms around his men, Troy let himself close his eyes.

WATCHING his two men slowly wake up, Troy let his hands rest on their chests. Letting them know he was with them, and hopefully keeping Bryce from getting too worried. He'd made it clear the night before that he was going to want Bryce's submission the next morning, but he knew it wouldn't be what Bryce was expecting.

Spanking and different types of erotic submission would have probably been Bryce's first guesses, but they would have been wrong. To Troy, the deepest and most honest submission came when it wasn't about arousal or sexual release. It was how he and Oliver had learned to communicate and to find their balance.

Troy hoped he was making the right call, but he thought it was time to start including Bryce in those traditions. The things that made Oliver and him work and grow. As Bryce turned and frowned when something didn't feel right, Troy settled in, ready to soothe Bryce.

His new sub rolled over, but when his leg didn't go far enough, one eye opened. There was curiosity etched on his face, but not worry, which soothed some of Troy's nerves. Bryce's feet moved under the covers and explored, trying to figure out what was going on. It didn't take Bryce long to understand.

He was tied to the bed.

Well, not exactly tied. Troy had elastic sports cuffs with hook and loop fasteners bolted to the end of the bed. One was wrapped around Bryce's leg and the other around a not-quite-awake Oliver's ankle. It would be very easy to sit up and remove the restraint, but he didn't think Bryce would.

Bryce frowned and lifted up the covers to peek down toward the foot of the mattress. It was almost comical. Troy could see legs and feet moving again. Then Bryce stilled and relaxed back down. He closed his eyes and wiggled around until he was pressed close against Oliver. One arm moved until it popped up beside Troy on the bed and reached for his hand.

Lacing his fingers through Bryce's, he let his sub fall back asleep. It had gone smoother than he'd expected, but he knew Bryce would have questions. He was hoping his conflicted switch would have lots of them. Troy was hoping it would show Bryce that it was okay to open up to them. They'd tried to make it clear they were looking for a long-term relationship with him, but it was easy to see he was sitting on the fence.

Troy just needed to pull him down on their side.

When Bryce settled back down to sleep, Troy slipped out of bed quietly and went downstairs. He and Oliver had purchased the house three months before, and they were still moving things around. The kitchen was Troy's favorite. Modern appliances mixed with old-fashioned elements made it perfect. It was what drew them to the house to begin with. Both he and Oliver were big cooks, preferring to eat at home instead of going out all the time, so they'd loved the kitchen right away.

Troy couldn't wait to see what Bryce thought about the house. From what they'd seen of Bryce's office, Troy thought they had similar tastes, as long as Bryce hadn't gotten someone else to decorate for him. Troy couldn't see that being the case. As Bryce had started opening up about his business, they'd learned more about the family dynamic and the little games of one-upmanship they played.

Gathering up a tray with coffee and some breakfast for the sleeping men, Troy made his way back upstairs. As he walked into the bedroom, setting the tray on the dresser next to his side of the bed, Oliver opened his eyes. He peered at Bryce and tugged on his cuff. "Does he know about the restraint yet?"

"Yes." A muffled reply came from Bryce, who was still pretending to be asleep.

Oliver grinned. "Is he mad?"

"No." Bryce pulled the covers over his head.

"Is he confused?"

"No."

He was tied to the bed. Troy thought the reason was fairly obvious, and evidently, Bryce did too. Oliver glanced up at Troy, a teasing smile on his face. "Do you think he likes being naked and tied up?"

Bryce snorted, refusing to answer that one.

Troy ran his hand over Oliver's head and shrugged. "I'm not sure yet. We can find out, though."

Bryce's eyes popped open, awake and curious. Troy cracked a smile. "Oh, look who's awake."

Giving Troy a wary look, Bryce sat up and moved to lean against the headboard. "Yes...Yes, Sir."

Troy nodded subtly, then reached over and ran his hand over Bryce's head. "Would you like a morning kiss, tiger?"

"Tiger, huh?" Bryce nodded, not even having to think about it. Troy gave him a smile and slid his hand down to Bryce's neck to pull him close. He started out light and tender, but slowly deepened the kiss, reminding Bryce who was in charge. Bryce melted into the bed, curling into Oliver as he kissed Troy deeply. A sudden squeak from Bryce had Troy pulling away in surprise.

"Oliver?" He knew his kitten.

Wide, innocent eyes looked up at him. "Yes, Sir?"

"What did you do?" That much effort into appearing adorable meant his kitten was definitely guilty.

Oliver shrugged like he was confused. "You said to check and see if he was turned on. He is."

"That's not exactly what I said." Troy shook his head. Bryce watched the discussion between them and was clearly trying to appear neutral, almost disapproving. He was failing.

"Oh? I'm sorry." He sounded sincere, but he didn't look sorry at all.

"What is this time for, kitten?" It seemed like Oliver needed the reminder, and it would be good clarification for Bryce.

Oliver sighed like it was torture. "To talk and cuddle with you, Sir."

"Were you supposed to touch Bryce like that?"

"No." Another dramatic sigh came with big puppy dog eyes. "He's just so tempting when he's naked." Oliver gave Bryce a long look. "He's a sexy tiger."

Bryce laughed, giving up the pretense of being disappointed in Oliver. He was still watching, though, not commenting yet, so Troy kept his focus on Oliver. "Why is this not play time?"

Another dramatic sigh had Oliver looking up at the ceiling, pretending to be bored with the conversation. "Because we can't have a good relationship just by fucking like rabbits every time you assert your dominance. We have to talk because good communication is important."

"And?"

"And we're not mind readers. We have to share our problems and needs." Oliver gave Troy a sideways look. "I was very naughty. I'm sorry, Sir. I understand if you need to punish me."

Bryce barked out a laugh again, and Troy shook his head. "No spankings for you. If you're naughty, I can find chores for you to do. Didn't we say all the baseboards needed to be cleaned? I think we have an old toothbrush—"

Oliver rolled over to curl into Troy's side. "I'll be good. Honest."

Troy laughed. "I thought you might."

Bryce relaxed and reached out his arm again so he was touching Oliver and Troy. "So you do this a lot?"

Troy nodded. "We broke up and got back together countless times when we were first dating because we weren't communicating. Once we started incorporating the BDSM aspects we liked into our relationship, this was a way to make us talk. We wanted to make sure that we were being honest and to make it hard to walk away."

"With me cuffed to the bed, I'd have to really consider how important it was to stop a discussion, and Troy can't leave me restrained because it's his responsibility as my Dom to keep me safe. It makes sure we're both held responsible." Oliver lifted his head and gave both men quick kisses. It was just enough to tempt Troy, but Bryce seemed surprised to be included in the tender peck.

"So most weekends we talk for at least a little while. Some weekends it goes for longer. Depending on how we're feeling, I'll move him downstairs and re-cuff him to the couch or somewhere in the kitchen. Those are usually play times." Bryce's eyes started to heat as Troy talked.

Did he like being restrained, or was it something else? They still had so much to learn about Bryce. "Next time, we might talk about your limits so we can understand what you need."

Bryce's eyes flew up to meet Troy's. "Like a contract?"

"Nothing quite that formal yet. I was thinking just the limits discussion first. We'll talk about contracts later, if that's something that interests you."

"Do you have one with Oliver?"

"Nothing that most people would call a contract." Troy shrugged. "We've talked about limits and rules, but nothing is written down. We thought about waiting to write out a formal contract so we could do it with our third."

"So you really want a third. Not just someone to play with occasionally or even on a regular basis? You want a true polyamorous relationship with another person?"

"Yes, a closed poly relationship with additional rules because of the BDSM aspects, but we want another life partner, not something casual." Bryce was still having a hard time with the idea, but he seemed more comfortable with it than he had at dinner.

"It was one of our first talk time discussions," Oliver piped up, starting to fidget. "We shared what we'd been thinking about and what we were frustrated with."

"I'm going to let you both go to the bathroom, but I expect you back here quickly. Do you understand? No getting distracted, kitten. You have one minute, or it's baseboards for you later." Bryce was trying not to grin as he nodded at Troy's instructions. "Kitten has a tendency to get distracted."

"I'll be good and come right back, Sir." Bryce looked serious and sweet, but he gave Oliver a little wink. "I won't get distracted. You won't need to punish me, Sir."

"Kiss-ass." Oliver mumbled low, blinking innocently when Troy gave him a narrow stare.

Cocking one brow, giving Oliver a serious look, Troy got off the bed and moved to the end to unhook the cuffs from the post, leaving both men with a leash of sorts. "Come right back."

His two sexy naked men hopped off. Bryce reached the master bathroom first and shut the door, leaving Oliver to curse as he raced for the hall bathroom. His men were going to be handfuls, but Troy had a feeling it would be worth it.

9

OLIVER

"Did you hear?" Oliver's excited voice rang out through the house as he ended the call. They'd been taking turns talking to Bryce, and Oliver was over the moon with excitement.

"Yes. I heard." Troy's dry voice came from the kitchen. He wasn't bouncing around like Oliver wanted to do, but Oliver could hear the pleased tone in his voice.

"He told his family about us!" Oliver tossed his phone onto the laundry basket full of clothes that were waiting to be taken upstairs and went into the kitchen to track down Troy. He walked, trying not to look like a teenager excited to be talking to their first crush.

Ever since the weekend Bryce had stayed over, their relationship had been getting more and more serious. At least, that's how it felt to Oliver. Troy kept telling him to relax because they weren't going to rush Bryce, but it was hard.

They'd talked most nights and had met for dinner several times. Oliver had even gone into the office to sign the new policies and talk through more of the fine print. To him, everything was moving along fabulously.

"It's a good sign, you're right."

"I'm always right. And it's a wonderful sign!" There hadn't been a good way to ask Bryce if his family knew about them, so it had come right out of the blue when he started talking about his brothers and mentioned that they knew. A completely casual comment that probably sounded innocent, but felt incredible to Oliver.

"Is he getting off work early enough to have dinner still?" Troy went back to stirring the pot on the stove, his calm expression betrayed by the pleasure Oliver could see in his eyes.

"Yes, he's on his way." He was coming over to the house to have dinner. Bryce had been making an effort to leave early enough to do things with them most evenings.

Troy had even left work early enough to make homemade pasta sauce. It was his obsession, so Oliver didn't even volunteer to make it. It was one of the things Troy did to show he cared. Oliver wasn't sure Bryce would notice, so he told himself he'd find a time to point it out. It had taken him too long to figure it out on his own, and he didn't want Bryce to suffer the same frustration.

As he walked around the kitchen, finishing the meatballs, Troy talked about his day and entertained Oliver with his stories. Troy was a consultant that helped small companies streamline processes and make things more efficient. Recently, he'd been working with a local chain of car dealerships that had been struggling.

He'd gotten home every night with stories about the stubborn employees and their insane reasons for not even following the systems they had in place. Most employees stayed with the company for years, and getting them to adjust to new things was more difficult than the owner realized.

"He didn't believe me when I told him how many month's

worth of receipts she had in her desk because she couldn't figure out the—" The ring of the doorbell cut Troy off.

"I'll go let him in." Oliver straightened and headed toward the door to the living room.

Troy laughed and went back to focusing on dinner as Oliver headed out of the kitchen. Opening the door, he gave a start of surprise when he was pulled into Bryce's arms. The deep, heated kiss made his toes curl, and he made a whine of protest when Bryce pulled back.

Bryce had a grin that was erotic and infectious. Oliver had flashes of naughty things going through his head as Bryce closed the front door behind him and pulled Oliver back into his embrace, this time tighter, with Oliver's body flush against his.

Oliver didn't fight the need to rub himself against Bryce. His new Dom wasn't a stickler for rules unless they were in a scene. He didn't mind getting Oliver worked up and making him beg. Troy, on the other hand—

"Oliver." Troy's firm voice came from behind Oliver. "What are you doing?"

"He caught you." Bryce's grin was pure wickedness and fire. Not a submissive bone in his body showed in that moment. Bryce looked up, shaking his head. "He came to the door and jumped me, terrible behavior."

Troy snorted, but Oliver peeked back and saw the laughter in his eyes. "We'll have to see about reminding him of his manners. I'm not sure he needs to be thrusting against you, demanding attention."

The control and censure in Troy's voice went right to Oliver's cock. He loved that naughty feeling that flooded through him when Troy looked at him like he should know better. If Troy had actually been disappointed, it wouldn't have been fun at all, but that mock disapproval was hot. Especially when Bryce set him up.

"I'm sorry, Sirs. I'll be good." He glanced back at Bryce. "I'll be *very* good."

Bryce grinned and smacked Oliver's ass, sending shivers through him. "Naughty boy."

Troy shook his head at both of them. "Come on, you two. Dinner is almost ready."

They headed back into the kitchen, Bryce teasing Oliver and making Troy roll his eyes. The smells from the kitchen hit them as soon as they walked in. Bryce groaned, sounding almost orgasmic. Oliver laughed. "If you actually learned to cook, then you wouldn't just about come every time you came over."

Bryce shrugged. "I'm not that bad compared to my brothers. It just doesn't stick. I can cook stuff like spaghetti with jarred sauce and a few things like that, but not much more."

He'd kept them in stitches at the restaurant the last time they'd gone out to dinner with stories about the things that his brothers had cooked. Even Troy had laughed upon hearing their antics. "I still don't see how your parents just gave up."

Leaning back against the counter, Bryce just lifted one shoulder in confusion. "I think it was a case of picking their battles. We all appreciate good food." He looked over at the mountain of food on the stove. "Cooking it just doesn't sound as good as eating it, maybe?"

Oliver just laughed, not understanding it at all. Seeing the food almost ready, he went over to the cabinet and grabbed the plates. Moving around the kitchen, he watched as Bryce and Troy eyed each other. There was still some awkwardness while they figured things out between the two of them.

Once the two men figured out if Bryce wanted to be more dominant or submissive in a situation, then things were easy. Until they worked that out, it was interesting to watch them. They each wanted to please the other, but weren't talking it out very well. Oliver thought he was going to have to be the one to cuff them both to the bed next time and make them talk it out.

Hopefully, it wouldn't get that far. He loved being tied to it and didn't want to give up his spot. He had the best fantasies about being Troy's love slave. Having to be the take-charge member of their little group wouldn't be fun.

They needed a calendar.

Oliver felt like a cartoon character with a light bulb over his head. *They needed a calendar.* One where they could plan out their roles. If something needed to change at the last minute, then they'd adjust it, but if Bryce knew he could be a Dom during the week and a sub with Oliver on the weekends, it might make it easier on him until the two men worked out their signals or could manage to talk without worrying about offending each other.

"Oliver?"

"Huh?" Bryce was looking at him questioningly, but Oliver wasn't sure what he'd said. "Sorry, I was thinking."

"I was asking about the job stuff and if you'd figured out what you wanted to do." Bryce walked around the kitchen and took a seat at the table. Oliver felt bad he'd zoned out and missed helping bring the food over to the table, but the guys didn't seem mad. Just curious.

"I'm not sure." Oliver walked over and took his normal seat beside Troy. They had a good-sized round table, but it felt like he was sitting between the two men. Sandwiched like that was perfect. "I've been looking around, but nothing is calling to me. I was talking to Troy yesterday about maybe going to grad school, but I don't know about that, either."

He'd been in the same position several years before when he'd just gotten out of college. At the time, he'd taken a job as an administrative assistant with a brokerage company. He wasn't sure he liked finance, but he was great with organizing and managing people, like his boss and the customers.

The first weeks of working for the older gentleman had been rough. He was an odd mix of charm and a sexist pig, with women and gay men lumped in the same category. He'd taken it personally until he'd realized that the man wasn't aware how offensive he was.

Before he could decide if he wanted to quit, one of the other assistants had approached him. She talked him through confronting the old fart and explaining what he could and couldn't say. Oliver's boss had never understood why what he said was so offensive, but it cleared the air and made things bearable. Oliver had actually come to enjoy their clients and his job.

When the old man died of a heart attack working late one night, Oliver decided to turn in his resignation instead of trying to find someone more open-minded at the firm to work with. Oliver only felt bad about George's death because over the years he'd worked with him, he'd heard George's wife say several times that she'd rather he died at work than retire at home.

She'd actually said something more colorful, calling him an old pig when she was yelling at him over the phone one time. So Oliver wasn't upset, but wasn't sure he wanted to live the drama any longer. Troy had agreed with him, telling Oliver that he should take time off to figure out what he wanted.

They made a good living with just Troy's salary, and Oliver never felt bad for not working. Bryce didn't seem disappointed that Oliver was technically unemployed, or maybe he was considered a house husband. House partner, maybe?

"Maybe you should find something to volunteer at if you just want to get out of the house." Bryce took a bite of a meatball and moaned, making Oliver and Troy both shift in their seats. Bryce was completely oblivious to it, but watching him eat made them both want to jump him.

"Huh?" What had Bryce said?

Troy gave a low chuckle. "Volunteering."

"Oh, yeah, it's not a bad idea." That just brought up more decisions, though. "I'm not sure what I would do."

Troy and Bryce both gave him understanding smiles. Bryce leaned over and gave his hand a squeeze. "It was just an idea."

"It's a good one. I guess I'm floundering a little. I liked the helping side of my job. I want a career, but I don't know what it should look like."

"You're smart enough to do anything you want." Bryce gave Troy's hand a pat and went back to eating.

"And staying home all day by yourself will make you crazy." Troy gave him a dry look that made Oliver laugh.

"It's already setting in." Aside from avoiding a few odd jobs around the house like the baseboards, it was usually clean, and they were starting to figure out where everything should go. He was quickly running out of projects.

They tossed around a few ideas from reasonable to ridiculous and finished eating, laughing and joking. As they started cleaning up the kitchen, Troy looked over at Bryce after he put away the leftover sauce. "You still staying for a movie?"

Bryce nodded, loading a plate into the dishwasher. "Yes. I don't have anything early tomorrow, so I'm not worried about the time." He gave Troy a grin. "I've been trying to manage my schedule better and not make as many early morning or late appointments."

"Evidently, you found something more interesting to do in the evenings." Troy gave him a heated look as he walked over to the table to continue putting things away.

"Much more interesting." Bryce looked at both of them,

making sure Oliver knew he was included in the *interesting*. They were so cute.

"I have to drive out to a few of the auto dealerships I'm contracted with tomorrow afternoon. The meetings are all going to run late, and one doesn't even start until after six. I was thinking that you and Oliver might want to have dinner out tomorrow." Troy nonchalantly tossed out the date like he was asking Bryce to pick up wine before he came over for dinner. Oliver knew it was on purpose to try to make it less of an issue, but the silence was overwhelming.

Bryce finally cleared his throat, considering both men carefully. "That sounds good. Do you want to try the French place we were talking about the other day?"

Inside, Oliver was squealing like a teenage girl at a boy band concert, but on the outside, he thought he looked fairly calm. "That sounds good, as long as I get dessert."

Bryce laughed, going back to finish loading the dishwasher. "I can agree to that."

Troy snorted, giving them a dismissive look. "I can't believe you're going to have your date at the French place. I thought you would take me there."

Oliver laughed so hard the drink of soda he'd taken started to come out his nose. Bryce gave them a look like they were both crazy. Then he gave Troy a flirty smile. "Wouldn't you like the sushi place instead?"

Scrunching up his nose, Oliver shuddered. "Eww, gross."

"You sound like my brothers."

"Then they have perfect palates because raw fish is gross and the green stuff sticks to your teeth." He grimaced, shuddering as he relived the taste of it in his mouth. "You two knock yourself out, but leave me home on that date."

Troy laughed. "It wasn't bad."

"It was. It was chewy and the texture...yuck." Oliver couldn't get the flavor out of his head. He took the last drink of his soda, but could still taste the memory of it. "I need something else to get it out of my mouth."

Troy walked back to the fridge, shaking his head, but Bryce walked over to Oliver and pulled him close. Kissing him deeply, sweeping his tongue deep into Oliver's mouth, Bryce had him sagging against his chest and hard in seconds.

When Bryce pulled away, he was smirking. "Did that help?"

"Yes, but just to be sure, we should try again." Oliver grinned and moaned as Bryce humored him, taking his mouth deeply again, pinning Oliver's hands to his side so he was trapped against Bryce.

By the time Bryce pulled away again they were both panting. Oliver was starting to think heading up to the bedroom sounded better than the movie, but hearing Troy clear his throat nixed that idea. "Movie, no sex."

"All right."

"Okay."

Oliver had to laugh because Bryce sounded just as disappointed as he was. They'd agreed that they'd hang out and not get distracted by naughty things. When they'd been on the phone with Bryce talking about the plan, it had seemed like a reasonable idea. In person, with Bryce looking at them like that, it was harder.

"You two." Troy didn't seem to mind their antics, though. Oliver thought he needed someone to help him relax a little more. Troy always took on too much, and if Bryce could help share some of his stress, Oliver would be grateful. He never felt like a burden to Troy or like a second-class partner in the relationship, but he knew Troy put too much weight on his own shoulders to make things work.

They'd talked about it several times, but Troy couldn't move past the taking-care-of-Oliver mentality. It was thoughtful, but it made Oliver worry. "Come on. You two are dawdling because you don't like the movie I picked out."

Troy and Bryce barked out a laugh. Troy looked at the room. "What did you do to help again?"

"I swept." Oliver gave them an indignant look.

"Sure." Bryce drew the word out, rolling his eyes.

"I have the broom." And he'd even moved around the kitchen with it. It wasn't his fault the two men were much more fun to look at than the dirt on the floor.

"That doesn't mean you did anything with it, kitten." Troy let the words rumble out in a deep voice.

"Do I need to be *punished*?" Oliver knew he hadn't managed to keep the excitement out of his voice. "I was naughty."

Wearing matching wicked grins, Bryce's just bigger than Troy's, the men looked at each other. Bryce nodded to a silent question Oliver hadn't seen. "You're right. I think he does need to be punished."

The way he said it sounded erotic and incredible. It made Oliver immediately suspicious, but horny, too. Before he could even ask, both men came toward him. Pulling Oliver so he was pressed between them both, Troy looked down at him. "Let's go watch the movie and I'll show you how we punish naughty boys who don't help with the chores."

Oliver almost purred. "Oh yes, Sirs."

10

BRYCE

"Um, sir?" The new temp, whose name he actually remembered, popped her head in the door of his office. "Yes, Rebecca."

She reminded him of an old TV show character. Fresh-faced and sweet, she seemed very innocent. She was a hard worker, and since he was having to look for a new assistant, she would have been a good choice if he weren't so worried about scandalizing her.

"Your mother is on line two."

"Shit. Are you sure?" He tried not to feel like a scolded schoolboy when she frowned at him and shook her head slightly. "Sorry."

"Thank you. And yes, I'm positive." She smoothed down her dress and walked back to the front, closing his door behind her.

She was nice, but she wouldn't work.

He took a deep breath and picked up the phone, hitting line two. "Hi, Mom."

"Don't you 'hi mom' me like you're so innocent. My babies are all falling in love and no one calls me?" Her voice was crisp, and he was right back to feeling like a kid.

"The guys said they called you."

Had she found out about him? Bryce wasn't sure what to tell her, so he'd hoped to stay under the radar for a little longer. He was past the point of fooling himself. He knew it was serious. His date with Oliver later in the evening was proof of that. He just wasn't sure what to call it.

Hi Mom, here are my lovers...

Hi Mom, meet my boyfriends...

HI Mom, meet my Dom and our sub...

Hi Mom, meet my friends...

The last option had him cringing. Luckily, she charged on, stopping his mental gymnastics. "I called Garrett twice this week from crazy places and where is he? At Wyatt's house. But all I'm getting is vague talk about getting serious and talking things out. Is he living with that boy without a collaring ceremony?"

"Um..." Bryce was going to play dumb with this one. He wasn't sure what she'd been told, and he wasn't going to be the one to tell her anything. He didn't even know what Garrett was doing, so he wasn't exactly lying. "I don't think so."

"We raised you boys better than that. When a Dom gets serious about a submissive, he or she has certain responsibilities. And that sweet boy shouldn't be letting Garrett get away with taking advantage of him. I'm going to—"

Bryce had to jump in. "Wyatt's thoughtful, but he wouldn't let Garrett talk him into anything that..." He wasn't sure what to say. He felt like he was having a 1950s-type discussion about a BDSM relationship. "I'm sure they're making good choices."

"How good? Do you know what they're doing? If I find out he's collared that sweet boy before I get home I'll—"

"I haven't heard anything like that." Wyatt and Garrett had been acting odd, though nothing he had to define, so he thought he was in the clear. Besides, Garrett would know better than to do something while she was out of the country.

"I'm starting to think I need to come home sooner than I'd planned." Her voice was thick with suspicion. She always had a sixth sense when they were up to something, and the way he figured, serious new relationships probably counted.

"Won't they miss you?" She'd planned the trip and organized just about all of it.

"No. I think they'll manage. Gerald will keep everyone in line. He's good with managing people." There was a quality to her voice that he hadn't heard in a long time, but he didn't want to know what it meant.

"That's good, but I don't want you to miss out on...Greece?"

"That was last week." She clucked her tongue. "I could disappear and my children wouldn't even know where I was supposed to be."

"I was close."

"No, you weren't. I'll resend you my itinerary. I should do that for all of you." She was going to start micromanaging their calendars again if he couldn't get her distracted.

"Grant met someone. He's dating Carter."

His mother sighed dramatically. "Yes, I had to hear that from Wyatt first and not Grant, but when I called Grant, he sounded very happy. I can't wait to meet his young man. All my boys are falling in love. Brent and Calen finally stopped dancing around each other, which is a relief. I thought I was going to have to intervene with them when I got back."

It seemed like a safer topic, so Bryce jumped on it. "They seem happy. Something seemed to be holding Calen back, but they've sorted it out."

"Now we just have to get you sorted out. I met a very nice young man when I was in Germany. He's a bit shy, but I think—"

"I don't need you to set me up."

"So you've met someone?"

Shit. He'd fallen for it. It was like high school all over again. "Mom, give me some space."

She made a disapproving sound. "When I give you boys too much space it turns out like cooking. You never figure it out on your own. You do better with someone to manage you. Take-out works for dinner, but not really well for sex. At least, not without getting arrested or a disease."

Bryce's head might have hit the desk.

"I'm not getting hookers or hooking up every night. Just give me some space."

"All right, until you're ready to talk to me." She sounded disappointed, but she could give Oliver a run for his money when it came to trying to manipulate people, so he didn't buy it.

"Thank you." Not that he was admitting he was seeing anyone. She seemed to be assuming that, though, so he had a feeling one of his brothers had talked. He was going to owe payback to someone.

"Now, I can't talk long. We're heading over to a tour."

He looked down at the clock. "What kind of tour?" He didn't know where she was. He'd just realized she hadn't answered that question. What kind of tour started this late? Wasn't it night in Europe? Was she even still in Europe? "What time is it there? What are you—"

"I have to go, sweetie. I'll talk to you later once I look at new tickets. I think you boys need a bit more supervision. Living together with no collaring ceremony, *lying* to your mother, the list could go on. Yes, you boys need your mother around." The lying part was aimed at him, but not telling wasn't lying. That was just the guilt talking.

When mothers said you needed them and they were going to come see you it shouldn't sound like a threat, should it? She was much more herself than she'd been when she'd first started planning the trip, but he was starting to remember why that wasn't a good thing.

"But Mom—"

"Don't worry about picking me up. I'll take a taxi or something. Oh, and I want to surprise your brothers, so don't mention our little talk."

Shit.

"But—" She'd hung up, and he was left talking to himself. His brothers were going to kill him.

HIS MIND WAS STILL REELING from the phone call from his mother when he got in the car to start driving over to pick up Oliver for their date. Between the news that she was coming home and the fact that Troy had given him permission to take Oliver out when it was just the two of them, his brain was flying around in circles.

Giving himself a short, internal pep talk, he picked up the phone and texted Troy.

You got a sec?

The answer was evidently yes because his phone started ringing in seconds. Damn. He tried to sound happy, but he knew it came out stressed. "You didn't need to call."

Troy gave a soft grunt that sounded like a snort. "Why would I text you when hearing your voice is so much better?"

Bryce laughed, secretly pleased but unwilling to tell Troy that. "I just had a question." Bryce paused, not sure how to ask it. The awkwardness of it was why he'd wanted to text about it to begin with. Not having to hear Troy's reaction would have made it easier.

Troy had been incredibly good about understanding what

Bryce needed, but how did you ask someone if it was okay to make love to their sub? "I'm getting ready to head over and pick up Oliver for our date, but I wanted to double check something with you first."

That didn't sound long-winded and vague.

Troy laughed. "Yes, Bryce. I expect you to fuck him so hard he can't move tomorrow. Was that your question?"

Bryce growled into the phone. "Yes, but it's not that funny."

"It is." He heard Troy shuffling things around in the background. "Because I just had the same conversation with Oliver."

Oh.

"You did?" It made him feel less ridiculous. "I've never been in this situation before, and I'm not sure what the rules are."

There had to be rules, but they'd never gone over any. They were going to talk about limits over the weekend, but nothing more specific beyond safewords and basic things had been discussed. It wasn't just the BDSM aspects that probably had guidelines. How things like sex were handled when it was just two of them together should be detailed.

"I'm not sure we need rules." Troy's calm words weren't what Bryce wanted to hear.

"The lifestyle has rules for everything. Some people wing it more than others, but still..."

"It's not a scene, though. It's three people getting to know each other first and sometimes having sex with a power exchange element. You and Oliver are going out on a date. You're going to flirt and tease and hopefully make him crazy. Then, it's up to you." Troy's voice was warm and soothing. It made sense, but it seemed too easy.

"So you really don't mind?" Bryce was having a hard time putting himself in Troy's shoes. Most of the time he could picture what someone was going through. Imagine how they were seeing a discussion. It came in handy when he was talking to clients. But with their developing relationship he couldn't move past his own issues.

"No. I want you two to be happy together. We told you this is serious for us. You'll have a relationship with him, just like you'll have one with me. The individual pieces will help strengthen the three of us together." Troy's voice dropped low, sending shivers through Bryce. "And if you behave on this date and keep it too nice, then I might feel guilty when I make our date very naughty."

Bryce's worries were like a balloon that popped under the pressure of his arousal. "I can't drive with a hard-on. Stop that."

It wasn't quite a chuckle, but Troy's low amusement sent waves of pleasure through Bryce. "I have to go to a meeting knowing you two are flirting and eventually going to get naked, while I'm talking to idiots who can't follow instructions."

"We're going to be very naked, and I'm going to drive him crazy in the restaurant. I made sure we had reservations for a table in the back and they have those long tablecloths that hide so much. I'll have him so needy by the time we get back, he will be begging to come." Bryce loved the frustrated groan that came through the phone.

"Now who's looking to get punished?" Troy's words were soft and growled out. He sounded like they were making love right then instead of talking on the phone.

"I was only telling you my plans for the evening. I wanted to make sure you knew what your boys would be getting up to while you were away."

"You were just keeping me informed, huh?"

"Of course."

"I want you to remember how good I am with paybacks." It was a delicious threat that made Bryce's toes want to curl in anticipation.

"I'll remember that when I'm sliding into Oliver later." He was trying not to let Troy hear how amused he was, but it wasn't working. "Have fun in your meetings. I have to go."

He disconnected as Troy was mumbling about him being a little shit.

Turning off the car, Troy stretched and fought off a yawn. Long days and even longer meetings were one thing, but when you had to say the same thing over and over it was even worse. He couldn't understand some people —and it wasn't just the employees.

The company's owner was turning out to be a bigger part of the problem than Troy had anticipated. The job was paying well and Troy knew he was worth every penny, but he was pushing against the tide. They just weren't ready for big changes.

He'd tried to explain that to the company owner, but he hadn't wanted to listen.

Troy told himself on the ride home that he would work with them for a few more weeks. Then he was going to terminate the contract if nothing changed. He'd been putting off several other offers from other local companies, and he wasn't willing to waste his time.

It hadn't helped his frustration to know that Bryce and Oliver were at home without him. He didn't begrudge them their time together, but a big part of him wished he was there, too. They'd needed it, though. He wanted both of them to be comfortable together with him and without him. It would never work if they couldn't communicate or negotiate scenes when it was just the two of them.

It was a conversation he'd had with both his boys.

He'd been expecting the call. That was why he hadn't let Bryce get away with a text. There was too much room for miscommunication when you couldn't hear someone's voice. He needed Bryce to understand that he was glad they were spending time together, and he wanted both of them to be completely wrung out from sex.

He'd hoped to have been home earlier, but it was late enough that even with dinner, they should have had time for a couple of rounds in the bedroom. Climbing out of the car, he headed up to the house, curious to find out what they were up to.

The fantasies and options had kept him hard for the long drive home. Getting out of his clothes and hopefully into one of his men sounded perfect. Closing the front door quietly behind him, Troy stood listening to see where they were.

The bedroom.

Troy set his bag down by the door and headed up the stairs. He could hear Oliver's desperate pleas and a low response from Bryce that he couldn't decipher but sounded wicked. Oliver seemed to both love and hate the words because his frustration mounted, but so did the desire in his begging.

"Please, Sir. Please. Oh, I need...oh, more..." A low moan stopped the rambling words. Oliver sounded so close to the edge Troy knew he would come any second.

Stepping into the doorway, he had to smile.

It was more wicked than happy. Bryce had found, or Oliver had shown him, the other cuffs that were attached to the four corners of the bed. He had their beautiful sub stretched out naked on his back with a pillow tucked under his hips to raise his ass up.

Bryce was kneeling next to Oliver, almost naked except for tiny little boxer briefs that had a silky texture. They'd been in the toy box because Oliver's cock was completely erect with a cock ring wrapped around the base and a long, thick dildo in his ass.

That was one of Oliver's favorites, but also the hardest because it had balls inside of it that would shift and move as the person writhed. The more he wriggled and worked his ass around the toy, the more turned on he would get as the balls rubbed against his prostate.

Bryce's wicked grin said he'd figured out the trick of the toy and was thoroughly enjoying it.

Troy couldn't wait to see how Bryce responded to it. He had a feeling it would be beautiful when he gave himself over to the torturous pleasure. Neither man had noticed him yet, so he leaned against the frame and watched.

"You know what we agreed, baby. You said you wanted us to wait until Troy got home. You wanted him to play with us, too. Don't you remember?" Bryce trailed his fingers around Oliver's nipples, alternating between soft caresses and little flicks that made Oliver cry out. As pink as they were, he had a feeling Bryce had been playing with them for a while.

"I didn't think it would be this long!" Oliver wailed out as Bryce pinched one nipple.

"We didn't specify a time. And you don't see me complaining, do you?"

Hmm, the way Bryce said that had sparks shooting through Troy. What was his boy up to? "Were my boys waiting for me?"

Troy let his voice go deep and reflect all the need that was surging through him. They were beautiful. Oliver gave a shout of pleasure like his team had just won a touchdown, and Bryce gave a small start as he looked over his shoulder to the doorway.

"We were waiting for you." Bryce's voice was low and sexy. Desire flashed through his eyes as he gave Oliver's nipple another pinch, sending pleasured moans through the house.

"I can see."

"Oliver agreed. He even got to come in the car as a reward."

"It sounds like you were extremely generous." Troy stalked into the room, reaching up to loosen his tie before slipping it off. Tossing it carelessly to the floor, he slowly worked his way down the buttons on his shirt while his men watched, transfixed.

When the shirt was off and had joined the tie on the floor, Troy toed off his shoes and reached for his belt. Oliver whimpered and stretched his head up to watch as Troy teased them both by taking his time. The pants finally hit the carpet with a low thud from the buckle and both men sighed.

Troy would have smiled if he hadn't been so turned on.

Hooking his fingers through his boxers, he bent over at the waist, pushing them down. He was facing the wrong direction for the men to be able to see his ass, but as he took off his socks and stepped out of the puddle of clothes, he heard both of them whimper.

Bottoming wasn't his thing, but he wasn't averse to a little ass play, and from the sounds coming from the bed, both men were in agreement. Straightening up, he ate up the distance to the bed in two long strides. He was done teasing. He wanted them.

Bryce moved to meet him, but Troy was too fast. Before Bryce had moved down to Oliver's hips, he had Bryce in his arms. Taking Bryce's mouth in a long, deep kiss, Troy reached out and let his fingers wander down the length of Oliver's trapped cock.

Oliver made a sound of half-pleasure, half-pain, and the begging started again. Troy pulled back, giving Bryce one last tender kiss. "It looks like you two have been having fun on your date."

Bryce's eyes almost glowed with pleasure as he looked down at Oliver. Reaching out, he moved his hand to join Troy's on Oliver's hard cock. "He showed me the toys."

"I'm glad." Troy teased down the long length to roll Oliver's tight, full balls in his hand. The noises from Oliver were incredible. "I think Oliver might be ready for more."

"You took longer than he thought to come home." Bryce smirked and flicked the head of Oliver's cock, making their sub almost vibrate from the sensation.

"What did you have planned, tiger?" Troy could envision countless perfect scenarios, but he wasn't sure what Bryce wanted, and he was going to do his best to let Bryce take the lead.

"Oliver and I talked at dinner. I went into great detail about what I wanted us to do. Kitten, why don't you tell Troy what we talked about?" Bryce let his hand stop teasing Oliver long enough for him to take a breath.

If he thought Oliver could give them a long, drawn-out account of the sexy torment Bryce had put him through, Bryce would have to be disappointed. Oliver pushed his hips up, shouting out, "You fuck him, he fucks me, please! Sirs, please!"

What? Troy stopped shifting the toy buried deep in Oliver. "It sounds like you boys made a wonderful plan."

Troy stretched out over Oliver and gave him a quick kiss. "Are you ready for Bryce to fuck you? Do you want him to go slow or—"

"Hard. God, hard and fast. Please." Oliver was nearly frantic, thrusting up and trying to reach for Troy. Giving his boy a kiss, he reached down and fucked him hard and fast for two or three quick strokes. "I think you're ready."

Oliver wailed and thrashed around, almost there, but

between the collar around his dick and being so close to the edge for so long, he couldn't come. Troy loved seeing him like that. "I think I need to get Bryce ready, though."

Oliver shook his head, but the words didn't come out, so Troy looked to a slightly nervous Bryce. Troy straightened to give him a kiss. "Are you ready for me?"

Bryce nodded, finding his confidence again because he turned and pushed down the tiny, tight shorts to bare his ass. The smooth skin of his bottom drew Troy's gaze, but so did the plug sticking out from between Bryce's firm cheeks. Bryce peeked over his shoulder, giving Troy a sassy look. "Oliver watched while I got ready for you."

A low, dirty chuckle escaped Troy. Knowing Oliver, it would have driven his kitten crazy to watch Bryce tease and stretch his hole but not be able to touch him. He couldn't wait to have them reenact it for him later. Troy reached out and put his hand low on Bryce's back. "Bend over for me. Push your ass up and let me see if you did a good job."

Bryce blinked at Troy, then bit his lip and nodded, surrendering to his Dom. "Yes, Sir."

Bryce's whole body shivered and a soft groan escaped as he leaned over and arched so his ass was offered up to Troy. Absolutely stunning. Troy trailed his hand down his tiger's back to palm Bryce's round ass. Bryce made a needy sound and squeezed his cheeks, working them around the plug.

"We need to get another dildo like Oliver's wearing. I think you boys would look incredible, side by side, with both of you filled and ready. Do you know they even make one with a cock on either end? I could sit back and watch you two fuck each other." Bryce gasped and his hands gripped at the bed covers as his body shook.

Oliver must have found the image irresistible because he moaned and his desperate thrusting rocked the bed. Troy gave them both a wicked smile. With that reaction, he wasn't going to be able to wait for long. Christmas was going to come *very* early to his boys. "Oh, I think my boys like that."

Pushing the briefs even farther down, Troy reached around to grasp Bryce's needy cock. Slowly jerking him off, Troy moved his other hand to pull the plug out almost all the way, then push it back in. "I want to make sure you're ready for me."

"Please!" Bryce moaned and danced between Troy's hands, fucking himself onto the plug and back into Troy's tight fist. Troy had been thinking about the two men for too long to extend the teasing any longer. He slid the plug out, watching as Bryce pushed his ass back, begging for more.

Troy gave him a light smack, and both Bryce and Oliver moaned in pleasure. "Naughty boy. If you want to be fucked, you'll need to show me you can behave."

"I'm sorry, Sir." Bryce shook and had to force out the words. "It was just...you're so...it was...please, Sir."

Troy felt the bed move again and looked over to see Oliver desperately working the toy with short, jerky movements while he watched Troy and Bryce. Troy glanced back to Bryce, who seemed shaky and nearly as needy as Oliver. "Grab the condoms."

Troy reached over to unhook Oliver's legs but left his arms restrained to the bed. Turning to focus on Bryce, he saw his boy's movements were jerky and uncoordinated. However, it didn't take him long to grab the condoms and find the lube where it had fallen next to Oliver.

Troy made both men watch while he sheathed and lubed the condom. Then, while they were both staring and shaking, he took his time doing the same thing to Bryce.

"Who does this cock belong to?" Troy growled out the words, smoothing the latex down over Bryce's rock-hard shaft with a possessive grip.

"You, Sir. It belongs to you." Bryce gasped the words out, fighting to stay still.

Troy spread the lube over his sub's hard cock, loving the feel of his tremors and the tight muscles clenched in anticipation. "That means I control how you get to fuck Oliver. When, how fast, how hard, do you understand that, boy?"

Bryce's hips jerked, thrusting his cock into Troy's teasing touch before he caught himself. "I'm sorry. Yes, Sir. You do. You control me."

"Good boy." Need and emotions swirled deep inside Troy, but he pushed them away. All he wanted to think about right then was his boys. By the time he was finished, his kitten was mewling and making the sweetest, neediest sounds and his tiger was fighting to stay still. It was a losing battle.

Giving Bryce's ass a swat just to make him groan and shake, Troy didn't make them wait any longer. "Kneel between Oliver's legs. Yes, like that, but I want yours wider. That's better."

Bryce shifted his knees so he was spread open for Troy. He moved behind Bryce and wrapped his arms around his chest, pulling his tiger back tight against him. He ran his hands over Bryce's pecs and firm abs, tweaking his pebbled nipples. "Are you ready for me?"

They'd played and made love in a variety of ways, but he'd never taken Bryce like this. Most of the time, they topped Oliver together. Troy knew he might have been too cautious, but he wanted to ease into their dynamics. It wouldn't just be bottoming as Bryce gave himself to Troy. It would be offering his submission. Troy wasn't willing to rush that, no matter how much he wanted to feel Bryce wrapped around him.

Bryce's head fell back on Troy's shoulder. Shaking, with every muscle tense, Bryce nodded. "Please, take me, Sir."

"Who's in charge? Who makes the rules now?" Troy knew the words came out rough and gravelly, but he didn't bother to hide how much he needed his tiger. Troy knew there were still things holding Bryce back. He wanted to get through to him how much they needed him.

"You, Sir." Bryce's muscles tensed, and it seemed to take everything he had to wait for Troy's commands.

A low growl rolled out of Troy, making Bryce and Oliver both moan. Troy let his cock slide between Bryce's cheeks, running the length of his dick over his hole to brush against his balls. Bryce gasped out and his control fell as he pushed and started to beg.

"Please...oh...yes...please...so long..." The broken words were breathy and filled with emotion.

Troy moved his hands to grip Bryce's hips. Holding him still, he moved his body back and lined his cock up with Bryce's readied hole. Easing the tip of his cock in, he kept his grip tight, refusing to let Bryce rush him.

"Yes...please..."

"Oh god, that's so freakin' hot." Oliver's outburst made Bryce laugh, but it was quickly swallowed by the moan that tore through him as Troy drove his hips hard, bottoming out inside Bryce.

He gave Bryce several long, slow thrusts, letting him get used to the sensation. He was stretched, but Troy knew he would still feel the invasion as he sank deep. When Bryce's breathing had evened out, Troy moved one hand around and brought it up to Bryce's face.

Turning him just enough to give him a gentle, tender kiss, Troy moved Bryce's face to look at Oliver. "Are you ready to make love to our kitten? To sink into him?"

A jerky nod gave way to another moan as Troy slid out of Bryce. "Lift his leg. He's all ready for you."

Bryce forced his body to listen and leaned down, pushing his arms under Oliver's legs to lift his ass even higher. It forced the toy to shift, sending the balls moving through the toy, and Oliver gave the most delicious cry of pleasure. Troy reached out and slowly pulled the toy out inch by inch as Oliver pleaded and Bryce watched, barely restrained.

Tossing the toy across the bed, Troy watched as Bryce sank into Oliver in one stroke. Oliver couldn't seem to decide if he was relieved to finally be getting fucked or overwhelmed by the pleasure. Conflicting emotions and needs flashed over his face as Bryce started to move inside of him.

Gripping Bryce's hips firmly, Troy forced him to stop, making both of his boys whine in frustration. Giving Bryce another smack to his ass that had gasps echoing around the room, Troy growled out orders. "Be still. Who's in charge, tiger?"

"You are!" Bryce threw out the words, desperate to please Troy.

"Good boy." Then Troy bit back a grin as he slid deep in his boy.

All three men were balancing on the edge, desperate to come but not ready for it to be over. Guiding Bryce's hips, Troy let him move again. Keeping an easy, painstakingly slow rhythm that made them all crazy, he watched his boy's frantic struggle to let him lead.

When Bryce's body moved faster, Troy gave him another smack that sent shock waves of pleasure through Bryce and Oliver as he thrust hard into the beautifully tied sub. "No." He waited until Bryce froze.

"I'm sorry. It's so hard. I...I need you."

"I know you do, baby, and you're going to have me. You're mine, but you only get to come if you're a good boy. You don't want to watch Oliver get to come without you, do you?" Troy whispered the heated words to Bryce, watching as his boy whimpered and shook his head.

"Next time we do this I'm going figure out a way to tie you

both up. I want to be able to control just how fast you can go as you make love to Oliver. And maybe I'll even find a way to *punish* you when you've been naughty and fucked him harder and deeper than you're allowed." Both boys whimpered at the wicked promise of punishments.

Troy flexed his hips, fucking deep into his boy. Bryce was pushed harder against Oliver, sending waves of pleasure through both men. Oliver wouldn't come as easily because he was still wearing the cock ring, but Bryce was rushing headlong toward an orgasm. Troy reached down between his two men and gripped the base of Bryce's cock.

"Do I need to get a cock ring for you, or are you going to behave? You can't come yet." Troy's words came out demanding and firm, but they went right to Bryce's cock because he gasped and his body started to demand they move.

"Oh god, please!"

Another swat to Bryce's ass had him still, but both of his boys were making the most incredible begging noises, words completely gone. Bryce finally nodded, but that seemed to be the extent of what he could manage to do. Troy brought his hand down again, loving the way Bryce's body jolted in shock. He'd jerk and shake, then would lean back against Troy like he was soaking up the feeling of being held, being taken.

Troy let his hand grip Bryce tighter. "If you forget, I'm going to lock your dick up for days."

That promise more than anything pushed Bryce even closer to insanity. Troy released his cock and started to thrust, pushing his tiger into his kitten and watching as they both came undone. They moved, crying out and racing toward their orgasm.

When his boys were begging for release, and Troy himself was barely holding his own orgasm back, he reached around and freed Oliver's cock.

"Come!"

Oliver went first, dragging a breathless Bryce right behind him. Troy felt his tiger's orgasm explode through his body as his ass clenched around Troy, fighting to keep the orgasm going. Troy kept fucking Bryce faster and harder, wanting to wring every drop of pleasure from both his boys.

When Bryce stopped shaking and his orgasm started to fade, Troy finally let himself go. Exploding into Bryce, filling the condom, Troy's orgasm burst through him. Bryce worked his ass and hips, riding Troy's cock to keep it going.

Finally spent, Troy slowly pulled out, and Bryce shivered from the sensation. Oliver giggled, then gasped as Bryce pulled out of him and carefully let his legs fall to the bed before reaching up to untie his arms. As efficiently as he could, Troy removed his own condom, then fought back a smile as Bryce blushed when he took his off as well.

Troy smiled as his confused tiger shoved his hands over his face. Throwing the condoms away, he pulled his boys into his arms. He kissed them tenderly, enjoying Bryce's bright face. His men were both very different, but both sweet and so important to him.

"Come here." Rolling around so he was lying on his back, Troy pulled them back into his arms. Yawns and warm snuggles had them all relaxing. It was everything he and Oliver had imagined but never really expected to find.

12

OLIVER

"Are you sure he said we could pick him up at the office?" Oliver looked over at Troy questioningly. He'd asked the same thing three times, so it didn't bother him when Troy rolled his eyes. Oliver just didn't think it was something that Bryce would do.

"His car is in the shop overnight. We're going to take him out to dinner, then drop him off at home." Troy sighed and glanced over at Oliver, reaching to take his hand. "It's not a big deal. We probably won't even have to go inside."

Oliver nodded and looked out the windshield. Bryce had gone on and on about how open his family and the people he worked with were. Even if they were just introduced as friends, it would be okay. He was probably overthinking it.

Ever since Bryce had invited them to the next family barbecue, Oliver's brain had been going in circles with what could go wrong. Troy had made him stop talking about the potential issues when they'd started to veer into the absurd.

He'd said the chance of aliens invading was too slim to worry over.

Oliver had to admit that one was over the top, but most of his worries weren't. Picking Bryce up at his work wasn't insane, but how many of his clients stopped by to take him to dinner? It couldn't be that common.

Was it Bryce's way of trying to be more open about their relationship?

He was still rolling the possibilities around in his head when they pulled up into the parking lot. At six o'clock on a Friday, he didn't think that many people would still be working, but there were several cars still around. When Bryce didn't come right out, they climbed out of the truck and headed for the door.

Entering the building, they heard the chime of a bell letting people know the door had opened. Bryce leaned out of the door to his office, holding his phone up to his ear, almost being strangled by the cord on the headset. He gestured to them to come back, then ducked into his office.

Oliver shook his head, smiling, and headed back. He didn't know why they were still using out-of-date phones. He should have had a cordless headset. Bryce moved too much to sit still, tied to a desk. As they reached his door, a woman in a long dress came around the corner, holding her purse.

"Oh, I'm sorry, I didn't know the door was still unlocked." She smiled at him, but it felt like they'd done something wrong.

"Um, Bryce is expecting us." Oliver pointed to Bryce, who was pacing around the office so much he'd tied himself in knots.

"I didn't see a note on the calendar. I'll mention that on Monday."

Troy made an odd coughing sound and shook his head. "It's personal. We're just picking him up."

Her gaze dropped down to Troy and Oliver's clasped hands. "Oh." Then she gave them a stiff smile and headed toward the front door.

Troy leaned down to whisper in his ear, "If she holds that bag any tighter it might pop."

Oliver snorted and whispered back, "It's protecting her from the big, bad, scary gay men."

Oliver might have looked fairly casual, but Troy was still in a suit. He looked like a lawyer or something. Shaking his head, feeling a little bit sorry for the mousy woman, he gripped Troy's hand tighter. "Love you."

"Love you too, kitten. Come on. Let's go see what has Bryce flying off the handle."

They walked in and sat down in the comfy chairs, watching as Bryce opened and closed his mouth several times. "But...I don't think...Surprising...Mom!"

Bryce finally raised his voice, waving his arms around like he was conducting an orchestra. "You can't just surprise everyone like that. What if someone has plans—" He snorted and let his head fall back. "No, I don't think anyone does. Nothing is happening behind your back."

He sighed and tried to untangle himself enough to sit down, but didn't do a very good job of it. By the time he was leaning back in his chair, the phone was at a precarious angle at the edge of the desk. Oliver wouldn't consider himself OCD or anything, but it was making him crazy.

Troy was just watching the circus unfold, trying not to laugh. He was quiet, but Oliver could see his shoulders jerking and silent laughter running through his eyes.

"But, Mother." He sat up in his chair. "I was not rude. You weren't listening."

Slouching back, barely catching the phone before it went crashing to the floor, Bryce sighed dramatically. "Yes, Mother."

Setting the phone down, he closed his eyes and took a deep breath. Pushing away his apparent frustration, Bryce opened his eyes and gave the men a forced smile. "Hi, guys. You ready for dinner?"

Oliver let go of Troy's hand after giving it a squeeze and went around the desk. "Come on, let's get you untangled. How did you do this?" Bryce was twisted up in the cord so bad, Oliver wasn't sure they'd be able to get him unstuck without taking apart the phone.

Bryce tried to shrug, but it didn't work. Laughing, he shook his head. "I don't know. She makes me crazy."

"Your mother?" Troy spoke up from the other side of the desk, still trying not to show how funny he found Bryce's predicament.

"Yes. She's decided that she's going to come in on Sunday to surprise everyone. She's going nuts about everyone settling down, and I think she's feeling left out. I'm supposed to keep her secret. She's planning on arriving when everyone is over at the barbecue. It's not my business, but we all think that Garrett and Wyatt are going to have some kind of announcement about their relationship. Telling everyone about their plans for a collaring ceremony or something." He sighed and stood up, letting Oliver move him around to untangle his mess. "She's going to take the focus off of them, but she's refusing to see it."

Oliver finally had him free, and he moved the phone back to its usual place. "I'm sorry she's putting you in the middle of it."

Bryce gave him a kiss on the forehead and sat down, pulling Oliver onto his lap. "Everyone will be happy to see her. It's just going to mess up their plans. I'm not one hundred percent sure what they're doing, but the announcement can't be that far out."

Oliver leaned over, giving Bryce another quick kiss, but jerked back when he heard a shocked gasp at the door. They all looked over to the door to see the rude receptionist, who was standing there looking ridiculously shocked.

Like his kiss was something you'd see on a porn site.

Bryce gave her a calm, questioning look. "Yes, Rebecca?"

"I forgot my books." She held up two huge books like a shield. "I have to say, I'm shocked to see such immoral behavior."

Huh?

"I'm sorry?" Bryce didn't seem like he was apologizing. No, he sounded offended. "Commenting on my personal life is not acceptable."

"I've stood by and held my tongue while hearing outlandish rumors, but to see it in person..." She didn't seem to know what to say.

Bryce did.

"I think it's best if I speak with the agency about sending someone else. We won't be requiring your assistance next week." He was calm and professional, but Oliver could feel the anger vibrating through him.

"I've never..." She shook her head, honestly flabbergasted. "Your behavior is—"

"My behavior is my business. For you to stand there and malign my partners is not appropriate." Bryce gestured toward the door with his head. "I will be calling the staffing company shortly."

She sniffed like some kind of old-fashioned matron and stormed out. "I never..." Her rant trailed off as she left the building.

Bryce sagged back against the chair. "I actually remembered that one's name, even if she was a judgmental bat. Why do they keep sending me idiots or crazies?"

"Why are you hiring temps?" Troy asked the question before Oliver could get the words out.

"I loved my previous admin. She handled a lot more than most receptionists and was really helpful. Her husband was transferred because of his job and it all happened quickly. I haven't found the right person to hire yet." Bryce looked like hiring an assistant was on the same level as hiring someone for NASA. "I need someone who's going to work well in the office and with the business, but not go off like that nut when something interesting pops up. If she thought this was bad, she should have been here the last time Grant came in talking about Carter."

Words were bouncing around in Oliver's head, but he wasn't sure if it was right to say what he was thinking. Troy didn't have the same reservations. "Why doesn't Oliver help you out? It doesn't have to be permanent if it doesn't work. But at least you know he's not going to freak out if you're making out with one of your partners."

Troy was teasing, but Bryce winced. "Sorry, it kind of came out."

Oliver gave him a cocky smile. "I could have thought of sexier things to call me, but that will work."

Bryce laughed, pulling Oliver close. "I can think of *loads* of interesting things when it comes to both of you. Not all of which need to be shared with assholes." Bryce rubbed his hands up and down Oliver's back and sides. "I'm sorry you had to see that. I knew she was off, but I specifically asked the temp agency for someone who would not have a problem with the LGBT community."

Troy snorted. "They must have missed that part."

"I'm not sure how." Bryce shifted, pulling Oliver closer. "The owner is a member of the club. He's not that active anymore because his partner is shy, but he's been part of the scene for years. He's going to have a heart attack when I tell him what happened."

Oliver laughed. "I'm sorry. I know it's mean, but I just don't see how she can be so hypocritical."

Bryce and Troy both looked at him like he was missing a few screws. "Didn't you guys see what she was reading?"

Both men shook their heads, confused. Oliver couldn't help but giggle. "Harry Potter and something about the collective works of D. H. Lawrence. A book about witches with a gay headmaster, and the other guy was absolutely scandalous when his books were first published. My kiss was nothing compared to the stuff in her books. It's kind of ironic."

Bryce barked out a laugh and Troy shook his head, a little smile peeking out. Oliver gave them both an impish smile. "I thought it was funny."

Still smiling, Bryce gave Oliver another peck on the lips. "I'm still sorry you had to see that. I've always made sure that my staff is open-minded and accepting of my family's lifestyle. Finding someone to take over the front office is harder than I thought."

"I still think Oliver would be a good choice." Troy gave them both a stern look.

Bryce looked at Oliver hesitantly. "I know it would be odd and weird at first, but would you mind? It's probably a waste of your skills but—"

"I don't think it would be a waste. I like working with clients and I'm good at dealing with the admin stuff. If your previous assistant did more than just answer the phones, then I should be able to help out just as much, if not more. I even have my insurance license for Virginia, if that helps." Oliver wasn't sure if the offer was wanted or if it would even be a good idea, but he wanted to help.

"I'd love the help, if you want to." Bryce seemed as nervous as Oliver felt. "You'll tell me if you hate it, though?"

"Yes. I'll be honest about it. You can't be any harder to deal with than my last boss." Oliver grinned at Bryce's expression.

"Your last boss wasn't worried about pissing you off and having to sleep on the couch." Bryce's words sounded like he was teasing, but something in his eyes made Oliver think he was serious.

"No sleeping on the sofa. I can't even imagine you demanding your assistant get you coffee. Much less saying something rude."

Bryce blushed. "No, I get my own coffee, but my last assistant would throw little candy bars at me when she thought I was getting grumpy, her take on that commercial. I once got a mini Snickers upside the head when I was arguing with Grant about something. She took his side."

Oliver snickered, then let his voice drop low and sexy. "How about I find other ways to keep you happy at work?"

Loud catcalls from just outside the door made him jump. What the hell was up with the people in Bryce's office?

"Go home!"

"We wanted to see what they look like." Random heads poked in the doorway as people filed by.

A short guy with blond hair grinned. "They're cute, boss."

Off-color jokes along with waves and grins were called out from the hall as the people in his office walked by. They'd waited late on Friday just so they could meet him and Troy? Oliver couldn't believe it, but Bryce was taking it in stride. "We're like one big family most of the time. They heard something from one of my brothers, probably, and it spread like wildfire. When I said I didn't need a ride home tonight, they started speculating right away whether you were coming. I've been trying to send everyone home for an hour, but they kept finding things to do."

He called out as his staff was heading out the front door. "I'm going to remember how busy you guys were the next time someone asks me for time off!"

Laughter and giggles flowed out the door before the office was quiet again. "They're..."

"Strange." Troy said it with such a dry, serious expression, Oliver couldn't help but laugh.

Bryce had to agree. "You'll find most of the offices are the same way. It takes some getting used to."

Bryce started to say something else, but a yawn stopped him. Oliver didn't like the feeling that was settling around Bryce. When they'd come in he'd been frazzled and stressed, but not unhappy. Now that was starting to change. Bryce looked at Oliver, then glanced to Troy. "I know we said you guys were going to come to the barbecue Saturday, but with my mother coming and interrupting everything..."

Oliver wasn't sure what to say. Troy cleared his throat. "We understand. We'll meet your family another time."

"Thank you." Bryce sighed, sounding torn and sad. "Can I still come over after, or..."

"Yes!" As worried as Oliver was that it wasn't just about Bryce's mother coming, he wasn't going to let Bryce find any reason to push them away. Despite how serious they were with each other, he knew it wouldn't take much to derail everything. It was still so new.

"You are always welcome." Troy said the words softly, but husky with meaning. "You need to remember that."

Oliver had a feeling Bryce was going to be tied to the bed again soon. Troy had that look. It was one Oliver had seen countless times in the past before he would wake up restrained to the mattress so they could talk. In a strange way, it made him feel better.

If Troy was planning something like that, then it couldn't be as bad as Oliver was imagining. It couldn't be. He tried to shove the sea of emotions pushing at him away. "Let's get you some dinner, then you can get a good night's sleep."

"Do you still want us to drop you off at home, tiger?" Troy's question was simple, and Bryce probably thought it was another way to make sure he knew they weren't upset at him, but Oliver had seen the tactic before.

"Yeah, I just need to relax. I'll be over to your house after the barbecue. Probably seven or so, depending on what time my mother shows up." Bryce either didn't get it or ignored it, but it had been Troy's way of giving him an out before making a bad decision.

Oliver generally got one "are you sure" kind of question before they talked and sometimes he got punished. He bit back a sigh. Bryce would learn. As much as he was saying he needed quiet, Troy clearly thought Bryce shouldn't run and hide from whatever was going through his mind.

After their rough start, Troy was a firm believer in communication and working things out. In his mind, no one got to run from whatever was making them miserable. They'd made that pretty clear to Bryce on their tied-to-the-bed-Saturday.

Oliver gave him a kiss on the cheek. "All right, let's go find food. I'm starved."

Bryce smiled, but it was a bit forced. "Me too."

The men stood, and Troy and Oliver went out to the reception area while Bryce locked up. Troy pulled Oliver tight to him. "You're worrying about this too much, kitten."

"I'm not sure I am. This feels wrong," Oliver whispered quietly.

"We're giving him some space, not letting him run. There's a difference. Besides, we have a secret weapon." Troy grinned, making Oliver suspicious.

"What?"

"We know where his family works. If he does something insane, we'll track him down. I think, from the stories he's told us about them, they'll be on our side." Troy's eyes had a naughty gleam. Even though he wasn't close with his family as an adult, he'd had several siblings close together in age. If anyone could relate to Bryce's brothers, it would be Troy.

"Okay."

He tried to look happy as Bryce came to the door. Bryce didn't comment, though. He just took Oliver's hand in one of his and Troy's in the other. "All set."

"Perfect." Oliver tried not to grip Bryce too hard, but he could almost feel him slipping away.

13

BRYCE

"Do you want to talk about it?" Wyatt came up quietly beside Bryce, watching the chaos as people tried to clean up after the barbecue.

"I don't know." Bryce had appreciated that everyone hadn't bombarded him. Wyatt and Carter had possessed enough common sense to hold Garrett and Grant back, so he'd been pleased not to get the third degree. "Maybe."

"Contrary to popular rumors," Wyatt said as he gave him a little grin, "I can keep a secret."

"I heard you were a chatty little birdie with Grant and Carter." Bryce cracked a smile, the first one in hours.

"I was not that bad." Wyatt sighed dramatically. "Carter needed a kick in the pants, so I gave Grant some hints to help him manage the crazy minefield around Carter's heart."

Wyatt grinned, very pleased with himself. "And it worked. Look at those two."

Grant was following Carter around, leaning close and whispering things that clearly made Carter nuts as they were trying to pack up the food. They were so different that he knew most people wouldn't have paired them together, but they worked and looked very much in love. Even if Carter seemed to be trying not to deck Grant.

They watched as Carter turned around, one hand on a popped-out hip, and waggled his finger at Grant. They only caught the word cookies, but Grant gave Carter a puppy dog look and shook his head. "He had to get out the big guns."

"Threatening to tell where the cookies are hidden is big around here." Wyatt giggled, enjoying the crazy.

"Grant's been making him nuts for the last hour. I think he's talking to him about the club." Bryce had caught them several times making out in quiet corners of the yard, while Grant whispered about the things Carter would see. "Do you think he'll be ready to go in two weeks?"

"Who, Carter?" Wyatt glanced at Bryce. "Yes, he's just nervous. It's really different from anything he's done before, and I think he's just building it up in his head."

"I hope he enjoys himself."

"He just needs a push." Wyatt sounded very sure, so Bryce tried not to worry. He could remember the first time he'd gone to a club, but he'd had support and a lot of friends in the lifestyle by that point.

"I told Troy and Oliver not to come today." He hadn't meant to throw the words out there, but they came out anyway.

"Because of your mother?"

"Yes, partly. How did you know?"

"She doesn't seem like the subtle type. I can't see her hiding it from everyone. And then there's the little bit about her knowing where to find you guys. I know you usually have a barbecue, but she couldn't have been that sure about everyone being here unless she'd talked to one of you."

"The guys are going to figure it out soon." Brent didn't feel like figuring out what they were going to do to him.

"Oh, yeah, I'd hide the cookies if I were you."

"The last time she put me in the middle, they pretended to understand and took me out for drinks. They got me stinking drunk, then dropped me off at home after they'd short-sheeted my bed and moved all the furniture around. Between my struggle to figure out the bed and trying not to freak out when I realized the lamp was on the ceiling, I thought I was going crazy. I had nightmares for days about accidentally walking into other people's houses and being abducted by aliens."

"How did you get them back?" Wyatt's eyes were lit up.

Bryce knew his grin was wicked, but it pushed back the worry. "I had a friend from college who owns a dog food company. He arranged for pallets of dog food to be delivered to Brent's house because he was the mastermind. They showed up randomly for months, just waiting in his driveway. One time, I even managed to get it in his living room. He just about killed me, but he couldn't prove I did it."

Wyatt giggled and said, "You guys are insane."

"Probably." Bryce just shrugged. "It also takes a special brand of interesting to join the family, though." He gave Wyatt an I-know-what-you're-hiding look.

Wyatt blushed. "This is not going to help convince you that I can keep a secret. But yes, we were going to talk to everyone about setting the date for our collaring ceremony. We'd planned on calling your mother tomorrow to tell her, but now we'll figure out something different."

"You could invite everyone over to a welcome home dinner for Mom?" Bryce glanced over at Wyatt to see his reaction.

"That's a good idea."

"It would be a lot of work, but—"

"No, it won't be that bad. Maybe later this week, so they don't think it's anything out of the ordinary." Wyatt's mind started to whirl as he began to plan. "But what about you?"

"Me?"

Innocent wasn't working on Wyatt because he shook his head, waiting. Bryce sighed. "I don't know. With her coming today, I didn't want to throw them into the chaos. And as much as I know she wants me to be happy and won't care about me having two partners, I worry about how it will affect the business. Did you hear about my temp?"

Wyatt nodded, regret etched into his features. "I did. Most of your insureds won't care or even notice, unless you guys get really crazy in the office."

Bryce snickered. "I'll do my best."

Wyatt snorted. "I'm beginning to see that doesn't mean the same thing in this family. It's more like *I'll try unless I can talk you into something else.*"

Bryce gave a low chuckle. "Oh yeah."

"What else happened?"

Bryce thought that was a very good question. One that he wasn't sure he had the answer to.

Confused, he started with what felt like the biggest thing in his head. "I just didn't like how it felt to put Oliver and Troy in firing range of someone like that." Bryce shuffled everything around in his head, trying to put it into words. "There are always going to be idiots who say something about us being gay, but this time it was because of me. She would have kept her ridiculous comments to herself if I hadn't added myself to the picture."

"So two gay guys should be acceptable but not three together?" Wyatt gave him an understanding look. "Who gets to define that?"

"I know, but—"

"There's always going to be someone who thinks me getting spanked or kneeling for Garrett is wrong. I can't let that stop me, though. Sure, it makes me nervous and I worry, but I can't let that fear keep me from living my life like I need to. Do you need them? I think that's what you have to decide."

Wyatt looked over to Garrett, who was trying to referee something between Calen and Brent. "I love him, but I also need what we have. I'm not going to lose that because of someone else."

Bryce threw one arm over Wyatt's shoulders. "When did you get so smart? It certainly wasn't hanging around this mess."

Wyatt laughed, shoving Bryce with his hip. "I love your family. Shame on you."

"Yes, he should be ashamed of himself. For several reasons." The sharp words coming from behind Bryce had him wincing.

Damn. How long had she been there?

He turned around. "Sorry, Mom."

"Don't 'sorry' me." She gave Wyatt a pat on the shoulder. "Wyatt, dear, why don't you go distract Garrett before Brent and Calen go after him?"

"Yes, ma'am." Wyatt gave Bryce a you're-on-your-own look and escaped.

"He's so sweet." She smiled as she watched Wyatt hurry away.

Bryce couldn't even respond before she continued, giving Bryce a disappointed look. "Of course, I didn't get to meet your young men."

He winced again. "There was just a lot—"

"Do not give me that line. Why didn't you bring them? I heard several people raise that question when they thought I wouldn't notice." She didn't seem to appreciate her children trying to keep it from her.

He tried to talk, but she barreled over him again. "Your father and I both would support anyone you love. No matter what they liked or who they were. It doesn't matter that there are two of them. As long as you're happy, that's all that counts."

He gave her a questioning glance, not even bothering to actually talk. She gave him another look like he was acting ridiculous and charged in again. "You may lose some insureds, but I think you'll be surprised. Enough about you boys' escapades has gotten out over the years that they can't be shocked."

Bryce looked away, afraid of what his face would reveal. He wasn't sure what she was talking about exactly, but he didn't want to start confessing things she might not know. She made another one of those mom sounds that always let them know when she was disappointed and frustrated.

"I think you need to go fix this, don't you?" She stretched up to kiss his cheek. "Go on. You shouldn't leave this. I bet they're worried."

He gave her a hug. "Thanks. Love you, Mom."

"Go on. You can't butter me up until you have your men so I can meet them. Go on, or I'll sic your brothers on you." She gave him a deceptively innocent smile. He couldn't help but think about how much Oliver would be able to learn from her.

He headed out to his car, grateful that people didn't stop him to ask questions. Bryce wasn't sure what he would have even said. Telling everyone he was going to Oliver and Troy's house to grovel didn't sound like something he needed to share—even if it was the truth.

The drive over didn't take nearly long enough. He'd thought the words would come to him on the drive over, but they hadn't. He hadn't even called them yesterday. They'd talked so often he couldn't remember a whole day going by recently where he hadn't at least talked to them on the phone.

What were they thinking?

Words and emotions were turning in his head as he walked up to the door. The countdown in his brain only had seconds left before he had to figure it out, and suddenly even those precious few were gone.

Oliver opened the door.

He was quiet, but Bryce didn't feel unwelcome, just sorry that he'd upset Oliver. "Hi, kitten."

Bryce watched as Oliver relaxed, finally giving him a smile. "You know you're in trouble, right?"

Now that he knew Oliver wasn't mad, he gave him a dramatic sigh, cuddling close and dropping his voice to a whisper. "Can't you save me from him? I'm sure you know just what to do. I'll make it worth your while."

Oliver giggled, shaking his head. "I can't give away my secrets. You'll have to learn them on your own."

"Will I get a spanking for being an idiot?" That didn't actually sound too bad. However, he didn't think it would be that easy.

Oliver leaned into Bryce's embrace. "No, worse, he's going to—"

"Make you talk it out." Troy's voice came from the doorway where he leaned against the frame, crossing his arms. "Upstairs, you two."

Bryce gave Oliver a quick glance. "We're going to get tied to the bed again, aren't we?"

"Yup." Oliver nodded, starting to head inside to follow directions. "And I know that look. He might have you tied up for a long time."

Bryce didn't understand the look on Oliver's face. He was missing something. "As a punishment?"

"No." Oliver's look turned tender as he walked up the stairs. "Until you understand we're keeping you."

Bryce fought back a smile. He didn't want them to think he found their reactions humorous, but it was adorable and made him warm inside. *They were going to keep him.* He wasn't sure he deserved them. All he'd done was question what he and they wanted. He still wasn't sure he'd made any progress, either.

Sandwiched between Oliver and Troy, Bryce walked up the

stairs, thoughts swirling. When it came out, would it really matter to the insureds in his office? He believed Oliver and Troy when they said they wanted a long-term relationship with him, but could they really make it work? Would he be able to sort out the dominant and submissive parts of himself that didn't always agree on who was in charge? He had more questions than answers, but he knew one thing.

He was where he needed to be.

"Strip down. You can leave your briefs on if you want, but everything else goes. Then climb up." Troy stood in the doorway and watched Bryce and Oliver. His expression was still guarded, but Bryce saw a warmth in his eyes that made him feel steadier.

Taking off his clothes, Bryce let everything fall into a pile and got up on the bed. He didn't bother keeping on anything. He didn't want any barriers between them and he didn't need to hide from them. Curling up into the pillows, he watched as Oliver joined him on the bed. They stuck out their feet and gave each other a grin.

As silly as it might have looked, Bryce liked the symbolism. He knew it was Troy's way of making sure Bryce understood how serious they were about communication, but it made him feel like part of their family. The idea that they wanted him enough to tie him down shouldn't have pleased him as much as it did. They might have been mad at him, but they still...wanted him... needed him...loved him.

Maybe.

Maybe he was overthinking it again.

When Oliver and Bryce were stretched out and patiently waiting, Troy calmly walked over to the bed and tied them down. The cuff would have been easy to remove, but Bryce liked how it felt. Secure.

Troy gave them both a long look. "Are you cold? Do either of you want a blanket?" He was calm and serious, but the heated glance he gave both men let Bryce know he wasn't unaffected.

Oliver shook his head. "You're like a big heater. I think we'll be fine."

Troy climbed up on the bed and, not even pausing, stretched out between the two men, pulling them close. He gave Bryce, then Oliver simple kisses on their heads and wrapped his arms around them. Bryce let his head fall to Troy's shoulder, enjoying his warmth and strength.

It made the submissive side of him want to curl up and purr beside his Dom and it made the dominant part of himself sit a little straighter. "I'm sorry for...for everything that I put you through the past couple of days."

Oliver peeked over Troy's chest and reached out to take Bryce's hand. "Are you ready to talk about it?"

"Yes." Bryce relaxed into their touch. "I'll admit there are a lot of things still floating around in my mind, but it's not going to keep me away from you."

"You should have talked to us about what was bothering you." Troy tightened his hold on Bryce. "Next time I know something's swirling in your head I'm not going to wait. You're going to get tied to the bed right away."

Bryce tried to smother his grin but it didn't work. "And I won't let it get that far without talking to you both."

"It's okay not to know everything. We just need to be able to talk about it." Oliver rubbed his fingers over Bryce's hand.

"That's probably part of the problem. I like knowing what happens. Whether I'm submitting or dominating, there's always an element of control. I might be giving that control to someone else, but it's still mine. You two just send everything in my head flying." Bryce wasn't sure it made sense, but Troy and Oliver seemed to understand. They nodded, and Troy reached up to run one strong hand down Bryce's head.

Not willing to hide, he decided to lay it all out for his men. "Do you want to know one thing I do know?"

Oliver's eyes twinkled. "Is it dirty?"

"Kitten, that's not helpful. Do we need to go over the rules again?" Troy gave him a long-suffering look, but the twitch at one corner of his mouth gave him away.

Bryce laughed. "No, but it's just as good."

"What?" Oliver's head came up and he smiled.

Bryce shifted and gave them both short, tender kisses. "I know that I love you two very much."

Oliver leaned over, wrapped his arms around Bryce, and gave him a silly, smacking kiss. "I knew that. We love you, too."

Troy laughed. "You're supposed to let me say that myself."

Oliver shrugged. "You took too long."

His men were funny, loving, and wonderfully his. "I think that means you need to punish him, Sir."

Troy snorted. "Don't look so eager. We're not done talking."

"We're not?" Bryce felt a little like Oliver.

Giving him a look like he must be crazy, Troy shook his head. "No. I plan on keeping you right here for a very long time."

Oliver smirked. "Told you so."

14

TROY

Troy watched his boys as they walked into the lounge. They were both striking but so different. Oliver lit up the room, flirting and bouncing around. He loved being noticed and knew just about everyone there. His bottom looked absolutely fuckable in his tiny little shorts, but the front was equally as eye-catching. The thin material didn't hide the long length of his cock or the thick ring around the base that kept him from getting hard.

When Carter first saw them as he and Grant walked into the lounge from the back hall, his eyes had nearly bugged out of his head. Oliver just bounced over to them both, giving them hugs and completely ignoring that he was nearly naked. Once Carter got over his surprise, he seemed to feel much more confident about his own outfit.

He looked almost fully dressed compared to Oliver.

Grant had mentioned that Carter was still unsure about what he would be wearing, but the feminine, sexy outfit covered the most important parts. That in itself, besides the fact that no one blinked over his feminine style, had him much more relaxed. He clearly wasn't going to go anywhere without Grant right there beside him, but he wasn't holding on for dear life, so Troy thought it was wonderful.

Bryce was wearing more clothing than Oliver, but unless someone was naked, it would have almost been impossible to wear less. He was wearing jeans, but was also shirtless and had the same bare feet that Oliver did. They'd talked about the visit to the club several times and had decided that Bryce would go as a Dom, but would let Troy lead for the evening.

It was their first trip up together, but he thought things were going well. As they walked over to the small seating area in the corner of the room, he saw the rest of the family hanging out and talking. Troy and Bryce settled down on the couch, and Oliver knelt on a cushion between the two of them. Wyatt was across from him, kneeling beside Garrett and talking a thousand miles an hour to Oliver and Carter.

Carter was perched on Grant's lap, cuddled into the Dom's arms. He stayed close to Grant, but was gradually getting more talkative and laughing at Wyatt's antics. Every so often, Carter would wave his hands around or say something, making Wyatt laugh. At first, he would look around to see who was watching them, but after a while, he didn't seem to even think about it.

Troy thought it probably helped that, aside from Oliver, they were the most conservative-looking group in the club lounge. The variety of half-naked to completely naked subs also included a handful of pups and even a few age play couples. Carter's lingerie and makeup were not the most colorful things in the room.

Brent and Calen were more laid-back. Brent was dressed very similarly to Bryce, but was kneeling on the floor by Calen. They were mostly lost in their own world, talking to and teasing one another. Their heated glances let everyone know those two would be heading off to find some privacy sooner rather than later.

"How are the plans going for next month?" Bryce leaned forward, talking to Garrett.

Garrett rolled his eyes, but Wyatt perked up and started talking a mile a minute with dramatic hand movements that made Troy want to smile. "It's good but a little frustrating, and we wanted something intimate but she wants something classy, and she's going a little over the edge." He took a breath, then charged right back in. "I kept it small, but she won on the clothing and she said you guys had tuxes but I wasn't sure, and I think it's going to end up being expensive and I've told her it's not a wedding but she's not listening. I'm not losing, though. Just on the tuxes and how formal it is."

Wyatt looked up at Garrett like he was starting to realize he might not have won after all. Garrett smiled, reaching out to stroke Wyatt's face. "You did wonderful standing up to that freight train. You kept it small and stopped her from renting that banquet room."

Nodding, Wyatt settled back down. "She's...Well, she's your mother, but..."

"She's a menace who needs a hobby." Grant spoke up, laughing when Carter frowned at him.

"Grant!"

"Hey, that's me being nice." Grant cocked an eye at Carter. "What were you saying last week when she came into the store?"

"Shh, I want her to like me." Carter looked around like he didn't quite trust the rest of them not to tell on him.

Grant just beamed like a proud parent whose child was finally learning about the world. Troy was starting to agree with Wyatt and Carter, Bryce's family was weird. But they were loving and open, so he was making an effort not to let them know how crazy they were.

Some days were harder than others.

Like the dinner where Wyatt and Garrett had announced

their plans to have a collaring ceremony. When Bryce's mother calmly asked if they were having an old-fashioned ceremony where Wyatt would be naked, Oliver almost fell out of his chair and Troy hadn't been far behind him.

Everyone else seemed to think it was normal, while Wyatt blushed trying to explain that they weren't going that far. Carter hadn't been much better than Troy and Oliver. He'd tried to cover his laugh with a cough, but he'd choked and Grant had gone overboard trying to make sure he was okay.

It had gotten Wyatt out of the hot seat, but it had taken Oliver forever to get himself under control. The whole collaring ceremony was turning into a circus and he thought most of the family agreed. None of them wanted to tell their mother no, though.

Looking over to his boys, Troy decided that when they had a formal ceremony, it would be done like an elopement and they would only tell Bryce's family at the last minute. He wouldn't fight with Bryce's mother about how it should be organized. It would be the closest thing he and his boys would have to getting married and he wasn't going to let someone else butt in.

Not that he'd mentioned it to the boys.

Oliver was starting to give him looks like he knew what Troy was thinking, but Bryce wasn't quite ready. In the two weeks since Bryce had come home, realizing they needed to talk about his concerns, things had improved dramatically.

Bryce was more open with what he was feeling and what he needed. Troy hadn't even felt the need to restrain the boys to the bed so they could talk since that evening. He was planning on rewarding both the next day when Bryce as well as Oliver was submissive.

As they'd talked, they'd found that having a schedule would feel better to Bryce and Oliver. Bryce thought that it would be too hard to change from being in control at work to submitting at home in just the course of a short drive. So they'd decided that, in addition to any time he was over at their house during the week as a Dom, he would spend weekends with Troy and Oliver where he would submit the entire time.

Waking up tied to the bed, even for a few minutes before Troy released them both, helped Bryce to switch over in his head. Troy had even stopped being such a stickler for dates being more about getting to know each other and less about scenes.

"You guys aren't going to do any better when she gets her paws into you." Garrett was frowning at the group, but giving special attention to Brent and Calen.

"What? Why us?" Brent shot him a frustrated look.

Troy was wondering the same thing. If anyone was going to be having some kind of a ceremony, he thought it would be Grant and Carter. Carter was still a little nervous, but Grant was determined to keep him close. There wasn't a better way to let a submissive know you were incredibly serious than to have a ceremony.

"Because she said she's been watching you two flirt for years and it was time for you to settle down." Garrett looked like he'd won the lottery when both Brent and Calen looked at him in shock.

"What?" They spoke at the same time.

Oliver was giggling as the drama unfolded. Troy could understand; it was always like watching a TV sitcom. He'd always thought his own family was frustrating until he'd meet Bryce's. They made his look easygoing and normal.

Their kind of special didn't make him feel unwanted or odd, though. It was something he appreciated.

As the rest of the group started debating Brent and Calen's love life, Troy looked down to his boys. He lowered his voice, focusing on Bryce but knowing he had Oliver's full attention. "I think I heard a rumor that the viewing room with the spanking bench is open."

Bryce cocked an eyebrow, looking intrigued, but Oliver nearly bounced off the floor. "It is?"

A low chuckle escaped Troy, making Oliver shiver. "Yes, it is, kitten." Troy reached out, trailing one finger down Oliver's chest, absently circling a nipple. "Does that sound like fun? Does my boy want everyone to see him getting spanked?"

Oliver's eyes had already started to glaze. Troy smiled at his little exhibitionist. Bryce made a deep humming sound, making it very clear what he thought of the idea. "I bet someone even had it stocked with toys."

"Oh, Sirs." Oliver's breathy words were filled with need, drawing smiles from the group. They ranged from sweet to curious to see what the three of them would get up to. Troy didn't particularly want Bryce's family to watch them now that he and Oliver were in a relationship with Bryce, but that was the joy of a one-way mirror.

As they played, they would never know unless someone said something later.

And because turnabout was definitely fair play in their family, he didn't think that would happen. Taking his boys' hands, Troy stood up. "You gentlemen have a good evening."

"Will we see you tomorrow at the barbecue?" Brent asked as they started to walk away.

"Yes, and we won't let him near the salad," Troy told him solemnly because he was well aware of what Brent was worried about.

"Thank you." Brent was so relieved that Troy had to fight to control his reaction.

They were so strange.

Leading Bryce and Troy toward the back hall, he could feel Oliver's excitement as it vibrated through his body. By the time they'd reached the private rooms, he was bouncing and nearly begging. His cock ring was the only thing keeping his dick from bursting out of the little shorts.

Eyes followed them into the room, only making Oliver's excitement worse. "They're watching you, kitten. Do you think they want to see you get spanked?"

Oliver nodded frantically, looking around the room and trying to figure out what would happen. "Do you think they want to see you plugged and teased while we spank you?"

The passionate sub shook as a wave of pleasure went through him. Oh yes, the ring had been a good idea and worth the effort. Bryce had spent nearly half the ride up trying to get Oliver soft enough to get the restraint on to keep him from getting erect.

He hadn't wanted to leave the ring on too long, but next time they were going to put it on before they left home, because driving with that going on in the back seat had been distracting. Pulling Oliver close, he nodded to Bryce to sandwich their kitten between them.

Letting Oliver feel exactly how turned on they were only made his need worse. Troy reached down, sliding his hands between Oliver's back and Bryce's chest. "You had everyone's attention out there, didn't you? These tiny shorts showing off your ass and your cock ring. I think next time you need a plug to go with the ring. What do you think, Bryce?"

Bryce's grin was wicked as he rocked his hips into Oliver. "I think it needs to be a big one. Like the fun one with the balls, making you gasp and beg as we walk around watching the different scenes."

"Wicked. You're just mean." Oliver didn't seem to mind, though. The words were too thick with passion.

"Only with you two, kitten. Just with you and Troy." Bryce's words were filled with more than need. "You know how much we love you. How much I love both of you."

Oliver purred and Troy wanted to as well. He smiled and leaned over Oliver to give Bryce a long, slow kiss. "Love you too."

Oliver shook and held tight to both of them. "I love you both so much, but I'm going to explode. Please!"

Laughing, Bryce thrust against Oliver again, looking up at Troy. "I think someone needs to be reminded of their manners."

Squeezing Oliver's ass one last time before releasing him, Troy nodded. "Up on the bench for you, naughty boy." Stepping back, they stared as a needy Oliver walked over to the bench, giving them a show as he climbed up.

Working his hips, flashing smiles filled with fire and lust, Oliver leaned over the bench, sticking his ass out and lifting his legs to kneel on the padded support. Troy nodded to Bryce, then started walking over to their boy. "I think we need to tie you down, just to make sure you don't fall."

Oliver moaned as they cuffed his arms to the handrest and put one more strap across his back. Running their hands down his lean body, they took their time teasing his skin and caressing him in long, smooth strokes. Kissing over his body, making him crazy with need, they worked him into a frenzy before they brought out the first toy.

Bryce walked over to the corner cabinet and took out lube and a thin plug that would slide in deep. It wouldn't stretch him much, but it would feel amazing as they reddened his bottom. Easing his shorts down to his thighs, Troy rubbed circles around Oliver's clenched hole as Bryce opened the lube.

When Bryce was ready, Troy moved his hand to squeeze Oliver's cheeks as Bryce started gently fingering their kitten. His sounds were beautiful as Bryce stretched him almost too slowly. Oliver shook, trying not to thrust back, but he was losing his control because his hips started moving as low mewling sounds were pulled out of him.

Bryce finally removed his finger and let the plug tease at Oliver's hole. Their poor kitten couldn't handle it any longer. He thrust his hips up, begging for more. Words that didn't make sense came tumbling out of his mouth. Bryce thrust the plug deep as Troy let his hand come down on Oliver's quivering ass.

Oliver cried out in painful pleasure.

"Naughty kitten. Look at you begging. Everyone's seeing you be a bad boy." Troy gave Bryce a wink and watched as he brought his hand down on Oliver's other cheek. "We need to make sure you remember how to be good."

Oliver was nodding, pleading, promising anything they wanted if they would just give him more. Troy gripped the base of the plug and pulled it almost out before plunging it back in while Bryce spanked him again. The pink flush that was starting to spread across Oliver's ass was beautiful, but the sound of his scream was incredible.

Over and over they took turns fucking him with the plug and spanking him until he was a quivering mess. He was so close to the edge, he just shook on the bench while his body danced for them. Moans carried through the room and out past the glass to whoever was observing.

They took turns teasing Oliver, telling him what people were seeing and how he was a naughty boy. With four hands, there was always one to tease his cock or caress the sensitive area around his hole while another hand came down on his bottom.

"Please...please...Sirs...love...please..." The words came out broken between gasping pleasure and moans.

"We're nowhere close to done, kitten." Bryce's grin was wicked as Oliver cried out in desperation. Bryce looked to Troy. "What do you think? Should we give him a reward for being so good? I think he's starting to learn his lesson."

Giving Bryce another subtle nod, Troy pulled the plug almost all the way out one last time. Fucking him with just the tip, he grinned and thrust it in as Bryce's hand slid under Oliver to undo the restraint around his cock. "Yes!"

Pegging Oliver's prostate, Troy watched as Oliver came undone. Screaming out his orgasm, sending long streams of cum shooting out to the floor, Oliver's orgasm went on and on as he rode the pleasure.

When he finally calmed down, sinking into the bench, his voice came out hoarse and low. "Love you. Both. Love."

"We love you too, kitten, but we're nowhere near done. We've got a long night ahead of us and neither of us has come yet." Troy caressed Oliver's cheeks in wide, gentle circles.

"More?" Oliver's brain didn't seem to be working well enough to make a more complicated sentence.

"We'll always have more for you, kitten." Bryce leaned down, giving their spent sub a tender kiss.

Troy knew what Bryce was trying to say. They weren't ready for planning the future yet, but that didn't mean they couldn't see it. It was clear and beautiful and would be waiting when they were ready.

EPILOGUE

Nora

HER BOYS WERE SO CUTE. Dressed in their tuxes, the nine of them looked so handsome that she took another picture. Wyatt had put his foot down on hiring a professional photographer, but she'd managed to get a few shots she knew were going to turn out beautifully.

As Garrett and Wyatt stood surrounded by their friends and family in their back yard, quietly reciting their commitments to each other, she couldn't help but tear up. When Wyatt knelt, in his bare feet and shirtless tux, she felt streaks of wetness run down her face. Her boys were growing up.

They were good men who she'd always known would love hard, but they weren't always the most mature. Not that she would have had them any other way. She loved the absolute chaos that had always echoed through their house as they were growing up.

Watching as Garrett placed a slim leather and silver

engraved collar around Wyatt's neck, she couldn't help but miss her Martin. He'd been her submissive for more years than she wanted to count. They'd discovered themselves with each other and had learned what real commitment and trust were together. Seeing Wyatt and Garrett start on that same journey made her heart ache.

As Garrett reached down to help Wyatt rise, she snapped another picture, ignoring her emotions. It wouldn't be long before the others would be ready for commitments of their own. The way they looked at each other, holding hands and exchanging sweet glances, said as much. It didn't matter if it was marriages, collaring ceremonies, or other personal commitments to their loved ones. She just wanted them happy.

All of them.

In the short time she'd known Wyatt, Carter, Troy, and Oliver, they'd become part of their family like Calen had when he first came around with Garrett. She knew it would take time for them to really accept that, but she wouldn't have it any other way. She'd done her best to give her own boys the confidence and strength to love the way they saw fit, and she wanted to make sure their partners had the same chance.

As Garrett pulled Wyatt close, giving him a tender, slow kiss, she knew they would always love one another.

ABOUT SHAW MONTGOMERY

Shaw Montgomery loves reading, traveling, and family. While not necessarily in that order, they all rank pretty close. Shaw has lived all over the United States and even Germany, and has finally managed to make it back to North Carolina.

Shaw reads an eclectic mix of genres, everything from Mystery and Sci-Fi Space Westerns, to traditional Romance and all kinds of Erotica. Currently the stories in Shaw's head are femdom romance and M/m BDSM, although there are some Sci-Fi/Fantasy that can't wait to come out as well.

Do you want to join the newsletter? Help with character names and get free sneak peeks at what's coming up? Just click on the link.

https://my.publishingspark.com/join/?show=239

You can also get information on upcoming books and ideas on Shaw's website.
www.authorshawmontgomery.com

ALSO BY SHAW MONTGOMERY

ALSO BY M.A. INNES

His Little Man, Book 1

His Little Man, Book 2

His Little Man, Book 3

His Little Man, Book 4

Curious Beginnings

Secrets In The Dark

Too Close To Love

Too Close To Hide

Flawed Perfection

His Missing Pieces

My Perfect Fit

Our Perfect Puzzle

Their Perfect Future

Beautiful Shame: Nick & Kyle, Book 1

Leashes, Ball Gags, and Daddies: A M/m Holiday Taboo Collection

Silent Strength (Coming December 2017)

Quiet Strength (Coming January 2018)

COMING SOON

DO YOU WANT TO SEE WHAT'S COMING NEXT?

Silent Strength
December 2017

MARCUS

"Are you on duty or just stalking someone over here?"

I was too well-trained to jump, but hearing Ben's voice come from behind me *might* have made my heart rate elevate slightly. "I have no idea what you're talking about."

"You're a better liar than that. Want to try again? And maybe this time try saying it when you're not still staring at him." The tone was teasing and light, but I could hear the curiosity in his voice—and possibly a little concern. "Not that he isn't cute, but still."

The boy was more than cute. With longer dark hair that gave him a slightly disheveled look, he seemed younger than he probably was. His lean build kept him from looking like jailbait, his body hinting at muscles as he moved around the room. He'd never be a body builder, but I had a feeling he'd be sculpted and would look incredible spread out and naked.

"I'm not going to do anything stupid. I realize he's here with someone else."

Ben snorted, coming around the side of the couch to sit down. "That's not something I'm worried about. But you've been watching him since he came in. Weren't you here to play?"

That's what I'd thought the plan was.

The goal for the evening had been to find someone to get to know, then possibly have a scene with. There were the same core members as usual, but lately, there'd been a steady stream of new ones too. I thought it was time I met some of them. Work had taken up too much of my time recently, and even I'd realized I needed a break.

"That was the idea."

In my peripheral vision, I could see Ben shaking his head, but my focus was elsewhere. There was something about the new boy that wouldn't leave me alone. To begin with, he'd been so unsure of himself I'd been worried. New subs, especially unaccompanied ones, radiated at least a mild level of fear when they started exploring the club for the first time.

This was different.

He set off the dominant part of me that wanted to take a sub in hand, but he also hit the button for someone in distress. It wasn't just nerves. He was afraid. He wasn't mine, and I didn't even know his name—but I wasn't going to leave him alone.

"There's something off."

That got Ben's attention and the teasing fell away. "What do you mean?"

"It's not just first-time jitters."

"I won't ask how you know that." Ben shook his head and turned his focus to the boy. "Tony said he was on the member's guest list and everything had checked out."

There was a strict background check for members. However, only a basic one was required for first-time guests. The club had an incredible reputation for protecting privacy. Newcomers were only allowed in the public areas on the first floor and were watched closely. If they wanted to come back a second time, then they had to fill out a much more detailed application.

It didn't surprise me to hear that Ben had already checked

up on the new submissive. He took the responsibility of running the club seriously. Too seriously. He was working every time I'd come in recently. Which wasn't that often, but it was something to ask him about. When I wasn't otherwise occupied with an anxious sub.

The boy hadn't seemed like trouble. As a nearly twenty-five-year veteran of the police force, I had a pretty good radar for that, but it was clear he had no idea what he was doing. "I don't doubt that—but he's frightened. His whole body language is off. I thought it would get better when the Dom he was waiting for finally showed up, but it's getting worse."

When he'd walked into the lounge, the bands on his arms had told one story, but the look in his eyes told another. The dichotomy was what kept my attention, even though he was off limits. He was wearing two bands, a white one signaling he was a submissive and a red one meaning he didn't want to be approached for a scene. It was usually a combination that indicated he was there to meet someone specific.

The level of stress coming from him had me concerned. This wasn't a submissive who was simply new to the club. He was new to everything. I was shocked that he was by himself. I'd never brought a new submissive there, but if I had, I would have never let them arrive alone. It wasn't how you took care of someone who was obviously inexperienced.

He'd wandered around the room, hands in the pockets of his tight jeans, trying to look calm. But it was a thin façade because his fists looked like only his death grip on the lining was keeping them in there. He was trying. I had to give him that. He'd even worked up the nerve to walk through the more *interesting* side of the first floor before coming back to settle down at a corner table with a drink.

Very casual.

Very confident.

Very much a lie.

By that point, I was hooked and not going anywhere. So I'd settled in to watch and make sure he would be all right. Maybe it was the Dom in me, or maybe it was the cop in me, but I had to know he'd be taken care of. He'd waited about ten minutes, swirling the ice in his glass and sweeping imaginary crumbs off the table, before the man he was waiting for walked in. I recognized him right away. Tall and lanky, he always introduced himself as Master Samuel.

The guy was a dick.

He hadn't done anything to get his membership revoked, but he seemed to prey on new subs. The cop in me knew he was trouble. He might not have done something wrong yet, but it was only a matter of time. He was that guy you knew would cross the line one day, but there was never anything you could do about it beforehand.

Once I'd seen who the boy was meeting, I was stuck. I couldn't leave him alone with that ass.

Things started off just fine. The nervous boy had been watching the doorway to the lounge and recognized the Dom right away, which had me feeling better. But as Samuel came over, the stilted greeting and the way the sub shook his head as Samuel pointed to the floor by his chair made me realize they didn't know each other well.

As nervous as the boy was, it was clear he wasn't ready to kneel for anyone.

Samuel either didn't realize it or didn't care, because I could see his attitude from across the room. Wishing I was closer, I had to make do with watching their body language since I couldn't hear their voices over the noise from the club. Most of the time, I found the low hum of conversations relaxing and the sounds of pleasure coming from the back rooms exhilarating, but at that moment, I wanted it all to quiet so I could listen.

Ben was now watching them intently. "How did he end up with that prick?"

"No idea, but it's not going good. The boy has scooted back from the table about six inches in the last five minutes and he went from blushing and nervous to ashamed. I'm not sure what that ass said, but I can't let it go on much longer."

The way he kept retreating was clue enough, but the look on his face made me want to gather him up in my arms and hold him. He was doing his best to hide it with a reasonably blank face, but he was crushed.

"Deep breath, Pops. He might just be pushing the boy a little."

"Don't call me that. And if he's testing limits, the sub doesn't realize it."

I was a "Daddy Dom" and freely admitted I had a lower limit for seeing subs in distress than a lot of other Doms. But even keeping that in mind, I was having a difficult time staying out of it. I preferred to see subs blushing and squirming, not shrunk back and nervous. Physical pain was one thing—every boy needed a spanking from his daddy occasionally—but what I was watching seemed like emotional pain—and that wasn't something I was comfortable with.

When Samuel rose stiffly from the table, saying something to the boy, I thought maybe their date was improving. However, the way he started gesturing with his hands and pointing toward the hallway that led to the private rooms made me realize it was only getting worse. Storming off to the back, Samuel looked like he expected the boy to follow him, but the sub wasn't moving.

Ben shifted and I could feel him starting to stand.

"No. I'll go talk to him." Rising, I ignored the grumbling coming from Ben and walked over to the table where the sub still sat.

He wasn't looking at the hallway any longer. He was staring

at his drink. I couldn't decide if he was upset or going into shock, but his blank expression made me nervous. Whatever had happened seemed to have pushed him to the limit.

There wasn't time to plan the best approach, so I winged it.

Reaching the table, I pulled a chair around to sit beside him. It seemed like he could use comfort more than space, so I put one hand on his shoulder. That was when he must have realized he wasn't alone, because he jumped and a cute little squeak came out of his mouth.

Giving him a squeeze, I let my hand stay resting on him. "Are you okay, Boy?"

He blinked at me with wide eyes before glancing down to the bands on my arm, black for Dom and green to indicate my willingness to play. "I'm fine...Sir?"

Pushing away thoughts about how cute he was, I nodded. "That will do, Boy. And you're really not fine. I understand if you don't want to talk about it. However, I need to make sure you're okay." Speaking calmly and trying for a soothing tone, I attempted to let him know it was safe to tell me anything that had happened.

He looked around and went back to playing with his glass, twisting it around in circles on the table. His nerves were still showing, but he hadn't pulled away from my touch. If anything, there was the lightest pressure against my hand where he was leaning into it.

Unconsciously seeking a soothing touch, or something more?

"You don't have to do anything here that you find objection-able. If someone makes you uncomfortable, he or I," I pointed to Ben, "will be glad to help. That guy over there is one of the owners, and he wants everyone here to be taken care of."

Tension radiated through him as he glanced over at Ben. He turned back to me. "There isn't a problem. I'm fine." He sighed and seemed to realize by the look on my face it wasn't going to be enough because he sagged down in his chair. "We were just meeting for the first time. We've been talking online, but this was supposed to be for getting to know each other more. I...I thought we were on the same page, but evidently not."

Since he'd started opening up, I didn't back off. "What wasn't clear?"

His cheeks reddened a touch, and he went back to concentrating on his drink, but eventually he answered, "I thought...I... We didn't want the same thing."

The stoic sub took a deep breath, obviously trying to pull himself together. "His profile said he was...well, he liked it too... but I might have misunderstood. Thanks for checking on me. I'm just going to—" His voice cracked and his hands started to shake. Putting the glass down, he set his hands in his lap and sat up straighter. "I think I'm just going to head out. This was a mistake."

He said it with such tired resignation I knew he would walk away from whatever he wanted. He'd end up being one of those guys who just shoved it in a mental closet and let it quietly die inside of him. "Hey, *he* was a mistake...but *this*..." I looked around the club at all the people who'd managed to find a place where they belonged. "This wasn't a mistake."

Sadness seemed to envelop him. "You don't understand."

Letting my fingers softly caress his shoulder, I tried to figure out what to say. "I think you'll be surprised. Aside from the occasional ass-hat, you're going to find that most of us are open-minded. There's a variety of people here, and I guarantee there's someone else that likes the same thing you do." The club had such a diverse group, no matter what the sweet boy was interested in, someone could relate to it.

I didn't know why I was fighting so hard to connect with him. I should have left him alone after I knew he was fine. There was just something pulling at me that wouldn't let me walk away. Yes, it was the right thing to do, but it was more than that. "Come over and sit with us for a while. Ben's looking for an excuse to goof off, anyway. I think he's probably got paperwork waiting for him in the office."

A questioning look passed through his eyes and I could see him weighing the options. Would he take the chance or was he done? How much did he want to find people who'd understand? I'd seen it over and over. With some people, the pull to discover a place where they belonged was stronger than the fear. But with others, they couldn't seem to push past it.

"I don't know..." He looked around again.

He wasn't refusing outright, so I pressed forward. "I'm Marcus. Come sit with us. At least let us give you a better memory of the club. You wouldn't want to hurt Ben's feelings, would you? This was a terrible first impression."

That had the ghost of a smile teasing at his lips. "For a few minutes." Then he took another deep breath and straightened. "I'm Eric. Nice to meet you."

Eric's story begins in Silent Strength, coming December 2017.

Printed in Great Britain
by Amazon

85580879R00347